INDIAN

SKY

THE ADVENTURE CONTINUES

In the beginning there was only the Legend and a mysterious "Sun" symbol that led them into a remote canyon in the Sierra Nevada. What they found was far more than they had bargained for. But it was now two years later, and there was a part of the mystery that still remained unresolved.

The adventure continues!

Yosemite Valley

INDIAN SKY

DARYL N. PATTERSON

CABIN BOOKS
PARADISE, CA.

This book is a work of fiction. Names, characters, places and incidents are either the products of the author's imagination or are used fictitiously. Any resemblance to actual events or locales or persons, living or dead, is entirely coincidental.

Published by Cabin Books
Paradise, California 95969
Printed in the United States of America

Additional copies of this book may be obtained from Cabin Books

ISBN   0-9646761-1-7

EAN-13   978-0-9646761-1-4

Library of Congress Catalog Card Number: 2009906797

First Printing: August, 2009

Second Printing – with Revisions: November, 2016

cabinbookspublishing@gmail.com (E-mail)

To my Family,
May Life Always be an Adventure

INDIAN SKY

IS A SEQUEL TO

MORE THAN LEGEND

ALSO AVAILABLE FROM CABIN BOOKS

TABLE OF CONTENTS

INDIAN

SKY

Tuolumne Meadows

1

BEYOND THE LEGEND

July 18, 1995
Tuolumne Meadows, California

The significance of the angry sky above the gray windswept heights of Yosemite's Cathedral group was lost in Bryan's thoughts as he contemplated the old Spanish helmet which he held in his hands. How did it fit into the two hundred year old mystery that was Captain Camino?

Eighteenth century history did not record the power struggle that he had with Spain and Mexico for control of what would become California, and much of the western territory.

Why were the exploits of Captain Maximo Camino missing from the pages of history? In the beginning there was only the '*Legend.*' But in the finale it had proven to be—*More Than Legend.*

A rumble of thunder carried over the crest from the direction of lofty Clouds Rest, bringing attention to a black mass that was visibly building in its heights. Streaks of lightning began cascading down the face of the dark granite range that loomed in the west. Thunder broke overhead with such power that it vibrated the whole granite mountain to its very core. As the storm intensified and advanced toward him, his thoughts drifted back to a painful recollection. To a day such as this one was, nearly a year before.

Suspended by climbing gear nearly two thousand feet above Tenaya Creek, a powerful thunderstorm had formed and clung to a granite dome a thousand feet above, dark, ugly—terrifying. Grumbling, it began spitting lances of white fire into the dome far above, followed by a pelting thundershower. A river of falling rock and water came cascading down the face of the cliff. He remembered pushing off from the cliff, dancing back and forth trying to miss the deadly projectiles. They became so numerous that he was unable to dodge them all. The pain was dreadful as they began to hit his shoulders, head, and then suddenly he blacked out. Coming to, after an unknown lapse of time he realized his partner was calling him from above. Black clouds still hovered overhead, but it was no longer showering. Being so wet and cold it took a moment for him to realize that he was bleeding. Blood from the top of his head ran down his face and onto his clothes. What a position to bleed to death in. But soon the bleeding stopped. Though weak and in pain, he was able to pull himself up the rope to his partner's location. Again he recollected passing out in sheer weakness and hypothermia.

From there he was rescued from the top. A helicopter evidently whisked him away to the nearest hospital. Rushing to the hospital his mother nearly passed out after seeing him lying there unconscious, covered in blood.

It must have been the next day when he finally regained consciousness. Still somewhat in a daze, he realized someone was holding his hand.

Thunder cracked overhead bringing him back to the present. A familiar voice called for him to hurry. That same voice triggered a return to his mental sojourn, lying there in the hospital bed, coming to.

He recognized Tammy, who had fallen asleep, her head lying against the side of the bed facing away from him. It surprised him to see her there. She initially came across to him as a carnivorous female. But there were times she would let a softer side show through. Squeezing her hand, he called her name. Startled she jerked up realizing he was awake. A happy smile filled her face, and the stars in her eyes began to shine like so many points of light. Then a blush came across her face as she became aware of the fact that she was still holding his hand, which she then released. Tammy called to his mother who was asleep in a chair in the far corner.

He couldn't remember much else after that, but one thing was for sure, he had mentally mapped every inch of her lovely face and strawberry blonde hair in his memory. Why did he keep thinking about her? They fought like cats and dogs half the time—just like sibling rivalry. And besides, girls were generally a nuisance anyway. So what was wrong with him? Nothing he couldn't correct, he told himself.

Dark haired and nearly six feet tall, he was attractive to the opposite sex, but shied away from any kind of social life, due to lingering feelings of distrust for the gender after his mother had left them some years before. She had returned since, but his feeling toward the female gender was slow in returning.

He had to admit though that Tammy was different than most other girls. She had spunk, which she demonstrated two summers before on a rugged mountain trek. However, on the other hand, her competitiveness bothered him; and besides—she was a *city girl*.

April 4, 1995
Stanislaus National Forest

After a lapse of two years, the fire to solve the unfulfilled mystery returned that spring. The latent impact of all those experiences was bound to arise again.

Riding across a high mountain meadow Bryan encountered thundershowers drifting down out of the high country, forcing him to turn his horse, Red, toward a stand of sugar pine to seek temporary shelter. Dismounting, he waited for a break in the storm under these noble giants. Leaning against a tree trunk he adjusted his raincoat and waited. Bryan contemplated the lack of precipitation in the upper zones of the Sierras. He attributed this to over-logging and recent fires; and felt a great need to do something about it.

As the shower passed, filtered sunlight moved across the meadow toward him. "Well Red, it's time to head up to the headwaters," he spoke up, noticing that the storm had let up. Remounting he headed northeasterly, skirting the edge of the meadow.

Bryan was nineteen years old, young, but hardened. He did not want to be taken away from the confines of these mountains that he knew so well. They were home to him. He found exhilaration among the towering peaks and beneath the distant stars that beckoned. Rambling through the mountains, shouting from the top of the highest peaks, he had the feeling of invincibility until his climbing accident humbled him and showed him otherwise.

His father was the proverbial mountain man who ran a successful mountain pack service. Bryan grew up to be an accomplished horseman himself, and because of his ability was offered a seasonal job with the Forest Service collecting specimens for environmental study. Two days a week he rode into some of the remotest parts of the forest. The schedule worked well with his college courses relating to Resource Management.

Coming up into a rocky windswept pass, he paused and stretched in the saddle. A remnant of snow still skirted the north side of the pass that divided the Stanislaus and the Tuolumne River Basins. Dark and gray saw-toothed peaks appeared and disappeared in the clouds in the far north. He could hear the peep of a ground squirrel carry from somewhere below.

Shafts of sunlight began to break through the overcast illuminating large volcanic domes that stood out from the surrounding promontories. Vertical basaltic columns tapered upward to their lofty summits. These astonishing island-like rock masses, the *Dardanelles*, were a natural landmark to early pioneers and Indians.

Bryan felt alone during times like this, wishing he could share this beauty with someone else. The breeze issuing through the pass seemed to whisper to him—how the earth was a constant, while time itself was fleeting.

His thoughts drifted back to his great-great-grandfather, Captain Camino, who was trapped by Indians, some two hundred years before in the 'Oro de Cañon.' But the lingering question still remained—had he succeeded in escaping? If so, could this possibly have been the "pass" mentioned in his diary? The fact was, because of the unknown nature of his disappearance, new life was given to the legend that surrounded him.

Red stomped his hoof indicating he was anxious to get down out of the chilling wind into the sheltered timber below.

"Okay Red, lets head on down," replied Bryan patting him on the side.

Pulling the reins, he directed him to the right side, following his old tracks from the previous week through the mushy snow. Halfway down the slope, he spotted mountain lion tracks meandering in out of the north, reminding him of stories he had heard in the past. Some were undoubtedly tall tales, but a few were probably based in fact.

His thoughts now raced ahead, and contemplated his close friend, Josh, who would be waiting for him at the end of the trail. He had been gone for several months, working heavy construction near Shaver Lake, on the Helms Creek Project. It was only after a phone call two weeks prior that he learned that Josh had a near fatal accident. While working on an electrical tower a freak electrical storm had backed in over the Sierra catching everyone by surprise. Lightning struck the tower, knocking him unconscious. Plagued with muscle spasms after the accident, they put him to work in the construction office shuffling papers, all to his distaste. So it was that Josh now returned home, at least for a while.

Descending beneath the snowline, a rugged canyon gradually revealed itself as he descended. Perched on a bench beside the deep rugged canyon was a small grove of red fir. These stately conifers were his last sampling location which was marked by the round yellow metal tag nailed to the trunk of one of the larger trees.

After securing the air, soil, and foliage samples, he quickly descended from his perch on the mountainside to the head of a sprawling meadow dotted with scattered lodgepole pines along its western fringe.

East Flange Rock and its associated volcanic ridge soon came into view. Its reddish cast sharply contrasted against the clearing azure sky. The pristine sky caused him to ponder how wonderful it must have been before industry and pollution had clouded the skies. He thought about how a person could be gobbled up by the beauty of these mountains—never wanting to return to the lowlands.

Suddenly, the ground shook violently, and a blast could be heard coming from over the west ridge. Startled, Red reared up.

"Woo! What could have caused that?" steadied Bryan.

His first thought was—earthquake, but it was more like an explosion. More disturbing yet was that it came from the direction of the Three Chimneys and the 'Oro de Cañon.'

"Oh no, someone wouldn't be that foolish?" he asked himself.

Looking at his watch, he calculated a diversion would get him into camp exceptionally late, but he had to know what was happening. Turning Red to the west they galloped toward the mouth of an unknown canyon. Kicking rocks left and right, Red clambered up into the rocky volcanic canyon. It took nearly thirty minutes to reach its head. Within the last quarter mile he had to hike on foot up over a series of steep and treacherous rock formations. The final leap required him to climb a narrow ravine to finally break over a sharp barren ridge crest. Exhausted, he plunked down on the narrow ridge, which was only about twelve inches wide. Rocks dislodged by his feet tumbled several hundred feet down the sheer face on the opposite side of the mountain.

Immediately he caught sight of his old nemesis, the dark, rocky spire known as the *Obelisk*, standing proud, aloof, and defiant. The Rock taunted him. There within its base, inside the hidden cavern was gold beyond belief. He had been there, he had seen it. It appeared to be about ten miles west, northwest.

Focusing his field glasses he could see the top of the 'Canyon of Gold' that curved away from the base of the Obelisk. Suddenly there was a plume of smoke and dust visible, but no sound. Then the ridge under him vibrated as the shock wave hit, sending a rockslide plummeting below. About five seconds later, the sound of an explosion blew past him.

"Those idiots!"

They must be using a case of dynamite per shot, he figured. Looking again at the spot where the smoke had appeared, he judged it to be near the entryway to the 'Canyon.'

"How stupid, they'll never be able to get in that way."

There's nearly a million tons of rock blocking the way, he reminded himself. Even though there was little chance of them succeeding, it still unnerved him. After watching a few minutes more, Bryan realized there was nothing he could do, and decided to slide back down to where Red was waiting. He would be late for his rendezvous with Josh at Deadman Creek. It irked him. They were treading on sacred ground so to speak. The best thing to do he figured would be to contact the rangers at Douglas Flat and put a stop to this.

Easing Red down the rocky terraces, they were soon back on the main trail.

"No time to rest, Red," sighed Bryan patting him on the side.

The course now wound down through scattered hemlocks and lodgepoles into Upper Relief Valley.

Today's incident seemed to awaken in him a latent desire to resume the search for the Captain. Truthfully, it had never left him. It had been two years since they had followed the clues and discovered the Captain's mines and the golden filaments within the Obelisk. The more he thought about it, the more it bugged him.

Passing beyond the brooding face of East Flange Rock, a piece of history now came into view. Beside the trail, secured by a heavy chain were the weathered remains of an old wheel rim from a prairie schooner abandoned there in 1853 by a party of emigrants attempting a Sierra crossing.

Relief Creek was roaring, swollen by spring runoff. To Red it was just a walk in the park as he crossed the stream twice on their way down into Lower Relief Valley.

Coming out of a mixed grove of aspens and lodgepole pines, the view spilled over into a deep gorge. The quiet roar of Summit Creek floated up to him on a breeze as a hawk became visible circling below. Sierra junipers on the rugged slopes gave way to Indian hemp and Huckleberry oak through a rocky section of trail descending to Relief Reservoir. Bryan dodged in and out of the small aspen groves located along the shoreline of this manmade lake.

It was reportedly here where emigrants were rescued and given "relief," thereby giving this area its name. In 1852 a wagon train attempting a late crossing was stranded by a snowstorm on the east side of the main Sierran crest. Abandoning their wagons they proceeded over what is now called Emigrant Pass, and down Kennedy Creek to the once upon a time meadow that is now at the bottom of the lake.

An old rusted steam donkey lay beside the trail, marking the way to the dam overlook and the powder house. A series of broad switchbacks quickly dropped them below the foot of the dam.

Crossing over an iron bridge, he could see the green pools of Summit Creek far below in the bottom of the deep gorge. Soon Kennedy Creek roared in from the southeast converging into a bending, leaping monster of power.

Bryan could see the enormous iron eyelets anchored high above in the granite wall. Cemented in by molten sulfur, they were used by the steam donkeys to drag themselves upstream to the dam site.

Coming out of the Jeffery pines into Kennedy Meadows, Bryan knew it wasn't much further. Cottonwoods along this stretch of the river showed signs of gnawing by the local beaver. Golden sunlight streaming through the trees highlighted two fishermen, reminding him that evening was quickly coming on.

The resort now became discernable beyond the north end of the meadow, hidden in the shadows of tall timber. Passing the cabins, his course took him over a forested knoll to Deadman Creek. Once on the upstream trail it took about five minutes to reach their secluded campsite.

He first spotted the horse trailer through the trees. Breaking into the clear, he noticed Josh bent over by the campfire, which instantly reminded him that he was hungry.

Joshua Knight, his friend seemingly forever, was a bit taller, blonde haired, and always wore a baseball cap. What would he do without his cap he wondered? Concerning that thought, he chuckled to himself.

Red snorted as they entered the camp, and Josh turned.

"Well, it's about time. You're late."

"Tell me about it," Bryan replied, dismounting.

"What have you been doing? Look at Red. He's plumb tuckered out."

"Got anything cooked yet?"

"You're not going to answer me are you?"

"Somebody is up at the 'Canyon,' dynamiting."

"What?"

"That's right; I climbed a ridge to take a look."

Josh sat down and stirred whatever he was cooking and thought about it. "Here, it's edible and it's hot," offered Josh. "You can tell me about it, after I take care of Red."

"There's not much to tell."

"You're sure talkative tonight."

"I guess I'm just tired."

Darkness closed in as Bryan related what he had seen from the ridge crest earlier that day.

"But how did they find out about the 'Canyon?' " questioned Josh.

"Probably from someone who was on the Sheriff's posse or the fire crew that came up when we were rescued. You know how talk gets around."

"Now that you mention it, I did overhear talk in town about someone going around asking questions the other day."

"Maybe that's what has stirred the pot."

"The man never identified himself. They did say he was a short middle-aged man and wore a suit."

"A suit?"

"Oh, by the way, look at this in today's paper," said Josh grabbing a newspaper out of the cab of the pickup.

"What? *NUCLEAR TESTING MAY RESUME AT YUCCA FLATS?*"

"No-o, here, *GOLD STRIKE AT SIXTEEN TO ONE,*" he pointed.   Turning the paper toward the fire, his eyes quickly devoured the article.

"Twenty-five hundred ounces of gold—I'm impressed!"

"Kinda gets the old adrenaline going again doesn't it?"

"You know it's strange, I was up on the Pass today, listening to the wind and I began thinking. It's like— I don't know exactly how to say it. But I feel that the intrigue, the beckoning has returned to resolve one way or another, my great-great-grandfather's two hundred year old mystery."

2

STRANGER AT DEADMAN CREEK

The forest lapsed into silence as the yellow light of the campfire flickered upon the trees. Josh moved the coffee pot off the fire and sat back down, thinking how quiet it had become. Bryan unrolled his sleeping bag. All that could be heard was the crackling of the fire and the shrill echoing cry of a bird somewhere deep in the woods.

Then out of the gloom came a blood-curdling scream. The scream of what seemed to be that of a man in anguish permeated the depths of the infinite forest. Or was it the whine of a stricken animal? The two froze in shocked suspense.

Suddenly a figure of a bearded man emerged out of the darkness, and stopped just inside the perimeter of dull light. His clothes and pack were mostly rags, and his dark hair hung down to his shoulders.

"Heads up, Josh," alerted Bryan.

"What the—"

"Who are you? What do you want?" demanded Bryan.

He staggered a step forward. "You have salt or flour that you can spare?" he requested in a low voice.

"Salt, flour?" repeated Josh under his breath.

"I've run out. It's been days," he explained in a shaky voice.

"Yes, we probably have something we can share with you," acknowledged Bryan sensing they were in no immediate danger. "Come and sit down," he invited.

While Bryan dug around in the supply box, the stranger stood at bay at the far side of the campsite.

"Are you camped nearby?" asked Josh. Paying no attention the strange visitor continued to stare off into the darkness.

"Before I give you these things, sit down for a moment," ordered Bryan. Finally he complied and sat on the end of a log facing them.

After a moment of silence Bryan reached over to set the supplies next to him. Suddenly, the man rose up and grabbed his wrist with an iron grip. Pulling him up close he glared into his eyes. "Tell me the truth, are you one of *them*?" he demanded.

"What are you talking about?" exclaimed Bryan glaring back at him. After a moment he pulled loose from his grip and straightened up. Who was this man? Was he hiding out from the law?

On closer examination, he did not appear to be very old. His face and neck were covered with small cuts, probably from being flayed by the brush.

"What is your name?" asked Bryan.

"Names are not important," he bluntly answered.

"Where are you from?"

The stranger pointed up into the mountains to the south. "Hells Mountain," he replied after a pause.

"Really, that's way down by Cherry Lake," realized Josh.

"You must be starved having come all that way. We still have some beans and franks in the pot, let me dish you up some," Bryan offered.

Lowering his head, he said nothing. Resting his elbows on his knees, he held his head and began to moan. "I've been in these mountains for so long I think at times that I'm losing my mind."

"I'll dish you up some," informed Bryan.

"Is there any place that we can take you, or someone that we should call?" inquired Josh.

"No, I have no one," he moaned again. "I can't leave; there is danger afoot." Almost like lightning his countenance changed. Raising his head as he looked into the fire, his face lit up with some kind of realization. Jumping to his feet, his face became distorted, terrifying. "I have been called to the mountains! But my past has not been granted for me to find," he screamed in agony. Collapsing to the ground he began to sob.

Taken aback by the behavior of this crazed man, Bryan set a tin of food next to him, and stepped back to where Josh had retreated to. While putting things away for the night, they mutually whispered their concerns.

"I don't think he's an axe murderer, but we better keep a close eye on him anyway," thought Josh. His partner silently nodded in agreement.

"There's something about him though—I mean beyond his craziness, that I can't put my finger on. I don't know, maybe I'm just jabbering," Bryan whispered back. At that point in their conversation they noticed that he was wolfing the food down like there was no tomorrow. Cleaning out the pot, Josh gave him the rest. He seemed to settle down after he filled his belly. With curiosity Bryan approached him again, finding him hunched over, scratching the ground with a stick.

"So, you've been up in these parts for quite a while," spoke up Bryan in an attempt to find out why he was living like a beast of the forest.

"Long enough to see some mighty strange things," he replied in a low voice.

"Like what?"

"High on the eastern flank can be found some of the most profound things. For example it can get so cold up here that the air sparkles—like glitter. The moisture in the air crystallizes and is held in suspension somehow. And the lightning! That comes down from the sky and travels along the ground like snakes. Not many people dare venture up into my domain, but there are a few who have, and they have tried to kill me."

"Why?" asked Josh.

"Plutonium!"

"What?" questioned Bryan.

"I'm not crazy! There is a group of evil men intent on smuggling plutonium out of the country, undoubtedly for monetary gain. I have known about this for quite some time. I even know where one of their secret hideaways is located."

"That's bizarre, they can't get away with that," argued Bryan.

"Believe me, they have."

"Someone needs to turn them in," replied Josh.

"No one knows who they are. You just can't walk in the front door and get results."

"How is it you know so much about this?" asked Bryan.

The stranger did not answer, but instead glared into the campfire, lapsing into a flashback of memory. If there was any truth to this, Bryan wondered if he too had been involved somehow.

"It was last autumn," related the man, "near one of the passes south of here. The first snows had come, clinging only to the higher peaks and ridges. I heard the sound of a vehicle beyond the ridge to the east. It took some time to get over to that side of the range. By the time I did get to a good vantage point, a four-wheel vehicle was already heading back down the trail. I was curious to where he had been, so I ventured down and found where he had driven up to a spot at the base of the mountain range. It was easy to see where the vehicle had turned around. At this point, it appeared that someone was just out four-wheeling. But walking around the bluff a well-concealed cave revealed itself. Rocks and juniper limbs were placed over the opening. Within were a row of bright yellow canisters marked—*DANGER, RADIOACTIVE PLUTONIUM.*"

"This is serious stuff, if what you are saying is true," reflected Josh.

"… and something else there," the man mumbled inaudibly under his breath.

"Besides this cave, have you ever seen anything that you might call unusual?" questioned Bryan, probing for information that could help them in their quest.

The bearded man looked at him strangely. "I have come across the remains of many people, some recent, some very old."

"The old ones, could you tell anything about them?" pressed Bryan.

Again the strange man regarded him with mystery. "They were travelers or prospectors, I believe," he bluntly answered.

"What about any rock markings of any kind?" asked Josh.

Suddenly, a strange transformation again came over him again. Grabbing his head he became very agitated, like he was fighting something from within.

Shaking his head in disgust, Bryan got up and declared he was turning in for the night. Fetching an extra blanket he laid it in front of the troubled man. Stirring the fire they went to bed. Both Josh and Bryan stayed awake for a long time, mindful of the strange guest who was curled up by the fire apparently asleep.

Waking at first light, they found that the man had gone, blanket and all. Rekindling the fire, they warmed themselves reflecting on the bizarre experience of the previous night.

"What was it he was saying last night? Something about searching for his past," recalled Josh.

"Appears to me his troubles are more in the present," commented Bryan.

Walking around to the opposite side of the fire, Josh methodically glanced up into the trees from where the stranger had come. Turning back, something on the ground near the end of the log caught his eye.

"Bryan, come over here and look at this," motioned Josh. "In the dirt," he pointed.

"In a warped kind of way it looks like the sun symbol!" thought Bryan, kneeling down.

"Possibly drawn upside down," noted Josh.

"Mm," squatted down Bryan. "Did he do this, or was this already here?"

Josh shook his head. There was no way to know.

"It's kind of interesting, though, that when you questioned him about rock markings last night, he seemed very agitated," reflected Josh.

"He's definitely a curiosity. I do sense something deeper about him though."

"His vocabulary, tells me that he's well educated," added Josh.

Packing up, they were soon ready to bid farewell to Deadman Camp till the following week.

Throwing Josh's newspaper onto the front seat of the pickup, a headline caught Bryan's eye: *FIRE BURNS DOWNTOWN BUILDINGS.*

"What's this, a fire?" asked Bryan.

"Oh, that's right. I guess it was Tuesday night. Pitt's Studio and a couple other stores in downtown Sonora went up in smoke. I guess every fire truck in the county responded."

"Wow, that was a chunk of history."

There was no traffic when Bryan drove the truck and trailer onto the highway to head down canyon and home. Leaving the river below, they slowly climbed Patterson Grade over the granite hump to Niagara Creek. From there the serpentine road followed the ridge tops beyond Pinecrest.

"You're still going with us down to Frisco, right?" questioned Josh.

"Yeah. But are you sure you don't want me to drive both ways?"

"No, the spasms in my left arm are nearly gone. I should be able to drive at least one leg of the trip."

"I hope you don't have any other ulterior motives in getting me down there?"

"Even if I did, what of it? You still owe me."

"Yeah, yeah."

Passing the sign that designated, Spring Gap, Bryan was prompted to change the subject. "Did you ever hear the story about the man who froze to death down at the Spring Gap Powerhouse?"

"You're pulling my leg!"

"No!"

"Now, let me get this straight. A fella froze to death at a powerhouse. Come on, he could have plugged in an electric heater or something, I'm sure."

"Well, you got me there. Maybe it wasn't at the powerhouse. He could have been a dam tender."

"What is it you called him?"

"Oh, get out of here!"

"Remember infamous, 3N01?" asked Josh as they passed the Long Barn turnoff.

"How could I forget that road after all those glorious days at Camp Clavey and Bourland Meadow?"

"If I close my eyes I can still see every curve in the road."

"Don't you dare!"

Bryan laughed. They again lapsed into their own thoughts as the highway descended one hill after another.

"After we get back from Frisco, I want to take a day off and go climbing. Are you up to it?" asked Bryan.

"No, not the climbing part, but I can sit on the ledge and watch."

"I want to practice bettering my time up to the 'roof.' "

The mixed forest of the upland soon changed to foothill oaks and grassy hillsides. Rounding a long descending curve, appeared the rustic gold rush community of Sonora, nestled in the rolling hills. The look of the town had not changed significantly since the eighteen hundreds. Brick and stone buildings still lined much of Washington Street.

A plumber stepped from a doorway carrying a pipe, reminding them that repairs were still ongoing after the big freeze that winter.

After crossing Woods Creek, Bryan could see the burnt skeleton of buildings and exposed rock foundations that had been mentioned in the newspaper.

Continuing uphill through town the narrow street soon brought them to the far edge of town, from which a number of roads scattered into the Purple Hills beyond.

As they approached Bryan's home, Josh commented on the new sign that was installed along the front of their property: *ANDERSON MOUTAIN PACK STATION.*

Pulling into the driveway, Bryan nearly ran over his father's new wrangler, Cal Bishop, carrying a saddle on his blind side. Cal glared at him from under his sweat-stained cowboy hat.

Bryan heard hammering as he came to a halt beside the house, reminding him of his father's ongoing project to add an extra room for his mother's working gallery.

As he unloaded his pickup, he thought about how she seemed to be happy enough now, working on her paintings, ordering supplies, and doing the scheduling for the pack trips. It kept her busy, to where it seemed she had a phone in one hand and a paintbrush in the other. Dusting off the old piano, she once again began playing as she had done years before. Though family life would never be the same as it had been before, it was nevertheless comforting to him.

Nearby curled up at the base of one of the large pine trees was Graffiti, their Golden Retriever, oblivious of all the surrounding activity.

"How was the trip, did you get soaked?" called out his father as he poked his head out of an unfinished window.

"It went fine. There were a few showers, but nothing out of the ordinary," replied Bryan slamming the pickup door. Briefly, the memory of the crazed man crossed his thoughts, but he dismissed it.

"I guess you've seen the fire downtown?"

"How could I miss it? Any clue to how it got started?"

"The talk is a gas leak, but the Fire Marshall is not so sure."

"I guess I'll take Red out to the back pen," called out Bryan as he got back in the truck.

"Okay. Welcome home."

"You didn't tell your dad about those guys dynamiting up at the 'Canyon,' " commented Josh after they drove to the back.

"No, it's best we don't bring it up."

"Why is that?"

"Well, my dad doesn't think I should be gallivanting after a dead man—as he puts it. It's a sore subject between us."

It wasn't long before Josh had his stuff packed up and left for home. After taking care of Red, Bryan gathered his gear and headed for the house. But before he could take two steps, a small freight truck swung into the driveway. The driver checked a slip of paper and got out.

"Is this the Anderson residence?" he asked.

"That's correct."

"I have a small crate here," said the short wiry man. Going to the back of the truck he slid the rear door up. Jumping up inside, he pushed the thin crate to the back of the truck. Bryan helped him slide it down to the ground. Pulling a tag from his pocket the trucker handed him a pen to sign while he closed up the back. "Catch you next time," he said jumping back into the truck.

Bryan noted it was marked fragile, and wondered what could be inside as he muscled it up to the house. Noticing a card stapled to the end, it proved to have his mother's name on it.

"Mom!" he called out. "There's something out here for you."

Soon his mother appeared in the doorway. "It's White Feather."

"What?" asked Mr. Anderson following right behind her.

"The painting, remember."

"Oh, that's right," he replied.

Laying the crate down they pried off the back and removed the padding to reveal the back of the painting.

"There's a marking on the back," noticed Bryan.

"Probably the painter's signature mark," informed his mother.

It was in the shape of a spur attached to a distorted C, shaped like a boot.

"Wasn't there someone mentioned in the Captain's diary that started with a C?" recalled Bryan.

"Yeah, I think you're right. Now comes the job of restoring the painting and the frame," she answered standing it up. "Soon she'll hang next to the Captain, as she should."

3

CITY GIRL

San Francisco, a city of ten thousand lights, twinkled in the black glassy bay that surrounded this great bastion of concrete and light. An endless artery of red lights crossed the Bay Bridge flowing into the megalopolis, like blood into a heart.

As Bryan glanced down at the glistening bay and the silent silhouettes of great ships lying in anchor, he thought of how things had changed. Over a hundred and fifty years before, this thriving city of shanties had mobilized to conquer the golden land with its seemingly endless resources of timber, waterpower, agriculture, and gold. Now the tide had turned. The impetus returned to the City in search of other kinds of gold, such as financial empires, notoriety, and power.

But he felt aloof, knowing that the secret of Captain Camino was by far the greatest thing that anyone at anytime had ever seen. It was still hidden after two hundred years. Only three persons alive had ever seen it. Besides himself, there was Josh, who was sitting next to him driving, and his cousin Tammy Holden who lived here in the City. He had mixed feelings about seeing her again.

Josh was fully absorbed by the traffic ahead, fretting to know which lane he had to be in. His mother sat nervously, but quietly in the back seat. She trusted her son's driving but this was his first time driving in the City.

She was to spend the day at the University of California Medical Center, receiving specialized ultra-sound training.

The hint of a murky sunrise now appeared in the east as they slid into the gray corridors and skyways that led to their destination. Following the directions given on a small map, they drove westward on Fell Street passing Buena Vista Park. As they proceeded on to Parnassus Avenue, tall white buildings now appeared gleaming against a gray sky.

"This must be it," announced Mrs. Knight.

"There's the driveway," pointed Bryan.

After finding a temporary parking spot, Mrs. Knight went in to the main desk, and soon returned with instructions for them to return later in the afternoon.

The view from the medical buildings overlooked the beautiful Golden Gate Park which stretched westerly for nearly two miles toward the Pacific Ocean. This continuous strip of green-forested canopy was broken in places by open landscaping and roadways.

"I guess we have a few hours to kill," stated Bryan looking out at the jagged skyline now coming into light.

"My aunt is at work so we won't be able to see her till later. The plan is to stop at their house before we head back this evening. Oh, I know, we could stop at Tammy's school at lunch break and surprise her," thought Josh.

"Are you sure that's a good idea?"

"Sure! She'll be glad to see you, right?" winked Josh. Bryan's tall lanky friend could sometimes be quite a tease. "Let's go down to the park and get something to eat," he suggested restarting the car.

Parking nearby, they walked along a flower-lined walkway through the picturesque Botanical Gardens, and quickly found their way to an immense stone columned building, the Steinhart Aquarium. Approaching the large entranceway, Bryan pointed up to a giant inflated balloon secured to the top of the building in the shape of "Godzilla." Josh thought it had to do with the "Dinosaur Days" exhibit as advertised on a large banner draped across the front of the building.

Near the Morrison Planetarium they found a hole-in-the-wall refreshment stand to satisfy their immediate hunger. Time flew by as they walked through the long echoing corridors of animal and mineral exhibits. Upon seeing a display of gold ore from the California Gold Rush, the boys were reminded how their journey of discovery two summers before had changed their lives.

"We better get back if we are to surprise Tammy," reminded Josh, looking at his watch.

"You know where the school is?"

"Yeah, it's just up the hill, in the Twin Peaks area."

"Twin Peaks, I've heard of that."

Leaving the Park, the route Josh remembered took them back through a mixed business district, and then uphill passing wall-to-wall, multi-colored residences, secured by wrought iron bars on the doors and windows. Nearing the top of the hill, Josh pointed out the large modern school just coming into view.

"Nothing like our old rundown school is it?" commented Josh.

"No, but at least we grew up in the real world," replied Bryan.

"Oh, come on, don't be so hard on these city kids."

"Why not, if the shoe fits."

"I think in your case one shoe fits all," laughed Josh.

"Yeah, you're right," replied Bryan, "I do need to consider that there is a possibility that something good can come out of this environment."

Josh glanced at Bryan and smiled.

With difficulty they found a parking space and walked down into the quad, an open area between the main buildings, where students collected to eat and socialize.

Bryan and Josh were strangely eyed as they approached in their plain contrasting clothing. Snickers, grins and students pointing made them feel a little self-conscience.

"Hey! What farm do you guys come from?" somebody yelled.

A nearby group laughed.

"This is not what I had in mind," whispered Bryan while noticing a prominence of gang-like clothing and insignias.

"Who are you and where are you from," demanded a grim faced young man wearing a black jacket, stepping out of the crowd.

"What's it to you?" challenged Bryan.

"Shh! Let me do the talking," cut in Josh. "We're just here to see my cousin."

Apparently they had stepped onto the turf of one of the gangs that frequented the campus.

Cousin? Who's that?" he further demanded.

"Tammy, Tammy Holden."

"Really? We'll see about that. Tammy!" he called out over the heads of the crowd, and then motioned for someone to get her. "Say, you better watch your mouth," the gang leader warned turning his attention back to Bryan.

"Who do you think you are?" snapped back Bryan.

"This is who I think I am," he replied pulling out a switchblade.

"O-oh, that makes you such a big man," taunted Bryan.

"Why you barnyard toad, I'll cut your tongue out!"

He was about to turn on Bryan when a girl slipped up close to him.

"What is it, Ben?" she asked in a familiaristic tone, not knowing what was happening.

"I'm about to dismember Johnny Hayseed here," he answered taking a step forward.

At that instant Tammy seen them, and the color in her face changed. "Wait, I know them!" she stammered catching his arm.

"Huh! Are you sure?"

"Yes! Now back off!" she demanded.

"Next time, compadre," he warned with his knife, and then backing away he disappeared into the crowd.

"Don't say anything more," cautioned Josh.

Bryan relaxed his arms and made no further comment. He couldn't but help notice the change of expression on Tammy's face from a serious look to that of a squelched grin.

"Tammy, what the heck is going on here?" asked Josh, a bit dismayed himself.

She pulled them away from the crowd before speaking.

"Don't be so naive. This isn't the back forty you know, this is how it is in the City. Either you play the game or you get hurt. I didn't expect to see you here."

"I thought it might be a nice little surprise," answered Josh. "But I guess I was wrong."

"Bryan, you shouldn't have challenged, Ben. You don't know what he's capable of."

"He's all mouth. No strength in his upper body. I could have taken him."

"Oh, you and your macho ego," she replied glancing away from him.

"Okay, okay, I'm sorry. I guess lost my head," apologized Bryan.

"Tammy, you look so different, in that short skirt and all that makeup around your eyes," pointed out Josh.

She turned away in a moment of embarrassment, her face flushing red.

"I don't have to answer to you, what I wear," she retorted.

"No, but who are you trying to attract with that getup?" seconded Bryan.

"No one! Say, you two can still really dish it out. Nothing has changed has it," she protested.

"All right, I'm sorry," apologized Josh. "Maybe you can show us around or something."

"Okay," she said wiping her eyes. "We have a few minutes before the bell rings."

"Are you sure we're not tarnishing your reputation," asked Bryan.

"And what is that supposed to mean?" she fired back, placing her hands on her hips.

The next several minutes whizzed by as they visited three of the main buildings where she had classes and even met one of her teachers.

Bryan reflected on Tammy and the habitat that she had grown up in. It seemed she had risen above it to become a better person.

Apologetically thanking Tammy for their brief and dramatic visit at her school, they bid her farewell till later when they would rendezvous back at her house.

Walking along the ocean beach they discussed the pros and cons of life in the big city, while they watched surfers in their wet suits riding the waves. As the sunny day waned, they could see a fog bank beginning to build off the coast.

Finding their way back to the hospital, Mrs. Knight soon appeared carrying an armload of binders and booklets.

"Whew! That was fast and furious," she exclaimed after Bryan had helped her into the back seat. "How did your day go?" he asked.

"Well, we spent most of our morning at the Park, and then went over and surprised Tammy at her school," replied her son.

"I think we were the ones that were surprised?" commented Bryan.

"How's that?"

"The gangs."

"That bad, huh?"

"Yeah, I'm afraid so," responded Josh as they pulled out onto the street behind a bus that had just roared by.

Meandering through the busy streets, filled with people heading home, they soon climbed above the rat race into the hills above the City. The sun began to set into the murky fog bank in the west.

Turning onto Glenbrook Avenue, they quickly located the Holden's modest home. It was a typical San Francisco row house, white, with tall windows on either side of a recessed doorway.

Someone peaked out at them beside a window shade.

"I don't see Aunt Janie's car, she must not be home yet," commented Mrs. Knight. "But Tammy should be."

Before leaving the sidewalk, Tammy's voice could be heard greeting them, and her feminine shape could be seen silhouetted in the open doorway.

"Tammy, let me look at you," her aunt exclaimed after embracing her. "You've grown into a woman already. I declare, what has your mother been feeding you?"

"I don't think it's what her mother has been feeding her," innuendoed Bryan.

"Bryan! Don't start in," she replied in a matter of fact tone.

As she turned toward him he could see a flush of color in her white cheeks. Her eyes seemed to sparkle with a thousand points of light, and her shiny hair seemed to dance upon her shoulders. She seemed to be transformed somehow from the person he had met earlier that day.

"Mom, will be here any minute, make yourselves comfortable. I've started dinner—I need to check on it."

Josh and Bryan looked at each other.

"Okay," grinned Tammy. "I know what you two are thinking. Don't think it! It was Bryan's stove not my fault that time."

"I wasn't going to say a word," laughed Bryan.

"Oh, by the way, what's this I hear about you going mountain climbing again? Didn't those rocks last time pound some sense into your head?" she half-scolded. Disappearing into the kitchen her voice echoed as she concluded her thought. "I think you need to see someone about your Peter Pan Complex."

"You speak from inexperience," replied Bryan leaning against the door frame. "There is no more powerful exhilaration or challenge. It's just you and the earth, up high and in peace, away from the maddening roar of humanity below. Besides, that one time was just a freak accident."

27

"I still think it's way too dangerous. What's it going to take to convince you?" she replied closing the oven.

"I'll tell you what, I'll show you the safety gear and how it works sometime."

"I don't think so," she rebuffed turning to leave the kitchen.

Entering the front room again, Bryan glanced around noticing the hardwood floors, the coved ceiling, and an older chandelier hanging in the center of the room. No doubt this was all contemporary to its time of construction back in the 50's.

Tammy's mother soon arrived carrying a bag of groceries, and in turn greeted them one by one.

After a delightful meal, the boys with little discussion washed the dishes while the ladies visited in the living room. Through the white curtains in the kitchen, the twinkling lights of the City could be seen. A scene that Tammy undoubtedly had seen thousands of times before. Bryan thought of the view out of his kitchen window—a view to the mountains. He preferred his. But the lights were yet intriguing somehow.

Drying his hands, Bryan stepped out into the hallway adjoining the living room. He slowly studied the pictures and the photographs lining the walls.

Suddenly Tammy's voice startled him from behind. "I guess it's your turn to study my walls," she stated.

Bryan smiled. "I don't see any pictures of your dad."

"No, you won't," she replied as some of the color in her face faded.

"I'm sorry, I should have thought first, before asking."

"That's okay. Have you made any progress in finding anything new about Captain Camino?"

"No, nothing new has turned up."

"I might be able to do some research at the Bancroft Library, if I can ever get over there."

"You don't have to do that."

"But I want to, I can really be a good detective, just as good as you guys, maybe better" she asserted.

Tammy's competitive spirit continued to annoy him.

"I'm sorry about this afternoon," he apologized, changing the subject.

"You caused quite a stir that's for sure. No one dares challenge Ben."

"I perceived by the way you talked to him, you must really like him."

"No! Not the way you mean. Besides it's none of your business."

"No, it's not. I'm sorry, again. I better keep my mouth shut or I'll be apologizing all night."

"You do seem to be doing a lot of that today. I know you didn't approve of the way I dressed and looked today. But don't you like me, like this?" she asked whirling around.

"Yes—I—do," he said stumbling over his words. It was all he could do to keep from revealing his true feelings for her.

"Well maybe there is hope for me yet, right?" she smiled, seeing how he floundered for words.

"Will you two stop, you're making me sick," bellowed Josh coming out of the kitchen.

Walking back toward the living room, the mood changed.

"Tammy, what's this I hear about you graduating here shortly?" asked Josh.

"That's true, I have enough credits to complete school this year. I took one of those accelerated programs they offer here."

"Wow, I'm impressed. I guess it proves that there are brains in the family after all," laughed Josh.

"Well, I wasn't going to let you guys graduate too far ahead of me. Don't you know whatever you can do, I can do better?" she declared glancing at Bryan kind of sheepishly.

"Oh, is that so?" Bryan questioned.

"Well boys, I think it's time we head back home, before the fog sets in bad," suggested Mrs. Knight getting up off the couch.

"Oh Auntie, you just got here, must you leave so soon?"

"Yes Tammy. You can visit sometime real soon, okay?"

"Okay," she smiled hugging her.

"Good dinner, Tammy," thanked Josh.

"That reminds me, do you have any antacid?" teased Bryan looking through his pockets.

"Stop, that!" whined Tammy, softly slapping him on the shoulder. She then whispered something in Josh's ear.

As they approached the door, Tammy slid her slender arm inside of Bryan's arm and gave him an affectionate squeeze. Smiling, she watched his expression, but was met with disappointment.

"I bet Ben likes that too," he whispered.

Pulling her arm back, she turned away burning from that remark. She felt like she had been dumped onto a hard concrete floor. But who made him judge and king? He'll be sorry, just wait, I'll show him, she thought to herself. We'll see who is worthy of whom. As they left she waved with little emotion.

"Tammy, where's that smile you've had all evening?" asked her mother closing the door.

"Oh, Mom," she replied hugging her. "Why is life such a pain?"

"Daughter, you must have it bad, don't you?"

On the way home Bryan thought how much of a sap he had become, letting romantic notions taking control of him. Pretty soon he would be wrapped around her little finger. How many others has she done this to? Perhaps it was better for him and her, if he just stayed away and disappeared into the mountains.

Nevertheless, he was climbing tomorrow and that anticipation seemed to infuse power into him and to wash away all emotions that seemed so distractive.

4

SUNRISE UPON A DISTANT LAND

His hand began to bleed again, as he beat the overhead anchor into the greenish underbelly of the protruding "roof." Dangling a thousand feet above talus and forest, Bryan studied the rock forms below, the ascending spires, and the bubbling domes of the opposite wall. How aloft he felt having conquered the great "wall." Sound from the roaring Merced River drifted up to him on a breeze. To the east he noticed clouds forming over the snow bound Cathedral group. Like a giant canvas, cloud and light continuously painted and repainted the magnificent granite walls of these mountains, and the infinite expanse of peaks beyond.

A certain sadness came over him, a loneliness, a feeling that there was something incomplete in his life. Could the search for the Captain help him answer the question—who he was, or what he was to become, and resolve this feeling of incompleteness?

The blue sky and the grandeur he viewed from this high station were nevertheless inspiring—aloof from the problems and strife of mankind.

Pausing in silence he soaked in the totality of that which surrounded him, and after a satisfying period of time he finally decided to rappel back down into the thin and troubling layer of humanity below.

The following week's high country trek was uneventful. The snow had retreated into the higher peaks; and more cougar tracks were visible along the north slope of the Pass.

Regarding the disturbing activity at the 'Oro de Cañon,' Bryan learned that the perpetrators had disappeared into thin air, apparently abandoning their futile pursuit.

Two days on the trail had given him time to ponder a resolution to the mystery that surrounded his great-great-grandfather. After returning to town, Bryan was anxious to put a plan together, so that the search could resume.

Remembering that Josh was filling in at the gas station downtown, Bryan jumped in his pickup and headed for town. On the way he contemplated the risks that came with pursuing this course. Traffic was light as he cruised down Main Street passing the narrow store fronts. The partially remodeled service station now came into view. Swinging into the driveway he spotted Josh hanging up a gas nozzle on the pump island.

Wheeling around, Josh spotted a familiar pickup pulling in.

"Hey Buddy! Make it snappy! I need some gas here!" yelled Bryan, razzing him a bit.

"Oh yeah, I'll give you some gas all right!" Grabbing the nearest gas nozzle with his left hand and popping the hood with the other, he proceeded to undo the radiator cap.

"Hey! You gone loco?" yelled Bryan jumping out of the pickup.

"It's not me that's gone loco!"

"What's that supposed to mean?"

"You need gas or not?" asked Josh putting the radiator cap back on.

"A couple of dollars' worth I guess. Say, we need to sit down and put our heads together and come up with some new strategy, if we are to revive the search for the Captain. We have till the snow flies."

"I was wondering when you would come back down to earth."

"Have I been that oblivious to things?"

"What do you think?" answered Josh leaning against the gas pump. "Ever since you've been on this climbing kick, your head has been in the clouds."

"Yeah I know, I've been on a real head trip recently," he confessed.

"You're telling me. Oh, before I forget, the other night I saw something that made my heart skip a beat."

"If it was at your house I would completely understand."

"Oh, thanks. No! It was at the airport, late Wednesday night. This dark colored jet-powered helicopter flew in to refuel. Now get this, it had no designations except for a small upside down "sun" symbol painted on its hindquarter."

"What? You're pulling my leg?"

"No, it was a perfect copy, except that it was upside down. I don't know who they were, but the pilot was just an averaged sized guy with dark hair and sunglasses, wearing an unbuttoned long-sleeved shirt. But anyway, they left as quickly as they came, roaring off into the darkness. And that was that."

Bryan stood there stunned. "Can it be just coincidence or has somebody stumbled upon something?"

"Hard to say."

"Well anyway, we better start crackin'. I'll come by your place later this afternoon. I don't want to get my dad's feathers all ruffled. You know how talk about the Captain gets him all riled up."

After Bryan pulled out of the driveway, and headed down the street, Josh realized that he forgot to pay. "Hey! You forgot to pay!" he yelled, waving his arms. But it was too late, he had already turned the corner, and was gone. "He did it to me again! How does he do that?"

Later that day, Bryan traveled the narrow road to his friend's house. Grabbing the folder of notes off the seat, he walked up to the front door and knocked, but there was no immediate answer.

Bryan opened the door and called inside, but there still was no answer. His Jeep was parked in the driveway. So where could he be? Then he heard his voice coming from behind the house. Stepping around to the back, he spotted Josh herding four chickens toward the chicken house.

"There you are," spoke up Bryan.

"Ha! I was rounding up some runaways," laughed Josh.

Wasting no time, Bryan stepped inside and dropped the diary notes on the dining room table.

"Let me find a tablet and we can make a list of all the pertinent clues," said Josh.

Bryan leafed through the papers and found copies of the Captain's translated diary. He gave Josh a copy to review.

"Here's our first clue: 'finding a breach in the lava tunnel,' and then they were to travel over an unnamed pass to the southeast," pointed out Bryan.

"Wasn't their destination, '*Whispering Valley*'?" asked Josh.

"Yes, and he says it's Paiute country with plenty of water and game."

"It mentions here, 'hot springs in the area,' and that this place was low enough to miss the first snows. Then they were evidently to make their way down to *Lake Monache*, or Mono Lake," added Josh.

"This is an important one—he would mark the trail back to this so-called Whispering Valley and—"

"And more instructions would be left there," finished Josh. "Is that all?"

"Appears so, but you know, all of this is contingent on their having survived," realized Bryan.

"Now that we have the list, what do we do next?"

CLUES TO THE TRAIL OF CAPTAIN CAMINO

1. ESCAPE THROUGH LAVA TUNNEL
2. OVER AN UNNAMED PASS TO THE SOUTHEAST
3. WENT TO A PLACE CALLED WHISPERING VALLEY
4. PAIUTE COUNTRY
5. PLENTY OF WATER AND GAME
6. HOT SPRINGS IN THE AREA
7. LOW ENOUGH TO MISS EARLY SNOWS
8. ROUTE DESCENDS TO MONO LAKE
9. MARK TRAIL BACK TO WHISPERING VALLEY
10. LEFT FURTHER INSTRUCTIONS AT WHISPERING VALLEY

"We could take the direct approach and search section by section, starting with an area just east of the Obelisk hoping to find the other end of the lava tunnel, that is if there is or ever was an exit," thought Josh.

"But that could encompass a hundred square miles, in amongst some of the most rugged canyons on the planet—I would say it's a practical impossibility."

"Maybe then, the first order of work should be to verify that they did survive. So we're not wasting our time looking for something that may not exist."

"That's a good thought," replied Bryan. "To do that, we would have to go to the east side, and intercept the back trail mentioned in clue no. 9, or even possibly locating clue no. 3, Whispering Valley.

If we could find any portion of that marked trail, eee-ha! We are on our way."

"As regards the location of this mythical 'Whispering Valley,' the description could fit any one of fifty different places."

"The Captain mentioned hot springs in the area, but I'm not familiar with any hot springs except for down in Owens Valley," commented Bryan. "We'll have to keep our eyes open."

"Don't forget, as we have seen before, things can change, things can be hidden or be forgotten over time," reminded Josh.

"I think your idea is the best approach. We just need to look for the Captain's marked 'back' trail. Do you have a map of some kind to look at?"

"There's a highway map here somewhere," Josh replied getting up to look. "Here we go," he said unfolding it.

"I'll just put a light pencil line on the map. If we draw a line between the Obelisk and Mono Lake, it would run southeasterly, like so," illustrated Bryan.

"The Captain's marked trail would logically run north from Mono Lake, so it makes sense to me to check the drainages from Mono Lake north. We should be able to intercept his trail along there somewhere, if it exists," figured Josh.

"Makes sense to me, let's plan to search these two drainages here, Lundy Canyon and Virginia Creek, first," suggested Bryan.

"Sounds promising, I guess we should plan for at least a three day jaunt this time," thought Josh.

"We'll have to wait till next week now," realized Bryan.

Different than previous trips this one was difficult to plan for, since they didn't know how much of the trip was going to be by trail. Finally the day was set. Wanting to leave earlier than Friday morning they opted to leave late Thursday afternoon, and camp below Sonora Pass at Deadman Camp, giving them a head start on the next day's adventure.

When Josh arrived about four o'clock on Thursday, there was already a significant change afoot.

"Josh, good, you're here. I've taken the liberty of a making a change to our program," informed Bryan, "which I think you'll agree with. First of all, I found out that, Bill Clifford, who is a chopper pilot for the Forest Service, will be flying to Bishop tomorrow. So I called him last night to see what his flight plan was. And low and behold, it just so happens that he'll be flying over Sonora Pass about seven in the morning. I asked him if I could hitch a ride part way and get a quick flyover from Green Lakes Pass down to Lundy Canyon. He said fine, it was on the way."

"That changes things dramatically. But is he bringing you back?" questioned Josh.

"No, he'll drop me off at the Mono Basin Overlook, and continue on his way."

"Hmm, that means that I'll have to drive from Sonora Pass all the way down to Mono Lake by myself."

"That's true, but think of all the work that it saves us," reasoned Bryan.

"You're beginning to sound an awful lot like a regular tenderfoot," teased Josh.

"Not at all, there's still plenty of hiking to do. It's just that this will help us eliminate some of the lengthier southerly routes."

"Now, let me get this straight. First, he'll pick you up at Sonora Pass, flyover Green lakes, Virginia lakes, and Lundy Canyon, to be finally dropped off at the Overlook. After which we'll head back for the one that has possibilities, or if nothing appears, I guess, the logical thing then would be to head up toward Twin Lakes. Is that the idea?"

"You got it," confirmed Bryan. "It could cover a twenty mile stretch and save us a whole bunch of time."

"Okay, it does sound like a good idea."

"If his flight plan should suddenly change, or if he doesn't show, we just go back to plan 'A,' I guess."

"Oh, by the way, your girlfriend called last night," teased Josh.

"Girlfriend? What are you talking about?"

"Girlfriend?" came the questioning voice of Bryan's mother from the adjoining room.

"Tammy, she likes you, haven't you figured that out yet?"

"Is this true? Are we making this official?" questioned Mrs. Anderson peaking around the corner to catch his expression.

"No! Josh, I'm going to brain you if you don't stop," he replied falling silent unwilling to reply.

"I told her and my aunt about our little excursion," informed Josh.

"I can imagine Tammy complained because we didn't invite her," thought Bryan.

"No, she didn't say a word about coming up. Oh, guess what? I think my aunt wants to move back up this way, closer to her relatives and all."

"Oh really?" questioned Bryan. "Did she say anything else?" he asked lowering his voice.

"Who, Tammy? No, but no wonder, at times you really put her off. Oh, something important, before I forget—Tammy has been doing some digging around on her own at the Bancroft Library, and discovered that U.S. Highway 395, that runs along the east side of the Sierra, was first known as '*El Camino Sierra*.' A historical footnote mentions that possibly, the name was romantically inspired by another road, El Camino Real, which means The Royal Highway."

"El Camino Sierra," Bryan repeated. "The Sierra Highway or maybe it's simply, Camino's Sierra Highway," he mumbled analyzing the phrase. "It's not a sure sign, but there is a strong possibility that there is a connection. El Camino Sierra," he repeated again.

"Our girl has come through again, maybe."

"I hate to admit it, but maybe she has. But I won't be convinced till I can come face to face again with one of the Captain's sunbursts," replied Bryan.

As the packing neared completion, Mrs. Anderson came out to check their outfit. "How about socks?" she said looking through things.

"Mom! Yes I have socks. You know that one pair can last me for a whole week."

"Ha, that's not funny. I'll get you an extra towel," she announced going back in.

Josh smiled at Bryan. "Stop that. She's only being a mom. It's better just to let them do their job, and everyone is happy," explained Bryan.

"I know, it's just so, déjà vu."

"You boys drive careful," requested Bryan's mother when she came back out with the towel in hand. She gave her son a long hug after loading up their gear.

Finally on the way, they waved as they descended the driveway and made the corner. "Oh-h! It feels so good! To get away and go exploring like the old days," exclaimed Bryan stretching his arms up in the air.

Catching Highway 108 easterly out of town their course wound its way through oak covered hills and fields of scattered wild flowers. Josh sped through 'Sullivan's curve' trying to break his old speed record.

"I swear, someday you're going to end up in the creek!" yelled Bryan.

Josh laughed, but said nothing. Slower than normal traffic was encountered as they drove past Standard Junction and the quiet community of Soulsbyville. Josh put the pedal to the metal as they approached Twain Harte Grade trying to gain as much speed as possible. Their momentum slowed quickly on the steep grade.

Twain Harte, named after Mark Twain and Bret Harte, was a cozy little town nestled in the pines; from which was the beginning of a gallery forest of mixed cedar, pine, and fir.

Tall stately Ponderosas towered above them through the curves that led up to the small village of Sugar Pine, which historically was the beginning of the Mono Toll Road built in 1867 to service the mining communities of Bodie, Dogtown and others on the Nevada side of the great Sierra Nevada.

Coming around a bend, a momentary glimpse of the distant rock formations known as the *Three Chimneys* came into view, bringing back memories from times past.

"The Chimneys look to be a million miles away today," commented Bryan as their course wound its way along the face of a volcanic bluff, evidenced by mud and breccia flows.

"I need to make a pit stop at Pinecrest for a minute," announced Josh as they passed Old Strawberry Road.

"If you insist," replied Bryan.

Descending down a long hill, they turned off at the Summit District Ranger Station, and proceeded straight along to Pinecrest Lake. Through the pines a large body of blue now became visible stretching to the far granite mountains.

"I'll be right back," said Josh as they pulled up adjacent to the restroom.

Bryan climbed out of the jeep to stretch and peer at the activity on the lake. Soon Josh emerged with a favorable report on the condition of the bathrooms.

"Let's take a quick look at the lake," suggested Bryan.

Walking on down under the tall ponderosa pines on a thick carpet of pine needles the view of the lake widened to the north. The white sandy shore was visibly crowded with people sunning themselves and young children playing along its edge.

Coming out from under the trees, the view was well worth the walk. The dark blue lake, contrasted beautifully against the magnificent white granite mountains that loomed in the north. Gentle waves sloshed on the beach, directing the eye along the meandering pine-edged shoreline to its upper limit. Catamarans with their colorful red and blue sails glided effortlessly to and fro across the lake.

"It's hard to imagine that there was ever a meadow under this lake," commented Josh.

"Strawberry Flat," recalled Bryan. "The old toll road went right up through there," he motioned with his arm.

"While fishing up here about five years ago, a friend of my dad's, who happens to be a geography teacher, was telling us a little bit about the history up here. You know how it is sitting in the boat all day long, rocking back and forth, and all there is to do is tell stories."

"Like the big one that got away, right?"

"Well, besides that one," laughed Josh. "This meadow was a meeting place and a summer camp for the Miwok and Paiute trading parties."

"I imagine things were usually peaceful back in those days," reckoned Bryan.

"Yeah, except for one altercation that happened back before the first 'white man,' had ever come to this area."

"What altercation?"

"I don't know, now, if anyone knows what really caused it. But a Paiute hunting party that happened to be camped here on the meadow was attacked by a band of Miwok braves. And the following spring, well, here come the Paiute braves to make a counterattack down near 'Little Sweden.' The Paiute braves ended up taking a group of Miwok woman and children captive, and promptly headed for the nearest pass to cross back over to their side of the mountains," recalled Josh.

"Didn't the Miwok, give pursuit?" questioned Bryan.

"They did, but as I recall the raiding party threatened to kill the infants one by one if they didn't turn back." And apparently, that was the way it ended."

"Wow, those poor women and the kids," thought Bryan looking into the depths of the lake.

Noticing that some people were beginning to pack up, it reminded them that they too had to be on their way.

On the road again they approached the modern day village of Strawberry located on the South Fork of the Stanislaus River. Located beside the cascading torrent was the center piece of the small hamlet, the brightly painted Strawberry Store—a local landmark. Climbing the ridge above the Pinecrest Basin afforded them spectacular mountainous views both east and west. Shadows were now noticeably lengthening in the vicinity of Cow Creek as the diminishing sunlight flickered through the trees.

"Those poor Indian women," spoke up Bryan after a long spell of silence.

"Are you still thinking about that?"

"It's burned into me; I can't get rid of it."

"Try thinking about something else."

"I'm trying, I'm trying."

Rounding granite bluffs soon brought them to the Eagle Meadows turnoff.

"If our trip to the far side falls through, we might have to go into Long Valley and conduct a search from there," commented Bryan.

"If we do, we'll have to go by and show our respects to the old *Bennet Juniper*. Remember back when they used to claim that it was 6,000 years old, and the oldest living thing on earth. But since then I think they have backed off on that."

"And don't forget the old autunite uranium mine, where we found those big chunks of petrified wood."

"That's still not active is it?"

"Oh, no, not for many years," answered Bryan.

The Dardanelles still bathed in golden sunlight, burst into full view as they rounded a curve in the road, which now descended into the North Fork of the Stanislaus River. They made good time on the steep grade leading down to Clark's Fork on the river. From there the easterly course bobbed and weaved parallel with the river for many miles passing through open meadows dotted with immense ponderosa pines, and skirting ancient basaltic lava flows.

Soon they arrived at their campsite on Deadman creek, which was conveniently located at the bottom of the steep grade that led up to Sonora Pass, some 9,626 feet above sea level.

Sitting by the campfire, and hearing the rush of the river nearby, Bryan thought of the stranger they had met there some days before. There was something about him that would not go away.

Rising early, they caught the sunrise at the Pass and what a glorious sight it was. The jagged edges of dark mountain ranges over one hundred miles away were contrasted against the intense opalescence of the rising sun.

"This is where east meets west," commented Josh.

"May our quest for a different sun rising prove successful in this wild and lonely land," replied Bryan looking down into its dark depths below.

In a figurative sense, Josh thought of the Captain's symbol—the 'Sunburst,' and how success would be theirs if they would once again feast their eyes upon it.

5

FLIGHT TO THE FAR SIDE

The pronounced rhythmic thud of an approaching helicopter alerted them to prepare for its landing.

"That must be Bill now," announced Bryan. "Help me stop traffic. And Josh, I'll see you at the Overlook in about two hours."

"Okay, but don't pile up somewhere," called out Josh as the chopper descended.

They could see the pilot looking both ways, watching for traffic, and then he continued his descent landing on the crest of the highway, which was the only half-level surface for many miles. The initial blast of air blew dust up the cut slopes and down the road. After the pilot powered down, Bryan ducked low and ran up to the side door and got in. After he buckled up, the pilot began to power back up.

Outside of the fact that the pilot wore sunglasses, all that Josh could tell about him was that he appeared to be in his mid or upper forties in age. With a final wave, they were off.

The chopper's engine wound up to a loud whine as it left the ground, the rear ascending first, pitching the machine as it were headlong into the rugged terrain below the pass. Soon the helicopter leveled out and banked southeast.

Bryan was amazed as trees and creeks whizzed under his feet. This was only the second time he had ever flown in such a craft. Josh and the highway quickly disappeared into the folds of the mountain behind them. In the northeast he could see white ashen mountains and off to their left was Walker Meadows, divided by the meandering Walker River. To the right, perched on a plateau of sorts was the most beautiful earthen mirror, *Leavitt Lake*. The blue oval was like a gem set in the rough, surrounded by reddish volcanic cliffs.

Soon as the whirlybird was out of sight, Josh jumped into the Jeep, and began his descent of the narrow ribbon of highway that soon brought him down to U.S. 395, the 'El Camino Sierra,' or at least its northerly extension.

Ascending a branch of the Walker River, he passed Fales Hot Springs and entered through the umber-colored Devil's Gate rock formation to descend into the lush green meadows of Bridgeport Valley, bordered by the magnificent snowbound peaks of the Sawtooth Ridge in the west.

Bridgeport was the County seat of this far-flung territory that extended from the icy peaks of the High Sierra to the lonely stretches of desert in the east.

Merchants in the small town were just opening up for the day's business, sweeping and setting out items along the storefronts.

Passing through a set of hills marking the south end of the valley, a historical monument on the right hand side of the road, faced out over a course-graveled creek. This was the site of the old mining camp of Dogtown, active in the 1850's. From there the road began a long ascent with a view of numerous green aspen groves scattered among the drainages and ridges to the west. Passing by Virginia Creek Road the highway finally crested at Conway Summit, on the dividing ridge that separated two geological basins.

After a short descent, Josh pulled into the Mono Lake Overlook, where he was to meet the helicopter in a very short time. The scenic viewpoint was busy with vehicles pulling in and out, and people lining up behind a stonewall to peer out over the vista that seemed endless. This was the vast Mono Basin. Perhaps even more impressive was the magnificent march of Sierran peaks that gradually disappeared some two hundred miles to the south. To Josh it seemed to be a brazen display of light, rock and ruggedness—on a planetary scale.

Below him sunken into the earth was a gigantic crater-like depression in which sat Mono Lake. The present residual body of water was about fifteen miles across. Its shape resembled in many respects like that of an amoeba. The light blue of the lake was accented by two islands, one volcanic black, and the other ashen white. Above the lake were terraces, evidently etched by waves beating against an ancient shoreline which gave evidence of a much higher lake.

Meanwhile, Bill and Bryan continued flying south. Skirting Forsyth Peak, Bryan could see over the crest of the Sierra into the Yosemite back country. He mentally noted to himself the abrupt change in geology along the northern park boundary. The white granite and glistening lakes of Yosemite's high country contrasted greatly with the reddish, barren, volcanic formations of the north.

Bill began to rattle on about how the Forest Service was going to 'ell in a hand basket. Because of economic pressures and the state of current forest management practices, an ugly scar was being left upon the forest that could take generations to clean up. Chatter from the fire lookout towers crackled on the radio. Bryan was somewhat caught up with all the current "forest gossip." Bill talked in depth on "forest" politics, cattle grazing, environmental issues and how "affirmative action" had taken its toll on the organization.

Bill banked the helicopter and adjusted his course more to the east. Glancing down, Bryan noticed something in the canyon below. It appeared to be a vehicle, but what made him think twice about the situation was the sight of two people running for cover.

"What canyon is that down below us," asked Bryan.

"I don't know, I'm not familiar with most of these canyons on the Toiyabe side."

Bryan was reminded of something that the stranger at Deadman Creek had told him.

Bill informed him they had to make a quick stop at the Bridgeport Ranger Station to pick up a parcel that had to be delivered to the Bishop office. With Twin Lakes just coming into view they veered easterly cutting across Bridgeport Valley to the new Ranger Station located along the easterly hills. After five minutes they were off again, circling over the compound and the adjacent highway, setting course again for Green Lakes.

Flying over the lush southern meadows, they passed over a major creek. Bill temporarily turned back to it in a moment of recognition. "That's right, this is Virginia Creek. Green Creek should be further to the west," he recalled veering back to the original course.

Within thirty seconds they had intersected Green Creek and began following its rocky course. Leaving the meadows, the terrain gave way to a rolling torturous landscape that was marked by aspen groves growing in the deeper drainages and protected areas.

Curving to the southwest, the yawning Green Lakes Basin opened up in front of them. Passing over a pack station with its familiar corrals and barns, Bryan spotted a campground ahead in the narrowing canyon. The creek below was intermittently hidden by scattered groves of aspen and fir. Bryan removed the field glasses from his pack.

"What did you say you're looking for?" asked Bill.

"Stone carvings, pictographs, that type of thing."

"The only ones that I'm aware of around here are down in Owens Valley."

"These are a little bit different."

"Uh."

"Take me right up to the pass at the head of the canyon and then from there we can slip over the ridge to Virginia Lakes."

Almost immediately three lakes came into view. One at the bottom of the canyon, and the other two interestingly perched left and right, on granite benches a thousand feet above.

"That should be Green Lake in the bottom of the canyon," thought Bill.

As they climbed past ten thousand feet, only sparse low-growing brush and pinyon pine could be seen scattered on the granite ledges. Slowly, approaching the end of the canyon, Bryan studied the slopes leading up to the top. Soon they had ascended to the eleven thousand foot pass, and gazed upon some of the wildest and most beautiful country that he had ever seen. The copter slowly pivoted counter-clockwise as Bryan took one last look. But nothing caught his eye.

Cutting between two tall peaks, they emerged over a breath-taking view of East Lake. Banking right, the course followed a string of small jewel-like lakes to the top of an intervening ridge.

"We're now in the headwaters of Virginia Creek," announced Bill as they came up over the top.

Out to the west exploded a view of the vast arena of the drainage systems of the Yosemite backcountry. And at their feet was Summit Lake perched at the Virginia and Yosemite divide.

"Let's follow the natural hiking trail down the canyon," suggested Bryan.

It was initially easy to follow the descending switchback trail on the glistening white granite slope below. A group of backpackers waved as they flew over. Rounding a corner, a string of beautiful dark lakes could be scene scattered about in the canyon below. The scenery sped by quickly as they passed over meadows and small lakes to finally swoop out into the main basin surrounding Virginia Lake.

"See anything?" asked Bill.

"Not a thing."

Dropping out of the Virginia Lake Basin, Bill made a wide turn banking south. Below them, Bryan could see the highway and Conway Summit. The Mono Basin Overlook where he was to meet Josh was now coming into view, just beyond the Summit.

Bill once again picked up with his pet peeves, pretty much where he had left off—discussing how they were eliminating all the outlying forest camps and centralizing everything out of the Supervisor's Office. "Well, here we are," announced the pilot breaking his own train of thought.

Bryan was awe struck with the vast theater that was flung open to them. The Mono Basin with its pale blue lake below was but only part of a vast panorama of sky, rock and infinity. The dark Mono Craters stood out obliquely in the south perimeter of the Basin. To the east beyond the outer rim of the basin, island mountain ranges disappeared beyond the horizon into the vast Nevada desert.

Banking to the right they descended into the great wall of snowcapped mountains that jumped up in front of them.

"This is Lundy Canyon that we're approaching. I know this place well—great fishing. I do believe the creek is called Mill Creek.

Bryan visually verified their location by observing that Mill Creek was indeed the first drainage to enter Mono Lake on its north side.

"There was a small flurry of mining back up in here in 1879 or so, as I recollect," continued Bill.

"What kind of mining?"

"Mostly gold and silver, but over here on the right is Copper Mountain, there was an active copper mine there for a while. But really, the real draw to this area, besides the fishing is the blazing fall colors that paint these hillsides red and yellow in the fall.

Dark blue Lundy Lake scarcely a half mile across, now came into view, extending more than a mile toward a wall of towering mountain peaks still draped in snow on their north and east faces. Small fishing boats dotted the placid lake, while the motionless figures in them kept vigil hoping for that one special catch. Scattered Jeffery pine and sagebrush growing along the north edge of the lake made an interesting mosaic from above.

The old town site of Lundy appeared to be just ahead at the west end of the lake. A number of small fishing boats were beached along the shore at the foot of the small village. Beside them the north wall of the canyon composed of a reddish metaphoric rock jumped up to over two thousand feet in height.

Weathered wooden structures half hidden, became visible amongst a grove of aspens that dominated the ascending valley. The first building to come into view was a small grocery with an old style gas pump standing like a lone sentinel along its front. Scattered among the trees were summer cabins, some well maintained, and others weathered gray and sagging.

"Somewhere up on this creek there used to be a power house. It was built back in the late 1800's to supply power to Bodie and the mines," recollected Bill. "It's gone now though, wiped out by a massive avalanche one winter."

Strange companionships were observed in the leeward side of these harsh and rugged mountains. Sagebrush grew to just short of the timberline, competing with communities of aspen, fir, and scattered white pine for precious water.

Avalanche damage was prevalent among the silvery aspens that flourished in the upper end of the canyon. Their course continued along the rocky north wall.

"Drop us down so that we're just above where the cliff meets the ground," requested Bryan.

Bill brought her down, throttling back. The copter seemed to glide effortlessly along the face of the cliff. Beneath his feet he could see the gauntlet of rock and brush, which would've presented a great challenge if they had been down there on foot. Clutching the field glasses, Bryan scanned the lower part of the canyon wall. Suddenly, an eagle darted out of the cliff ahead of them, undoubtedly being frightened by the helicopter's approach.

Bryan put down the glasses and rested his eyes for a moment. A trail was intermittently visible below them winding between scattered groves of aspens.

Gradually Lundy Canyon curved to the south and climbed steeply toward a distant pass. Bryan thought his best chance to find anything would be in the throat of the pass. Directing Bill to pause and turn slowly in the pass, he closely examined the rock formations on both sides. Through the gap in the mountain, Bryan glimpsed what was probably Saddlebag Lakes.

Seeing nothing, they descended the south wall continuing the search. Their course soon wrapped them around into Lake Canyon, intersecting high up on the main canyon wall. Almost immediately, the remnants of a mining operation came into view along the east side.

"That's the famous May Lundy Mine if I'm not mistaken," guessed Bill.

Remains of old buildings and machinery lay scattered in the snow drifts. On the opposite slope were mine tailings; but again nothing significant was visible. Dropping back into Lundy Canyon, Bryan spotted something he hadn't notice before.

"Bill, up there at the top of the north wall, it almost appears to be a pass of some kind," pointed Bryan.

"Woo! That's way back up on top," commented Bill peering up through the top edge of the windshield. "Well, we do need to climb back up part way anyway. So here goes."

Banking left, the helicopter curved its way back up canyon. Circling, Bill brought them back around in close proximity to the north wall. Slowly they ascended to the jagged pass, when suddenly a strong updraft jolted them, nearly turning them on their side.

"Whew! That was close. We could've been slammed into the cliff if we had been much closer. I'll back off a ways. We should be fine now."

Bryan released his white-knuckle grip on the frame and raised the field glasses to inspect the rock-shattered surface of the pinnacles adjacent to the pass. Dark mineral stains flowed out of the pass like a tongue, which faded to a point about one hundred feet down the cliff. Back behind some of the peaks, pockets of snow still remained.

"Hmm, nothing—nothing," concluded Bryan putting the glasses down.

Curling away from the mountain, they dove down the center of the canyon passing back over Lundy Lake to finally reenter Mono Basin. Banking left their course veered toward the Mono Lake Overlook.

Several cars and one trailer appeared beyond the overlook wall as they ascended from below. Bryan finally spotted the Jeep and Josh at the east end of the parking area. Josh waved as they drew closer approaching from the east along the highway alignment. Bill quickly descended and landed in the vacant east end of the parking lot.

After thoroughly thanking Bill, Bryan bailed out of the cockpit. Ducking down he cleared the rotors and backed off to a safe distance. Giving him the all clear sign, Bill powered back up, blowing dust and debris everywhere. Lifting off he gave one last wave before falling forward into the Great Basin beyond. He stood there watching him for a moment sweep out and disappear into the great void.

Walking toward the Jeep, Bryan noticed that all the sight-seers along the overlook wall were staring at him, making him feel a bit self-conscience.

"How did it go?" first asked Josh.

"It went well enough, but my head is still in a whirl," he replied putting his pack in the rear of the Jeep. "Why are those people staring at me like that? They're just plain gawking at me." He then noticed that Josh was trying to conceal a smirk, but was failing. "Okay, what's going on?"

"Ha ha ha, I couldn't help myself. I told them you were a secret agent," he finally blurted out, starting up the vehicle.

"What? You're crazy! That's embarrassing." But looking back as they pulled out of the parking lot, he broke into a smile and had to laugh to himself.

"Well, what did you see, flyboy?"

"Basically nothing. We zoomed in and out of the passes, and I looked at all the major rock faces that seemed appropriate."

"The process of elimination has begun."

"Yeah, but in the end, it could all be eliminated—it's easy to miss things."

Bryan recounted the sights and scenes of his trip as they climbed the steep grade to the top of Conway Summit. At the Virginia Lakes turnoff, they descended the long grade into Bridgeport.

Nearing the center of town the old Victorian style Courthouse painted white and trimmed in red loomed up against the blue eastern sky. Strategically placed was an old Civil War style cannon that faced the street.

Pulling into the parking lot of a local grocery store, they watched with intent while two men tried to unlock a station wagon, after apparently locking the key inside.

"I've been thinking as of late that I need to get my own contractor's license," commented Josh stretching his legs.

"There's money to be made in the trades, that's for sure," thought Bryan. And if you work for yourself, you don't have to take all the guff."

"Yeah, but it's all that paper work that I hate."

Noticing how high the sun had risen in the sky, they decided to hurry along their business in the store and continue on the way.

Twin Lakes Road was handily just across the highway. The narrow county road first angled south then west across the restful green meadowlands toward the wild jagged crest of Sawtooth Ridge. At the edge of the valley an alluvial wall forced the road to wind its way along its face to the top of what was apparently a plateau. Their course followed a meandering creek that dodged around scattered pockets of aspen trees that hid a number of small campgrounds. Knife-edged peaks leaped up just ahead. Snow still choked the deep vertical crevices that ran down the face of the great granite wall.

Reaching the mouth of the canyon, white caps on a dark blue lake became visible. This was no doubt the first of the Twin Lakes. The road narrowed to proceed along the north edge of the two lakes.

The resort of Mono Village now appeared along the west shore nestled in a grove of pines. A boat launch and dock were built along the shoreline with a restaurant and store set further back at edge of the tree line. A campground and a scattering of quaint little cabins were spread throughout the forested area behind.

After getting directions at the store, they realized it was already mid-afternoon, prompting them to hurry up their preparations. Parking the Jeep in a designated parking area they prepared their gear for the overnight stay.

"Did you hear that guy in there talking about a 600 pound bear that's been raising havoc up here?" asked Josh.

"No. What did he say?"

"Apparently he's so strong that he's been pushing over those big garbage dumpsters looking for food. Even a full-sized pickup pulling with a chain could barely get it up-righted."

Bryan shook his head as he studied a map. "That must be Matterhorn Peak up there," he pointed, "12,281 feet high."

"It does have that Alps look," agreed Josh as he slung his pack onto his shoulders.

A white pickup pulling an aluminum fishing boat passed by them as they made their way across the parking area to head into the pines. Hiking through the campground, the path intersected the main trail near Robinson Creek. Upstream a Forest Service sign warned them they were now entering a bear habitat. Food storage was to follow very strict guidelines.

Further along, small groves of aspen trees began to mingle with a thinning coniferous forest. Coming up onto a rise, they could clearly see the treeless upper end of the valley, carpeted by sagebrush and mule ear. Pulling out the field glasses Bryan began a visual search for symbols along the canyon walls.

After a brief respite, the trail soon led them up to a sign that designated the beginning of the Hoover Wilderness area. A magnificent view to the south drew their gaze up into the majestic peaks of Little Slide Canyon, which contrasted greatly with the sweeping aprons of rock debris on the north slope of the valley.

After snapping a couple of pictures, they continued on their way through the sagebrush, kicking up the dust. At the upper end of the valley a forested area gave them a break from the glaring sun. From there the trail climbed a brush-covered slope to pass through a cluster of aspen and snowberry. The course curved southwesterly paralleling a fork of Robinson Creek. A flower garden made up of red Indian paintbrush and fireweed, greeted them as they crossed a small gravelly creek.

A gradual climb into an ever-deepening canyon brought them to the north shore of Barney Lake. The diffused reflections of the high peaks streaked across the water toward them, as they walked along its rocky shore. The magnificent stature of snowbound Crown Point, dominated the scene at the south end of the lake.

"Look what the beavers have done," pointed Bryan as they came up on a rise overlooking the inlet to the lake. "They have dammed up the creek, flooding the meadow way back up into the lodgepoles."

"My arm is beginning to hurt. I'm going to have to stop and take the weight off my shoulder for a bit," informed Josh holding his arm.

"Sorry, I keep forgetting about your arm," apologized Bryan.

"Wish I could," Josh responded pulling his pack off and sitting down on a log. "If this was the Captain's route, this would be the perfect spot for marking the trail," he commented, changing the subject.

"True, but the Captain's methods didn't always follow the obvious," replied Bryan as he eyed a large white fleecy cloud drifting overhead.

Back on their way, the trail climbed through a dense forest of lodgepole, white pine, and red fir. As anticipated, another series of switchbacks appeared, that would carry them to the next level above nine thousand feet. The slope was covered with glacial till; giving evidence this had been the scene of an ancient glacial battlefield. Climbing through a large rock outcropping they soon reached a windy pass.

"Where the wind blows," Bryan uttered to himself.

"What's that supposed to mean?" asked Josh, feeling how tender his arm had become.

"I've always felt that on one of these wind-swept passes, I would someday find an answer to what we've been looking for, but alas all I see is just bare granite."

"Well, you didn't expect to find a flashing neon sign up here did you?"

"No, but I was hoping," laughed Bryan.

Crossing a glade, the trail intersected Peeler Lake Creek, which continued upstream through a windy ravine. Climbing to the top of the next ridge, the windswept surface of Peeler Lake broke into view. A jumble of huge stones sat in the outlet of the lake, effectively damming it.

"This is it–base camp!" declared Bryan.

"None too soon," commented Josh, still hurting.

Beyond the dazzling blue lake, the surrounding rugged snow-laced peaks were beginning to fall into shadow. Pockets of aspen groves looked promising as shelter along the meandering shoreline. In the second cove, they found a nice spot decorated by patches of blue-violet Delphinium.

"We better get camp set up first," thought Josh glancing around at the deepening shadows.

"Rest that arm. I'll get things set up," offered Bryan. After putting up the pup tent, he quickly set up the kitchen and prepared the fire pit. Josh mentioned he was getting hungry. So Bryan proceeded to build a fire, but the damp wood created more smoke than heat.

A hot meal of black beans and rice seemed to satisfy their hunger. After sipping some hot green tea, Bryan declared he was going on a jaunt and would return shortly.

Scrambling around on the adjacent domes and outcroppings he finally wandered back to a high spot just above their camp. The darkening voids between the peaks began to creep down the mountainsides joining as they descended.

Calling down to Josh, he asked him to come up and look around. While Josh made his way up, Bryan noticed a near full moon rising behind Kettle Peak to the east.

"What a wild and wonderful place this is," commented Bryan as Josh finally worked his way up. Colors sprang forth in the eastern sky, in brilliant reds and mixed purples. "What a sight—the ascending moon in among the dark rugged peaks. Brings back memories, doesn't it?" questioned Bryan.

"Indeed it does, but it seems that our lives will be soon be moving in different directions again. At least it worked out we could be together on this one adventure." They became silent reflecting on their conversation and the rising moon before them. For a frozen moment in time, Josh felt that all things were as they should be, and he smiled to himself.

"You didn't happen to hang the food up did you?" asked Bryan.

"Ahh—no," realized Josh.

Leaving their perch they quickly scampered down to camp. "I'll stoke the fire if you gather the food," offered Bryan.

"I guess we'll have to pack up the cooking utensils and plates, dirty, tonight," realized Josh. "You can wash them in the morning."

"Me?"

"Yeah. But I need your help in hanging these items in that tree yonder?"

"Yonder? Where did you pick up that jargon?"

Josh laughed, "A fellow I worked with—"

Snapping tree branches nearby caused them to freeze. Suddenly, a large dark shape appeared at the edge of the trees. It was a very large brown bear.

"Dang, we haven't got our food hung up yet," quietly spoke Josh.

"This bear must have an understanding of camp schedules," thought Bryan "Let's bang some pans together—that usually works."

"They are over there in the pack. What do we do now?" queried Josh.

The bear sniffed in their direction as he advanced into the campfire light.

"Stand big and impressive, and yell as loud as you can," recommended Bryan.

"It's not going to wor-r-rk!" hollered out Josh running for a large tree at the back of the campsite.

"Don't turn your back to it!" warned Bryan quickly backing away as the bear lumbered up to their packs tearing them apart. Scrambling up the tree, they peered down on the devastating sight. He seemed to be unhappy with his find, and looked in their direction. Raring up on his hind feet, he approached the tree.

"Uh oh!" voiced Josh.

The bear was immense. Grunting he pounded with his upper body against the tree, pushing with his large forepaws. After several attempts of trying to shake them loose, the bear seemed frustrated, and returned to the packs. He occasionally looked back at them as he rummaged through their stuff.

"Now look what you have done!" spoke up Bryan. "You didn't pack anything the bear liked."

"Well, frankly I'm glad. But he sure was looking at us with those big hungry eyes."

Soon the furry marauder faded into the darkness carrying off his prize.

"Whew! Close one," commented Bryan, finally climbing down the tree. With Josh right behind him, he asked, "What was that he carried off?"

"Our breakfast!" replied Josh, disgusted.

"I guess, I don't need to worry about doing the dishes now," commented Bryan.

Quietly they picked up what was left of their packs and the food, and hoisted them up into the tree in case the bear should return. With guarded sleep it was a long night before gray dawn and the beginnings of a new day.

After making makeshift repairs to their torn packs, they nourished themselves with what little food was left while basking in the first rays of the early morning sun. Sitting on a granite bench they overlooked the calm glassy lake. The cold early morning breeze carried the shrill echo of a peregrine falcon from the canyon below.

The crystalline blue lake was like a darkened mirror that had been melted into the upheaved gray cement of the earth. It was a sea of light and perfection, rendering everything beyond of lesser glory.

"It's so peaceful here, but I reckon we better get back to business," reminded Josh.

"I was presumptuously expecting to find something between here and Barney Lake," reflected Bryan. "But from here on up, the possibilities scatter to the four winds."

From Peeler Lake, the rough trail traversed down a slope into the upper end of Kerrick Meadow, whose meandering creek drained into the South Fork of the Tuolumne River many miles below. Their final hour of search took them to the rugged head of the canyon at Buckeye Pass.

Looking up at the elongated summit of Ehrnbeck Peak, quite some distance away, and the unknown canyons that lay beyond, Bryan felt the beckoning to go to them. But what was the use? Beyond these passes, the chances of finding anything was even more remote. Bryan felt the disappointment set in. It was time to return to the lowlands.

6

HIGH DESERT RENDEZVOUS

It was nearing midday as they pulled back onto Highway 395 headed for home, feeling frustrated and downcast. Both were silent and deep within their own thoughts as they paralleled the meandering river and sped through the curves. Suddenly, a loud pop aroused their attention. Within seconds the right rear tire began rumbling and vibrating.

"A flat!" Josh rang out over the road noise. Coming into view just around the bluff was a white building. It appeared to be a roadside diner of some kind.

"Hopefully, they have a phone," stated Bryan.

Josh coasted the Jeep to a halt in front of the old weathered structure. Through a series of windows they could see tables. To their left, two rusted gas pumps that probably hadn't run in years, stood as a monument of times past. Along the edge of the highway a weathered, paint-peeled cafe sign made a sizzling sound as the light bulbs flashed on and off.

"Is it open?" questioned Josh.

"Looks like it, there are a couple vehicles parked around the other side," answered Bryan jumping out of the Jeep.

Opening the squeaky screen door they entered the small cafe, whose decor must have dated back to the fifties. The screen door clapped shut behind them. An L shaped counter with green revolving stools dominated the room. Overhead, a lazy ceiling fan whorled slightly out of balance. At the far end of the counter sat a man dressed in white, who was swatting flies—evidently the cook! Bryan glanced at Josh with a smirk on his face. In front of the windows were small tables. An older gentleman sat at one of the tables looking out, drinking coffee.

"This place is almost like a museum," whispered Josh.

"There's the phone over there," pointed Bryan. "Do you have a couple quarters?" While Josh dug through his pockets, Bryan flipped through the phone book.

"If you're looking for someone to fix your tire," spoke up the middle-aged cook, "Jensen's is your best bet around here."

"Jensen's—okay," acknowledged Bryan.

"The number is up on the wall behind you," he pointed as he turned to go into the kitchen.

Bryan thanked him and dialed the number. Flies buzzed in the window as he waited for someone to answer. In the meantime Josh turned the revolving postcard rack glancing at the scenic pictures. Leaning his back against the edge of the window frame, Bryan noticed a number of old Polaroid photographs tacked onto the yellowed knotty pine wall. Their condition was very poor, but something caught his eye. Finally someone answered the phone, and he turned away looking out the window. After having made the arrangements to get their flat fixed, they sat at the counter and ordered a couple of sodas. Josh noticed an autographed picture of Art Linkletter on the wall behind the counter.

All at once, the old man sitting along the windows began to babble out loud. "It's up there, I know it!" The boys glanced at the old man, then over at the cook.

"Don't pay any attention to old Abe. He comes and goes like that all the time."

"What's wrong with him?" whispered Josh.

"Stroke, I reckon. He's prospected all through these mountains in search of some fabled gold mine."

Josh didn't have to look at Bryan to know what he was thinking. But really, there could have easily been other lost mines in the surrounding area.

The repair truck pulled up, and Josh sauntered out. Bryan spun around on the stool, and dropped to the floor to follow, but halted long enough to get a closer look at the old black and white pictures. Most were badly blistered by the dry desert air. But something familiar caused him to look closer.

"Say, do you know who took these pictures?" he asked the cook.

"Ah—those old snap shots? Yeah—there was a fella who brought those by. I guess it must have been about two years ago. He was looking for some old rock inscriptions or something of the sort."

"Do you know his name?"

The cook shook his head. "I don't remember."

"What's going on?" inquired Josh coming back in.

Bryan waved him over to the pictures. "See this picture—it has the "sun" symbol, but it appears to be upside down," he explained in a hushed voice.

"Really? Where were these taken?"

Bryan blinked, "I don't know, but let's see if we can track this down."

While Bryan quizzed the cook further, Josh examined the photos more closely. The cook recollected that he was about thirty years old and wore gold-rimmed glasses. Beyond that there was little he could remember.

"Say, there's something written on the back of this one," discovered Josh, lifting it up.

"What's it say?" queried Bryan.

"B.L. Coleman, 691 West Elm Street, Bishop. Phone number—760-872-6xxx."

"Let me get that down."

"I wonder if that phone number is still good?" questioned Josh.

"Well, one way to find out," answered Bryan, reaching for more change. The phone rang, but a recording came on informing him it was out of service. "No, it's no longer active," he sighed, hanging up the receiver.

Thanking the cook, they charged out the door to settle up with the tire repairman.

"This could be what we've been looking for, proof that the Captain did survive and did leave a marked trail," Bryan excitedly pointed out as they jumped back into the Jeep.

"If this Coleman fella left those photo's here, then logically this must be in the general area they were taken, right?" figured Josh.

"Makes sense to me. But, are they though? We need to get down there and find him."

"Have you considered that he may be searching for the same thing that we are? And that he may not even give us the time of day," stated Josh.

"True, but no one can know as much as we do, can they?" replied Bryan.

"Well, not unless there's another side to Captain Camino's life that we don't know about. Or, maybe he has just accidentally stumbled across his trail."

"I guess it's even possible that the Captain's hidden instructions at 'Whispering Valley' may have been discovered," concurred Bryan.

"These pictures are nearly two years ago, but what has happened since?" pondered Josh as they pulled back on the road headed south.

Glimpsing the image of the old cafe in the chattering side mirror, Bryan wondered how many times he had unwittingly been by here in the past.

Approximately two hours later a gust of wind sent a cloud of dust and a number of tumble weeds across the highway as they approached Bishop. It was an island of green in an arid region sandwiched between the rugged White Mountains to the east and the Sierra Nevada to the west. The small town was situated along the banks of Bishop Creek—its life blood. Traveling through the business district they soon found Elm Street and turned west toward a broad and magnificent view of the Sierra Nevada. Counting down the addresses they neared their goal.

"This must be it," said Bryan pointing to a cluster of white buildings trimmed in green. Behind the main house were a number of apartment-type buildings.

"It's the right address all right," confirmed Josh.

"Let's try the main house first," suggested Bryan. Parking beside a timbered retaining wall, they followed a narrow sidewalk up to the house. Knocking on the door brought no immediate response.

"Here, let me knock, I'll show you what knocking is all about," spoke up Josh. Boom! Boom! Boom! Josh literally pounded on the door. "That oughta do it," he concluded. And certainly it did for in a matter of seconds the door suddenly jerked open part way.

"Who's trying to break my door down?" came the raised voice of a woman.

"Sorry to bother you ma'am, but we're looking for a B.L. Coleman, does he still live here?" asked Bryan.

Slowly the door opened to reveal a thin older woman with a scarf wrapped around her head, holding a broom. "You know Ben?"

"No, but we would sure like to talk to him," reiterated Bryan.

"About what?" she snipped.

"Well, it's concerning—some photographs of his," answered Josh.

After a long pause she stepped outside. "Okay, apparently you boys haven't heard. Ben disappeared over a year ago, and hasn't been seen since."

"Disappeared?" queried Josh.

"Yeah, he drove out early one morning and never came back. He left me with all his stuff and no rent money!"

"Really? If that doesn't beat all," replied Bryan looking at Josh.

"I guess his relatives were contacted," commented Josh.

"That's the strange thing. I didn't have a clue to the whereabouts of any of his relatives so I reported his disappearance to the Sheriff's Department, and an officer came out and took a report. And about two weeks later this tall thin guy appears, claiming to be his uncle. He agreed to take charge of Ben's belongings and pay up the rent. But after an hour or so, I went back to check on him, and he was gone! All of Ben's stuff had been ransacked. No telling what he took. Now here is the clincher. One of the deputies from the Sheriff's Department later called back and said they were still trying to locate his relatives. Well, there you have it."

"Hmm. What ever happened to all his stuff?" questioned Josh.

"It's up in the attic. I'll probably end up putting it in a yard sale and hauling the rest to the dump."

"Is it possible for us to look it over, we might be interested in buying something," asked Bryan giving his partner a sideways glance.

"Sure, why not. By the way, my name is Ida."

"I'm Bryan, this is Josh," he replied, returning the introduction.

Putting the broom down she led them around to the side of the house and up a staircase to an attic door. Unlocking and opening the door, bright sunlight poured into the dark room.

"His stuff is all back there and along this side," she pointed. As the boys waded through all the things stacked on the floor, she sat down on a trunk. "Weeks before he disappeared I had a feeling that something wasn't right," she continued as she watched them rummage through the various boxes.

"Really?" acknowledged Josh, half paying attention.

"Yeah, he quit his job, and then he began going off for days at a time."

"That is kind of odd," agreed Josh.

"Do you have any idea what that tall fella could have taken?" asked Bryan.

"I recollect that Ben had a file box, you know one of those small portable ones with all kinds of papers or maps in it. That turned up missing."

Bryan now realized there was someone else interested in Ben Coleman's research. But who? And to what extent?

"Look here," said Josh holding up a framed certificate of some kind.

"What is it?" asked Bryan.

"He was a graduate of the Colorado State School of Geology."

"Geology, huh. Makes sense."

"He was always dragging some kind of rock specimen home," commented the landlady.

Sifting through a box of miscellaneous items, Bryan came across an identification card. It had been torn in two. The words: *CLASS 3 SECURITY CLEARANCE* caught his attention. "What kind of work did he do?" he asked.

"Something to do with the government, I'm not sure," she replied.

"You can tell a lot about a person by what he reads," said Josh going through a box of books, which was mostly comprised of geology, chemistry and other reference manuals, and even a Japanese cookbook. Under a pamphlet on Indian Petroglyphs and a textbook on radioactive minerals, he pulled out a thick book entitled "Western History." It fell open to where a "Ski Aspen" brochure had been placed as a marker. He observed that several lines were highlighted dealing with accounts of early crossings of the Sierra Nevada.

"Was Ben, tall or short? What did he look like?" asked Bryan.

"Oh, I guess you would describe him as a medium build, but husky, with dark brown hair, and he also wore glasses—that is most of the time. I might add he was a very reserved, quiet person," she recalled.

As she continued speaking, Bryan began looking through a small maple dresser. After a few minutes, Josh declared he was done looking, coming away with just the one book. Finally Bryan stood up.

"How much for the chest of drawers?" asked Bryan. Josh gave him a funny look, and walked over to where he was standing.

"O-oh, ten dollars," she replied.

"You don't want that old dresser," argued Josh.

"Yes, I think I do," countered Bryan. After paying the women they hauled their treasures down to the Jeep and laid the dresser on its back and tied it down on top of their camp gear.

"What kind of vehicle did Ben drive?" queried Josh.

"It was like a Blazer or something; light brown in color as I recall."

"If you should hear anything more about Ben, please call this number," requested Josh handing her a slip of paper.

Back on the road again they headed north through town. "I'm glad you remembered to ask for a description on Ben's vehicle, that may come in handy later," commented Bryan.

"I gather from what the landlady was saying, that the tall fellow she mentioned must have swooped in and cleaned out all of Coleman's research," spoke up Josh over the wind noise.

"The whole thing stinks—could be foul play. And another thing, if he worked for the Government, they should've had all his records, next of kin and all that," Bryan replied back.

"That's true. But did you notice there wasn't even one picture of him anywhere? Say, what's the deal with that stupid dresser anyway?"

"I'm not sure, but there appears to be a false bottom beneath the lower drawer. I got a glimpse of something white under there. I guess the worst that could happen is that I could be out ten dollars."

"Could be just shelf paper," speculated Josh.

"Well, let's find out. There is an exit ahead at Tom's Place," replied Bryan.

Once off the highway it was a short distance over to the "old road" and the small community of Tom's Place. Near the rustic general store was a wide spot that offered a bit of shade. Wasting no time, Bryan untied the rope securing the dresser. He pulled the bottom drawer up out of the dresser and set it on the ground.

"There is something under here, all right," reported Josh peeking down into the dresser. Reaching down inside he pulled out a number of photocopies and an old photograph. After dropping the drawer back into place, they adjourned to a nearby picnic table to examine the contents of the dresser.

Bryan picked up one of the photocopies and began reading: "Philadelphia Independent, Philadelphia, Pennsylvania, May 12, 1798."

"1798!"

"That's what the heading says."

"Look at the girl in this old photograph," demanded Josh. "She looks a lot like your mother—and you."

"Really?" asked Bryan without looking. Suddenly the color went out his face. "Josh, I can't believe what I'm reading. Listen, to this! I'm serious, listen! 'A distinguished gentleman of Spanish descent is reportedly meeting with government officials behind closed doors this morning. There is no word on what his mission is, but speculation has it, that it concerns the western territories from which he came.' "

"The Captain?"

"I don't know, let me read on," answered Bryan grabbing the next sheet. Josh picked up the remaining one, squinting at the blurred print. "Here's more, listen to this: 'No official could be reached for comment on the closed door talks being conducted with a certain Spaniard reportedly named Camino.' There it is—the proof!" exclaimed Bryan, pausing before he read on. " 'Rumor has it, he is here to muster support for an American involvement in areas of the far west.' "

"There is more on this photocopy too," excitedly discovered Josh. "It says: 'Officials continue to refuse any kind of comment concerning Camino's petition for help. But word on good authority has it, that talks have ended without any agreement, reportedly due to the present conflict with France over areas west of the Mississippi, and the feeling that it would not be wise to oppose Spain at this time. However, Camino did turn many ears about claims of great wealth—gold and silver, all in connection with a great mountain range in the West. One eyewitness claims that Camino, and his wife who is heavy with child secretly left last night. If true, it may have been a smart move on their part, due to his revelations of western wealth, and the fact that the greedy and the opportunist would surely follow.' That's it."

Bryan stared off into the distance, watching a flock of birds flying north, as it all sank in. "Let's take this from the top. We know that the Captain was run out of Spanish California. So apparently from this, he goes to—Philadelphia, which was the capitol before Washington D. C., and there he tries to get the United States Government to help him take away California from Spain."

"But it appears they didn't go for it. They probably already had too many irons in the fire so to speak. The article mentioned France, and it wasn't until 1803 or thereabouts when the Louisiana Purchase was negotiated?"

"Yeah, I think your recollection of U.S. history is correct. And if that was the case, it makes sense, because it would be another five years before the issue with France had been settled," realized Bryan, checking his watch. "We better hit the road, while we continue this. Can you believe it! I can't!"

"I thought you were crazy, when you bought that dresser," confessed Josh, getting back into the jeep. "But before we go you've got to look at this picture."

Bryan stared at the picture for the longest time, amazed by the face that stared back at him. He noted that the name Florence was scribed across the bottom.

"Don't you realize, if White Feather was pregnant again, there may be another branch to your family out there somewhere, and this girl here could be one of them," explained Josh as he accelerated up the road.

"That would be incredible if that's true. This whole thing is more than I ever bargained for."

"One thing is for sure, the Captain did survive, and therefore the back trail to the 'Oro de Cañon' must exist in reality."

"Truly said, but we have no leads, no trail. We're still stumped."

Passing the Mammoth Lakes turnoff, they soon coasted back down into the Mono Basin.

"What about this Ben Coleman? Could he be a relative of yours?" questioned Josh breaking a long silence of contemplation.

"I don't know. But I sure wish, I could find out where he took those pictures?" replied Bryan as he glanced up Lee Vining Creek toward Tioga Pass. Traffic slowed through the small town of Lee Vining, and picked up again as they skirted the westerly shore of Mono Lake. Before long they had passed over Conway Summit, and through Bridgeport Valley to again approach their point of origin, the old cafe.

"Let's stop and ask the owner if we can have those old pictures," suggested Bryan.

"Doesn't look like anyone is around," observed Josh as they pulled off the road in front of the buil
ding.

Bryan hopped out and peeked in through a window, while rapping on the doorframe. But there was no answer. Not even a light was left on inside. Bryan looked at his watch, which showed it to be nearly six o'clock.

"There are no cars around either," noted Josh.

Bryan stood on the porch for a second, glancing back inside. "Guess they don't get enough business to stay open much."

"I don't think this is what you would call a four star restaurant," laughed Josh.

"More like—four hour. Well, I'll tell you what, I'll drive for a while, then you can drive the last leg of the trip home," offered Bryan.

Josh happily agreed. Once on the way he opened up Coleman's book to the page where he had certain passages highlighted. "Listen to what Coleman marked in this book: 'Ensign Gabriel Moraga reaching the San Joaquin River in 1806, found a group of Indians who told them that a few years before, soldiers from the far side of the mountains on a forced march through the foothills had killed many of their number.' "

"Think about that for a moment. A number of years before 1806 could possibly be about the time the Captain was back east," commented Bryan.

"Or after."

"Yes, exactly. Maybe a secret detachment of soldiers was dispatched to find Camino's gold after his foolish disclosure, destroying any who got in their way."

"That doesn't sound like any of the Captain's tactics. You're probably right."

"I think we better keep this information between us for a while," recommended Bryan.

"Why?'

"My mom and dad would probably freak."

"You'll have to tell them eventually," replied Josh

"I know, but we have to be careful not to make any waves. Things are too preliminary at this time. I have a feeling we have a long way to go to get to the bottom of this."

"I don't know if I can sit on this, it's going to be burning a hole in my gut."

7

AT THE FOOT OF THE GREAT
TISSAACK

"**S**he found what?" exclaimed Bryan.

"Tammy thinks she has run across a hot lead," answered Josh over the phone.

"Now what?" asked Bryan, who was somewhat in a bad mood.

"It has to do with a piece of Spanish armor that was found years ago, but she won't give us any more information, because she wants to take us there this weekend."

"Dang! We can't let her take control of our operation, can we?" questioned Bryan.

"No, not take control, but she can help, right? Or, shall I just tell her to forget it?"

"No-o-o! But it's just getting annoying," he responded hanging up.

Josh hoped Bryan would have forgotten all those feelings after his mother had moved back, but apparently not.

Three days later on a Friday evening, Tammy and her mother arrived just before sunset. Mrs. Holden dreaded driving at night, and made a point of avoiding it.

Josh called up Bryan to inform him that they had arrived and everything was a go. "Just be here at 6:30 in the morning," he requested.

"Do you know where we are going?" Bryan asked.

"No, they won't divulge a thing. It's like they've got us over a barrel or something," chuckled Josh.

"All right, I'll see you in the morning," sighed Bryan. Frankly, he didn't know what to think about the situation, but figured he had better play along just to see if anything important did turn up. What should he take he wondered? As he picked up his trusty, but worn out pack, he thought of the many places it had accompanied him, including the 'Oro de Cañon.' Would he be able to bask in its glory once again? Only time would tell.

Tammy's competitiveness bothered him. In reality, he realized in many respects he should be grateful for her help, but her aggressive attitude reminded him of a sibling rivalry.

Next morning after a quick breakfast, he was out the door and on his way. While driving over, he mulled over the thought of the Spanish armor. Did it have anything to do with what they were looking for? The chances were very slight.

Pulling into their driveway, he spotted the Holden's yellow Chevy Nova parked next to the house with the trunk lid up. Parking off to the side, he approached the doorway he knew ever so well. Mixed voices coming from inside met him as he knocked.

"That must be Bryan," someone said from inside.

"It is," replied Josh. "Come on in."

"Hello," said Bryan as he opened the screen door. Walking through the living room he could see everyone busy in the kitchen. "Good morning, Mrs. Knight, Mrs. Holden," he greeted sticking his head in the doorway. At the same instant Bryan spotted Tammy working at the breadboard. She wore a dark blue shirt and faded blue jeans. Glancing up she smiled, as their eyes briefly met. He wondered what female conniving was hidden behind that smile and those pretty eyes. Exchanging a subdued greeting he stepped inside.

"Good, your here," acknowledged Mrs. Holden, giving Tammy a quick glance. "We're almost ready to go."

"Mmm, something smells good," commented Bryan leaning against the doorjamb.

"Applesauce cake," informed Josh's mom. "A little bird told us it's your favorite," she added smiling at Tammy.

"Well then, what more do we need, let's get the show on the road!" exclaimed Bryan.

Mrs. Holden smiled at him, but Tammy remained expressionless except for the right side of her mouth that was slightly turned up.

"Help me carry out some of this stuff," called Josh from the front room. "There's enough stuff here for an expedition to Everest."

After loading the trunk, they stood by the car discussing aspects of their recent discovery. Tammy soon appeared in the doorway carrying a picnic basket.

"Say Tammy, where is this place that we're supposed to be going to? What's the big secret about anyway?" questioned Bryan.

"It's not that it's a secret, it's a surprise! I thought maybe it was something you would appreciate."

"Appreciate? How can you expect me to appreciate it if I don't have the foggiest what it's all about?"

"Get this through your thick head buster. This could be one of your precious little clues."

Mrs. Holden and Mrs. Knight stopped just inside the doorway to overhear the majority of their heated conversation.

"Will you listen to that, you would think they were married the way they carry on," commented Mrs. Knight. Her sister uttered a half-chuckle and clapped her hand over her mouth.

"We are going to the museum at the visitor's center in Yosemite. You, you, who has to know it all, ooh!" she finalized trudging off.

Josh's mom would not be going with them as planned. The hospital called, needing her for the afternoon shift. So it was only the four of them that prepared to leave. Bryan decided to take along some climbing gear just in case the opportunity afforded itself. The boys sat in the back seat with Tammy and her mother in the front. Bryan was surprised, when Mrs. Holden handed Tammy the keys. He nudged Josh.

"Aunt Betty, you're not letting Tammy drive are you?"

"This is her trip," she answered.

"She could drive us—over the edge," said Bryan under his breath.

Tammy turned and stuck here tongue out at Bryan, and started up the car.

"You better tighten up that seat belt," recommended Josh tugging on his own.

Pulling out of the driveway they traveled down the winding country road to the main highway south of town. Dominating the landscape on their journey south was a blending of green pastures and the reptilian lava flow called Table Mountain. Turning off onto another side road, scattered oak trees escorted them across a rocky landscape among rolling hills.

"You guys probably know a lot of the history of the places we'll be passing through today, the old historical towns and mining camps," queried Mrs. Holden.

"Yeah, quite a bit I guess," replied Josh watching the fence posts whizzing by.

"Good, that'll make the trip more interesting," she smiled.

Turning left onto Highway 120, they passed the old Gold Rush town of Chinese Camp with its colorful history and many stone buildings.

"They originally called this place, 'Little Peking,' " informed Josh.

"Did they actually mine gold here?" asked Tammy.

"Yeah, but these were dry diggings. So what they had to do was haul the gold bearing dirt down to Six Bit Gulch or to another nearby stream to get sluiced," answered Josh.

"Out that same way," pointed Bryan, "toward the west, was the site of a tong war between clashing Chinese clans."

"Tong war?" questioned Mrs. Holden.

"It was more of a colossal brawl than anything else. There was about two thousand Chinese involved, fashioning homemade weapons out of whatever they could find. You know, like brooms and gardening tools. But only one person was killed as I recall," he answered.

"The road that is leading off to our left is the old Jacksonville Road," pointed out Josh. "I am told there were a number of holdups down on what's called the Shawmut Grade, namely by Black Bart."

"The 'Gentleman Bandit,' " recalled Bryan.

After a pause of silence, Mrs. Holden asked Bryan about his college classes and what kind of career he was thinking of.

"Well," laughed Bryan, "that's a bone of contention between me and my dad. He has a viable business and feels that I should take it over someday. Which is fine, but I feel the need to do something greater. My father thinks I'm foolish for spending so much time trying to find out what happened to my great-great-grandfather. The mystery is intriguing, but I don't believe it will have a big affect on my future. But anyway, what I really want to do is to effect positive changes in forest practices management, not only here, but also globally. Things just have gone too far in the demise of our forests and altered climates."

"Wow, I'm impressed," commented Mrs. Holden.

Tammy glanced at him in the mirror.

"Tell them about Eagle Shawmut," spoke up Josh.

"Oh yeah. Over to the left, along those hills is the Eagle Shawmut Mine, which was where my grandfather worked, back in 1908. It has one of the deepest 'glory holes' in the region," informed Bryan.

"What exactly is a 'glory hole?' " asked Tammy.

"It's the main vertical shaft," answered Josh.

"The old timers said you either go to glory or you go to—well, somewhere else," informed Bryan stumbling on his words.

After a pause, Bryan continued, "Just out of sight below the mine was a boarding house where my grandmother worked as a cook. That's where they met."

"Gold seems to be the common thread in your family," commented Mrs. Holden.

"Just as it was with the Captain and White Feather," recalled Tammy.

"Bryan, with that kind of record, I would be careful, some gal could be ready to hog tie you most anytime," warned Josh as he hit the back of Tammy's seat. Mrs. Holden gave him a questioning look, but Tammy gripped the wheel and remained expressionless.

Descending through the hills and scrub pine, they found themselves paralleling the upper end of Lake Don Pedro, and facing larger mountains ahead.

"What's this place up ahead?" pointed Tammy's mom.

"Moccasin," replied Bryan socking Josh in the arm when no one was looking.

"Ow!"

"Must be a power station—look at all the power lines," guessed Mrs. Holden, pretending not to see the hit.

"It's the City of San Francisco's hydro plant," answered Josh holding his arm.

"Look at the big pipes coming down the hill," noticed Tammy. "Must be the penstock." she finally realized.

"The pressure in those pipes is so great that a pin-hole leak could bore a hole right through you," informed Josh.

"Really?" commented Tammy's mother in amazement.

"There's a turn off up ahead, which way do we go?" asked Tammy.

"You better go left. Old Priest's Grade is not for the tender hearted," recommended Bryan.

The course now climbed a switchback up the fire scarred and toyon covered mountain, soon rising to a thousand feet above the powerhouse. Tammy was noticeably driving slower.

"You okay?" asked her mother.

"Ye-ah," she replied slowly.

"Not exactly city driving is it?" stated Bryan.

"Scared of heights, eh?" prodded Josh.

"No! I'm not, I'm just being cautious," she retorted. The truth was she was getting very nervous, and her hands were beginning to sweat. Tammy didn't realize how scary these mountain roads could be. Rounding a sharp curve, a pang ran through her as she glanced up, and could see the road notched into sheer bluffs far above. Her mom was not going to be of any help. Her nails were dug into the armrest as it was.

Bryan, sensing her nervousness decided that he had better come to the rescue. Leaning forward, he told her first to relax, and ignore what was below or above, and to just concentrate on each section of the road at a time. After a bit that strategy seemed to work. She was able to loosen up and breathe regularly again. The confidence in his voice had a calming effect on her, and she took note of it.

Finally reaching the top of Priest Grade, the course left the steep canyon behind and veered left, ascending a meandering draw. The toyon and manzanita of the lowlands gave way to the beginnings of a pine and black oak forest. Pulling off in front of a cafe near the top of the grade, Tammy let the traffic that had piled up behind her go by.

"We're getting close to Big Oak Flat," announced Josh.

"Anything exciting happen around here?" questioned Mrs. Holden.

"Not too much," answered Bryan. "Big Oak Flat was originally called 'Savage's Diggings,' named after James D. Savage, who you'll hear more about in Yosemite. But what's kind of interesting, is that he was the one who built the mill race at Sutter's Mill where James Marshall found the gold nugget that started the whole she-bang."

"Sounds like quite a colorful character," commented Tammy's mother.

"Yeah, but what Bryan didn't mention was that he had several wives," added Josh.

"What?" questioned Tammy.

"The truth is the poor fella probably didn't have *any* color left in him," laughed Josh.

Scattered stone buildings now came into view. Many of these were principally built of native rock layered and cemented together by lime mortar. One such two story building which stood near the edge of the road had five weathered iron doors. Scattered among the old buildings were old straggly apple and pear trees, partially dead and partially in bloom.

Steadily climbing beyond the small town of Groveland, magnificent views of the forested mountains and the snowbound peaks of the high country met them around every turn.

"Isn't this beautiful, Mom?"

"It certainly is. Makes you wonder why we're still in the city," she answered looking off into the rolling forest.

"I know of an interesting place to stop and stretch if you want to. And it's not too far off the beaten track," suggested Bryan.

"Sounds good to me," answered Tammy meaningfully glancing at her mother.

"Yeah, good idea," she agreed. "Is there a store or service station nearby?"

"Matter of fact there is," answered Josh.

"Watch for a sign that says: Hardin Flat. The old road is on the right. It's narrow but paved," instructed Bryan scooting up in his seat as far as he could.

After several minutes they finally reached the designated road, and descended its steep winding narrow course to finally burst out of the trees into the flat.

"That was a roller coaster of a ride! Let's do it again!" whooped Josh.

"No way!" was the volley from the front seat.

On the opposite side of the picturesque meadow they pulled off the road at a small store to make a necessary comfort stop. Getting out, Josh stretched his legs and noted the numerous cabins that were scattered all along the periphery of the meadow.

Returning to the car they continued on up into the forested hills beyond Hardin Flat, and came to an unmarked road that led back into what had been *Crocker's Station*.

"This was a 'way station' for travelers going to Yosemite. But there are no buildings left," informed Bryan.

"Look at all the sweet peas blooming," noticed Mrs. Holden as they drove through the trees into a clearing. A small meadow now became visible off to the east adjoining the clearing.

"This must have been some place in its day," commented Tammy bringing the car to a stop by an old scraggly apple tree.

Getting out of the car, Bryan showed them about where the main house sat. Walking along a line of old gnarled apple trees he stopped to look up hill amongst the scattered evergreens. "Up there, about four hundred feet was a small barn and down here was a number of out buildings. And even further over, is an old dump, where people have dug for bottles and things."

"Did you ever try digging over there?" asked Tammy.

"Yeah, but the only thing I came away with was burned fingers from battery acid. Apparently, someone threw an old car battery into the debris."

His thoughts changed as they slowly walked back to where the old house sat. "Can you imagine what it must have been like here a hundred years ago? Envision perhaps an elevated porch on the main house that extended out this way and the individuals who were probably seated there conversing and looking out over the meadow and the forest beyond. Perhaps a grazing deer could be seen on the far side along the trees. The smell and sounds of cooking inside would drift out of the doorway. Stop a second and visualize. Can you see it?"

"Okay, I see a couple men wearing hats seated on the porch talking about the consequences of the new Tioga Pass Road. The one doing the talking has a mustache, and he is pointing up the stagecoach road that probably ran around the edge of the meadow," imagined Josh.

"That's good, that could easily have been a reality," commented Bryan.

"Let me close my eyes and see what I come up with," said Tammy. "In the kitchen there are two women in long dresses talking around a wood cook stove. You know, the ones that have the cast-iron top with the round lids. One whispers to the other, something about how her husband drinks too much, and shows her a couple bruises on her arm."

"Tamm-y! You're too young to be thinking of such things," her mother objected.

"Really Mother?"

Bryan glanced at Josh. Was this a glimpse into a side of Tammy's life he had no clue to? Was this partly the reason she acts the way she does?

"Life can be cruel sometimes," replied Mrs. Holden realizing her daughter was no longer a little girl to hide things from.

"We better get on the road," suggested Josh. Returning to the car in an ominous silence, they got in and buckled up.

"You ought to be a tour guide Bryan," commented Tammy's mother.

"Me? No-o. It would be fun though, but as I've been reminded, I shouldn't be spending too much time dwelling in the past while the future crumbles in our hands," he replied.

Tammy gave Bryan a funny look as she turned the car around. She was about to say something, but realized she might be revealing something she didn't want to admit even to herself.

Leaving Crocker's Station they soon crossed Soldier Creek, which Josh explained was named after army soldiers that patrolled the region in the 1880's. Meeting the main highway again, the scenic route climbed the side of a long ridge with a spectacular view up into the granite domes that seemed to gleam in the rarified sunlight.

Passing into *Yosemite National Park* they soon arrived at the entrance kiosk, and paid the usual auto toll. A friendly ranger handed Tammy a couple brochures and wished them an enjoyable time. Tammy's mom carefully read the leaflet that gave warning about the bears. Passing the adjoining rest area, the highway again ascended through a gallery forest over the divide that separated the Tuolumne and the Merced River watersheds.

Numerous long curves now brought them down to the junction at Crane Flat. "Tuolumne Meadows," read Mrs. Holden off of a sign that pointed left. "We went through there many years ago when it was virtually just a wagon road. I had my nails dug into the armrest almost the whole way," she confessed.

Tammy giggled to herself, remembering the same coming up the hill that morning.

"Oh, look down there a round meadow! But the forest is burned all around it, what a shame," exclaimed Mrs. Holden.

"That's Big Meadow. We're coming into that bad burn they had here a couple of years ago," replied Josh. "The fire roared around the meadow and straight up the hill past us."

"This is a perfect example of why better forest management is necessary," commented Bryan.

"What a waste," agreed Tammy glimpsing views between the burned trees.

"Look, there's the Merced River Canyon—Yosemite Valley is just around the corner," pointed Josh.

"Good, my back is getting stiff," said Tammy stretching in her seat.

Reaching a point above the Merced River Canyon, the road turned easterly to descend through tall conifers and granite outcroppings along the canyon wall. Large gray granite mountains loomed above them across the shadowy deep gorge.

"Waterfall ahead," announced Josh.

Almost immediately a loud roar became discernible. Coming into view were cars slowing and people standing adjacent to the road looking up to the left through alternating heavy and fine blowing spray. Approaching the bridge, the power of a thousand tons of water could be felt and heard as it pounded and roared down the slope hundreds of feet above them.

"Cascade Falls," read Tammy off of a small sign.

Ducking low they peered upward into the boiling mass of white fury.

"The power almost smothers you," commented Mrs. Holden.

"This is only the beginning," informed Bryan.

After descending into the deep granite-walled valley below, the road followed the raging white water of the Merced River upstream. Cedar and dogwood decorated its rugged banks.

"The waterfall that's just across the canyon is called *Bridalveil Fall*, if I remember right," spoke up Mrs. Knight.

"I believe you are correct," answered Bryan.

"I understand that young unbetrothed women are not allowed on the trail that leads up to that waterfall," stated Josh with a straight face.

There was a long pause of silence, and then everyone exploded into laughter.

Crossing to the opposite side of the valley, the magnificent gleaming white granite monolith, *El Capitan*, rose to breathtaking heights. Quickly coming into view was the three tiers of *Yosemite Falls*, all 2,425 feet of it. The contrasting gray granite cliffs seemed to form a buffer of sorts between the dark blue sky and the warm greens of the meadowscape.

The traffic began to grow heavier as they neared Yosemite Village. "We need to find the Visitor Center according to the information I read," informed Tammy.

"Okay, just take the road into the Village, and we can park behind the store," directed Bryan.

"You know your way around here pretty well I take it," commented Mrs. Holden.

"I've been here a time or two, rock climbing," he replied.

"You're going to give us a demonstration later aren't you?" she further asked.

"Yeah, I was hoping to."

Getting out of the car, they immediately heard the roar of Yosemite Falls high above them, occasionally cracking against the cliff as the winds shifted.

"This is so nice," commented Tammy.

Walking between two buildings faced with wood and stone, they emerged along the main walkway that fronted along the gift shops, restaurants, and lastly the Visitor Center. Along the way a small crowd gathered to watch two teenage boys in worn-out Levi jackets playing Hacky Sack. After pausing to watch for a moment they approached the building they were looking for, which was largely constructed with a gray granite exterior.

Once inside, they decided to first look around. Displayed under glass was a genuine handwritten page from one of John Muir's journals from his ramblings into the High Sierra. Old paintings or at least prints of them depicted the glowing impressions of some of the first white men who visited the valley. Toward the back wall were a number of rock specimens and pictorial interpretations of the geological history of the area. The Indians that once lived here were well represented by exhibits of artifacts and dress.

After quickly looking around and not finding the armor, Tammy inquired at the information desk. A female ranger informed her that the exhibit was not ready yet. She then asked if they still could see it, but was met with a negative answer.

Bryan caught the jest of the conversation as he came up. Putting his arm around Tammy, Bryan further explained that they were on a research project and that Tammy had graciously driven them all the way up here to see the armor. "Can we not just look at it?" he pleaded.

"Let me see if it's possible, I'll be right back." replied the ranger in a reluctant tone.

"I could have handled it," Tammy replied to Bryan, removing his arm from around her.

The woman quickly returned. "The ranger in charge said it would be okay, follow me," she announced.

Calling the others, they went through a doorway behind the counter into a large room filled with tables and artifacts. They were taken to a large table where they found the dark tortured curved piece of metal. It was approximately eighteen by twenty-four inches in size. Its corners were badly deteriorated by blisters of rust.

A Ranger sat behind a desk in the corner engrossed in viewing a stack of photos. Finally he noticed them. "Interesting piece isn't it?" he said getting up and walking over. "It's definitely Spanish, but that's about all we can tell about it."

"Where was it found?" asked Josh.

"Right here in the Valley, at *Indian Caves*, back in 1924."

The Ranger, introduced himself as Bill Smedley, he was tall, lean, and hardened.

Putting on a pair of gloves he turned the armor over, pointing to something on the opposite side. "There are markings and writings on the inside, but no one knows exactly what they mean. Another thing that's quite unusual was the presence of a waxy substance coating the metal. It's been removed now, but somebody went to a lot of trouble to have it preserved."

Seeing the markings, Bryan's eyes lit up. "Are there any other pieces?" he asked.

"No, this is it. Anyway there it is, look at it, but don't touch. The acids from your skin are very damaging. I'll be back in a minute." As he left, Mrs. Holden walked out with him asking questions about another exhibit.

"Well whata-ya think?" asked Josh.

"Tammy do you have any tissues in your purse?" asked Bryan.

"I think so," she said digging in her purse. "Here."

"What else you got in there?" he asked peeking in.

"None of your business!" she replied snapping it shut, her face turning red.

Bryan grabbed the armor and turned it so he could see the markings better.

"Bryan! He said don't touch it!" exclaimed Tammy.

"Quiet, I'm not touching it with my bare hands. Josh, quick, we need a pencil and about four sheets of paper. Let's pencil trace these inscriptions real fast, before he comes back."

Quickly and nervously, Josh placed overlapping sheets of paper and pencil traced the markings. Tammy watched at the door, nervous and upset. Completing the task, Bryan turned the piece back to the way it was, but accidentally bumped it just as Tammy warned of their return.

"Are you kids ready to go?" queried Mrs. Holden.

"Yes Mom, we're ready."

"Say, did you find anything helpful in your research?" asked Ranger Smedley.

"Exchanging glances with Bryan, Josh answered, "Not really, there's not that much to it."

"Has the age of it been estimated yet?" asked Bryan.

"In rough numbers—it's about 200 years old."

Again there was an exchange of glances.

"Would it be okay if I snapped a couple pictures?" asked Josh digging a small flash camera out of his bag.

"Ah-h, sure," he replied after a pause.

Thanking the Ranger, they left the building. Turning around, Mrs. Holden noticed her daughter and Bryan arguing.

"Is everything all right, Tammy?" she asked.

"Just a difference of opinion," she replied not really wanting her to know the real crux of the argument.

"Where is this place called Indian Caves?" Josh wondered aloud as he unfolded the Park brochure.

"It's further up the valley near Mirror Lake. We can catch a shuttle and go up there, but it might be a good idea to bring our lunches with us," recommended Bryan.

Agreeing, they returned to the car, and then strolled back out to the bus stop. Within in a few minutes a shuttle arrived that would take them on the Mirror Lake loop. Seating was hard to find and scattered. Tammy sat across from Bryan. As she sat there she contemplated what kind of person he was. She thought she knew him. The bus driver announcing each stop finally proclaimed they had reached their destination: "Indian Caves, Mirror Lake next stop."

"It's just a pile of boulders," first commented Josh as they walked across the road.

"That's exactly right, it's a talus cave," stated Bryan

"I was imaging a mysterious cave with all kinds of hidden clues," confessed Tammy.

"The advantage that a talus cave has is that it has good ventilation. It won't trap moisture like a regular cave. Therefore it would be more ideal for preservation," remarked Bryan.

"It is dark in there, things could be easily hidden," commented Mrs. Holden, stooping down, peering into the darkness of the cave.

Josh noted that a park ranger's vehicle had pulled up a short distance down the road. The person inside appeared to be looking at a map.

"Look up here, Half Dome, the great *Tissaack*," pointed Bryan. Up through the tops of the sprawling oaks the massive sheer face of the great dome towered far above them.

"Is that supposed to have any significance?" asked Tammy.

"I don't know. 'Tissaack,' according to Indian legend was an Indian maiden, who watched over the valley," recalled Bryan. "See those black stains that run down the face?" he pointed.

"I do."

"That's her hair hanging down, and between there, some say you can see her face looking out."

"Hmm," was Tammy's only comment.

"In winter time, inhabitants of the valley would watch the height of the clouds along the face of Half Dome and could pretty well tell what the weather was going to be like. Some even called it the '*Tissaack barometer*.' " added Josh.

Finding a nearby picnic table, they wasted no time in unloading and divvying up the food. A period of silence fell upon them as they meditated on the day's journey and their beautiful surroundings. A pair of stellar jays squawked from a nearby cedar tree, their high-pitched voices echoing deep into the woods.

8

THE MAIDEN'S MIRROR

"Remind me to marry someone who can cook," bluntly stated Bryan. Tammy and her mother stopped and stared at each other and then back at him. "What?—I meant someone who can cook like this," he explained.

"With comments like that, you may never get the chance," replied Tammy.

"Not to change the subject, but did any of you notice how the ranger back at the Visitor's Center was heavily scrutinizing us when we left?" asked Josh.

"He did have curious eyes, if you know what I mean," commented Tammy.

"He was very nice," thought Mrs. Holden.

Had the ranger noticed that the armor had been tampered with, while he was out of the room? Bryan wondered to himself.

"I'm dying to find out what those inscriptions are on the armor," stated Josh pulling out the tracings. "No wonder no one has deciphered these, look at these scratches, what a mess."

"Where did you get those tracings?" asked Mrs. Holden.

"Ah-h, from the armor, while you and the ranger were out of the room," answered Josh.

"I told them not to do it," stated Tammy.

"We could have been booted out of the park," rebuked Mrs. Holden in a serious tone.

"Check for reverse writing. Hold it up," suggested Bryan.

"Well, it could be," thought Josh, holding up one of the sheets. "Tammy, what do you think?"

Wiping her hands she came around the table and held the paper up to the sky. For the longest time, she kept turning it and squinting her eyes. "I'm not a Spanish expert, but I think we have something here. Mom, what do you think?" she asked passing it to her.

"It would appear that there is something written through this area here," pointed out Mrs. Holden. "But my eyes aren't as good as they used to be."

Bryan studied it for a minute and then passed it back to Tammy. "I'm not sure, but I think there is a 'sun' symbol toward the bottom."

"There are two words at the top of this sheet that I believe I do know," ventured Tammy.

"Show me," asked Josh.

"Here," she pointed. "Doncella and espejo. Doncella is—"

"Is like, damsel, a maiden or young woman," answered her mother.

"And espejo is—mirror," finalized Tammy.

"Maiden's mirror," voiced Bryan.

"The other writings are so much more difficult to read, they will take some time. See, how good a detective I am," she spouted off.

Bryan shook his head. "Yes, Tammy, of course you are. Say, Mrs. Holden, how much would it cost me to hire out your daughter as a detective this summer?"

"Oh, I don't know. How much are you offering?"

"Mom!"

"Well, Tammy, with a swelled head like yours, you probably would be completely useless around the house anyway."

Bryan reached for his wallet, and pulled out a ten-dollar bill. "Is this enough?"

"Close enough."

"I'm pretending that I'm not hearing this!" Tammy announced.

Mrs. Holden laughed.

"I'll fix you a place in the barn to sleep," stated Bryan.

"Bryan, you're the one who has the ego problem," she asserted. Everyone stared at her. "Okay, okay, so I'm not miss congeniality twenty-four hours a day. You know, two can play this game," she smiled in her own little devious way. "You have to feed me, buy me some new clothes, and let's see—I need some new shoes, and my hair needs done too."

"I'm out of here," replied Bryan jumping up. "Women are sure high maintenance, even more than my dad's livestock."

"Are you comparing me, to your mules?" she protested.

"Only if the shoe fits," he grinned.

Wadding up a paper sack, she threw it at him.

"Anyone up for a walk to the Lake?" asked Josh.

After a positive response, they packed up and began their walk along the oak-shaded roadway. The roar of nearby Tenaya Creek drew their attention away from the trees and cliffs to its pounding, wild descent. A steady but pleasant climb soon brought them up into a parking area adjacent to the lake. Beyond a low granite wall, a breath taking view of sky, rock, and the reflective lake dazzled their eyes.

"It's easy to see how *Mirror Lake* got its name," commented Tammy.

A nearby sign explained how it was gradually turning into a meadow. Part of a geological cycle that covered generations of time.

"Let's walk around the lake," coaxed Bryan.

Mrs. Holden said she would stay and enjoy the view from the wall. Walking on down to the lake side trail, Josh decided to venture out onto a rocky point to get a better view, while Bryan and Tammy continued along the path. Tammy felt somehow idyllic in this beautiful place.

The soft reflections of sky and cliff were ever changing in the placid waters of the lake, being framed and reframed by the low hanging branches of the many trees that lined the shore. The dogwood was in full bloom; their large pink blossoms being much larger than Tammy's small hand.

"Look at the ducks," pointed out Bryan.

"It's a whole family—aren't the little ones cute?"

"They're called ducklings, for your information."

"Stop being so technical—can't you just enjoy them?"

The brown mottled ducks soon paddled their way into the next alcove and out of sight.

Following in the same direction, the shoreline trail meandered around a group of boulders to curve among the trees. Crossing a small gurgling brook the path turned toward a bare stretch of beach, from which a picturesque view of the lake opened up. A certain quietness seemed to prevail over the lake. The shining face of Half Dome reflected brilliantly on the glassy surface.

"Bryan, didn't you say, 'Tissaack' was a young woman or maiden?"

"Yes."

"Well, there's her mirror," she pointed.

Bryan glanced up at the reflected image of 'Tissaack' on the water. His eyes seemed to smile even before the expression reached his face. "Tammy! You've solved the first clue!" he exclaimed throwing his arms around her, lifting her off the ground with a hug.

"Bryan! Careful, Mom is watching," she blushed.

"I'm sorry—I just got carried away."

"Don't be sorry—silly. Tammy looked up at the face of Half Dome that towered far above them. "I can see her face. It's right there between the weathered streaks, between her dark flowing hair."

"It must be a female thing, I don't see a thing. Is she happy or sad?"

"I think that is yet to be determined, partially by those around her," she answered giving him a meaningful glance.

"You realize how unique this situation is?" asked Bryan.

"How's that?"

"Well, it took a maiden to look into the 'maiden's mirror' to solve it. If the answer had been any closer, we would have fallen into it," laughed Bryan.

Suddenly the silence was broken by a discernable splash and a yell coming from nearby.

"Sounds like somebody did," commented Tammy.

After exchanging glances they ran through the trees back to the water's edge and spotted Josh crawling up onto a rock, soaked to the skin. Hurrying they scrambled over the rocks toward him.

"You all right?" asked Tammy.

After a few unfavorable comments, he affirmed he was fine.

Bryan began laughing and Tammy soon joined in.

"What's so funny?" asked Mrs. Holden, walking their way. "Oh, no!" she exclaimed.

Bryan squatted down next to him still chuckling. "So I see you wanted to take a closer look at the 'maiden's mirror.' "

" 'Maiden's mirror?' " questioned Josh.

"Yes," spoke up Tammy, "there's the maiden, 'Tissaack,' and there's her mirror, the lake," she pointed.

"I told Tammy: 'If the answer was any closer we would have fallen into it.' Then we hear this big splash! And here you are!" recounted Bryan.

Josh laughed. "Mirror Lake, eh?"

"We better head back and get you dried off," stated Mrs. Holden, a little dismayed.

Once on the trail leading up to the parking area, they spotted a shuttle bus picking up a small group of visitors, and a ranger on horseback talking to a colleague on foot.

Waiting for the next bus, Josh sat on the rock wall sunning himself, while the others enjoyed the peace and serenity that surrounded them.

Returning to Yosemite Village, they treated themselves to an ice cream cone. Tammy had to laugh at the way Bryan and Josh licked their ice cream.

Returning to the car, they discovered that it was unlocked, and their belongings had been gone through.

"Mom, I'm sure I locked the door before we left," recollected Tammy.

"I think you did too. The dregs of humanity are everywhere even in paradise," replied Mrs. Holden.

"Anything taken?" questioned Bryan.

"Everything looks to be here," commented Josh as he went through his things. "Wait! My camera! Where's my camera?"

"It's not up here in the front," replied Tammy.

"It was in this bag," recalled Josh. "It's gone."

"Well, the good news is that nothing else seems to be missing," concluded Mrs. Holden after they had gone through everything.

To get their minds off of the negative, Bryan reminded them about the short demonstration on rock climbing, if they were still interested. Tammy was reluctant to go along with it, on two counts. First, it was a futile and dangerous sport, and secondly it was just another chance for him to show-off. Somehow she was hoping to rid him of his Peter Pan complex. Tammy's mother however, thought it would be very interesting to see. So as they neared the base of El Capitan, Bryan directed them into a shady parking area under a group of large overhanging black oaks.

Bryan pointed out an immense granite boulder about thirty-five feet in height standing just out from the base of El Captain that would work splendidly. Carrying his gear over to a nearby picnic table, he began sorting it out. Finding the athletic tape, he began wrapping his hands. While doing so, Bryan, glanced upward to watch the dynamics of the cloud masses crashing into the gray soaring spires of Yosemite's north wall.

"Look at your hands," noticed Tammy grabbing his left hand, "all the scars and scabs."

"They'll heal."

"This is another reason why you need to quit. You're hurting yourself." Her facial expression was one of dismay as she rubbed her fingers over the scars as if healing them somehow.

"Okay," spoke up Bryan—changing the subject. "We use wedges, called chocks, and 'friends' are these cams that expand into the various sized crevices, besides the good old fashion piton that's hammered into a crack," explained Bryan.

Suddenly, a climber with a ponytail stepped out from behind the large boulder distracting them. In an agitated state he threw his gear to the ground and stalked off babbling something about "a soul-death job in L.A."

"He must have freaked," guessed Josh.

"Ready to go up?" asked Bryan.

"You think I'm scared, but I'm not. I can do anything you can do."

"Oh, is that so? Let's find out. Put this belt on."

Bryan, by use of hand and foot holds quickly worked his way to the top of the boulder and set a cam in a crevice to secure the two ropes they would be working off of.

While he descended, Tammy glanced at her mother, frowning. Her mother had to laugh to herself, at what her daughter's big mouth had got her into this time.

"She'll be okay," assured Bryan catching the concerned look. "I'll be right next to you, you can't fall."

"Is that a promise?"

"You trust me don't you?"

"Sometimes," she responded, looking up into his eyes for a reaction.

Ignoring her implication he went on to show her how to control the rope through the belt loop.

"Place your right foot there and push off to gain a hand hold."

After a successful try, she went again.

"Make a fist this time in the crevice, it will hold you. Try another reach."

Grunting she pulled herself up. "I must have a hole in my head. What am I doing this for?" She pulled and pushed herself off a couple more times, and made the mistake of looking down which caused her to freeze to the rock.

"You shouldn't have looked down, imagine you're only a foot off the ground," encouraged Bryan.

"It's too late, I can't."

"Hang on." Bryan inched over and drove a piton into a crack next to her and secured her to it.

"You all right?" he asked squeezing her shoulder.

Her dark eyes spoke to him. "I'm fine now."

"Hey! Are we idiots or what?" Josh yelled up to them. "The biggest clue of all is right here, *El Capitan*, the Captain," he pointed.

"You know he's right," realized Bryan glancing up at the towering monolith that was now coming into shadow.

"Glad to finally meet you!" hollered Tammy.

"It appears we have a tie. You and Josh are now tied in the clue solving department," informed Bryan. "Now stay put. Let me show you another thing."

Pushing off he placed both feet against the bare granite, and pushing off again he skipped toward her. She screamed when he bounced over her and rebounded on the opposite side.

"Sometimes, you have to move across the face of a cliff to get to another route," he explained.

She closed her eyes and hugged the rock as he went back over, but this time he kept going and disappeared around the side of the boulder.

"Br-yan! Don't you dare leave me here!"

All of a sudden he appeared on top of the boulder looking down. "Hi, gorgeous," he grinned.

"Br-yan," she whined, being disarmed by that comment.

"This is called rappelling," he demonstrated sliding down.

"Watch out there's some red ants over there," she warned.

"Grease ants. Don't crush them if you can help it."

"Why? What will happen?"

"They give off a rancid smell that sets off the whole colony into a wild biting frenzy. It can be a painful experience, believe me. I'm now unclipping you, and I want you to rappel down with me. Control the rope like I showed you earlier. Okay, let's go."

Following his example she gracefully glided down with him. Her mom and Josh clapped in applause. Coming to a stop about five feet from the ground, she lost control of her guide rope and slowly turned upside down. After a short scream, she began laughing.

Bryan reached down and grabbed the bottom of her polo shirt and pulled it through Tammy's climbing belt, saving her from an embarrassing situation. "And what do you think you're up to?" he asked, flopping upside down too.

"Oh, just hanging around."

"Here grab my arm, I'll pull you upright. We're not quite down yet."

Back on the ground again she was quickly congratulated by her mother. "Welcome back to planet earth. Look at your cheeks, their beet red."

"Whew! What a rush. I thought my heart was going to jump out of my chest." Taking a deep breath she looked over at Bryan who was talking with Josh concerning the fact that the Captain must have made his presence known in this valley. That is if this monument of granite had been actually named for him. How quickly his mind had shifted gears, while she was still calming down—just to be able to speak.

After packing the climbing gear, Bryan asked her for her honest opinion.

"It certainly is a thrill ride, but I still think it's much too dangerous, especially when you get up real high. And besides look at what it's doing to your hands."

"I did have that one accident, but that was a freak of nature. The margin of safety is the same up there as it is down here."

Tammy shook her head. "I do want to thank you though, for being a gentleman, if you know what I mean," she whispered.

A pleasant breeze stirred the trees. Looking up into the rustling leaves and the darkening cliffs above, she felt a certain serenity—that everything here and now was right—joined with those she cared about.

But it was now time to go home. Tammy readily accepted her cousin's offer to drive on the return trip.

Checking out of Eden, they climbed the north wall of Yosemite Valley as the late afternoon sun shone yellow upon the opposite cliffs, and upon the great 'Tissaack' which glowed brilliantly at the far end of the valley.

Bryan gazed back into the giant rent in the earth, into the place where the Captain must have stayed for a time. He wondered why the armor and the clues it held were so far removed from the Obelisk and the 'Oro de Cañon.'

"So, Bryan and Josh," spoke up Tammy, "what do you have to say now? Did I not come up with the first proof that the Captain did survive?"

"Well, not exactly," replied Josh.

"What do you mean, 'not exactly'?"

"Josh!" exclaimed Bryan.

"Oops."

"Br-yan!" exclaimed Tammy.

"All right, all right," stammered Josh. "On our last trip, we came across some old photographs that showed the 'sun' symbol," he explained, hoping that would suffice.

"Then what? You followed up on them, right?"

Josh paused, not knowing what to say at first. "Yes, but the person who took them has been missing for a long time."

"Why didn't you tell me?" she asked directing the question to the ringleader.

"I asked Josh not to," explained Bryan.

"So you two could have a head start?" she fired back.

"No, it's my Dad. Let me explain."

After doing so, Tammy sympathetically replied, "You still could have trusted me."

"You're right, I should have shared that discovery with you, and I'm sorry. But there's more, and I don't know how I am going to break it to my parents," conceded Bryan. For the next half hour, Bryan and Josh revealed what they found in the dresser drawer—the newspaper articles, the historical research, and the photographs.

Mrs. Holden couldn't believe what she was hearing. "Do you comprehend what you are saying? If this is true, there's a whole page of American history missing," she commented.

"And do you realize, you may have a whole 'nother side of your family out there somewhere?" reflected Tammy.

"Yes, and it puts me in some kind of a quandary as to what to say, and when I should do it."

"It still bothers me that you thought you couldn't trust me."

"Nothing personal, it's just I didn't want to take a chance."

"Well, nothing personal, but I'm not talking to you either," she finalized crossing her arms, leaning against the door away from him.

After many miles of silence, Josh noticed his aunt nodding off. Glancing in the rear view mirror he was surprised to see Tammy slumped over, sleeping comfortably against Bryan, her head lying against his shoulder. Bryan had dozed off also.

9

ABOVE THE OWL'S FACE

I t was another beautiful day in the high country. Red guided himself along the now familiar trails. Spring had gone and the warmth of summer was evident.

Unknown to Bryan, on that very day another plot was unfolding that would eventually collide head-on with his search for the Captain. But for the moment everything seemed to be moving in a positive direction.

On a downhill slope, sun glinted off an object through the trees, catching his attention. Drawing closer he could make out a four-wheel drive vehicle parked on an old logging road just below. Changing course to intercept, he found himself at the edge of a clearing. Out in the open, a man dressed in a surveyor's vest was busy leveling a satellite dish on a bright yellow tripod. The man appeared to be middle-aged. As he approached he could see that his face was red from prolonged exposure to the sun.

"Howdy," he greeted looking up from his task.

"Hi," returned Bryan. "What kind of signals are you trying to pick up?"

"GPS."

"Oh, that's right, it's the Global Positioning System, I heard a little bit about it at a briefing at the S.O."

"You work for the Forest Service I take it then?"

"For the summer," Bryan answered dismounting. "I'm Bryan," he introduced.

"Just call me Mack," he returned shaking his hand. "We're under contract to increase the densification of the GPS net, which will serve as a basis for a regional GIS database."

"That's a mouth full. If I remember right, this is utilizing the military satellites, isn't it?"

"That's right. Look at the display on the receiver right here," he pointed bending down. "Right now I'm tracking 6 sv's, short for space vehicles, which are the satellites that are above the horizon. I need a minimum of four to get good readings."

"I take it these satellites are constantly transmitting."

"Yes, they transmit time in increments of a billionth of a second; and without getting too technical, the carrier wave cycles are counted and translated into an exact distance, which in essence creates triangles between the satellites and earth. The result is— triangulation."

"Wow, I'm impressed."

"It's amazing technology for sure. Say, that's some horse you have there."

Before Bryan could answer, the receiver began beeping.

"Oh, no, don't tell me. They're doing it to me again!"

"What?"

"Something big must be going down. The military is retasking the satellites. It happens every so often. Well! It appears I'm done for the day!"

After helping him break down and load the equipment, Bryan departed and regained the trail, anxious to finish the day out.

A number of miles away, the trail curved sharply at a promontory of rock that overlooked miles of forest. A discernable sound out of the west made him pause as he looked out over the green expanse. It sounded like the whine of a turbine engine, growing ever louder. Then over the treetops they came, two black turbine powered helicopters, racing at full throttle. They quickly descended into the depths below, banking right. He realized they were heavily armed gunships, flying low and avoiding radar recognition. What could be happening? Recalling what Mack had said about the satellites being retasked, made him wonder even more. There was a high altitude Marine base some miles away on the east side; but what kind of maneuvers were these?

A week later on a warm evening, Bryan was unexpectedly beckoned to Josh's. Apparently Tammy had called earlier and said something was up. Not knowing what could be so urgent they waited in anticipation. Josh jumped when the phone finally rang. After a brief greeting, Josh switched the phone to speaker mode.

"I have good news and bad news," she started out. "First, the bad news. Yesterday afternoon I came home, and found someone in our house going through things. He apparently heard me come in, and escaped out through my mother's bedroom window. I ran out of the house and spotted someone rounding the corner on the next street over. Hurrying, I got down there in time to see a tall man getting into a black Mercedes, which quickly sped off."

"This doesn't sound like your common garden variety burglar," commented Josh.

"Did he take anything?" asked Bryan.

"No, not that we can tell. He went through the desk and both bedrooms. But anyway, the police came and made a report. But they were of little help."

"But what about the papers with the tracings on them?" queried Bryan.

"Their safe, I had them tucked away in a place that no one would have thought to look."

"Good."

"Assuming that is what he was looking for, how did he know to come here?" she wondered.

"Your license plate number," answered Bryan.

"Your right," she realized. "They'll probably soon figure out your location too."

"Remember how my camera was stolen right out of the car, the one that had the pictures of the armor in it?" recollected Josh.

"That's right, and we had the tracings with us when we went up to Indian caves and Mirror Lake," recalled Tammy.

"But the ranger didn't object to the pictures," pondered Josh.

"No, he wouldn't have, that is if he didn't want to shed any negative light on himself," replied Bryan.

"Right now, I'm calling from a friend's house just in case they have tapped into my home phone. Now, for the good news. Bryan, you were right, the sunburst was there, hidden in the lower right-hand corner."

"That's good, but I am wondering how this figures into the Captain's original scheme of things?" pondered Bryan.

"This could very well be another set of clues. Besides, geographically speaking, Yosemite just happens to be straight across from the El Camino de Rancho, which is where the Captain's heir, your great grandfather lived and was raised," commented Josh.

"Perhaps given the circumstances of the time," thought Bryan, "the reality being that no one could ever access the Canyon of Gold from the west side again, it would be prudent to add another set of clues that would shed light on the 'back door' approach to the Canyon."

"Are you two ready to hear more? You're just rattling along with speculation without hearing all the facts. This was no walk in the park you know," cut-in Tammy.

"Go on," both replied.

"There are seven phrases that comprise the body of the text. The first is the 'maiden's mirror' as you already know. The second is 'the lake of the shining rocks.' Third, is a 'mineral spring.' Now the fourth one is a strange one. Listen closely. 'Where the puma and the whale face the owl.' "

"Whale?" questioned Josh.

"That's correct, the Spanish word is ballena. Now, number five is simply, 'above the owl's face,' and sixth is, 'at the ram's head.' And finally the last one translates as 'armor helmet.' "

"That's it! We're looking for a Spanish helmet, that's what all this leads to. It must contain more instructions," burst out Josh.

"I guess the first question is, where is this lake and the mineral springs?" wondered Tammy.

"The lake is *Lake Tenaya*, and the springs are at *Tuolumne Meadows*," answered Bryan.

"Are you sure?"

"The Indian name, Pywiack, means 'shining rocks.' There's a conical granite dome at the head of Lake Tenaya that has the same name. The glacial polish on this and the other surrounding granite domes makes them very reflective. You'll see climbers practicing on them quite frequently."

"I think Bryan is right about Tuolumne Meadows. Years ago it was commonly called 'Soda Springs,' " recalled Josh.

"It fits doesn't it?" Tammy realized. "Starting down in Yosemite Valley at Mirror Lake, then following upstream to Lake Tenaya, and then over the hill into Tuolumne Meadows."

"This may prove to be a trail of armor of sorts. Maybe there is another piece beyond the helmet. But I think what we're going to have to do is go up to the Meadows in order to figure the rest of this out," thought Bryan.

"There's a nice campground up there," informed Josh.

"I won't be able to go till Friday, because of work," stated Bryan.

"I may be able to go up sooner, if I can arrange some transportation," Tammy thought out loud. "My mom works most of the week. I may be able to talk one of my girlfriends into going."

"Getting a head start on us will you?" commented Bryan.

"Swallow your pride; in the end it benefits you anyway. How about a little incentive? Whoever solves the most clues wins a prize," proposed Tammy.

"Prize?" questioned Bryan.

"I'll call if I can get things arranged," she stated.

After exchanging goodbyes the informative phone call ended.

While Bryan was gone on his weekly trek through the mountains, Tammy had called stating that she was going up on Wednesday with a friend. But her friend had to leave on Friday and return to the City. So the plan was that Tammy's mom would come up to Columbia on Thursday and the boys would join her on Friday to go up to the Meadows.

Josh had pretty well predicted Bryan's reaction when he got back. "She's taking over! Give her an inch and she'll take a mile."

Friday finally came, and they left on schedule, with Bryan behind the wheel. Whisking through the curves between Big Oak Flat and Groveland, Mrs. Holden had something on her mind.

"Now that we're by ourselves, I have a question for you, Bryan, and I want you to be frank with me," she asked.

"Sure."

"It seems to me that Tammy likes you a lot. What are your intentions toward her?"

Bryan felt his chest cave-in. He couldn't breathe. "Ah—frank answer, uh? Well—this is in strict confidence isn't it?"

"Just between us."

"I do like her, but at times she drives me up the wall."

"Ah ha!" exclaimed Josh. "You admit it!"

"She does that to me too," laughed Mrs. Holden.

"I'm kind of backward in my social skills, and pretty slow at this boy/girl stuff," he confessed.

"That suits me just fine. You can understand a mother's concern, right?"

"The way we clash at times—you may have nothing to worry about."

"Don't kid yourself. Take it from another woman, she sees beyond that, and apparently likes what she sees. Let me tell you something. I don't know what happened to her two years ago, but when she came back home she was different, quiet and thoughtful."

"We probably scared the living daylights out of her," remarked Bryan.

"No, it was you, I'm pretty sure. You two are a lot alike, smart, headstrong and competitive. But I think you went one up on her, and no one has ever done that before."

Briefly stopping at Olmstead Point, they gazed at a view to the north side of 'Tissaack,' and the blue jewel that was *Lake Tenaya* which was just below them to the east. The bubbling granite domes at the far end of the lake—were a striking example of geological architecture. One of which was Pywiack, one of the "shining rocks." Furry marmots languished on the rocks attentive to any food that would be thrown their way.

Skirting along the edge of Lake Tenaya, Bryan explained that before the road was dynamited out of the rock along the north shore that travelers with their horses and wagons had to venture out into the lake along the shallows to get around the granite bluffs.

Within minutes they had passed over the hump and began their descent into picturesque *Tuolumne Meadows*. What an attractive place this was for the mountain traveler to recoup within this fortress of rugged pinnacles. The sprawling green meadows, the fields of wild flowers, the crystal clear streams, and the towering spires of the Cathedral Range, all but forced you off the road to embrace its beauties.

Nearing the Tuolumne River, a sign directed them down a narrow road to the campground. Pulling up to the entrance kiosk they found a note on the message board directing them to campsite 22. Following a dusty road that paralleled the river a short distance, it soon turned into the pines. Arriving at the designated site, they spotted Tammy sitting at a picnic table, reading. She wore tan hiking shorts and a blouse to match. Bryan noticed as she approached that her face was pleasantly bronzed by the sun.

"Bryan, you drove all the way?" she asked.

"Guilty as charged."

"How did he do, Mom?"

"Tammy, if he can pull a horse trailer up and down these mountains, today's drive is just a country stroll," commented Josh.

"Bryan is a good driver, I didn't even get nervous," she responded.

Bryan didn't even bother to catch Tammy's reaction as he got out of the car.

"Been waiting long?" asked Mrs. Holden. "When did Rachel leave?"

"About two hours ago. We couldn't get her car started for a long time because—"

"Because at this altitude carburetors have a tendency to flood, right?" guessed Bryan.

"Yeah, you're right," she acknowledged. "I'm really glad you guys are here. There is a creepy guy who came over to help us; he keeps watching over here."

"What is this you're reading?" asked Bryan, flipping the book over that was on the picnic table. "A romance novel! Mrs. Holden your daughter is reading romance novels. You better have a talk with her!" Tammy's mother laughed.

"A girl can dream can't she?" replied Tammy.

"No, life is exactly what you make it," Bryan bluntly replied.

"Oh, mister realist here."

"Say, Miss Jane Goodall, have you made any discoveries yet?" he questioned as he carried the tent equipment over.

"No, one only knows I've tried. I've been up in Dana Meadows, Lyell Canyon and even downstream toward Waterwheel Falls."

Bryan was relieved. He was ready for her to rub it in.

"Bryan Anderson! Do I see you smirking?"

"Who me?"

"Just because I haven't won this battle doesn't mean I won't win the war."

"What war?" asked Bryan.

"War of the sexes. Where have you been?"

"Oh, that war. I've been in the woods, where it's peaceful, no war out there. Except perhaps the other day. Besides you can't win."

"Betcha I can."

"Okay, what'll you bet?"

"I bet you one week— being your personal slave, and you have to bet the same."

"Deal, shake on it," answered Bryan.

Their eyes locked for a brief second, prisoner of a feeling that was stronger than gravity.

"I suspect the first place we need to visit is the Soda Springs and go from there," recommended Josh, coming over with an arm load of gear.

"I've already been there," replied Tammy.

"Josh is right, I think we need to start there to at least get orientated," felt Bryan.

"You kids go and play Sherlock Holmes, I'm going to take a nap right here, under this tree," announced Mrs. Holden, setting up a lounge chair.

Electing to walk, they followed the west bank of the Tuolumne River, whose emerald green waters led them down to the Tioga Road and to an arched rock bridge. Crossing over the bridge, a short hike on the shoulder of the Sierra highway brought them to a graveled road at the base of *Lembert Dome*. Proceeding north past the horse stables soon brought them to the trailhead. Entering onto the meadow, ground squirrels were busily darting across the trail. An impressive view of the Cathedral Range opened up to the southwest with the shimmering waters of the Tuolumne River reflecting in the foreground. Beyond, stretched lush green meadows that extended to the far boundary of white granite domes and peaks.

Proceeding around a rocky protrusion, white and rust colored mineral deposits along a southerly facing slope marked the location of the Soda Springs. Traversing over the damp adjoining ground, clear bubbling pools came into view, adjacent to and beneath the remnants of an old cabin.

"Did you taste the water yet?" Bryan asked Tammy.

"Yes, try it, it tastes like Alka-Seltzer."

"Aaa-h, your right," agreed Josh.

"Let's fill our canteens for tonight, just in case Tammy tries to cook something," Bryan whispered to Josh.

"I heard that!" she responded.

Josh laughed. "Now that we are here, we need to consider the next clue. Where the 'puma and the whale face the owl,' " recalled Josh.

"Let's walk out toward the middle of the meadow, and consider what fits the clues," suggested Bryan.

"Well, they are all animals, one walks, one swims, and the other flies," summarized Josh.

"My thought was that 'water' is the common thread between all the clues," disclosed Tammy. "Two mountain lakes and a mineral spring, and from here, if you literally follow the drainage, it would take you down the Tuolumne River into the gorge," disclosed Tammy.

"That's good reasoning," complimented Bryan. "The mountain lion and the owl are creatures of the mountains, but the idea of a whale completely throws this whole thing out of whack."

"The description indicates a place. The puma likes the high rocky terrain, right, and the owl of course likes to be in the trees. All logical until you get to the whale," thought Tammy.

"Whales live in the ocean, a hundred miles that way, to the west. It doesn't make any sense," agreed Josh.

Getting the field glasses out of his pack, Bryan scanned the surrounding area, and handed it to Tammy who wanted a turn. Crossing a small log bridge, they slowly sauntered further out into the meadow. Silently they admired their surroundings, the wavering grasses, the song of a blue bird, and the restful quiet itself.

"Look!" exclaimed Tammy. "Over there," she pointed.

"What?" the boys asked in chorus.

"The crimson flowers, look at them dance in the breeze," she pointed.

"Woo-o, I thought you found something," breathed out Josh, holding his hand on his chest.

"Oh, you just can't stop for a minute and enjoy life, can you?"

"That's why they made women to point these things out to us, right?" replied Bryan.

"So you think that the real reason we were put on this earth is to be subservient to you buffoons," she snapped back.

"Sounds good to me."

Tammy curled the edges of her mouth up in dismay.

"They are called penstemon, and yes they are pretty," finally agreed Bryan. "You shouldn't be so sensitive."

"Women are sensitive; we use both sides of our brains, not just the left side."

"Quantity is not always quality."

"Whoa! Time out—this is going nowhere," broke in Josh. "I just had a thought. What if the Spanish word rendered, 'whale' could have been also used in a more general sense. Like—a big fish."

"It's possible, I guess," thought Tammy.

"If that is the case, there is the possibility there is a lake up here somewhere that has large fish, nestled in among these high ridges with trees surrounding it," concluded Josh.

"For only half a brain you are working wonders," winked Bryan.

Ignoring that comment Tammy glanced at her watch. "We'll probably have to wait till tomorrow to check that theory out."

Pulling a map out, they located all the lakes in the surrounding area.

"Ladies first, I pick this one, Elizabeth Lake. The gender is right, anyway.

Bryan kind of laughed.

"What?" she asked.

"Nothing," he replied, grinning. "I'll tell you what, let's go check out the rumor that there's a natural water slide in the river next to our camp," he suggested, changing the subject.

Working back toward the campground along the river, they soon located the natural flume. On a sweeping curve, the rivulet of white water would carry the willing participant through a granite channel into an emerald green pool of frothing water. Air bubbles raced to the surface with such a violent effervescence that it appeared that the river had come to a boil.

"Looks like fun," said Tammy.

"I brought some cut-offs," remembered Bryan.

Josh and Tammy agreed, and away they raced back to the camp to change. In the warm afternoon sun, the water was cold but refreshing. Besides trying the natural water slide, they explored a number of potholes that had been carved out of the granite bedrock by the swirling currents. Some were large enough to sit in. Others were smaller, but all had a similar collection of small rounded stones.

Tammy had a sore bottom from slipping and falling on the slick rock adjacent to the slide. She was glad that the boys didn't make fun of her, as she tried to rub the pain away.

Returning to camp, they found Mrs. Holden preparing an early dinner, declaring that she was famished. They quickly seconded the motion.

After the meal was over, Josh and Bryan teamed up to wash the dishes.

"Who taught you guys how to wash a spoon?" scolded Tammy, holding one up. But before she could continue, a ranger named Ken, handsomely dressed in his uniform and ranger hat stopped by reminding campers that the campfire program began at dusk. The subject that evening was "The Vampires of Tuolumne Meadows."

Josh laughed and envisioned some guy running around the meadow and the adjoining forest, wearing a cape, scaring people. The others speculated it had to do with bats.

Hurrying to finish up with chores, they gathered jackets and flashlights, and lit out for the campfire circle which was only a short walk through the trees. Up a rise, the paved semi-circle had wooden benches laid out radially facing the rock-lined fire pit. Gradually the seats filled as family groups and couples trickled in from all directions. Tammy couldn't help but notice the variety of the apparel that seemed to fill the complete color spectrum. Snuggling up against her mom she closed her eyes.

The ranger they had met earlier soon arrived and began building a fire, declaring that none of his wood was soaked in kerosene. As the fire sparked to life, he mentioned he was a ten year veteran of the Meadows. Before going into that night's subject, he had the audience shout repeatedly as loud as they could, "campfire!" and then to sing a warm-up song. The vampires of Tuolumne Meadows they soon learned were none other than the lowly mosquito. But these little monsters did have one redeeming value, which was their role in pollinating wild flowers.

As darkness ensued, the glowing fire reflected upon the ranger's face, leaving a memorable scene as he related many stories of life in the wilderness.

But it was the "States" song, which really set the audience off. The enlivened audience began singing such lines as, "where has Or-e-gone?" and "what did Ida-hoe?" The body of the song grew as a new state and phrase was added each round.

Before dismissing for the night, Ken reminded everyone about that evening's star watch program that would be starting shortly. In the diminishing light of the campfire, he remained for a few minutes answering questions, mostly relating to bears and food storage.

Tammy was excited about going to the star watch and finally talked her mom into going. With the aid of a flashlight they walked down the dark roadway that led to the main highway, and met with the waiting group. Two cars traveling the lonely dark highway temporarily blinded them with their headlights, as they whizzed by and disappeared into the night.

After a few minutes, the ranger arrived introducing herself and explaining that in order for their eyes to adjust to the night sky, all lights would have to be left off, from here on out. She led the group across the highway and along an unperceived pathway that wound its way through the trees into an open area in the meadow. Dimly, in the light of the night sky, a flat granite area became visible that would be ideal for watching the stars from.

Gathering in one general area, everyone began looking for a comfortable spot to lie down and face upward on the bare rock. The four of them laid out side by side, with Bryan and Tammy sandwiched in the middle. The ranger began the program by relating some stories from the Indian lore. Such as, how the stars were actually woodpecker holes in the ceiling of the night sky.

The most common constellation was the *Big Dipper*, made up of seven bright stars. In North America and in Europe it was commonly perceived as a bear. The first two stars in the handle were braves in pursuit, and the last star was a boy carrying firewood. The wood was to be put under a nearby celestial pot to cook the bear. Lining up with the two pointer stars on the front of the Big Dipper, their eyes were directed up to a faint yellow star that proved to be the *North Star*, also called Polaris. An old Indian story related that this was one of Coyote's eyeballs that he juggled to impress his lady friends, but somehow it got stuck and remains there till this day. And above Coyote's eyeball was a set of stars that made a horseshoe, this was believed to be the cave that the bear hibernated in.

"Did you see that?" whispered Tammy swatting Bryan in the chest. "Two fallings stars just went right through the Big Dipper."

"What would the Indian stories have us believe as to the significance of that?" he whispered back.

Other constellations were pointed out to them such as the Summer Triangle and the Teapot which rested just above the southern horizon. The distance to some of the stars were over a thousand light years away and others much closer. One of the last subjects covered by the ranger was 'meteor dust.'

Returning to camp, tired and sleepy, they prepared to retire for the night.

"Josh," called Mrs. Holden who approached the boys' tent.

"If you're looking for Josh I think he went down to the bathroom," informed Bryan poking his head out of the tent.

"I'm worried about Tammy; she went down there about fifteen minutes ago and hasn't returned. And I just heard someone say they seen or heard a bear. Could you go down there and see if she's all right?"

"Sure."

Finding his flashlight, he made his way down the dark dirt road. He noted that the campground had grown quiet. Very few were still up. Rounding the stone structure that contained the bathrooms, he called Tammy's name as he neared the doorway.

"Who is it?" questioned Tammy's voice.

"It's me, Bryan. Your mom sent me down to check on you."

"Oh, great."

"Well, if that's the way it is, I am heading back to the tent."

"No, wait!" she exclaimed. "There may be a bear out there, I think it may have followed me here."

"Ha, ha. Oh come on. You're just being silly. Let's go."

Tammy slowly crept out of the dark doorway, looking both ways. "Okay, lead the way. I'm right behind you."

He could feel her hand on his back as she did literally stay right behind him, peeking over his shoulder. Bryan wondered if Josh had picked up on some of his old tricks.

Suddenly, the bushes just ahead began shaking. They stopped and shined their lights on the disturbance. Tammy dug her nails into Bryan's left arm.

"I think somebody is playing games with us," confided Bryan.

113

Dragging Tammy along with him they soon arrived back at camp unscathed.

"You okay now?" he asked, as they approached her tent.

"Yes, thanks to you. How will I ever repay you?"

"Oh, I'll figure something out one of these days," he replied.

Good thing it was dark, for her face grew red hot with a blush.

"Say, I want you to know, I generally don't make it a practice to pick up girls at campground bathrooms," he laughed turning to go back to his tent.

"I hope not," she replied.

Josh soon returned, but was unusually quiet as he went about getting ready for bed. Bryan's suspicion was confirmed later that night when he overheard Josh mumbling in his sleep—something about "a bear in the bush, ha ha."

Tammy was up early the next morning. "Hey you country boys, raise and shine, you're not going to let a city girl beat you to the punch are you?" she taunted, trying to rouse them. Not hearing a response, she swatted the side of their tent.

"Little chance of that," remarked Bryan from the other side of the campsite.

Startled, she turned around to see them approaching with towels draped around their necks. "And why do you say that?" she demanded, seemingly a little dismayed.

"Well, because city folk seldom get up that early," he answered.

"I'm standing here right now in living proof that's not true," she countered.

"There could be two possible reasons for that. One is that this is just a fluke—"

"Fluke! I'm not talking to you," she replied stalking off.

"Uh oh, now you've done it," commented Josh as they stepped into their tent.

"A little dose of truth never hurt anyone, did it?"

"Little dose? Hardly. You may have single handedly vanquished romanticism forever."

Bryan spotted Tammy leaving with her pack in a huff, and felt regret and resolved to apologize to her at the next opportune time. "I guess I should have given her the second reason first."

"And what was that?" asked Josh.

"That she's not a city girl but a country girl after all."

Her mother soon appeared wondering why her daughter had left so quickly. Bryan at that instant learned something new about Tammy. She didn't run to mother for every little thing, she was truly her own person.

Hiking to the Lembert Dome parking lot, the boys split up in their individual quest for the mythical animals that would reveal to them, the secrets of the forgotten past. Josh headed up the trail to Dog Lake and points beyond. Bryan caught a ride up to the ranger station at Tioga Pass, and reasoned that if he took the trail up to 13,050 foot *Mount Dana* that it would give him the very best view of the whole region. Looming up, barren, and powerful, along the Sierran crest, its reddish tinge told him of its volcanic origins.

Crossing the meadow, Bryan considered the reflective small glacial lakes that were scattered principally down the western slope. Like framed mirrors, they afforded him varying views of the surrounding mountains. Soon above the timberline, the trail degenerated to debris fields of shattered metaphoric rock. It zigzagged, steep, and relentless with little clue at times of where the true location of the trail was.

The beauty of *Dana Meadows* sprawled out below him. His eye followed the ocean of green that flowed southerly down into Tuolumne Meadows. Clouds were already forming in the dark ranges to the south of Yosemite, where the crest of the Sierra rose an additional thousand feet; it being a bastion of rock and ice. With the possibility of a thunderstorm forming above him, he realized he had to hurry.

Higher yet, the view allowed him to look down into a granite basin of blue lakes, into which Josh was somewhere hiking. Recognizing Saddlebag Lake in a deep canyon to the north, a flashback instantly linked him with memories of the ranges beyond.

Well above the timber line, there was no shade, the sun glared down on him. Overheated and tired he slowed. The sound of water rushing under his feet intrigued him. Somewhere, perhaps ten or fifteen feet under the great jumble of rock that clothed the mountain, ran a gushing stream of cold snow water.

After another half hour of climbing, he reached a plateau of sorts. A rock mound marked the trail. Above him stood the final ascent of the great dark rock mass, now partially shrouded in a gray cloud. Worn to the bone, he slung his pack against the mound and laid against it. A gusty wind whistled up the slope. He closed his eyes and tried to take a catnap, but he kept having the sensation that he was whirling around. It was probably the oxygen debt that was affecting his brain. Opening his eyes he felt dizzy. Taking a deep breathe, Bryan sat up.

Digging out his field glasses, he focused on the Cathedrals and the smaller intermediate ranges.

"There must be something absolutely unique that we're missing," Bryan told himself.

Realizing he was just below a low point in the rocky spine of Mount Dana, he slowly made his way up to look over the eastern precipice. The dull blue form of Mono Lake first caught his attention several miles distant, and at his feet there was a sheer drop-off of at least two thousand feet. Emerald green lakes lay nestled in the hollows below, and traces of snow lingered in the shadows of the north slope.

It dawned on Bryan that he could see both trails of the Captain's from this point. Could they be tied together somehow? Turning his back to Mono Lake, he focused westerly toward Tuolumne Meadows. What were these animals they were looking for? Were they something real or figurative? he wondered. Lembert Dome was perhaps one of the few discernable objects that he could focus on. The Soda Springs was hidden directly behind it. He again focused on that area. The granite domes behind came in and out of focus. Then something jumped out at him.

"The 'Whale!' There she blows!" Bryan exclaimed. "No, wait. It's oxygen deprivation, I'm seeing things." Looking again, it was still there, laying on top of an elongated dome. He was now convinced he had found the first one. Slightly to the right and on the side of another granite dome was the shape of a mountain lion, arched ready to spring.

"Bingo! We have confirmation." They were mountains in the shape of animals. How else would a whale be up here? he realized. What next? The Owl. It faces them, he mentally pondered.

"I have to get back down to the Soda Springs—the answer was staring us in the face all along," he again spoke out loud. "E-e-ha!"

Returning to his pack, he glanced in the general direction of mosquito-ridden Elizabeth Lake, and figured Tammy would soon be back down at the campground. It would probably take Josh another hour, and for him it would take at least two hours to get back down. Still a bit stiff, he clamored down the trail, sliding on the loose rock which proved to be as fatiguing as the ascent. Dropping below the timberline, nature's sentinels, the marmots, were out in number perched on rocky protrusions facing west out over the meadow. Crossing a small creek lined with delicate yellow flowers, the trail quickly descended into the lush meadow and meandered through the sparse trees.

At the ranger station, Bryan caught a ride from a park ranger who was heading back down. The ranger stated he had spent over thirty years in the area, and wouldn't dream of going any other place. Paralleling Dana Meadows he pointed out to Bryan, the approximate location of where old wagon wheel ruts still could be found.

Back in camp, Bryan found that Josh had come in about twenty minutes before, dusty and tired. Tammy had come and gone. Getting back early she had decided to go on a ranger walk.

"What is that look on your face?" questioned Josh. Oh, no, don't tell me, you figured it out!"

"My face seems to be an open book. Well, yes, the answer was right out here all along," Bryan answered pointing out toward the meadow. "I've located the 'whale' and the 'mountain lion,' but I want you to be the one to solve the whereabouts of the '*owl.*' "

"You know it's not going to make any difference in the end. These little games you two play, the meaningless arguments. Ever since the very first day I brought her over to your place, I could tell she was hooked on you. She wanted to know everything about you. Are you blind? Can't you see what's going on?"

"No, not completely," Bryan replied.

Soon, Tammy returned with a piece of rope she had made with reeds, just as the Indians of old would have made. She seemed to be excited about the things she wanted to share, but stopped short when she read their faces.

"You've, figured it out?"

"Yes. We need to go back out into the meadow near the Springs," informed Josh.

"We have to find the 'owl' next," added Bryan.

"Josh, you figured it out?" she asked.

"Well, actually no," he confessed.

She twisted her mouth and shook her head. "Well, I guess it's a good thing. That's why we're here, right?" she responded with mixed feelings.

Tammy's mother joined them in their journey of discovery, excited and curious. Tammy was unusually quiet on the way out.

"This is as good a place as any," stated Bryan, coming to a stop in the meadow about a quarter mile out from the Soda Springs. After whispering something in Josh's ear he went on. "Look due west at the various granite domes. The 'whale' sits up there and the 'lion' is to the right," he pointed.

"I see them," acknowledged Mrs. Holden, "they are huge figures cast in stone. This is so surreal.

"The 'mountain lion' is all arched up ready to attack," observed Josh.

"The 'owl' has to be behind us than," realized Tammy. Before she could turn around, Josh had already spotted it.

"There on the fractured face of Lembert Dome," he pointed.

"Bryan, you had me set up," complained Tammy, giving him a glaring look. "I can play this game too, the next clue directs us to *'above the owl's face'*, there, high to the left is the *'ram's head.'* "

"Your daughter learns quickly," commented Bryan.

"She has learned from the best," Mrs. Holden replied winking at Bryan. "But I would like to point out one thing to you three, if you haven't figured it out already. You are first of all a team. You may continue with your competitive game but realize, Bryan, that you needed Tammy to do the deciphering and break the first clue; and Tammy, you needed him to make the next big breakthrough. You need each other."

"Tammy, I need you," declared Bryan holding his arms out to her, jokingly.

A pang ran through her, as she realized she was tempted to comply. "I'm not talking to you, remember."

"But I apologize, please forgive," he begged smiling, getting down on his knees.

"Stop that, you're just plain off the wall," she giggled. "Rise Sir Bryan, you have been forgiven," she announced tapping him on the shoulders and the head. Everyone laughed.

"We need to return to camp and make preparations to ascend the Dome," reminded Josh.

"The Spanish helmet is near the 'ram's head,' " Tammy recalled.

"We'll have to smuggle the metal detector up there. This is a national park you know, they don't take kindly to that sort of thing," commented Bryan.

"We may have to wait till after dark before we can begin the dig," thought Josh.

"After dark! May I remind you that one false step up there could be curtains," Tammy warned.

Dark lazy cumulus clouds drifted ever so slowly, eastwardly over the piercing peaks of the Merced watershed, far in the south.

Returning to camp, they excitedly began their preparations for the ascent of Lembert Dome. Josh broke down the components of the metal detector and distributed them among their packs. Bryan packed a small folding shovel along with some small hand tools. Tammy would carry a small battery powered lantern and a flashlight, in anticipation of working after dark. Josh remembered his replacement camera that he brought along and slipped it into his pack also.

After getting a quick bite to eat, they set off along the river to the stone bridge.

Josh turned around and smiled. "Doesn't this remind you of something?"

"Like old times?" guessed Bryan.

"Yes. But this time I'm ahead in solving clues," answered Josh.

Tammy made a face at Bryan in disapproval. Bryan smiled and said nothing.

Just south of the Lembert Dome parking area, Tammy pointed out the location of numerous mortar holes in the granite slope that the Indians had used for food preparation.

Glancing up, they noted that a group of people who had been gathered near the trailhead were now dispersing. They seemed to be disappointed somehow.

Further up the highway the young adventurers intercepted the little used east fork of the Dog Lake trail. The route from that side of the mountain proved to be steep, winding its way up into the upper limits of a lodgepole forest. Huffing and puffing, the oxygen debt soon caused them to slow to a crawl. At an insignificant pass, a stencil-cut iron plate sign pointed uphill to the west, to the top of the dome. Within minutes they broke out onto the back edge of the granite mountain.

"You okay?" asked Bryan.

"Yes, thank you," replied Tammy.

"You know, some things have changed," commented Josh.

"How so?" lackadaisically responded Bryan, climbing the first set of granite steps that led up onto the main part of the dome.

"It's you two. You argue like the old days, but you actually make up and sometimes you're even nice to each other."

"Are you complaining?" asked Tammy.

"Frankly, I used to get a big bang out of the way you two used to carry on."

"Don't lose heart Josh, I think there's still plenty of potential," responded Bryan.

"And what do you mean by that?" demanded Tammy, stepping her way along a granite terrace.

"Well, we haven't argued about money yet. That's always a hot subject."

"Sometimes it's not just the money," she commented. "My Dad had a problem with booze and gambling. We went hungry more times than I want to admit."

"Sorry to hear that," replied Bryan.

"But otherwise if things are budgeted—I really don't see where there would be a problem," she stated.

"Sounds like you need to marry an accountant," concluded Bryan.

"No way! I can't imagine being married to someone like that. Besides, if I did marry someone, they would be like—well, it wouldn't be a boring accountant.

"You see what I mean," spoke up Josh. "Your arguments don't have the same entertainment value anymore."

Bryan laughed. "Let's continue on up to the 'ram's head.' "

"Did any of you notice that this evening's Lembert Dome nature walk appeared to be canceled?" queried Tammy.

"Now that you mention it, there was quite a bunch of people leaving," recalled Josh.

With evening coming on, hikers were now coming down from the top of the dome anticipating the time it would take to get back to camp before darkness fell.

Walking along the southerly slope of the dome, they looked down upon the campground and the white water of the Tuolumne River below. A gentle-down canyon breeze now became noticeable. Climbing the slope they soon reached the top of the elongated rock mass. The immensity of the view held them for the longest time as their gaze swept from the glistening domes of the west, to the red and black volcanism along the main crest of the Sierra Nevada to the east, and then southerly over the rugged ranges of the Merced Basin, glimpsing an occasional flicker of lightning out of a brewing thunderstorm. The salt and pepper granite underfoot was weathered and grooved. Continuing along the upper lip they found dwarf trees growing in protected pockets.

"This must be the 'ram's head,' " thought Josh, "but from this angle it just looks like an ordinary granite protrusion."

Bryan stepped around to its side and confirmed they were in the right location. Dropping their packs in a common spot, they spread out to look around in the declining sunlight.

After about fifteen minutes, Bryan circled around and returned to the west side of the dome. He spotted Tammy sitting out near the face of the dome, just below him. Working his way down, he noted her head was bent over, leaning on her knees.

"Beautiful view isn't it," he said approaching.

Raising her head, she wiped her face with the back of her hand, and looked up at him.

He noted dried tears on her face. "What's wrong, are you hurt? Is it something I said?"

"No-o, it's just me—my emotions. I was sitting here admiring the view, and began thinking about what a mess my life has been. I don't know why I'm telling you, you're just going to make fun of me."

"No, I won't." he replied sitting down next to her. Her sadness had a dramatic effect on him. He felt the same pain—he had been there before. "The anger concerning your father is coming to a head again, isn't it? I was pretty bitter when my mother left a few years ago. I came to the sound and undeniable conclusion that all women are treacherous and can't be trusted. But since I've met you, I've come to realize that's not completely true. You are not at fault. Tammy—look at me. You're probably the smartest girl I've ever met, you have drive, and you have good looks."

"Ha, you're just saying that. You haven't known enough girls to make such a comparison."

"I mean it," he replied, putting his hand on her bare shoulder. His touch seemed to have an electrifying effect. "Look at the bright side. Because we came out of broken or partially broken families we realize how precious a good relationship is. The best years of your life are just about to begin," he added, purposely forcing her to make eye contact. She momentarily lost herself in his eyes, as she listened with her ears and heart.

With a deep sigh she responded, "You're right!" Another tear appeared in her eye, but this time it was a tear of happiness. She smiled at him. "I declare Bryan, you seem to have some kind of power over me at times. But it seems to be a good thing."

"Hey you two, no slouching on the job," called Josh from above.

"Come on," coaxed Tammy, slapping him on the knee, "Let's go find that helmet."

Bryan smiled and helped her up. Climbing up to Josh's position, they looked back over their shoulder to where the sun was dropping below the horizon. A gusty breeze blew from below, as a shadow devoured the mountain of rock. With the advent of darkness coming on it appeared that everyone had finally left the dome.

"If you ask me, the only place where anything can be buried up here, is in these joints or crevices in the granite that have opened up. They're filled with decomposed granite," pointed out Josh.

"No telling how deep they go," commented Bryan. "But you're right, there is no other place to bury anything."

"Metal detector time," suggested Tammy.

"Let's start at the 'ram's head' and work our way out along each of these crevices," agreed Bryan.

Returning to their packs they assembled the detector and let Tammy start out on the most westerly crevice. Walking with her down slope, the boys patiently listened. After two hundred feet the fissure closed up. Josh tried his hand at the only other crevice that was wide enough to bury an object. After several minutes he too came up empty.

"What now?" wondered Josh, scratching his head. "It would take days to dig through these trenches."

"Okay Bryan, where's that so-called superior male intellect of yours now?" challenged Tammy.

"Right here," he replied pointing to his head. He stroked his chin as he thought. Tammy wondered if he could pull this one out of the fire. "I wonder—a penny for your thoughts?"

"No insults please," she responded.

Bryan laughed and threw a penny into the cleft between the rocks. "Run the detector over it."

Josh passed the round disk of the metal detector over the coin without a sound.

"It appears that the detector is simply out of adjustment," concluded Bryan.

Adjusting the sensitivity of the ground balance knob, Josh finally got it to beep.

"Not so fast! Ladies first," she demanded. "I know what you two are up to—trying to let Josh win. You'll be my slave for a week yet!"

"Ooh, she's really got it in for you," commented Josh.

"We can't let her win, she'll probably make me go shopping or something," whispered Bryan.

"Oh, that would be so-o cruel," sarcastically remarked Josh.

Starting at the 'ram's head' again, she slowly swung the detector back and forth. The boys again watched her progress as a last shaft of light temporarily lit up the top of the dome and the Sierran crest beyond in a reddish cast.

"What was that?" Josh questioned.

"What was what?" asked Bryan as he watched Tammy, making sure she didn't miss a spot.

"A flash over that way, toward the east," he pointed. "Somebody could still be up here."

"Better go check it out," recommended Bryan.

Below the 'ram's head' the slope leveled off and the crevice widened into a round bowl. Directly in the center of the bowl, the metal detector beeped once. Tammy froze.

"Try it again, keep low," directed Bryan.

A faint glow still illuminated the high country. Below, it had grown dark, campfires were now visible scattered throughout the trees in the campground.

There was a definite tone each time she passed over the spot.

"This could be it," she thought.

"It's still too light to start digging," stated Bryan. "Continue on down, keep checking. I'll go and check on Josh."

Before he had gone far he spotted Josh coming toward him. "I didn't see anyone, but you never know," reported Josh.

Faint on the breeze was the distinct yell, "campfire!" Recalling last evening's ranger program they glanced down toward Dana Circle and the flickering campfires among the trees.

"Those clouds are really getting dark behind the Cathedral's," pointed out Josh as they hurried back. Before they had gone much further, a rumble of thunder carried from across the canyon.

"It's coming this way, we better hop to it," realized Bryan as they neared Tammy's position. "Find anything else?"

"Yes, a strong reading right here," she pointed.

'I'll get the lights and we can start digging," anxiously spoke Josh.

"Keep an eye out, Tammy, I'll start digging and then we can trade off," proposed Bryan.

After five minutes he had a hole dug into the hard packed decomposed granite about eight inches deep, when something dark came into view.

"Careful," he warned himself. Catching the edge, it moved. "An old tin can!" he recognized turning it over.

Lightning bolts lit up the southern sky as they filled the hole.

"One down, one to go—let's hurry," beckoned Josh jumping up.

"Josh, you start this next one and I'll keep watch," volunteered Bryan.

The latent thunder finally swept over them. Josh dug the trowel in and bit by bit scraped away the loose granular rock. Progress slowed as he got into the packed material. He tired after ten minutes and then let Tammy chisel away at it. After three minutes she was holding her aching arm. The hole was now about fifteen inches deep. Thunder and lightning now began to grow increasingly violent beyond the Cathedrals. Exhaustion came quickly as they went through another round of turns. The storm made them nervous at it bore down.

At twenty-four inches in depth, Tammy stopped. "I think I hit something," she announced. A dark surface appeared in the white granite, as she scooped out the loose material. "It's the helmet, I know it!" she excitedly exclaimed.

"Quick, dig around it," prompted Bryan.

Soon the top fin was exposed, verifying their find. It took another fifteen minutes to extricate the helmet. Bryan and Tammy carefully lifted it out together. Bryan dusted it off and inspected it in the light. A sudden crack of thunder caused all of them to jump.

"Wow! Look at this! The inside is inlaid with gold and there appears to be some kind of a map etched into it," realized Bryan handing it to them.

"There's writing around the inside of the rim, with stars and 'sun' symbols around the interior," discovered Tammy.

"There are also radial lines running up to a point in the top of the helmet," pointed out Josh, getting a quick look. "I'll get the paper and pencils to do the trace," he volunteered, scampering off into the darkness to retrieve their packs.

"Want to try it on?" offered Bryan.

"No, but here, let's see how you look," she replied, taking it and gently sitting it on his head. "If you look anything like the Captain, he was very handsome."

"Here we go," said Josh, rushing back. He gave a short laugh after seeing Bryan. "The Captain lives!"

After carefully completing the tracing due to the soft nature of the inlaid gold, they took another turn closely examining it.

"Josh, if you have your camera, let's try taking a couple shots inside the helmet and perhaps a group shot with all of us together," suggested Bryan.

"Bryan, that such a nice thought," commented Tammy.
As they went about taking the pictures, the winds shifted as the storm neared and intensified.

"We better go," urged Tammy.

But before reburying it, he held it and thought about the man who wore this helmet two centuries before.

10

PAOHA

 light shower misted from the diminishing thunderstorm as they clamored into camp, exhausted and dirty.

"How did you get down so quick?" wondered Mrs. Holden, "I just saw a light up there."

"We left about fifty minutes ago," informed Bryan.

"Look! She's right. Someone is up there near the top of the dome, up near where we were," pointed Josh. An unsteady, winking light could now be seen high up on the dark bulging silhouette of Lembert Dome.

"Somebody must have been following us," realized Tammy.

"I've had that suspicion ever sense we were down in Yosemite Valley," commented Josh.

"Did any of you notice how there was an absence of ranger patrols this afternoon and the fact that the nature walk at the Dome appeared to have been cancelled?" questioned Bryan.

"Uh, I noticed that too. It's almost like somebody is giving us a wide berth," thought Tammy.

"Yeah, letting us figure it all out, and then swooping in and cleaning up," commented Josh.

"They can't do that, and get away with it," angrily responded Bryan, throwing his pack down. "I'm going back up!"

"No! You can't. You don't know how many of them there are, and besides, you're already tired out," argued Tammy, grabbing him by his right forearm, trying to hold him back.

"I have to try," he told her, looking her straight in the eyes.

She knew she couldn't stop him. "Okay, then I will go with you."

"No, it's too dangerous and you wouldn't be able to keep up," Bryan replied. Her mom also protested.

"I'll go," finally announced Josh.

Within seconds the boys had disappeared into the darkness. Tammy looked concernedly at her mother.

"Get used to it," she replied. "I'm going to lie down. Let me know when they return."

Tammy was starved, but she couldn't eat. She just walked to and fro in the damp coolness around the camp, looking up at the dark mass that seemed to fill half the night sky. After twenty-five minutes the blinking light no longer could be seen. Bright stars again appeared in the northern sky.

After forty-five minutes, Josh returned, exhausted and alone. Tammy ran to him, and gave him a quick hug.

"What happened? Where's Bryan?" she begged.

"I don't know, I lost him about half way up. I couldn't keep up, and of all things I lost my way."

"What?!" she reacted, pushing him away.

"Ow! My arm."

"I'm sorry."

"You're more nervous than the proverbial long-tailed cat."

"I know," she whined.

"I barely had the strength to get back," informed Josh hobbling to the picnic table and laying his head down.

So the waiting began again. Tammy sat next to him and noticed he had already conked off. She too soon nodded off.

"Huh! What!" responded Josh and Tammy after being nudged.

"You better turn in, no more can be done tonight," informed Bryan, who had just returned.

"Take me to bed," muttered Tammy still half asleep. "Bryan! You're back! You okay?" she asked excitedly.

"I'm more dead than alive."

She found him to be soaked in sweat and very weak. His muscles were hard and strained.

"I was too late, they had already descended via the north trail, but I could make out that there were two of them. They also have the helmet."

"Oh no," reacted Josh. "I guess we should have brought it down with us."

"Here, let me help you get these wet things off," offered Tammy, as she helped him with his shirt.

"Thanks, I'll take it from here," half laughed Bryan. "Let's get some sleep, I have a feeling things are about to jump to light speed.

Tammy at first had trouble getting back to sleep, pondering Bryan's last statement. What would the celestial-like map found in the helmet reveal? Bryan's dried sweat on her hand smelled just like him, and she didn't mind.

Bryan woke up late and found everyone sitting at the picnic table.

"Hey, sleepy head how are you?" Tammy called out glancing his way.

"Sore."

"Sit down, I'll get you something to eat," she offered.

"Enjoy it while you can," whispered Josh. "After the vows all you get is a box of cereal stuck in front of your face."

"Don't make me laugh, it hurts," he replied.

"Say, we've been going over the tracings from the helmet and came up with an idea," continued Josh, pulling the sketches in front of him. "The irregular object in the middle was at first baffling. But Tammy thought that these two shapes within could be islands. Then I thought about Mono Lake with its two islands, but the shape isn't right."

"That's when Mom," spoke up Tammy, "interjected the thought concerning the City of Los Angeles and all the water that has been drained off and piped south."

"You're right, and all the water wars that have ensued since," recalled Bryan.

"Then the recollection hit me," related Josh, "that the terraces that I had seen from the Mono Lake Overlook must have marked the shore of an ancient lake. I think this shape shown here would closely match that of an ancient—Mono Lake.

"And look here, inside the lake. It looks like an x scratched across the larger of the two islands," pointed out Tammy.

"You know, since today is our last day up here, perhaps we should make tracks over the hill and check this out," thought Bryan. Another glance at the x told him it was near the southern end of the island.

Tammy set a tin of scrambled eggs and potatoes in front of him.

He thanked her, and she smiled back. "Tammy have you had a chance to look at the Spanish words that circle the rim of the helmet yet?"

"Yeah, briefly. Let's see, the one at the back right of the helmet means 'cottonwood trees.' And this one in the front starts out kind of bold with an "au," but the rest is indistinguishable. On the front left, I have no idea what it means, and the back left—there are lines like flowing water."

Bryan pondered the meaning of the "cottonwood" trees, while he ate.

"I wonder if there is a way we can get over to that island?" spoke up Bryan after a spell of silence.

"I think we can rent a boat at Lee Vining," thought Josh.

Mrs. Holden unfolded a road map she found in the car, and spread it on the table. "Well, it doesn't seem to be that far," she realized.

"Look," pointed out Tammy, "the big island is called *Paoha*."

Bryan quickly finished eating, as the others put things away and prepared to leave.

Excitement was high as they left the lush green meadows and made their way up to Tioga Pass. After passing two scenic mountain lakes the grade descended steeply into Lee Vining Canyon, whose character gradually changed from granite to volcanic and from pine to sagebrush. Josh got a whiff of overheating brakes just as they neared the bottom of the grade. Their first view of Mono Lake was unimpressive—a low slung basin draped in sagebrush, barren and desolate. The lake and the islands laid low in the pit of the basin. The smaller island to the north was called Negit. Its composition was black basaltic in nature. Paoha was a completely different animal, shrouded in white sediments.

Turning left onto the highway that led into Lee Vining, they found a local tackle and bait shop in which to inquire about boat rentals. Being directed to the outskirts of town, they drove past the scattered businesses strung out along the highway to a marked driveway that descended to the edge of the lake. A dirt and gravel lane led them down to a set of small red cabins trimmed in white with a boat house to match.

Coming to a stop, they noticed some movement under a nearby weeping willow tree. Apparently, they had awakened a man who had fallen asleep while reading a newspaper. Knocking over a half empty bottle of beer and cursing under his breath, he stumbled to his feet.

"What can I do you folks for?" he asked. Mrs. Holden laughed.

"We need a boat and some information," spoke up Bryan.

"I can rent you a boat, but no guarantee on the information," he replied bending over, peering into the car. Mrs. Holden waved her hand to clear the air. The man's foul alcoholic breath was getting to her.

"Sorry ma'am, I just had brick-fest a bit ago."

"A full course meal, I'm sure," she replied.

Having agreed on a rental fee for a fourteen foot boat, the three quickly checked their packs in preparation to depart. Tammy's mother decided that a boat ride out to a desolate island was not her cup of tea, so she decided to go back up into town to browse through the local gift shops while they went out on their excursion.

"What do you know about the history of the big island," Bryan inquired of the half-sober man.

"Not much to tell. Some Frenchman tried hatching chickens over the sulfur steam vents for a while. In the early nineteen hundreds, it was homesteaded for a few years. And in the forties, they tried establishing a sanitarium out there, but that was a crazy idea, right?"

"Yeah," Bryan chuckled.

"The only other thing that I can think of is that someone hauled a drill rig out there sometime before the First World War looking for oil, but they never found any."

Tammy found the rented aluminum boat moored to a small dock adjacent to the boat house and set her pack in the bottom. Stepping into it she nearly made it capsize.

"Sit down!" warned Josh.

The boys soon joined her. Josh pulled the start rope on the motor and it surprisingly jumped to life on the first pull.

"Ow!" complained Josh. "There goes my arm again, you better take over," he informed Bryan. Holding his hurting arm he sat forward.

"I guess it's a little late to ask if you know how to handle a boat?" questioned Tammy.

Powering up the outboard motor, the boat dug in and plowed through the brackish water.

"Tammy, you trust me, don't you?"

"You keep asking me that. Yes, I trust you, but that doesn't mean something couldn't go wrong."

"If it does, we'll have to live the rest of our lives out here, I guess."

"Adam and Eve, huh?"

Bryan made no reply. Tammy felt they needed to talk, but somehow the time wasn't right yet.

"Listen to what this brochure I picked up in the tackle shop says on Mono Lake," spoke up Josh over the roar of the motor. "First of all, 'it's a terminal lake, it has no outlet. The water is three times as salty as the ocean. There are 280 million tons of dissolved salts in the lake, primarily carbonates, sulfates and chlorides. Mark Twain once said: 'It's sluggish waters are so strong with alkali that if you only dip the most hopelessly soiled garment into them once or twice, and wring it out, it will be found as clean as if it had been through the ablest washerwoman's hands.' Oh, listen to this, the name of the Lake came from the Yokut Indian word for the Kuzedika Paiute, meaning fly people. They would harvest the alkali flies in their larval stage, which would turn the beaches white due to their great abundance.' It says they were also 'excellent basket weavers.' "

"Oh my, larvae-eaters! That's horrible," commented Tammy.

"Hey, don't knock it. They could be like crunchy snacks," teased Bryan.

"Sick."

"What about those odd-shaped formations up on the shore that look like towers of cement slag?" wondered Bryan, pointing toward the northwest corner of the lake.

"Those are—'Tuffa Formations, made up of calcium carbonate that formed from mineral springs bubbling up from the lake bottom. But because the lake level has dropped some forty feet, they now stand on the present shore.' Here's what it says about Paoha: 'It's about two thousand acres in size, layered in lake bottom sediments. The only thing that grows there is greasewood and cheat grass. There are active steam vents that hiss with noxious vapors along Hot Springs Cove.' "

"I see them," pointed Tammy.

Nearing the island, Bryan throttled back and idled slowly along the shoreline, passing what was undoubtedly Hot Springs

Cove. A sulfurous mist blew from the gurgling waters inside the cove. Barely visible high up on the shoreline was an old handmade brick tub. Finding a gentle beach area, they landed and pulled the boat up on shore.

"What a strangely beautiful place," thought Tammy. "It's almost like we've gone back to primeval times."

"It's going to be hot, there's no shade anywhere," realized Josh, as he swung his pack on.

"If everyone is ready, let's hit the—" began Bryan.

"Dusty trail," the others chorused and laughed.

Working their way south, a gust of wind sent a dust cloud scurrying to the north end of the island. Sea gulls floating on the breeze observed them from above as they squawked among themselves. The terrain they meandered through was a gauntlet of mounds and gullies that gradually steered them inland. Noticeable along the way was a small dry lake bed whose sides were stained a light shade of red.

"Stop! Get down," warned Bryan.

"What is it?" the others begged, dropping low.

"Two people, along the shore on the southeast side of the island," explained Bryan in a hushed tone.

Josh dug out his field glasses. "It's a man and a woman. They have a boat nearby. They are digging in the sediments along the upper beach."

"Let me see," asked Tammy. Refocusing on the subjects, a realization hit her. "Oh no!"

"What?" asked Bryan.

"It looks like the park ranger and the woman that we talked to at the Visitors Center in Yosemite. They are wearing regular clothes."

"Let me see," Bryan requested. After a moment, he paused for comment. "You have good eyes for a —"

"For a city girl, right?" she responded. He half laughed. "I know you all too well, mister."

"Is that good or bad?" he asked making conversation while he continued to peer through the glasses.

"Well, some is good, and some could be better."

"The man is tall just like the ranger," confirmed Bryan.

"Tammy didn't you say, that the person who broke into your house was tall also?" remembered Josh.

The expression on her face clouded. "Josh, you're so right," she replied. "Let me see again." After a long look, she turned and sat down. "This is so odd."

"Now wait a minute here," Bryan realized. "This is all kind of circumstantial, but this is fitting a pattern. Follow me on this. There were two people last night up on the Dome that snagged the helmet. And Josh, how did the lady in Bishop describe the guy who claimed to be Coleman's relative?"

"Josh's eyes lit up. "He was tall and partially bald. That's right!"

"Bingo, we have our man. Apparently, this park ranger is the one behind all the subterfuge," concluded Bryan. "I don't know what he knows about Captain Camino, but I sense we have some serious competition here."

"We literally came knocking at their door," realized Tammy. "What have I done?"

"Exactly as you should have done," replied Bryan.

"They must have interpreted enough of the helmet to get this far," commented Josh. "They keep looking around. I suspect, they think we wouldn't be far behind."

"What's this about you visiting some lady in Bishop?" questioned Tammy.

"Woo, things are getting serious, the first signs of jealousy," laughed Josh.

"Stop it!"

"It's not important now. I'll explain later," answered Bryan.

Not important! You could have a wife and kids in Bishop, and that's not important? You go off on these trips, two or three days at a time. Anything is possible," she argued.

"Get a hold of yourself. I told you before, you have to trust me. We went to Bishop to talk with Ben Coleman's landlady. That's all," replied Bryan defending himself.

"I know. I was just trying to get your goat," she finally confessed, chuckling to herself.

Bryan shook his head. "Young lady, you're on report."

"Ha."

"Enough," finalized Bryan. "This is what we need to do. Cut back to the west and get behind the high ground that's just ahead, and continue our search just out of their view."

"They may have found something, but it may not be what we're looking for," thought Josh.

"They're probably trained archeologists," speculated Tammy.

"Come on let's work our way along the backside of this volcanic ridge, up to higher ground. I believe it's the most logical place to look," coaxed Bryan.

Ducking low, they crept through the maze of gullies behind the ascending ridge. Stepping their way up successive layers of sediment and volcanic debris, they came to the edge of a caldera.

"This is the highest point on the island, and we are definitely near the south end as shown in the helmet," declared Josh.

The others shook their heads in agreement.

"Look! There's an opening up there," pointed Tammy.

Climbing a few feet more up the pyroclastic slope, a tall jagged gash in the volcanic wall allowed them access into the crater.

"Be careful," Bryan warned Tammy, while he helped her through. "You don't want to cut your pretty little legs on these razor-sharp rocks."

"Pretty?"

"I thought I said—gritty."

"No-o, I heard it plain," she affirmed.

"Will you look at that," called out Josh, interrupting their conversation.

"A pool of water," observed Tammy as they joined Josh near the center of the caldera. "And it's bubbling from the bottom, just like the Soda Springs at Tuolumne Meadows."

The crater was for the most part circular, about one hundred feet in diameter. And the walls were mostly basaltic, accented by white-orange sediments having collected in the voids and niches. Along the upper wall, four small V shaped notches about thirty inches in height were noticeably spaced around the crater. A natural bench ran around the interior just above the water level, being slightly offset to the northern end of the crater. They marveled at the glassy reflection of sky, cloud, and rock. Climbing around the walls, Josh peered out through the notches around the perimeter.

"Someone has camped here before," discovered Tammy. "Look at the stones that formed a campfire ring."

"Fire fractured and blackened too," noticed Josh. Putting foot pressure on one of the stones, it easily crumbled.

A flock of sea gulls suddenly took to flight and noisily departed. Bryan turned and looked at the pool watching the various strings of bubbles racing to the surface.

Suddenly, the ground shook violently, and thousands of gas bubbles viciously boiled up from the bottom of the pond giving off a definite sulfuric smell.

Tammy grabbed Bryan by the arm. "What's happening?" she yelled in his ear.

"It's probably an earthquake."

After another fifteen seconds, it all stopped.

"There's been a lot of seismic activity down in Mammoth Lakes recently," recalled Josh.

"And a number of earthquakes over near Markleyville too," added Bryan.

"We have to leave!" demanded Tammy.

"Wait!" protested Bryan. "Something has changed." Walking to the east side of the pool, he peered at something beneath the water.

"All the bubbles have ceased," observed Josh.

"Didn't you hear me, we have to leave!" Tammy exclaimed in a concerned voice.

"Will you stop? Just come here and look!"

"My word! What is that?" she asked glancing back up at him.

"It looks like a circle of stones laid out in the bottom of the pool," replied Bryan who was kneeling down close to the edge of the water peering into its depths.

"There appears to be arms radiating out from the circle," spotted Josh.

Slowly Tammy walked around the pool, her eyes fixed beneath the water. "I count four. It reminds me of the pattern in the helmet in a crude kind of a way," she observed.

"If that's true, you should be standing right on top of one of the symbols shown in the helmet," speculated Bryan.

Scraping away the sediment and dust that covered the bench, course grooves soon appeared in the black rock.

"Wow! It's true!" declared Tammy. "It's the 'sun' symbol, but it's upside down."

"That would match the reverse 'sun' that we k on Coleman's photos," recalled Josh.

"I believe we have finally tied into the so-called 'back trail,' the one that we've been looking for," realized Bryan.

"Of course, it all makes sense, doesn't it?" jumped in Tammy. "From the west, looking east, the 'Canyon ot Gold' was marked by the sunrise, but here on the east side looking west, it's the sunset." The boys nodded in agreement.

Excitement overtook them as the realization of their discovery sunk in. Lining up with the other pointers, they quickly uncovered the other three symbols. To the northwest, in the general direction of where the literal Oro de Cañon would be, was carved the outline of what appeared to be the top of a mountain, a mountain shaped like that of a crater. To the west, wavy lines pointed back toward Tuolumne Meadows and Yosemite. Lastly the figure of trees pointed southeasterly, past the Mono Craters into the vast Nevada desert.

"Tammy can you sketch these symbols, while Josh and I take some compass readings?" asked Bryan.

"Sure, good idea."

"Soon as we're done, we better cover them back over," thought Josh.

"You know something, these V notches in the crater wall line up with the pointers," noticed Bryan.

"Huh, this crater must be a directional beacon of some kind," pondered Josh.

"It would seem we're at the geographical hub of Camino's empire." agreed Bryan.

Josh took magnetic bearings along the four sightlines and referenced some of the existing mountain peaks.

"What is it with these birds, they're circling around us again," complained Tammy, worried she might get dumped on.

"Their definitely drawing attention over this way," thought Josh.

"Oh no, we've forgotten to keep tabs on the two rangers," remembered Bryan. "Get the symbols covered back up, while I sneak a peek."

Climbing up on the inside of the crater he slowly rose up and peered out toward the beach. The boat was still there, but he couldn't see either of them. A sudden noise close by drew his attention. Then he saw them, about a thousand feet to his right and closing. Jumping back down, he waved them over toward the crater entrance.

"They're almost on top of us, we have to leave now," Bryan frantically informed in a hushed voice.

"I've finished the sketches," declared Tammy.

"And I covered the symbols the best I could," added Josh.

"Let's get going, back the same way we came," Bryan ordered.

At that instant, the ground began to shake again. It soon ended as abruptly as it began. Powerful jets of gas again bubbled forth, clouding the pool and putting out a sulfurous odor.

"Wait," remembered Tammy, "the fire ring."

"Should we destroy it?" asked Josh.

Bryan made a face. "Just scatter the rocks," he suggested

After scattering the evidence, they quickly exited the crater and retraced their route. Soon, they were able to cut back over to the opposite side of the volcanic ridge, dropping into the adjoining gully. From there they made their way back to the boat without being seen.

Having floated the boat, they jumped in, and paddled toward the north end of the island. The afternoon wind had appreciably increased, making the lake surface somewhat choppy. Having reached the end of the island, they fired up the motor and made a wide arc northwesterly, curving back toward Lee Vining.

"I don't know if our attempt to keep our visit to the island a secret will pay off, but we had to try," commented Bryan, looking back.

"The ranger must have left his vehicle on the south beach. I see a couple rigs parked down there," observed Josh.

"I'm tempted to go down there and get even," considered Bryan. "But I think it's better we just fade away, like we were never here, and cover our tracks from here on out. Tammy, you're so quiet, are you okay?"

"I'm fine, just emotionally spent."

11

THE FORGOTTEN SISTER

With incessant heat, the dog days of summer had arrived. But the presence of the Dog Star at sunrise would soon yield to the days of autumn. Summer was slipping away quickly.

It had become increasingly difficult for Bryan to hide the truth concerning Captain Camino and the possible existence of family elsewhere. He felt it was a card he had to play at the right time.

It was early morning, nearly a week after their return when the phone rang. Bryan's mother called him to come into the house.

"It's your girlfriend," she informed as he came in.

"M-om," he complained.

"Well, she is a girl and she is a friend, right?"

"No comment. Hello, this is the home for the criminally insane, how may I help you?"

Tammy laughed. "Bryan, do you really want me to comment on that?"

"No, I guess not," he laughed back. "What's up?"

"It looks like we're going to be neighbors."

"What? No way!"

"We've sold the house, and have to be out in a week."

"That's fast. Do you need any help?"

"Matter of fact, yes. We're covered at this end, but we can use your help when the truck arrives up there."

"Up here?" he asked.

"You didn't know? We're in process of buying that vacant house that's just around the corner from you on Columbia Way."

"The Benson place? No way! Isn't this going to make it hard for your boyfriends to visit?"

"Ha, what boyfriends?"

"Well, like Ben."

"Oh don't start that again." After a brief pause she continued. "My mom wants to thank you for being able to help us. She thinks of you as family. You know, like the son she never had."

"Really? That's very kind. If my dad kicks me out, I may need to find another place to stay."

"You're not serious, he wouldn't do that, would he?"

"It's possible, if he finds out about all the time I've been spending following leads on the Captain," whispered Bryan.

"Well then, I better just tell him, so you can come live with us," she laughed.

"Tammy!"

"I was joking."

"One thing is for sure, I won't be able to call you 'city girl' anymore."

"Well, maybe not completely. I'll be taking a few classes at Berkeley this fall, and I'll be staying with Rachel while I'm down there."

"Berkeley! Wow, I'm impressed. I can't compete with you; you're definitely in the fast lane. I'll probably end up shoveling horse manure the rest of my life." His mother gave him a dirty look, having overheard that statement.

"Bryan, don't say that. It's just circumstances. You're a very smart person, and if things were different, you would be here too."

"Oh, before I forget, did you happen to figure out what that remaining Spanish word from the helmet was?"

"Yeah, I think so. The closest word I could find has the meaning of a caldera, a crater-like basin, usually caused by volcanic activity."

"That does seem to fit the corresponding symbol we found on Paoha."

"Have you made any sense of the compass bearings yet?" she asked.

"No, not yet. There's got to be something radically wrong with our readings, because the lines are projecting out into oblivion. I tried looking further out, but there was nothing out there either. Say, what about the 'au,' is there anything more on that?" wondered Bryan.

"Au, is the atomic symbol for gold," she recalled.

"That's interestingly true."

"Oh, by the way, I talked to your mom about having a party at your place after we move up. I'll be inviting some of my girlfriends and their families up. It'll be like a post-graduation party, before we all scatter to the four winds," she informed.

"You want to have it here?"

"Yes, it'll be perfect. Your mom thought it would be good for business too. She's going to talk to your dad about it.

"But, all those girls!"

"Does that bother you?"

"Well, yeah. Girls are a pain in the—well you know."

"Oh is that so?"

"Yes it is."

"Bryan, if you haven't noticed yet, I'm a girl."

"That's true, but you're different."

"How?"

"Well-l, you're just different."

"Can't you say something romantic, even if you don't mean it?" she complained.

"Me? I don't know."

"You know something, you're an oaf, a stick in the mud. I'll talk to you later, bye," she finalized, hanging up.

He was a little miffed at her continuing criticism, but she was right, he did have a problem in expressing his feelings.

The search for the Captain had entered a new phase, but none of the new leads had yet panned out.

Bryan was buffaloed by the errant compass readings. Sitting down with his maps and compass, he pondered the problem. His mother who had been busy in the kitchen came out and set a small box next to him on the table. At the same instant, Bryan noticed how the compass turned toward the box.

"Mom, what's in this box?"

"Refrigerator magnets," she replied.

"Of course, what a fool I've been. Thanks Mom, you may have solved my problem."

"Don't let your dad see you playing around with that stuff. I think he's already getting a little suspicious about your recent excursions," she warned.

Studying his marked up map, he realized that local magnetic fields due to iron ore deposits on or below the island, could very well have the same effect, pulling the compass needle off course. Erasing the old pencil lines that were based on the standard 16 degree deviation between true and magnetic north, he rotated everything to align with one of the sighted mountains, which he realized he should have done in the first place. As per this new base line, Bryan laid out the other lines based on the original internal angles. He understood that three of the sightlines would remain nebulous, unverifiable, at least for a while. But the Yosemite leg depicted by the wavy lines—like waterfalls, should align with Lee Vining Canyon or Bloody Canyon—and it did, matter of fact quite well.

"Bingo it works," he told himself.

The caldera leg, extended over the mountains into Bridgeport Valley, but how accurate could that line really be? he wondered. At the very least it was showing the general location of where the 'back trail' would lead. But they had already searched the headwaters of Robinson Creek. That directional clue was still too vague.

Bryan was mainly curious about the sightline that was designated with the upside down 'sun' symbol. He reckoned that this was the way that had to be followed, but to where? The line passed well to the east of Bodie, the old ghost town, and went clear off the map into Nevada. It was interesting that the bearing on this particular line was perfectly aligned with true north. Was this just by accident?

Finding another map that covered the whole region, he redrew the line well out into the desert. Tracing the line with his finger beyond Bodie, he stopped at a small obscure name that was more than familiar. "*Aurora*," he read out loud. He stood up almost in shock. Repeating the name several times, he contemplated its significance.

Then he remembered the 'au.'

"So it is true, a second 'Aurora,' " he told himself.

In the Captain's diary, the Stanislaus River was called "Aurora" meaning "golden dawn," and in that common time frame the area surrounding it also became associated with that name. Intertwined by forgotten history, these two Auroras must be sisters. It was clear to him now that Camino had built up a mirror image empire on the east side of the Sierra Nevada with the Obelisk and its sister peaks being the dividing spine.

But what about the pointer to the south, designated as the "cottonwoods"? On the larger map, Bryan penciled in the "cottonwoods" line and extended it all the way to the edge of the map. Retracing its course he found it passed through a restricted military area and far into the Nevada desert. Nothing along the route seemed significant, except possibly one jerk water place along Highway 93 in eastern Nevada that was named, *Alamo*, which in Spanish was translated as cottonwood.

After Josh returned home that evening, Bryan called to tell him to pack his bags, because they were soon to be off to

Nevada. They realized that there was a need to do some quick research on this new site.

So it was, after three days they set out for the high desert in search of the long lost empire of Captain Camino.

They had it in mind to stop at the old cafe to retrieve Coleman's pictures, but coming around the curve in the highway, they were met with a shock. The cafe was no longer there. It had completely burned to the ground. Coasting to a stop near the blackened sign they gawked at the remains.

"It seems we've been allowed to see, but not to touch," commented Bryan.

"This was our first big break that led us to Coleman, and proof that the Captain and White Feather had survived the incident at the 'Oro de Cañon,' " recalled Josh.

"We were fools for not gathering up those pictures when we had the chance," sighed Bryan. "But anyway, let's go find this forgotten sister."

"Oh, by the way, I dug up some information on Aurora and this map here that shows all the mines," remembered Josh. "One of the mines is interestingly called 'The Rising Sun' and another is called 'Sunset.' "

"That's interesting indeed," considered Bryan. "That will be at the top of the list for us to check out."

On the road again, the route led them north of Bridgeport, along the East Walker River to finally turnoff onto a remote dirt road. Flocks of sea gulls circled overhead as they traveled easterly into Nevada. The river again became visible over a rise, angling sharply.

"According to my map this was called 'the elbow,' an old stage stop," informed Bryan.

"More like sage stop," laughed Josh.

Entering a greenbelt they passed Nine Mile Ranch, part of the sprawling cattle empire of Nevada. Horses stationed in front of the stable were saddled and ready to ride.

Sagebrush covered hills jumped up in front of them as they approached Bodie Road. At the crossroads, an old weathered sign pointed easterly up into the umber colored hills. The continuing dirt road wound its way for miles up into a rocky canyon. Reds and yellows seemed to dash across this semi-volcanic landscape. A large red cinder cone became visible in the northeast, and according to their map it was called Aurora Crater.

"We must be getting close, look at the large smelter off to our left," pointed Josh.

"Wow, look at the size of it. The stack must be six or eight feet in diameter," estimated Bryan.

"Some big time operation for sure," commented Josh.

The dark plated smokestack towered far above the large stone supporting structure that stood out prominently along the slope of the mountain. Almost immediately the road forked to the right, and ascended an eroded slope that was once apparently one of the main routes into Aurora.

Reaching the top of the hill they found a cemetery nestled in the nut pines. Brown-rusted iron fences surrounded the white gleaming marble headstones that were etched with lambs and lilies. And below them were the ruins of an ancient city, *Aurora*.

"According to my research, this mining camp was also called, 'The Golden City of the Dawn,' pertaining to the meaning of the word Aurora; but the mining didn't last long," recalled Josh. "The veins proved shallow."

"Aurora, our fair sister," remarked Bryan. "Back home, the Aurora we knew was eventually replaced by other names, but here the name stuck—through all the intervening history."

The ruins of Aurora sat in a V-shaped valley, surrounded by lofty sage-clad hills, broken along the ridges by rock outcroppings.

Descending the hill, frightened quail darted across the road and scattered into the brush. Coasting to a stop at a crossroads in the center of town, they gazed upon the devastation—the rubble-filled basements, the piles of broken brick, and the charred and weathered timbers.

"According to the old map the courthouse sat up here to our left and the Exchange Hotel was built on this bank to our right," pointed out Josh.

"Let's set up our tent on the courthouse site, it's pretty level, and devoid of sagebrush," suggested Bryan.

"Seems appropriate," agreed Josh.

"These dang deer flies!" complained Bryan swatting his neck, "They sure bite."

After getting the tent set up, they strolled up the dirt road that was Antelope Street.

"Mark Twain's cabin was supposed to be along here somewhere," indicated Josh, looking up from his map.

"Ha, where hasn't he been," laughed Bryan.

"And up here at the head of the street, was the Dunlap house," informed Josh.

Nothing was left but a set of stone steps that led up to a debris laden building site. The top step sat precariously on the slope. Bryan gave it a push and it tumbled down the bank.

"Hey, look here," discovered Josh, "a small bottle."

"That's an old umbrella ink well. You know—quill pens and that sort of thing," recognized Bryan.

Josh turned the white speckled aqua-marine bottle round and round inspecting it. "I wonder what things were written out of this bottle?"

"Oh, probably the usual things—the weather, the productivity of the mines, murders, hangings, and perhaps an inquiry about news from the front lines of the Civil War—that type of thing."

Chatting as they went, they retraced their steps back to the center of the once lively mining town, and ventured up an eroded roadway that led up into an obscure side canyon.

"Somewhere up in this gulch is where 'The Rising Sun' and the 'Sunset' mines are supposed to be located," informed Josh.

A small dry wash led the way through the rock and sagebrush. Looking upward a wedge of snow was visible on the far northeast side of Brawley Peaks. White weathered remnants of old cabins that backed up to the stony wall of the canyon were laid open and exposed.

"The mines should be right along in here, in the east wall," pointed Josh glancing up from his map.

"Looks to me a landslide has covered most of this section," observed Bryan.

Walking further as the canyon curved to the left, a solitary plank with a cross marked on it was visible half way up the bluff.

"Must have been the site of a fatal cave-in," guessed Bryan.

"I think we've come too far," believed Josh. "We're getting up into some of the other mines."

"You got some dynamite and a backhoe?"

"Wish I had."

"Hmm, well I guess all we can do now is hike these canyons and look for the standard clues," concluded Bryan.

"It's too bad, there's no access. I was hoping this could be something that would directly tie in with Captain Camino," Josh commented disappointedly.

At dusk they returned to camp to eat and prepare for the night's stay. With miso at the top of that night's menu, they kept their meal quick and simple. After dishes, Bryan walked through the sagebrush behind their campsite in the dimming light to dump the dishwater, and noticed a big gaping hole in the ground. It looked more like a collapsed tunnel. Hurrying back to the tent, he got a flashlight and brought Josh back with him to investigate.

"It's lined with brick," first discovered Josh. "Back in the old days they did use a lot of brick in constructing sewer and storm drain systems."

"I bet you're right."

Returning to camp, they began settling in for the night. A light breeze buffeted the tent as Josh turned on his radio, and adjusted the tuner. Far away stations drifted in and out.

"What a lonely forsaken place," commented Bryan, looking out at the dark silhouetted horizon. Soon the stars began appearing one by one in the great expanse.

Nearly an hour later, just before turning in, the distant roar of a nearing vehicle caught their attention.

"Turn out the light," spoke up Bryan. Stepping outside they intently listened in the darkness.

Soon headlights could be seen ascending the slope toward what was called the Del Monte Mine, up in the east canyon. The vehicle stopped somewhere up on the mine tailings.

"Desert stargazers maybe," thought Josh.

Several minutes transpired and nothing happened. But after another ten minutes, a powerful searchlight snapped on and began rotating, round and round.

"What's that all about?" questioned Bryan.

"You got me."

"Do you hear something?"

"Yeah, like a high pitched whine," replied Josh.

The sound grew louder and louder; and finally bright lights emerged above the mine. It was a jet powered helicopter and it quickly descended to land on the mine dump. As the chopper's engine shut down, there was frantic movement by those present. All but one small light went off. There was the sound of something heavy being moved. After a good three minutes, the one light went off, and the vehicle they first heard started up and descended the road, and finally was gone.

"What in the world was that?" questioned Bryan.

"I don't have the foggiest," Josh confessed.

"The helicopter landed but did not leave."

"Apparently, they are hiding it up there."

"Strange for sure. I don't know what they're up to, but we can't let them interfere with what we're doing."

"What are you saying?" asked Josh.

"Well, it might be best if we break down the tent before it gets light; and coast the Jeep down into the willow patch in the gully and hide it," thought Bryan.

So it was, before dawn they had packed up and rolled the vehicle down out of sight amongst the tall willows in the creek bottom. Sitting in the jeep as the sun came up; they ate a cold breakfast and contemplated their next move.

"It bugs me that we can't get into the 'Sunset' or 'The Rising Sun' mines, because I think that's where we'll find what we're looking for," stated Josh.

"Well, there is one remote possibility. The arched brick sewer that we ran across may have also been used to drain some of these mines, including the two in question," theorized Bryan.

"We could at least look at that possibility."

"Okay, let's get our stuff and check it out."

"No telling what could be down there," commented Josh.

Bryan laughed.

Observing the area around the Del Monte Mine briefly, they could see no movement of any kind. Assuming it was safe they ventured back up on the main road and over to the collapsed sewer.

"Chances are we won't get very far," thought Bryan as he peered into the cavity.

"We've got company," informed Josh, "Look! Up there on the mine dump, someone is running, they must have spotted us."

"Dang, let's jump in. Quick! They probably won't be able to figure out where we disappeared to," said Bryan.

Dropping into the bottom of the hole, they immediately turned on their flashlights, and proceeded into the dark tunnel. The bottom of the arched brick sewer was covered with soil, and littered by scattered rock, brick, and dead branches. Their footsteps echoed into the unknown depths. Climbing over a partial cave-in, they soon encountered a branch line that seemed to run in the correct direction. Out of this side sewer ran a small but discernable trickle of water. Josh knocked a couple of broken bottles out of the way as he entered the smaller line. Along the way, side connections about thirty inches in diameter were visible in the walls. After a good thousand feet, the size of the sewer shrank to about forty eight inches in width.

"We must be getting pretty close," figured Bryan, breaking the silence.

After another thirty feet, a brick lateral appeared on the left, being about thirty inches in diameter.

"There's another one just ahead," informed Josh flashing his light around. "But the main line looks like it's caved in about fifty feet ahead."

"End of the line," confirmed Bryan.

"I'll check this first one out," said Josh getting down shining the light back in. "It's collapsed about ten feet in, so it appears," he reported after a few moments.

"There's a trickle of water coming out of the second one," noticed Bryan.

"I'm beginning to feel like a sewer rat crawling around down here," commented Josh.

"This one seems okay for a ways," reported Bryan. "I'll crawl in on my hands and knees and take a peek." After half a minute or so, Bryan stopped. "It's partially blocked," he yelled back, his voice echoing. Dirt and debris is acting like a small dam. I'm going to break it loose, watch for the water that'll be draining your way."

Bryan tried to stay out of the path of the dirty water as it gushed down the pipe. After two or three minutes the flow was reduced to a trickle. In the wet they crawled an additional one hundred feet before coming up into a definite mine tunnel. A small clear stream of water gurgled out of the darkness beyond.

"If we're in the right place this could be the 'Rising Sun,'" coughed Josh.

"Fifty-fifty chance. Let's see if we can find out something," replied Bryan.

After walking for a couple hundred feet they found nothing except for a twelve inch quartz vein in the ceiling that the tunnel was undoubtedly following.

Suddenly, three pounding explosions shook the mountain. Dust blew in through the drain line filling the mine tunnel.

"They must have blown up the sewer main. And we're probably trapped," realized Josh, coughing. "What do we do now?"

"They must have ran across our footprints," concluded Bryan. "We're definitely in a real pickle this time."

"Here we go!" discovered Josh. "Look it's the sun symbol," he spotlighted with his flashlight on the wall.

"Upright sun, yes, this confirms that we must be in the 'Rising Sun' mine," believed Bryan.

"The Captain was definitely here," concluded Josh.

Bryan flashed his light back and forth, then onto the ceiling. "There's a transition here. Do you see the change of mining aspect about ten feet past the symbol?"

"What do you mean?"

"It appears whoever extended this tunnel used different tools and techniques, than the original miners," replied Bryan.

"Oh, so what you're saying is that the Captain and his miners were forced to stop for some unknown reason," understood Josh.

"Yes, and someone later, perhaps in Nevada's own Gold Rush times made the rediscovery and continued on with the mining."

"If that is true, there may not be anything related to the Captain beyond this point?" commented Josh.

"That may be, but let's look around," replied Bryan.

"I would hope we don't have to go back into the brick sewer and try to dig our way to the surface," pondered Josh.

"That would be difficult," agreed Bryan. "Let's check out the rest of this tunnel first before we have to go tunneling."

Venturing further back into the mine they passed through a series of unremarkable rock formations and came to a partial cave-in on the right side. Part of the ceiling had fallen in and created a steep ramp of loose material below a conspicuous hole that lead upward out of sight.

"What do you make of that?" asked Bryan.

"Danger, if you ask me."

Bryan flashed his light down the tunnel. "I'm going to poke my head up in there and take a look," he announced.

"Be careful," warned Josh.

"As always," replied Bryan.

Stepping his way up the debris pile he could make out the existence of another tunnel running at an angle above the present mine.

"This has possibilities," realized Bryan. "We need to get up there and take a look."

"I hope it's a way out," replied Josh.

"Give me a boost, and I'll see if I can work my way up into the tunnel."

"Alright, here goes!"

Bryan grabbed onto whatever he could grab hold of as Josh pushed him upward as high as he could. Finally, Bryan was able to climb through the hole to the next level.

"Yes! I'm up," exclaimed Bryan. He looked both ways, and then shut off his light.

"What's going on?" asked Josh.

"I think I can see light up here to our left," responded Bryan. "Stay put, I'll be right back."

"Yeah, like I can go anywhere," commented Josh.

Three or four minutes went by as he waited. Then he heard Bryan going back down the tunnel toward the opening.

"The good news is, yes, there is a way out," confirmed Bryan.

"What's the bad news?"

"You just need to get you up here."

"Let's do it!" agreed Josh.

Reaching down he helped Josh fight his way up into the new tunnel. After catching his breath, Josh went up to check out the escape route, while Bryan searched the tunnel in the opposite direction.

Josh could see a dim light several hundred feet up the passageway. Nearing that location he noticed abandoned tools and supplies lined up along the left wall. He discovered that the light was coming through a crack between two large rocks set in an irregular opening in the ceiling. The floor to ceiling height at this point was barely five feet, causing him to stoop down slightly.

Bryan trudged down the dark corridor noticing increasing pitting in the walls. Descending slightly the tunnel came to an abrupt end in a wall of rock. Black smudges were evident out ahead of this blockage. To him it appeared that a blast had been set off closing off the passageway.

Something in the rubble caught his eye. It looked metallic. Removing the loose rock he found it to be long and slender. It was a sword.

"U.S. Cavalry?" questioned Bryan. "Wow!" he commented. Hurrying back, Bryan was anxious to show Josh what he had found.

Josh could hear the clamber of his footsteps as he neared. "Bryan, look at this on the wall," he spoke up flashing his light on the wall.

"What is it?" questioned Bryan.

"An upside down 'sun' symbol, but notice someone has gouged a shape over top of it," pointed out Josh.

"The Obelisk," recognized Bryan.

"What's that in your hand?" he wondered.

"A sword. U.S. Cavalry, I think."

"Really? This is intriguing," commented Josh.

"Whatever happened here did not go down well. This could be an indication that they had to retreat back to the mountains or the 'Oro de Cañon,' " theorized Bryan.

"I think it's time we make our own retreat," added Josh.

"Agreed, let's try pushing up on these rocks and see if they'll give."

Remarkably, the large stones seemed to have a propensity to roll upward and back allowing them to squeeze through to the surface.

It was early in the afternoon when they finally climbed out amongst a large rock outcropping. Hidden from view, they found a route that descended back down into the side canyon. Crawling along the bottom of the dry creek soon brought them into the willow thicket.

"So far so good," whispered Josh peeking through the branches.

Within minutes they made it to the Jeep, which apparently had gone undetected among the willows. "They must not have flown the helicopter since last night," concluded Bryan, "or they would have surely spotted it."

"Once I start this thing, we have to go for it," stated Josh.

"If they pursue, keep the petal to the metal," seconded Bryan.

"Okay, here goes."

At first it made a funny grinding noise and did not start. They looked at each other in shock. Turning the engine over again, it finally roared to life. Easing out of the gully onto the road, Josh gunned it. Flying up the hill past the cemetery, and down the canyon the dust flew. Skidding onto Bodie Road, Josh raced north.

"Which way?" he demanded.

Grabbing for a map in desperation, Bryan realized there was no time. "What a time to ask me for directions!" yelled Bryan. Throwing the map down he looked behind. "Go right, toward Lucky Boy Pass."

While ascending the bumpy long grade, dust was spotted about four or five miles back. Once over the pass they flew down the opposite side and sped across the desert toward Hawthorne. No further pursuit was visible. Josh glanced at the gas gauge and then over at Bryan.

"It seems that our interpretation of the Captain's celestial map must have been all too correct," Josh commented.

"Yes, but really what have we discovered? Originally, the Captain said he would mark the way to 'Whispering Valley,' and give instructions from there to the 'backdoor,' " recalled Bryan.

"So I guess the question is—is 'Whispering Valley' and Aurora one in the same place?" stated Josh. "I'm not even sure we've crossed paths with the original 'back trail.' "

"By virtue of the Captain's original diary, it doesn't seem so," replied Bryan.

"In the helmet, the Captain referred to this place as Aurora, not as 'Whispering Valley,' " recalled Josh.

"That is true, and the other directional lines from Mono Lake appear to point off to other things."

"If they're not the same, than we're still missing a link in the chain—between Aurora and 'Whispering Valley,' " stated Josh.

"The trail of clues has suddenly turned cold, very cold."

"Yeah, but how many times have we said that?" reminded Josh.

Bryan kind of laughed and agreed.

"Well, we're headed in the right direction; do we still want to run out to the place that translates as Cottonwood?"

"I guess if we didn't, we would always wonder what we missed," replied Bryan.

"I have to stop somewhere and get a shower," insisted Josh.

"Tonopah," replied Bryan sticking his foot up on the dash and laying back.

Later that evening after checking into a motel and cleaning up, Bryan took a stroll outside and found a postage stamp sized piece of lawn with a picnic table behind the building. Sitting on the table he looked across the silent lonely desert toward the darkening distant mountains. Tammy's face appeared in his mind's eye above the far horizon. Thoughts of her seemed to strengthen and fill him. He sensed that the pursuit for the legendary Captain Camino would soon come to an end, and he would have to make things right between them. How could someone who could climb mountains and stare death in the face be afraid to show his feelings? The joke was on him.

Next morning the day dawned clear and bright. Traveling a hundred miles more or less through some of the most desolate wasteland, they finally pulled into the wide spot in the road that was called Alamo. Surrounded by gravelly barren hills, all that comprised the town was a gas station and store on the left side of the highway. Old dilapidated houses, long abandoned, were scattered along the hillside beyond. The weathered wooden sides of the store were supplementary surfaced by galvanized metal sheets in places.

"There's your cottonwoods," pointed Josh.

On the opposite side from the store, scattered cottonwoods were lined along a meandering dry wash. Their leaves gently rustled in the morning breeze.

"Let's just ask around and see what we can come up with," suggested Bryan.

Walking into the cluttered store, only one other customer was present.

"You boys lost?" asked a tall slender man from the back. Stepping forward he was visibly bronzed by the desert sun.

"No, we just need some information," answered Josh.

"What kind?"

"Who would know about the history of this area?"

"History?" he laughed. "What history?" After a pause he continued. "Well, old Pappy, out at Argosa wells might talk to you, if he's in the mood," finally considered the storekeeper.

After receiving directions they were off again, backtracking thirty miles to near Hancock Pass, to follow an old dirt road into some of the most forsaken country either one of them had ever seen.

"Who would want to live way out here?" wondered Josh.

"Someone who doesn't want to be around people, I guess."

Paralleling a dry wash their course curved through eroded purplish hills. And finally after working their way to the top of a small pass, there below them was Argosa Wells. It was a desolate valley nearly ten miles in diameter, framed by yellowish-brown mountains in the north and west. Sculptured sand dunes dominated an area in the southern reaches of the basin. Wild burros could be seen browsing on the meager foliage along the weathered hillsides.

The road wound its way down to two homesteads about a half-mile apart along the basin's north side. Both places were glutted with old trailers, abandoned cars, and what looked to be the head works of a mine on the far west side. An old hermit at the first place directed them on to his neighbor. Again they received the warning that he may not talk to them.

The old wooden house they approached was dark and tattered. A piece of tin banged in the wind. Knocking on the door brought no response.

"Back here!" yelled Josh, pointing up behind the house.

A lone figure was visible sitting in a chair looking out toward the west. He wore an old green and black plaid jacket and a ruffled hat. The white whiskered old man did not turn as they approached.

"Excuse me, sir, do you have a minute to talk to us?" first asked Bryan kneeling down to his level.

"I may be nearly blind, but I heard you coming. I heard you even before you set eyes on this valley. You wasted a trip; I don't talk to strangers."

"We're told, of all people, you would know the history of this area," explained Josh.

"Go away! History is dead and gone."

Bryan thought he would try one last thing. "Have you ever seen this before?" he asked as he drew the 'sun' symbol in the dirt in front of him. The old man refused to look.

"Come on," beckoned Josh.

"Yeah, there's little chance he knows anything about Captain Camino anyway," replied Bryan getting up.

"What name did you say?" the old man stammered.

"Camino—Captain Camino."

He looked down at the ground to where Bryan had drawn the figure. "How is it you know this? Has the empire arisen?"

"Empire?" questioned Bryan, looking at Josh.

"You carry the sign of the old empire!"

"Yes, I guess you could say that," thought Bryan.

"Where have you seen this?" demanded the old man.

Bryan realized he would have to risk some information, to get him to talk. "Captain Camino was my great great grandfather." Digging the medallion out of his pocket he handed it to him.

The elderly man held it up and studied it. "It must be true," he mumbled. "You must be the one! The old stories say that someone would eventually come and restore the empire. Have you come to take possession of what was the Commander's? If you have, it's too late."

Bryan and Josh looked at each other.

"Well, the primary reason why we're here is to find out what happened to him," replied Bryan.

"I don't think anyone really knows. Reportedly, cavalry troops were pursuing him from the south. He left two maybe three men here to keep guard. They were told to wait for his return, but he himself never did. Word was later sent that someone would come and eventually restore the empire. Apparently, it was Camino's ambition to establish an independent territory," revealed the old man.

"How did this area fit into the scheme of things?" asked Josh.

"This was just a stopover along a strategic route, but to where I do not know."

"Then this wasn't the end of the trail," realized Josh looking meaningfully at his partner.

"My father used to say, the old trail came through *Stonewall Pass*, which is in the far west. From there it worked its way over to Groom Lake not far from the old mine. That whole area was added to the Nellis Testing and Gunnery Range some years back. That area now is all restricted government land."

"Groom Lake!" exclaimed Josh. "That's where the legendary Area 51 is supposed to be located."

"I have heard that, but I really don't know," replied the elderly gentleman.

"Groom Mine, what's there?" asked Bryan.

"Nothing much. It was in the summer of '54, unseasonably hot it was. The Government went to a great deal of expense to fence off that whole area. There was a large caravan of army trucks that came by here, some of them carrying heavy equipment. Military aircraft began daily reconnaissance flights over the whole region. A neighbor of mine happened to be watching through binoculars from a nearby ridge top. On the surface it looked like a regular military exercise, but something wasn't right. The heavy equipment was digging, drilling and blasting near the old mine. Soldiers appeared to be guarding their operations. On the third day, whatever they were after, they found. The trucks soon left, heavily guarded. Then there was one final blast that leveled everything. They locked the gate and have never been back to the site since."

"I wonder what they were after at the Groom Mine?" questioned Josh.

"Whatever it was, it wasn't at the old mine itself, but nearby. However, before they left they also ended up dynamiting the old tunnel shut as well," he further explained.

"If that is Area 51 over there, they must have built a road in from the other side to construct the air strip and other facilities," thought Bryan.

"I haven't seen one military vehicle pass this way in years," confirmed the whiskered man.

"Is there anything else you can remember?" asked Josh.

"I don't remember much and since the Great War I haven't cared much about anything anyway," he commented.

"World War II?" asked Josh.

"No, the First. I couldn't live in a world like that anymore."

"I'm sorry, I wish things had been different," consoled Bryan. "I'll tell you what, when we get this all figured out, we'll come back and fill you in."

"You better hurry; I don't have many days left."

Turning out of the old man's driveway, the name on a sign caught Josh's attention—Smedley. There was something about that name. What was it?

Curious about the Groom Mine site, they continued west along a rough corrugated road until they came to the locked gate and a wire fence that stretched for miles. White blistered and rusted signs declared that this was a U.S. Government restricted area; violators would be prosecuted to the fullest extent of the law.

Josh tugged on the rusted chain and lock. Surprisingly the lock fell to the ground.

They looked at each other as if to say—do we dare?

"The old man must have been right, no one has been in here for years," commented Bryan.

Josh looked at his watch. "Against my better judgment—let's try it."

This was certainly a whole new chapter that they knew nothing about. Fixing the gate and chain behind them, they roared down the dusty road several more miles to an apparent mine site which was situated up against a nameless broad mountain. It was pretty much as they had been told, the main tunnel itself had been blasted closed. Additionally, they found a second site nearby that also had been extricated. It appeared that adjacent rock faces at this location had been shattered by explosives. Long shadows now crept out from the adjacent mountain in the late afternoon sun.

"Josh, I wonder if this could be where the Captain stored the gold that we believed was missing from the 'Oro de Cañon,' remember?"

"From what the old man said that could very well be true. But what bothers me is that the Government came in here under a covert shroud of secrecy, removed the gold and destroyed any historical evidence that may have been connected to Captain Camino. Why?

"You're right, why is there a cover-up? It can't be just to hide their infinite greed could it?"

Waiting for dark they prepared to leave under the guise of night. A slender moon appeared in the eastern sky. Suddenly Bryan sat up. He heard something.

"It's a helicopter and it's headed this way," realized Bryan

"Uh oh."

"The only way they can see us is with night vision scopes or infra-red. Just remain still."

The roar intensified, and finally a black body moved across the darkening sky toward them with no running lights and very low. As it banked and turned to the northwest, a dim greenish glow could be seen coming from the cockpit. Maintaining a low profile thy slid between the desert mountain ranges undetected.

"That was no military patrol," concluded Josh.

"What goes on here?" seconded Bryan.

"The desert hides its secrets well."

12

SUMMER PARTY

Returning home about three weeks later from his scheduled mountain trek, Bryan pulled into his driveway with the horse trailer in tow. His heart went clunk, when he spied a group of girls busily decorating for Tammy's summer party.

How quickly time had passed. Tammy and her mother had finished moving up and were settling in. He remembered her sadness, leaving the house that she had grown up in, but declared that she would not live life looking in the rear view mirror.

The girls were stringing up Chinese lanterns between the tall ponderosa pines. Tammy pretended not to see him as she talked to his mother.

Stopping in the driveway next to the old barn he let down the tailgate on the horse trailer. Backing Red out of the horse trailer, he instantly became the center of attraction. Tammy's friends flocked around the horse taking turns petting him.

"You must be Bryan?" one of the girls asked, diverting her attention to him.

"Yes, that's me."

"Oh, Bryan, I've got to meet you," said another girl slipping through the crowd. "I'm Roxanne," she self-introduced, making curious eyes at him. "I've heard all about you," she kind of drawled.

"Hopefully it was all good."

"Wel-l, yeah," she replied glancing at Tammy who had just wandered over.

Tammy seemed a little distant; she did not smile. "You might as well meet everyone else," she finally spoke up. "This is Rachel, who I'll be staying with this coming semester."

"Glad to meet you. Tammy speaks of you every now and then." He noted she was a little taller than Tammy with long blonde hair.

She also introduced, Summer, whose freckles and warm smile made her seem very pleasant. Dark haired, Kristi, proved to be the shy one, but lastly there was, Jodie, who with all her eye-makeup, gave him the impression that she was a little on the flirtatious side.

After a few minutes of small talk, Bryan walked Red over to the corral, while the girls made their way back toward the house, chattering as they went.

"Tammy, he's so handsome, no wonder you've been hiding him from us. I'll be tempted to take him away from you," teased Jodie.

"Jodie! Stop it. I swear you can be such an animal at times. Besides it's not like that anyway. I'm not sure at times if he even likes me."

"I guess the question is, do you like him?" asked Rachel, popping into the conversation. "Be truthful."

"Well, yes, but we got this little war going on."

"Oh, I see, he's one of those, macho type," guessed Roxanne. "Hey don't fret, there's lots of men out there, some you can easily control. The night is still young."

Bryan thought he would make himself scarce. There had to be things that would take him elsewhere. But it wasn't long before the partygoers sought him out to get a ladder and help them string up more electrical cords.

The actual party was to be Saturday night, giving them a couple days to prepare and enjoy the country setting. There was to be live music and dancing. Family and friends from the City were to come up and mingle.

Bryan could feel the mood of things changing. The end of summer was near bringing an end to his job. But it was his inability to completely solve the mystery of Captain Camino that made him somewhat depressed. Tammy was soon to be off to Berkeley and he was stuck with a few dismal classes locally.

Next day he was corralled into giving the guests a tour of the ranch. Half-heartedly he began at the tack room, explaining the purpose of the various types of saddles and harnesses. Leading them out to the corral, he showed them the pack animals, and explained a little about the personality of each. After a while they begged him to teach them how to ride a horse.

"I wouldn't mind a little lesson too," coaxed Tammy, winking at him.

"Tammy, what are you saying?" laughed Summer.

Bryan sighed.

"We'll be most grateful," begged Jodie.

"Okay," he smiled, "I'll tell you what, I have to be gone for a while, but I'll meet you back at the corral after lunch."

"Goodie!" they applauded.

In the back of his mind he figured he could get his mom or perhaps one of the hands to fill in, if he should mysteriously get delayed. But in checking around, everyone had made themselves scarce. "Uh oh, what have I done?" he realized.

After lunch, he finally wandered toward the corral, hoping they wouldn't be there. But alas! There they were, giggling and carrying on.

"One at a time, whose first?" he called.

"Me, me!" responded Summer, all excited.

Bryan brought out a small mare and showed them how to saddle and mount. While Summer took her turn, and Kristi stood by, the others scampered off while they waited. He learned that Summer's father was a successful stockbroker, and she too thought someday of doing the same. Bryan found out that Kristi really wasn't as shy as she seemed, actually very talkative.

Jodie raced up to be next. She was more interested in who liked who than in learning to ride. After a brief ride along the hillside behind the barn she returned to the corral and prepared to dismount. Unnoticed by her, Tammy and Rachel approached from the house. Attempting to swing her right leg back, it appeared her foot was caught in the stirrup and she began to fall. Bryan caught her in his arms.

"You're so strong," she said as she laid her head against his chest.

"Jodie! What are you doing," scolded Rachel.

Tammy with a confused look on her face was speechless.

Jodie's face turned all kinds of colors. "It was an accident!" she tried to explain.

"Rachel, go ahead and take your turn," finally spoke up Tammy.

After Jodie slipped away, Tammy and Bryan exchanged glances. Turning she returned to the house.

"Is everything going to be all right?" asked Bryan after he helped Rachel up.

"Yeah," she smiled. "Tammy might be a little irritated for a couple of days, but that's classic Jodie." Changing the subject she turned her head to address him more directly, "I'm glad to finally meet you. I've heard so many things about you over the last couple of years. Sometimes the way I hear it, you can walk on water. Other times, well—you can guess."

"She thinks I'm too domineering and not very romantic."

"One is genetic, the other can be fixed," she whispered.

All the girls had taken their turn, but Tammy, who did not reappear. Gradually work resumed on the party preparations.

That evening with yellow lights shining out of the windows, Tammy slipped out of the house to find Bryan talking with one of the ranch hands. After they finished, Tammy stepped forward. "Chilly tonight, isn't it?" she commented rubbing her arms.

"A little."

"Soon you'll be starting your classes and I'll be off to Berkeley. Seems like we're always going in opposite directions," she commented.

"You don't have to be you know."

"What do you mean?"

Suddenly, there was a call for help from behind the house. Apparently someone was falling off of a ladder.

"Why is it that every time we get to talk something happens?" she complained.

A few wispy clouds became visible over the high country peaks as the light of a new dawn crept silently over the mountains. Bryan mentally noted the strange quietness, like the quiet before a storm. That evening, according to plan was when the summer party was to begin. Additional guests would be arriving in the afternoon.

Remembering Tammy's missed riding lesson, Bryan invited her to ride with him before all the hubbub began. She gladly accepted, hoping to get a chance to talk to him alone. Meeting him in the barn they prepared to go.

"Nice outfit," he complimented as they rode out.

"Oh, it's just a little something I brought up for the occasion."

"If you were one of our pack guides, I know our business would double."

"Bryan, you're actually complementing me."

"It's not like I haven't done it before."

"You just need to do it more often that's all."

Riding on through the trees, a view of the forest and canyon opened up to the north. Distant cirrus clouds seemed like accent marks over the mountains. Soon they came to a breath-taking vista at the edge of the canyon.

"It's so beautiful, peaceful, and dreamy," responded Tammy.

"Dreamy?" questioned Bryan as they dismounted.

"Yeah, it's a perfect place for a house to sit, looking out over the forest." she answered finding a comfortable place to sit gazing out upon the magnificent view.

"Dreamy," he repeated. "That's not necessarily true."

"No?"

"It doesn't have to be just a dream. We own the property."

"Really?" Her eyes seemed to smile at him. In the back of her mind a little voice was wondering how many other girls had he brought up here? But she needn't ask, she already knew the answer to that.

"But there's one problem, I may not be around here much longer."

Suddenly her smiling countenance was gone. "Why?"

"It's because I'm considering making that trip to Philadelphia to research those newspaper articles on the Captain. But in doing so I will have to tell my parents and run the risk of getting booted."

"I don't understand why your dad has such a problem with it."

"I don't rightly know either, it almost seems like he's afraid of something."

"Maybe you should wait."

"The truth has to come out sooner or later. And what if I wait too long, there could be family members that could pass away before we would have a chance to meet them? And besides that, there are others in pursuit of Camino's treasures."

"There has to be a way to get your dad to be more understanding."

Bryan smiled. "Come on we better ride back."

Reluctant to leave, she slowly mounted her horse and swung around to look out of an imaginary window, from an imaginary house, but it all quickly vanished as she came back to reality. Catching up with him she asked, "What's your impression of the girls? No city girl comments, be honest."

"They do have those two strikes against them," he laughed. "But they seem to be a good bunch. But now, Jodie, I'm not so sure what makes her tick."

"Boys," she answered.

"Rachel seems to have a good head on her shoulders, she'll do well."

"What about me?" Tammy asked.

"You're different."

"You keep saying that, but what do you mean?"

"Catch me and find out," he laughed as he galloped ahead.

"Wait up cowboy!"

Guests were arriving by the carload. Most were dressed in semi-formal attire to meet the occasion. The girls had spent most of the morning doing up their hair and nails; and what a show they put on in their long gowns.

Bryan's parents greeted the arriving families and friends with an eye on prospective customers. Bryan too met many of them, including younger brothers and sisters. He noted that about half of the families had only one parent, including Tammy's. He realized it was still a sensitive issue to him.

"Where is Josh?" complained Bryan looking around.

Finally he showed, plainly in a hurried manner. Tammy straightened his collar.

"Come meet the girls," she coaxed.

After a few minutes, Bryan overheard Roxanne tell Tammy that her cousin was no slouch.

Before the festivities started, Mr. Anderson gave a brief tour of their facilities and explained what areas and activities their pack services covered.

Soon the band arrived and began setting up. Tables were covered with red checkered cloths and prepared for the evening meal. Many of the men talked business, while the women discussed office politics and family.

At dusk, dinner was served. Mr. Anderson rang the triangle and called out the traditional announcement. The tables quickly filled with hungry guests. Bryan's dad said a few words of greeting and waved Tammy over to officially kick off the party.

She was so nervous, that she could hardly speak. Not having prepared anything in advance she decided to talk from her heart, explaining how it seemed like a good idea for close friends to come together before they all scattered to the four winds, wherever life would take them. Pausing and looking down thoughtfully, she glanced over at Bryan and smiled. "So, enjoy yourselves and remember the good times we've had together. And above all, don't forget to keep in touch."

Everyone was moved by her short heartfelt speech and applauded. Then someone yelled, "Let's eat!"

Tammy's head was still whirling while she walked over to where her mother and Mrs. Anderson were conversing.

Bryan's mom reached out and hugged her. "You know if I had a daughter I would want her to be just like you."

Tammy smiled and thanked her. She thought to herself maybe someday she could become the next best thing to it, but on the other hand maybe not.

The girls waved her over to sit with them. Sitting down she purposely left a vacant seat next to her and nonchalantly looked around for Bryan. Rachel and Summer, seeing the situation, got up and escorted him over to the empty seat.

"What a pleasant surprise," Tammy responded.

Bryan glanced at the two girls. "Yeah, it is, isn't it?" He noticed how flushed her cheeks were and how pretty she was. For an instant he flashed back to a memory of her on Lembert Dome. Though beautiful in form he wondered what she had filled her heart with all these years.

"Say cowboy, now that I've got you corralled, whisper in my ear why you think I'm so different."

"You really want me to whisper sweet nothings in your ear?"

"No-o, not nothings."

Before he could answer, his dad called him.

"Gotta go."

"Bry-an!"

The band played soft background music while everyone dined and conversed. Bryan finally returned, finding that mealtime was over and that all the tables had been cleared off. Looking around he spotted his mother and Tammy coming toward him from opposite directions with plates full of food. They laughed on discovering their mutual intent.

"Well, looks like you have two women—looking out for your well-being now," Mrs. Anderson commented.

"Thanks, I'll try to eat what I can," he replied taking both plates.

"If you have something to say to me, I'll be over here," Tammy informed, abruptly turning away.

Mrs. Anderson gave her son a funny look and walked away also.

Things livened up as the dancing and merriment began. But Bryan did not come out to dance. Tammy watched him as she took a number of turns. Finally the girls came to the rescue and forced them to dance. At first they held each other far apart and did not talk, only studying each other's eyes, looking for a clue to what the other was thinking or feeling.

"I think my mom has really taken a liking to you," finally spoke up Bryan.

"I like her very much too."

He noted how her eyes sparkled. They were like fountains of stars. Swinging around, she drew closer to him, but said nothing.

Bryan noted headlights down on the road next to the driveway. Pausing in their dance he observed a young man with sandy hair coming up into the light. Jodie must have recognized him, for she ran over and they began conversing. Even though he was uninvited, no one said anything and let it go. She seemed excited to see him at first. But his demeanor did not appear to be a happy one. Falling back into the rhythm of the dance they quickly forgot about Jodie's visitor. But after a few minutes they heard them arguing. Bryan thought he heard the stranger say something about "this ... forsaken place." She must have said something disparaging to him for without warning he grabbed a bottle off an adjacent table and smashed it, leaving him with a lethal weapon. Bryan lurched, and everyone froze. Tammy put her hand on Bryan's arm in a cautionary gesture. To Bryan it seemed that time had stopped as he focused on the broken bottle. He knew what he had to do, and he had to do it now. Bryan observed the intruders arm begin to move, and he bolted toward him quickly closing the distance. The enraged young man turned toward him as he neared. With his left hand, Bryan grabbed the arm holding the bottle and straight-armed him with the other, pushing him backwards with startling force. Backing him up to a nearby tree, Bryan flung his arm up to smash the bottle out of the angry young man's hand, and continued pushing him all the way out to where the cars were parked, throwing him to the ground. The young man came up swinging. Bryan ducked and sent him sprawling on the ground again. This time he paused and fled into the darkness. Soon a vehicle was heard starting up, followed by squealing tires as it roared down the road.

Coming back to the party, he was surrounded by the guests, asking if he was all right, and then they began chattering among themselves. Josh came over and remarked: "That was some piece of work." The band began playing music again. His mother and Tammy were pale white.

"You could have been seriously hurt," his mother scolded.

Tammy took a deep breath. "Always the hero," she commented shaking her head.

"It seems to me, Jodie's coquettish ways are catching up with her," Bryan remarked.

"I'll talk with her, I invited her," sighed Tammy looking in her direction.

Soon the girls had whisked the hero off to dance. Bryan noticed that Josh seemed to be hitting it off with many of the female guests. He noted too that Roxanne had been spending a lot of time lingering outside the dance area.

Reporting to the punch bowl for a drink, Roxanne motioned him to follow her.

"I need to ask you a favor," she whispered dragging him back into the trees. "I'm embarrassed to ask, and I don't want the other girls to know—I can't dance."

"You're asking the wrong person. I'm not a good teacher."

It appeared to him that she was going to cry.

"Now stop! Okay, let me try. I'll give you a few basic steps. Here, take my right hand and put your right foot forward, now follow me through this routine. Step one, two, three, and four."

"Let's try that again," she requested.

"Stand about this far from your partner," he illustrated, holding her waist. Suddenly someone appeared through the trees.

"Bryan! Roxanne! You two? Bryan you always asked me to trust you. How can I now?" cried Tammy, turning to run away.

"Tammy, it's not what you think," called Roxanne after her.

"I'm not blind, I seen his hands around your waist, you can't tell me he was just checking your hula-hoop size!"

"I asked him to teach me a few dance steps. I was embarrassed and didn't want you guys to know. I'm sorry, I didn't realize you would go into a jealous rage."

"Jealous? Is that what I've become?" Drying her eyes, Tammy quickly turned and left.

Dancing continued under the soft lights of the Chinese lanterns into the wee hours of morning. Bryan and Tammy drifted apart and never spoke again that evening. Josh finally escorted the giggling girls over to Tammy's house as it was getting late. However, for Tammy and Bryan the party ended on a sad note.

Bryan was depressed about things in general; and was a little ticked off by a remark his dad had made earlier. That was when he had left the party during mealtime. His father discovered that two animals had not been put in for the night. The remark revolved around how he wasn't pulling his weight around there anymore. That irked him to the point that he finally had to seek a resolution to it. Finding his dad inside the house, he demanded to know what was behind that comment. His dad's comments were not settling. Besides the work that he had been neglecting, his father mentioned Bryan's secretive excursions that were troubling him.

"I'll tell you what!" exclaimed Bryan losing his demeanor. "On one of those secretive excursions as you put it, we discovered that Captain Camino not only survived, but there is a very strong possibility that there is another part of the family in existence."

His mother came in on the tail end of his comments. His father was at first quiet, and then he blew up and came all apart. It was like something latent in him had awakened.

"Did I not tell you to leave well enough alone?" he yelled leaving the room. In a fit of anger he stalked back in and told him to pack his bags and get out.

His mother protested, believing what he may have found could be of vital importance.

"No excuse," he replied. "Are you willing to give up on this thing here and now?"

"No! I've got to see this thing through."

13

IN A CITY FAR FAR AWAY

And so it was, after two days he found himself looking out of a window of an airliner headed east, to an unknown future. He felt strangely alienated from his old life, and didn't know where it would all end. In the meantime, Tammy, and most everyone else continued on with their daily lives as usual, unaware.

Glancing out of the window, the sea of clouds parted, revealing an unrecognizable portion of the Nevada desert. He recalled what the old man at Argosa Wells had said about how it was foretold that someone would come and reestablish the empire. It was a bit of escapism to dream about how that could ever come to be. Political boundaries, federal, and state had been built over top of the old empire. It was an empire that perhaps only existed in the minds of its proponents.

Late in the morning—Eastern Standard Time, it was announced they were approaching Philadelphia. The city filled the window as far as the eye could see. Buildings, bridges, and rivers were all cemented together by a sea of green trees. Traffic was on the move everywhere. This was undoubtedly a city of big business situated along the banks of the Delaware River.

Before long they had landed and he was standing in the terminal, temporarily lost and confused. People hurriedly rushed by almost in a panic. At least they knew where they were going.

Locating a phone book and looking through the yellow pages, he found a listing of the local newspapers, but there was no newspaper by the name of the Philadelphia Independent listed.

That was a long time ago, the name could have changed, he told himself. Dialing one newspaper at random, he found out that the Philadelphia Times was probably the oldest in the City. But a call to them revealed that they only went back to 1851. They suggested trying the library. Jotting down the address and getting directions, he caught a taxi ride downtown.

"West coast accent," commented the driver, pulling out into traffic.

"Yes, that right."

"Did you say the library?" he asked again kind of quizzical.

"That is correct—the Central Library. I'm tracking a man that has been dead for nearly two hundred years." The driver gave him an alarmed look, and asked no further questions.

Entering downtown, tall gray buildings closed in and blotted out the sun. Soon they pulled up in front of the city's main library. Bounding up the concrete steps, he entered through swinging glass doors to step in front of a black marble countertop. He noted brochures on the Liberty Bell, Independence Hall, and the Betsy Ross House as he waited for help.

His inquiry was met with a rude reply, but he apparently hit pay dirt. A librarian led him to a back room lined with shelves of microfiche tapes, and to a particular section to begin his search. Dropping his bag, Bryan sorted through the tapes, but the dates stopped at the year 1800. Hesitantly he asked for help again.

"I think I'm ready to go postal," remarked the female assistant. "Do you ever get the impulse when you want to just start strangling people?"

Bryan raised his eyebrows. "No, I can't say I've had the pleasure."

"What date are you looking for?" she asked.

"July 1799." That date must have struck a nerve, for she gave him a surprised glance. "What's wrong?"

"There are no tapes prior to 1800," she explained. "What are you specifically looking for?"

"Basically, just information on my great great grandfather."

"Follow me," she sighed.

Weaving their way through a maze of hallways and descending into the basement, they came to the entrance of a large vault. After dialing in the combination, the large steel door began opening automatically, revealing a long room nearly one hundred feet in length, lined with metal cabinets on both sides. Pulling open a particular drawer, the librarian rummaged through layers of specially sealed jackets containing newspapers.

"Do you know the exact date?" she asked.

"Oh, about July fifteenth to the twentieth."

"Sorry, those dates were seized by the U.S. Government some years ago. Matter of fact we're supposed to report anyone that requests that specific information."

"Really?"

"Don't worry, I'm not going to. You're just looking for some information on a family member."

"Thanks. Who is it that this is supposed to be reported to?"

Looking down she read the information off of a card taped to a divider. "A Frank Marlow, FBI Special Investigations."

"Why would they want those old newspapers?"

"I don't know," she confessed.

"Is there any other sources of information here in Philadelphia from that same time period?" he asked in frustration.

"Not here, but you can try the National Archives in Washington D. C."

"Hmm, thanks for the tip."

179

Bryan leaned against the cold course granite of the building, looking up at the clouds that were moving overhead. He felt strangely alone. Had he foolishly thrown away home and family to go on a wild goose chase?

Pigeons scattered as he scampered down the steps. He figured it was useless to stay in Philadelphia. Approaching a street corner, a commuter bus ground to a halt in from of him. After a number of people exited, he sought the advice of the driver on the best way to get to Washington D.C.

Before long he was aboard the Muni-Rail headed southwest. The train passed under increasing stormy skies through the river related cities of Wilmington and Baltimore, on a ninety-mile journey to the nation's capital. Noting the dark ominous clouds that now loomed over the city, he checked his watch, and realized there was still time to locate the Archives and check their business hours.

Taking a bus he was soon standing on Constitution Avenue, lined with the massive buildings of the Federal Government, including the Justice Department, the Internal Revenue Service, and the National Museum of Natural History.

It now began to rain as he hiked up the steps to the multi-story building that he sought. The doors were already locked for the day. Mentally he noted the business hours and hurried back to the bus stop as the storm escalated to a heavy shower, soaking him to the skin.

Back on the bus he headed for the hotel district. Crossing Pennsylvania Avenue he got a glimpse of the stately Capitol Building a couple miles distant down the corridor.

After receiving a tip from another passenger, Bryan stopped at the Blair Hotel, which was reportedly clean and modestly priced. Checking in and finding his room on the seventh floor, he wasted no time in removing the wet clothing and getting cleaned up.

How strange it seemed, being alone in an unfamiliar room in a strange city, far far away from home. But then again, he really didn't have a home anymore.

Peering out of a large window, he could see the Washington Monument towering above the surrounding structures, reminding him of the Obelisk, which also was a monument of power.

In the pouring rain he thought of Tammy, and their unsettled relationship. He kind of laughed at himself for thinking he could use a hug from her right now.

Under a partly cloudy sky the next morning, he retraced his steps back to the National Archives, hoping that somewhere within this vast building there were a few molecules of ink that would shed some light on his great great grandfather.

Finally gaining entry into a series of large echoing rooms with magnificent vaulted ceilings and marble columns, he located the main directory board. The listings were endless. Nothing seemed to fit the right category. Next to the listing for the Bureau of Indian Affairs was Governmental Affairs (General), which he thought would be a good place to start. But his inquiry ended up leading him up to another floor of the building that specifically dealt with records prior to 1900.

Some of the records he looked at were on hardcopy and others on microfiche. Excitement built up as he approached the target dates, but changed to disappointment as he found numerous designations of classified material or missing documentation. Most of the notifications of classification carried the date of March 3, 1954. What happened in that year? Then it hit him. That was the approximate date when the Groom Mine was plundered. He noted that there were a large number of classified documents throughout that narrow band of time. Looking forward and backwards a number of months, he couldn't find anything that compared to it.

Another area of research next caught his eye—US Army Special Operations—Western Region. There were two ways that the documents were indexed—by year and location of field operation. There was very little from the early years surviving. More troubling notes now came to light as he crossed into the

1790's. Many of the documents—listed by number were destroyed by Executive Order.

Another dead-end he thought. They covered their tracks well. What were they trying to hide? Was it more than the gold?

Flipping through the pages dedicated to specific field operations and their commanders, the name, *Anderson*, jumped out at him. He recalled his dad mentioning something about a relative of theirs that had been a soldier in the Indian Territories. Could it be? *John Anderson*, captain, assigned to Fort Smith under *Major Benjamin Grinstad*, dated July 2, 1835.

A series of reports were listed under both of their names. Paging through them, Bryan noted that Anderson's patrol took them to a place near Neches, Texas Territory on October 14, 1835. Nothing of significance was noted. Another report dated February 22, 1836, indicated that a full garrison had camped near the Brazos River. But a third chronicle read strangely different. Grinstad orders Anderson by courier on March 10, 1836, to pursue a renegade band of Spaniards and Indians on a search and destroy mission. Was this perhaps one in the same pursuit mentioned by the old man at Argosa Wells?

Was this Anderson related to him? His thoughts suddenly clouded. Oh my! Could this be the reason why his dad had always acted strangely as regards Captain Camino? If this was true—it would mean his great great grandfather on his father's side was pitted against the Captain. Perhaps even instrumental in his demise or death. No wonder his dad didn't want this to get out—for his wife's sake.

Nevertheless, he realized regarding the Captain himself, there was no paper trail left for him to follow.

In asking one of the clerks about the possible reasons why such old records would be classified or destroyed, all he got was a shake of the head and a vague explanation about Executive Privilege. The clerk hurried away and disappeared into a back room. That's when Bryan noted the blinking surveillance cameras scanning the room.

Realizing he had again come to a dead-end, he slowly made for the door still somewhat in a daze. The glass door jarred closed behind him. Part way down the hallway, he heard the same door open and close. After several steps, a man's voice hailed him to stop. Turning around, an older man approached.

Looking over his shoulder he spoke. "I overheard you talking in there. Follow-up on this name and address, this person may be able to help you," informed the gray-haired gentleman. "Be careful and keep an eye out," he further warned.

Bryan thanked him and wondered what he meant. The well-dressed man turned and proceeded down a side corridor. Bryan listened as the sound of his footsteps gradually faded away. Looking at the note, he reckoned he was off to the community of Georgetown in Washington D. C. But before seeking further transportation, he checked his wallet and discovered he was running a little short, but he had to see it through. Bryan recollected he still had an emergency stash for the return trip.

After catching a bus he soon arrived in Georgetown. Disembarking, Bryan checked the address: 3003 Cherryhill Drive. It was probably another three blocks. Walking the street, he studied the varying styles of architecture and yard landscaping. Arriving in front of a large brick Tudor styled house, he told himself this was the place. Ringing the doorbell the first time brought no response, nor the second. He paused, considering whether to ring again. Trying one more time, there was only silence. Bryan turned to leave and walked a few steps when he heard a thump behind the door.

The door opened partially and a stern voice called out, "What do you want? Whatever it is—I don't want any!"

"I'm looking for a Mr. Gorbly. Someone at the National Archives gave me this address."

After cursing, he grumbled about having his name being given out; and ordered Bryan to leave.

"Wait, I need to know if you know anything about a certain Captain Camino."

There was a definite pause. "Did you say Camino?"

"Yes, Maximo Camino."

The door opened revealing a short elderly man with rounded facial features, mostly bald with tufts of hair above his ears. The man scrutinized him carefully after putting on his glasses.

"You're so young, but you may be the one. We can't talk here. My house is probably bugged. Meet me in an hour at Rock Creek Park, one mile east of here, near the old mill. You can't miss it." He hesitated, and then closed the door.

What did he mean by the phrase, "... you may be the one"? Bryan contemplated this as he continued down the street. Checking his watch he noted the time. The next hour seemed an eternity as he quickly found the park and the old mill. On the banks of Rock Creek the partially restored structure boasted a new undershot wheel and new planking. Finding a vacant park bench under a large elm tree he waited. The minutes ticked by. The rendezvous time came and gone. Was he even going to show? Standing to stretch he was startled when he noticed Mr. Gorbly standing mute behind him.

"I want to know why you're asking about this man?" he demanded.

"He was my great great grandfather."

"You have proof?"

Digging out the golden medallion he showed it to him. Slipping his glasses on to study it more closely, Mr. Gorbly stared at it and then fixed his attention back on him.

"What's all this cloak and dagger about?" Bryan asked.

"Because frankly, there's billions of dollars of gold involved."

"But what about Captain Camino?" asked Bryan. He went on to briefly explain what he had come to learn from the old newspaper articles.

"Those newspapers have been unavailable for at least half a century. Are you committed to knowing the truth?"

"Yes, that's why I'm here. I want to know why the Captain was painted out of the history books, and get it corrected."

"I must warn you, you will probably be followed just for meeting me today, and an attempt will be made to question you. Don't you understand! It's the gold. It was the gold then, it's the gold now; apart from them protecting their own stinking reputation of course."

"Our time is short. Listen carefully." Mr. Gorbly proceeded to disclose details of the attempted surveillance of Camino during and after his visit to Philadelphia; but he and those with him disappeared in the middle of the night. They were interested in his stories of gold, but not in opposing Spain at the time. But, many years later they began looking at Camino in a different light, when his attempt to take the western territories away from Mexico took a serious turn, besides the fact that their efforts to find Camino's gold had failed. With greedy eyes, the Government again renewed its desire to attain the gold to support its ambitions of expansionism. Evidently your great great grandfather backed a revolt from Mexico in the Southwest, thinking that if it was successful, that the entire Mexican Government would collapse, allowing him to take possession of the West. But something happened—"

"Someone is coming," warned Bryan.

"It's them all right," he confirmed looking around. "I've got to go," replied Mr. Gorbly.

"You're not going to tell me the rest?"

"There's no time. Perhaps it's better you know little at this time, just in case you get caught. However, if you do get away— go to the Lincoln Memorial tonight before eleven p.m., and locate the Gettysburg Wall. When the floodlights go off, certain letters will glow for a few minutes. They will inform you of where you must go to unravel the rest of the mystery. Frankly, I don't have all the answers. Think about what I have told you, and maybe we can yet get the truth out in the open."

Bryan stood there bewildered after Mr. Gorbly shook his hand and disappeared just as he came. Men in suits approached on a trot. He decided to go in the opposite direction to divide their number. The only thing he could think to do was run through the trees along the creek. Bryan was fast, but it appeared they already had him hemmed in. Sliding down the rocky bank into the reeds, he noted that the channel was about one hundred feet wide. The reeds grew well out into the water and provided shelter as he slid down among the plants.

"Get the dogs," someone ordered.

Bryan knew they would find him quick, if he didn't keep moving. Eying the murky stream, he silently slid fully into the water and slowly drifted downstream almost completely submerged. He did not know how long he had held his breath, but it felt like an eternity. Rolling over for air, no one was visible. Paddling to the opposite shore, he again hid in the reeds. After a minute he heard someone upstream yell something about a duffle bag. Which no doubt was his, the one he dropped at the edge of the creek. Glancing around, Bryan crept out of the reeds and up the bank to hide behind a tree. So far so good he thought to himself. The water drained out of his clothing. But something inside his shirt was moving. It was a small fish, but nothing seemed funny to him now.

Realizing they would soon be expanding their search area, he walked on through the trees to the edge of the riverfront park. A woman pushing a baby stroller eyed him strangely as he passed along a paved walkway.

Suddenly, a helicopter swung in overhead and spotted him. Running again, Bryan ran toward a concrete headwall. Swinging over the railing, he jumped a good eight feet into a dry concrete channel. Two large pipes approximately six feet in diameter disappeared into darkness. There were sirens—numerous vehicles were approaching.

Bryan clamored into the pipe on the left side with an echoing boom. His eyes were slow to adjust to the darkness, but he perceived a pin dot of light quite some distance down the line.

About a thousand feet in, cool air could be felt entering from a forty-eight inch pipe on the left side. Crawling into the smaller pipe, over a small deposit of gravel he pretended he was in a lava tube under the Obelisk. Periodically there were flashes of light overhead, where drain inlets daylighted to the street above. It must have been a good half-mile until the slope of the pipe finally allowed him to reach up and lift off a grate. Lifting himself up he felt something sharp dig into his side as he climbed out. He didn't have time to inspect the wound, but kneeling and looking around he found himself at the corner of an intersection. Everything looked clear till he turned around. A small freight truck was bearing down on him. Springing up, Bryan tried to get away, but it was too late. The truck driver tried slamming on the brakes, but the impact was almost instantaneous, throwing him into a metal signpost. He heard his ribs crack and felt the pain as his head also hit. Curling up with pain on the sidewalk, he could hardly breathe.

Over the ringing in his head he heard someone talking about calling an ambulance.

"No, I'll be fine. Can someone give me a ride?" begged Bryan.

"You shouldn't be moved. I'll call an ambulance," replied the truck driver in a foreign accent.

"Do what I say or face a lawsuit," grunted Bryan as he got up on his knees.

Bryan noted that a small crowd had formed as the driver helped him into the cab of the truck. After they drove away from the intersection, he could see a police car with blinking lights in the side mirror stopping at the accident scene. Bryan could see people pointing down the street toward them. The car swung around the corner with sirens wailing and the pursuit was on.

"Whatever you do don't stop," Bryan ordered.

"It's the police, I have too," he protested.

"Keep going!"

"I can't!"

"Then get out!"

Coming to a screeching halt, he opened the door and Bryan shoved him out. Pain shot through him as he slid into the driver's seat and jammed the truck into gear, speeding on. The police car closed in, undoubtedly soon to be joined by his brothers. He had to change direction. Making a high-speed turn to the right, the truck nearly flipped over. Cargo in the back of the truck slammed against the left wall. Besides the pain on his right side he now sensed a sensation of wetness. He figured he was bleeding, but there was nothing he could do about it. Accelerating down a broad avenue, and erratically weaving to keep the pursuers from getting around him, Bryan caught sight of flashing lights ahead. He realized he was getting in deeper the more this thing went on. Somehow he had to disappear.

A drawbridge appeared ahead, its warning lights were blinking, indicating it was about to rise. Police lights reflected in his side mirrors. Bryan sped toward the blinking lights, not knowing what would happen. But in seeing that the bridge was beginning to tilt up, he stomped on the brakes, sending him into a skid through an intersection, snapping off the bridge cross arms and sliding up the ascending ramp. Gritting his teeth, Bryan could see the gap widening in front of him and the dark green river some fifty feet below. He grabbed the door handle ready to bail. The truck sailed across a gap of twenty feet or more and impacted on the lip of the opposite span. Objects in the back of the truck slid forward and hammered the back of the cab. The rear wheels caught the edge of the deck and the vehicle hung there, facing down the elevated roadway. It took a moment for the shock to wear off. The slope continued to increase, as the truck remained perched in its precarious position. Opening the door and holding onto the window frame, he reached over and grabbed the pedestrian railing and proceeded to climb down the span. Hurting, Bryan jumped down on the approach deck. The truck hung ominously above him. There was no time to linger, he had to get away. Startled by the frightful scene, traffic jammed the intersection with horns blaring. Weaving through the gridlock and across a landscaped median, Bryan sought refuge in the maze of buildings and alleyways that loomed up in front of him. He heard a loud crash from behind. Glancing back, the freight truck had fallen a hundred feet or more. Sparks flew everywhere as it flipped forward landing on its back, sliding to the bottom of the ramp and two hundred feet down the approach. The truck stopped just short of striking a car.

The pain was tearing him apart, but he had to go on. Eventually, he found a safe hiding place in an out of the way alley. He was forced to stop, rest, and tend to his wounds. Leaning back against a brick wall he could see a band of blue sky and clouds floating overhead, reminding him of the '*wandering sky*' and to what it had led him.

After three hours, daylight began to wane. The only company that Bryan had in the intervening hours was a stray cat looking for food. In an adjoining alley someone threw a bag of old clothes in a dumpster. Rummaging through them he found a shirt that would temporarily work, and disposed of his that had become bloodied. The wound on his side finally stopped bleeding.

After dark, he sought and found a small shop to purchase a baseball cap and a sweatshirt to help disguise himself, and a notepad and pencil for later use.

Keeping to the shadows he walked the street. Whenever a patrol car approached he mingled in the crowds and kept moving. Every so often a helicopter would pass over.

A good three miles and two hours later, Bryan finally stumbled onto the Lincoln Memorial grounds. The floodlights still shone upon the Parthenon-like structure. Thirty-six marble columns surrounded its perimeter. The seated white marble statue of Abraham Lincoln nearly twenty feet in height looked out over the lengthy reflecting pool toward the obelisk-like Washington Monument in the distance. The stalwart figure appeared to look down and solemnly scrutinize him as well.

On the south wall was the Gettysburg Address: "Four score and seven years ago, our fathers ...." Glancing to the north side, Lincoln's Second Inaugural Address was likewise impressed into the wall.

His watch was smashed and broken, no telling how much longer he would have to wait. Sitting in a dark corner of the structure he waited. A fiery pain burned in his ribs and the side of his face was tender to the touch. Bryan sharpened the pencil with his pocketknife, and sat ready to jump the instant the lights went out. He contemplated what his next move might be. A half-moon ascended beside the Washington Monument, reflecting in the glassy pool.

Suddenly, sooner than expected, the floodlights clicked off. The surrounding streetlights continued to burn. Standing back from the wall, his eyes adjusted to the darkness. Sure enough, just as described, there they were. A dull phosphorescence highlighted scattered letters throughout the wall: "A, L, A, M, O." Bryan double checked it, and ran out under a streetlight to examine what he had recorded.

"*Alamo*?—This can't be right, I've been there—done that. Unless, it's the one in Texas? He did mention something about a revolt in the Southwest. Could this be right? "

14

AT THE COTTONWOODS

S an Antonio, Texas. It was hard to believe that he was standing there basking in the early morning sun peering out on the airport tarmac from the glass-paneled lobby. This was definitely a surprising destination; but he figured he did well in getting there seemly undetected, by catching a flight in the wee-hours of the morning.

But he now realized he didn't have enough money to get back to California. He couldn't call home. Should he call Tammy? After their last go-a-round, she may not even want to talk to him. But maybe she would at least get a message to Josh. He found her new number written on the back of a business card in his wallet and dialed it up. There was no answer in Columbia, just an answering machine. Punching up the digits for Rachel's apartment in Berkeley, he remembered it was a good two hours earlier on the West coast. Finally after about five rings a female voice answered. It was Rachel, she was still half asleep, taking a long time to answer his inquiry about Tammy. He overheard some banging, and Rachel warning Tammy not to be so excited, "play hard to get."

"Bryan, are you all right?" questioned Tammy. "I heard about your dad kicking you out," she asked still fumbling with the receiver.

"Are you still talking to me, you're not mad?"

"Mad? No, I'm not mad. Where are you?"

"That's why I called. I need to get a message to Josh, to wire me some money. I'm in San Antonio, Texas."

"San Antonio! Why?"

"Well, to make a long story short, I went to Philadelphia, then Washington D. C., and ended up in a pickle with the police chasing me all around the city."

"That was you? It was all over the national news last night!" She stopped to tell Rachel. "Are you hurt?"

"I'm pretty badly banged up, but I'll survive."

"Okay, where are you exactly?"

"At the airport, there's a Western Union office here where the money can be sent."

"I'll do what I can, and Bryan, promise me you'll stay put and won't do anything crazy."

"It seems I have little choice."

Tammy said something to Rachel before saying goodbye, and it seemed to him that they were arguing about it.

Even though he hadn't slept much, it was broad daylight, and he had to keep a vigil. A pang in his stomach reminded him that he hadn't eaten all that much.

Near one of the main doors a large color-coded map of the city caught his eye. The Alamo was easily locatable. From a bank of tourist brochures, Bryan selected one, advertising the historic structure. Carrying it into a cafe, he read it through while his meal was being prepared.

The rest of the day, he stayed as serene as possible, taking catnaps and checking the Western Union office every couple of hours.

Sometime after nine o'clock that night, he was startled awake by someone nudging him and calling his name.

"Tammy! What are you doing here?"

"There was no one else, and besides you're hurt and needing attention."

"Does your mom know?"

"No, she's off on one of her club cruises. I left a message," she answered. Tammy put her hand over her mouth and began giggling.

"What?" Bryan asked, checking himself over.

"Your sweatshirt—'I love cherry blossom time.' "

"Oh, yeah," he laughed. "I bought it in Washington, after my other shirt became soaked with blood."

"I brought a first aid kit in my bag. If we need something more I can buy it. Let me take a look and see how bad you're hurt. But probably not in here," she realized looking around.

Stepping outside, a partial moon shone down from a cloudless sky. Finding a bench along the dimly lit side of the building, it seemed to be just what they were looking for.

"What a place for a moonlight rendezvous," commented Bryan.

"Bryan Anderson! Are you making a pass at me?"

"No-o."

"No? Well, maybe you better," she mumbled under her breath.

"I better what?" asked Bryan who only half caught what she had said.

"Never mind."

Helping him to remove his shirt, she looked at the cut on his right side.

"It's a nasty slice, and a bit messy with all the dried blood." She bit her lip as she reached for the kit. "Does it hurt?"

"I get sharp twinges every now and then. My ribs and the side of my face are still very tender after I collided with a steel post."

"My poor baby what have they done to you? Turn your head a little, let me see."

Feeling his cheek, her fingers brushed across his unshaven face. Their eyes met for a meaningful second. She smiled and went about cleaning up his wound.

"Ouch!"

"Hold still. I'm just about finished."

"I still can't believe you came. You'll be missing your classes, and think of the expense."

"Bryan, I came because I was worried about you. We're still a team, right?"

"Given the same circumstances, I would be there for you or Josh," Bryan agreed, slipping his shirt back on. After a pause of thought, he laughed.

"What's so funny?"

"I'm a little embarrassed to say, but when I was staying overnight in Washington, I felt down and wished you were there to give me a hug."

"Bryan, that's so sweet. You need not feel embarrassed. We all need comforting from time to time, even you."

"Yeah, but real men are supposed to be independently strong, empire builders."

"Oh, that's your manhood talking. But, now wanting a hug shows me that you have a good heart."

"I probably shouldn't have told you. Now I'll never hear the end of it," he remarked holding his head in his hands.

Tammy sighed, "How do you feel now?"

"Rotten. How am I supposed to feel?"

"Like this," she replied giving him that hug. "Bryan, won't you hug me back? It's just what the doctor ordered."

Bryan slowly complied. "You'll not spread this around will you?"

"No, if it so worries you."

"How can you be so soft and tender, and other times be so sharp?"

"I'm a woman, my emotions run deep. I have trouble controlling them myself sometimes."

"I guess, I can't think of you as that young girl from the city anymore."

"Nor do I think of you as just as that tersely opinioned country boy."

Pulling his head back, his left hand slid down her back to her side. He could tell her emotions were stirred. "Thanks for coming and for the hug. How can I repay you?"

Mimicking one of Bryan's past responses, "I'll think up something one of these days," she smiled.

Bryan darted her a funny look and laughed.

"Oh, by the way, the hugs are free."

It seemed to Bryan that relationships with women could be likened to handling dynamite.

"It's getting cold out here, let's go back in," she coaxed.

Sitting in the back row of the waiting area, Bryan related much of his Washington D.C. adventure including the meeting he had with his mysterious benefactor. But before long, weariness caught up with both of them, especially Bryan.

As Bryan laid there asleep beside her, she studied his face. Reaching over she gently felt his whiskered cheek, thinking to herself how different men were both physically and emotionally. Why did he make her heart pound so? They were always fighting about something. Or was it fighting at all?

And so it was the next morning, their first argument of the day ensued. He wanted her to go straight back, and not miss any further classes on his account, but she insisted on staying with him to return together.

"But you're aiding and abetting a fugitive."

"Baloney!"

Finishing breakfast, Tammy snapped her purse closed and handed Bryan the money to pay the bill.

"This is kind of embarrassing, you paying my way," commented Bryan.

"My pleasure," she replied smiling. "Besides you helped me more than once."

Taking a bus, they soon stood in front of the old stone structure called the *Alamo*, with its fluted and spiral stone arches and pillars.

"So, this is where the proverbial trail leads," stated Tammy.

"So I'm told."

The building and associated grounds covered an entire city block. Behind the perimeter sidewalks were stone walls inset with metal bars creating a modern day fortification around the site. A large wooden double door, segmented into vertical and horizontal panels, opened into the interior of the building. Walking inside, nothing seemed remarkable to them at first glance.

A museum of sorts detailed its fiery history. They learned that it was originally called: San Antonio de Valero, named after the Viceroy of Mexico, and built around the year 1750. Later when it was occupied by the Mexican Army, they changed its name to Pueblo del Alamo.

"The word los alamos means the cottonwood trees," reminded Tammy.

" 'The Cottonwoods'? That's right!" recalled Bryan.

"Of course, the route from 'Paoha,' " she also remembered.

"There is a very strong possibility that there may indeed be a connection here," he realized.

Reading on, they learned about the power struggles that ensued as Mexico became independent from Spain in 1821. In the meantime 30,000 colonists had moved into Texas. In 1833, Santa Anna became President of the Mexican Territory. Stephen F. Austin, a leading colonist was imprisoned after hostilities began to heat up between the colonists, the Mexican Government and the local Indians. Eventually a rebellion on the part of the colonists broke out on the Brazos River. General Cos of the Mexican Army took up position in the Fort in 1835. The New Orleans Greys, a volunteer force surrounded General Cos and captured the Fort on December 12, 1835. A small group of volunteers then assembled under Davy Crocket, James Bowie, and Colonel William Travis.

Bryan turned to Tammy, "Remember the Alamo?"

"In history class."

Stepping to their right, they continued reading. February 24, 1836, Lieutenant Colonel Travis sent a letter in a plea for help, just before they were surrounded. March 6, Santa Ana attacked with 4,000 troops at five a.m. and the battle was over by six-thirty a.m. One hundred and eighty eight men were dead, only women and children were left alive.

"Sometimes being a woman has its advantages," commented Bryan.

"Those women lost their husbands; I don't think they would agree."

"Apparently, this must have been the revolt that Mr. Gorbly referred to that my great great grandfather backed. We need to find something that would clue us in, what he did and where he went."

"The obituary list might be the next thing to check," suggested Tammy.

"Good idea."

After cruising down the long columns of names, none of them caught their eye.

"I didn't expect to find his name here," stated Bryan.

"Let's look around. If the Captain was here, he would have left us something," she encouraged.

On the wall were numerous historical items of note, including written documents, photographs, and maps of the fort layout as it changed through time. In glass cases were old guns, coins, buttons, and leather goods. Examples of uniforms and dress were also on display.

"Look at the paintings," pointed Tammy. The recognizable front facade of the building was captured on canvas in the first large painting. "Must be a well in the courtyard," commented Tammy as she viewed a second painting. "The painter is listed as unknown."

While Tammy went on to the next one, Bryan continued studying the second painting.

"Tammy, wait." Reaching for her arm he pulled her back. "As you said the painter is listed as unknown, but look here in the corner, a signature of sorts that looks like a boot spur. The yoke of the spur is like the letter C."

"Yeah, I see that, but is that significant?"

"It's the same thing that was on the back of White Feather's painting."

"Really?"

"Now, what to you looks to be the central focus of the painting?" he asked.

"The well, with the courtyard in the background," she replied after first stepping back.

"Yes, the well, let's go out and take a look."

Working their way out into the open area next to the building, the well was nowhere to be found. Asking, they were directed to the granary in the back area of the Alamo.

"This can't be right," thought Tammy. "It's all closed in with walls."

"Back to the drawing board. Apparently we need to go back and look at those historic layouts one more time," Bryan replied.

"Here we go again!" excitedly exclaimed Tammy.

"What? Are you all right?"

"Yes," she replied, slipping her hand under his arm. "It's just I'm getting that giddy feeling again. The same feeling I get just before we make a big discovery, and it's always when I'm with you."

"That's nice, but it's not just me. It's the both of us and sometimes Josh—working together. But I think on my end of it, I've really made a mess of things this time."

"I feel guilty that perhaps my jealousy may have contributed to that."

"It was a decision that I made, and I have to live with the consequences."

Back inside, they compared the site maps.

"There are two wells," reaffirmed Tammy. "But where is the second one?"

"It had to have been in the plaza area, next to the Alamo building."

"That's out in the street," she realized.

Venturing out of the main entrance they stopped at the curb to peer out to where the plaza would have extended, but no manhole lid or anything was visible to mark the well's location.

"It must have been filled with dirt and paved over," concluded Bryan.

"It would seem so," she agreed. Well, how are you going to pull this one out of the fire?"

"Let's go back to square one, I mean—well one," he answered.

Back in the granary, wavering sunlight filtering through the foliage of nearby trees highlighted irregular areas of the enclosure. Nothing seemed remarkable about the circular stonewall of the well which stood about three and a half feet high. Tammy leaned over and peered through a protective grating into the dark depths below.

Bryan mumbled something as he also peered through the well grating. Looking toward her a thought occurred to him.

"Tammy, do you have one of those little hand mirrors?

"What do you have in mind?" she wondered.

Fishing around in her purse, she handed him a small round mirror. Reflecting the light down the dark shaft he could see water about thirty or more feet down. Then other details along the wall caught his eye. He gave her a quick glance.

"What?"

"When does this place close?" he asked.

"Six, I think. What did you see?" she begged. On her tiptoes, she peeked over his shoulder.

"See that?" asked Bryan.

"Hand and foot holds. But this is not the well that was in the picture."

"There is the possibility that they could be connected somehow. Let's go to lunch and figure up a plan."

At an open air café two blocks away they found a place to rest and share a meal.

"What does this Mr. Gorbly, know about all this," asked Tammy.

"I don't know, he didn't have a chance to tell me very much. He said I should be able to figure it out."

"How safe is it going to be to climb down in there?" she asked.

"It doesn't look too bad. I'll go slow."

"You're already hurt, don't push it. We can always come back."

"I need a flashlight, and for you to keep watch while I go down and back up," he replied without acknowledging her concerns.

Sharing personal thoughts on various subjects, the afternoon waned. By waiting till late, they hoped that the number of tourists would have greatly diminished. Tammy clutched Bryan's arm as they slowly walked back to the Alamo.

"You know, I've really enjoyed our time together; and it seems to me that we've been able to relate more openly since we've been by ourselves," commented Tammy.

"If the FBI catches me I'll be relating through jail bars."

"Not if we hide you—somewhere, maybe in the City."

"No more city. It's out of my element."

"Ha! You had the whole police department and the FBI buffaloed. And how did you escape that truck falling from the top of the drawbridge?"

"I'll tell you later—let's finish the task at hand first."

Back inside, they casually strolled back to the granary. Bryan rechecked the flashlight and made sure his notebook was safely tucked away. With no one around, Tammy begged him one more time to please be careful as she helped him lift the safety grate. Getting his initial foothold, he began a slow descent. Closing the grate over him, she walked about trying to appear like an everyday tourist. Returning to the well, she peeked down into the dark hole to see his light moving around. Soon there was silence and no light at all.

Suddenly, she was startled by a voice from behind. "Careful miss, don't get hurt on that metal screen, it has some sharp edges," warned a young man dressed in a tan uniform.

"Thanks for the warning," she replied nervously thinking about Bryan somewhere below her feet.

He kept asking her questions such as where she was from and who she was with. It seemed to her that he was trying to put the make on her. She had to get rid of him quick. Walking away from the well, Tammy informed him that her boyfriend would soon arrive and that he was a very jealous person, and had a police record.

"Funny you should mention that, we just got notice from the FBI to be watching out for some fella that may be in the area," he informed. Excusing himself he was quickly gone.

In the meantime, Bryan had descended about twenty feet into the rock lined well. He could hear grit and debris falling into the water below. Suddenly, there was no foothold below. Matter of fact there was nothing below. Feeling around with his feet, he stepped onto the floor of a side tunnel. The bottom of the arched tunnel was eroded; telling him it was dug to bring water from one well into the other. After quite a distance the tunnel grew smaller, ending at a mound of earth in a vertical shaft.

He realized this must be the second well. Shining the light upward he could see concrete and rebar far above forming a cap over the old well. Evidently after many years the backfill material had migrated down the tunnel. Climbing up onto the mound of rock and dirt, he surveyed the wall above him. No hand or footholds were visible, which surprised him. Flashing the light along the dirt line on the opposite side, there seemed to be some lines in the rock. Scooping away the earth a familiar sunset symbol appeared. A recollection flashed through his head concerning the bottom half of the golden medallion that would correspond to the sunset. An opening now appeared below the symbol. It had to be another tunnel. Digging even more vigorously he opened up a hole big enough that he could slide down into the black void.

"A room!" he announced to himself.

The chamber proved to be about ten foot square and a bit elevated above the floor of the second wall. The sidewall on the right carried both sun symbols, sunrise over sunset, separated slightly. A map was painted out just below utilizing some kind of black pigment. The main ridge of the Sierra Nevada was clearly depicted. His heart pounded as he studied it further. From the Alamo he followed a fairly straight line that led northwesterly to an unknown site and from there across a desert, designated by three or four cactus symbols. Somewhere in the middle of the desert was a mountainous region where a second site was located, and beyond that there was a significant pass indicated. Bryan figured these had to coincide with Groom Mine and Stonewall Pass to the west. From there the trail continued on the same general course as before toward the central Sierra Nevada. In a cradle of mountains was what appeared to be Mono Lake with the Island of Pahoa within. A north arrow reckoned him to look further.

"Aurora," he spoke out loud.

There was a prominent sun symbol and the name. Toward the west was another name, very hard to read. It appeared to be two words: valle susrar. Proportionally it looked to be about half way between the Sierra Nevada and Aurora.

"Valle," he pondered out loud. "Valley, of course, but susrar?" Tammy would know he thought.

To the left was a message sprawled out on the wall. It appeared to be hurriedly written. The only word he recognized from the Spanish text was the name Major Grinstad.

"Grinstad?" he repeated out loud. That was the name mentioned in the report he had read in Washington. If this was true, the implications of this could be shocking, but there was no time to think about this secondary issue. Bryan quickly copied the message as accurately as he could make it out.

Finding no further information on the walls, Bryan turned his attention to the back of the well. The tunnel continued, but after a hundred feet it ended in a cave-in.

Returning to the second well he crawled back over the mound of earth. Bryan kept repeating to himself the Spanish phrase he had discovered on the wall as he lumbered down the tunnel toward the light. Reaching the first well he switched off the flashlight, and stuck it in his back pocket. Bryan reached up and grabbed a handhold and spun around to continue up the wall. About five feet from the top he called Tammy's name. She was only a step away. Raising the grate she helped him out. Breathing heavily Bryan plunked down on the edge of the well.

"We have to go, the FBI has the word out on you," Tammy whispered loudly.

Bryan made a face. "Tammy, what is the Spanish word, susrar mean?"

"Susrar? Oh, susurrar. It means to talk softly."

"Like whisper?"

"Yes."

"Tammy, I know where Whispering Valley is," Bryan excitedly revealed.

"That's great; but you sure got dirty down there," she observed.

"Tammy! Don't you understand how important of a find this is?"

"Yes, but look at you! You're a sight!"

15

WHISPERING VALLEY

rriving back in San Francisco in the wee hours of Saturday morning, Tammy drove Bryan back to Columbia under the guise of darkness.

"The stars are always so pretty up here," she commented glancing up through the windshield.

"I'll probably be seeing a lot of them in the near future. But it's good to be back and I have you to thank."

"Don't worry about that now. Go to where Josh is camped at Lyon's Dam. I'll come up tomorrow. My mom may be back. If she isn't, I'll erase the message that I left for her on the recorder. Oh, by the way, you're welcome. I've enjoyed our time together, but I must admit the circumstances could've been better."

Nearing the dark silhouette of Josh's house where his pickup was parked, it all seemed so strange. It wasn't that long ago when he had visited Tammy and Josh here, seemingly in a whole different lifetime.

Tammy placed her hand on his knee and begged him to be very careful.

"I will," he promised placing his hand on top of hers. Leaning over he kissed her on the cheek. "Thanks for everything."

"Hey, you actually kissed me!" she exclaimed as he got out.

Closing the door, he disappeared into the shadows. Driving to her house she sensed how the car had become suddenly so very empty. Taking a deep breath, a rush of conflicting emotions seemed to well up in her. How was this all going to end?

The sun was just beginning to break through the trees as Bryan drove into the forested camp at Lyon's Dam, which was just coming alive with activity. Smoke from the cook shack drifted into the woods beyond. A small generator could be heard running nearby. Amongst a small city of tents and campers, he found Josh's vehicle and his tent. Josh was preparing for the day's work as he made his presence known. He was surprised, but happy to see him. Seeing that Bryan was exhausted and under much duress, he told him to just sleep, and they would talk that evening. That sounded good to him, but he ended up sleeping all that day and through the night.

Come morning, he finally awoke to the sound of familiar voices outside the tent. Peering outside he spotted Josh and Tammy conversing a short distance away.

"No more sawing logs, eh?" teased Josh noticing him up.

"I must have been worse off than I thought," Bryan answered.

"Tammy was filling me in on what's been going on, and I must say you sure haven't lost your flare for the dramatic."

"I've stirred up a hornets nest, and I may not survive," he soberly commented.

"So, I hear you know where Whispering Valley is?" queried Josh.

Before answering, he looked around to see if anyone was within listening distance, "It's approximately fifteen to twenty miles west of Aurora."

"That's not even in the Sierra."

"No one ever said it was. We just assumed it was."

"Bryan," broke in Tammy, "there's something you must know. I happened to go by your house first thing this morning and there were two men in suits at your front door. It looked like they were questioning your mother."

"The FBI is already here," Bryan concluded. "Now what am I supposed to do? They'll soon be up here. I have to go, that's all there is to it. Might as well head over into the desert, hide out, and search for Whispering Valley all at the same time," he contemplated.

"Promise me if you do locate it, that you'll call us before doing anything dangerous," demanded Tammy.

"I have a feeling it's all going to come to a fiery end soon anyway," he answered.

"No!" she protested. "That is not the way it has to be."

"Now don't panic, I may have a possible ace up my sleeve, that not even you two know about."

"What's that?"

"I'll explain later, but I need to borrow some food and money for now."

"I can muster some food but I don't have much cash," volunteered Josh.

"I have some money, but I don't feel right letting you go out on the desert by yourself," confessed Tammy.

"It's better this way. I'll call you at Rachel's in a few nights."

"Bryan! It's like we're sending you off into exile," complained Tammy.

"Don't worry, I think this will work." In retrospect it crossed his mind how Coleman had disappeared and was never seen again.

By noon he was on his way. The farewell for Tammy was somewhat emotional. This whole thing was increasingly more difficult for her to cope with.

Stopping at Sonora Pass, he dug out a set of maps that covered the area from Aurora to Bridgeport. Bryan noticed how the eastern sky was streaked with cirrus clouds, as he unfolded one of the maps. He noted numerous cow camps and springs scattered throughout the mountainous terrain. Many were in small secluded meadows, scattered throughout this isolated island of mountains that was well separated from the main Sierra

Nevada Range. Circling several possible locations that were due west of Aurora, he figured to begin the search at the most easterly location, and work west.

A momentary breeze gusted over the pass as he prepared to depart. The sun was warming, giving a false sense of complacency. Winter in the high country was not far away.

Traveling down the steep grade to Leavitt Meadow, Bryan noted the contrast between the pinkish cast of the volcanic mountains with the dark blue skies. The aspens were just beginning to turn color.

Remembering a poem he had written many years before, he tried to recite it:

> *Green shall become yellow in the flight*
> *of the autumn winds.*
>
> *Chasing away the summer with its*
> *dreams and whims.*

He wondered if this somehow was going to be some kind of self-fulfilling prophecy.

Traffic was light as he turned south onto the "El Camino Sierra Highway." At Bridgeport he retraced the same route that they had taken before to Aurora, along East Walker River. Dust flew as he made his way east along the old stagecoach road. Before reaching Nine Mile Ranch, Bryan decided he had gone far enough east, and turned onto a narrow side road that led up into the brush-covered hills to the south. Range cattle were scattered about as he ascended the often rutted and almost nonexistent roads through the sagebrush. Water drainage from nearby springs made for an occasional muddy crossing.

Bumping his way over a low saddle in the hills, a small oval shaped meadow opened up below. A cattle chute sat alone at the far end. No cattle were present. This late in the season vegetation was scant. Circumnavigating the oval, he stopped to study his map. If he was where he thought he was, he was now on a line due west of Aurora.

From the low saddle Bryan followed a promising side road till it turned into a cow trail. Foolishly he continued and soon found himself high centered and stuck. The sun was low in the west. He called himself an idiot as he got out to see how bad it was. Using a small folding shovel to dig himself out, it wasn't long before he was free and was able to back track. It was nearly dark when he finally made camp.

Three days passed as he crawled through the brushy hills looking for the fabled Whispering Valley. He was soon to run out of mountains in which to search for the illusive valley. His gas gauge read slightly below the quarter mark; and he was nearly out of food. Things looked glum.

The wind was picking up. A storm was brewing in the Sierra, coming in out of the west. Looking at his tattered map while driving on a lonely dirt road, Bryan noted that the next site was called *Masonic*. On an uphill curve, a marker indicated he was now crossing back into California.

Rounding the rolling hills the road wound down into a small valley. Old cabins and stone foundations soon became visible. A small but active creek flowed northwesterly toward the Walker River. There was abundant evidence that this had been once an active mining camp. Besides the presence of mine dumps and rusted heavy equipment there was the towering head works high on the mountain to the south. A bit further he spotted a historic plaque, mounted in stone detailing the town's history. Bryan learned that Masonic was actually three towns—divided into Lower, Middle, and Upper Towns.

Meandering groves of bright yellow aspens followed upstream to what must have been Middle Town. Only a few foundations were remaining, half hidden in the sagebrush. Curving on around to the south, the small valley widened and continued ascending.

Nothing was evident at the Upper Town site, only a grove of aspens growing along a meandering creek at the upper end of the canyon. Bryan thought it would be an ideal place to camp for the night, adjacent to the gurgling stream. Selecting a site, he parked and set out on foot to scour the area.

Returning to Upper Town late in the afternoon, he was tired and cold. The weather was continuing to change for the worse. The wind having picked up was driving the aspen leaves into a flutter. Approaching his truck a pang ran through him as he noticed a wet spot under the engine. It smelled of gasoline! Bryan opened the hood and found a fitting on the fuel pump leaking. Finding a wrench, he tightened it and the leak seemed to stop. As Bryan closed the hood thoughts ran through his head concerning the dilemma he would be in if he really did have a serious mechanical problem. He sat in his truck and contemplated his situation. Throwing the map down he realized failure was eminent. He had nearly run out of locations to look. His food and fuel ran dangerously low.

How dismal he felt; the stars didn't even shine that night. His sleep was restless and troubled. Near dawn he finally awakened to the gurgling of the nearby stream and the wind as it buffeted the tent. Bryan laid there and listened to the melody. It seemed to him there were voices in the creek; many of them low like a whisper. Then it hit him. " 'Whispering Valley,' of course! It has been whispering in my ear all night. This has to be the place."

Crawling out of his sleeping bag, he walked down out of the aspen grove to view the valley. The wind had deposited a carpet of golden leaves during the night. Storm clouds were continuing to build in the Sierra. Looking down canyon toward Middle Town, he figured he needed a different perspective on the valley and its components. Strolling back to camp, Bryan prepared a meager breakfast.

With only a warm jacket he was off to scour the west side of the valley, especially a series of bluffs opposite the Middle Town site. About noon, fine snow began to fall, forcing him to return for warmer clothing. Sitting in the cab of his truck he napped while the snow flurry continued. An hour or so later, the snow shower had passed. Clouds raced overhead.

Digging in his coat pocket he found a familiar notebook. It was the one he had in San Antonio. Flipping it open, he came to the page on which he had scribbled out the message in the well. Tammy must have translated it for him and stuck it back in his pocket while he was asleep in the plane.

Running over what she had written—a strange truth glared back at him. Apparently a plea for help had gone out to a detachment of U.S. Army troops under the command of Major Grinstad, camped on the Upper Brazos River. Their request was rebuffed. If this was true, it meant that the U. S. Government allowed the massacre at the Alamo to happen, which in turn caused the rebellion backed by Captain Camino to collapse.

What a stink this would be if it ever got out. No wonder so many documents was classified or destroyed by Executive Order. This information could prove to be valuable later he realized.

It was coming clear now why his great-great-grandfather was painted out of history. And additionally, he believed he understood now why his father didn't want any of this getting out.

Frustrated, Bryan drove to the top of the mountain where the large head frame stood, overlooking Lower Town far below. It was a bare rocky summit. Meager plants grew in amongst the red rock. But what a view! The storm-shrouded bulk of the Sierra Nevada Range jumped up right in front of him. It appeared to be so close, or was it just plain immense? Somewhere across the way was Camino's trail.

The wind gusted over the 8,400-foot summit. Bryan walked around the top of the mountain looking for clues, but soon was chilled to the bone and had to give up. Thinking about fuel, he noted how low the gas gauge needle registered. Bryan reminded himself that Bridgeport was just down the mountain to the left. He would drive in under the cover of darkness and refuel. The storm seemed to be breaking up over the Sierra, allowing sunshine to flicker through. The position of the sun was just above the horizon and was beginning its descent into the darkening hollows between the snowbound peaks.

Bryan was reminded of the significance of the sunset. The low sun angle sent shadows sprawling across the landscape. He sighed and leaned his head back, closing his eyes. Soon a shaft of glaring yellow light roused him from his catnap. Getting out of the truck he walked up to the crest of the mountain, and faced the great panorama of light and shadow laid out in front of him. Clouds raced southeasterly across the Walker River Valley below. Turning his back on the diminishing sun, he noted his shadow extending hundreds of feet down the rocky hillside. As a cloud passed in front of the sun the light faded and the shadows flickered.

That's when Bryan realized what he was seeing. He was standing in the midst of alternating bands of light and shadow that closely resembled that of a sunburst. Walking on he discovered a curved dike of rock neatly slotted that ran on for a couple hundred feet. This couldn't be natural he told himself. If this was the circular shell of the sun symbol, where was the theoretical Obelisk? Looking back toward the golden sunset, Bryan stepped over to the edge of the sheer cliff. Walking the fringe, the wind buffeted him as it ascended from below. His hair whipped against his forehead stinging him as he looked about.

Then he seen it—near the center of the site, two crudely notched lines running parallel about two feet apart, coming to a blunt point about ten feet away from the cliff edge. The lines disappeared over the edge of the precipice. He crept up to the edge and peered cautiously down as far as he could see. But due to the in-slope of the cliff, he couldn't see anything after about a foot or so. It was however a drop of several hundred feet to the bottom. What could be down there he wondered?

Bryan worked his way along the top of the cliff to where it curved toward the west. It was most difficult to find a place to view the face of the adjoining cliff. But in a low saddle, lying flat on his belly he was able to get a distorted look. He had to guard his eyes from dirt blowing up from below. About two hundred feet down, there appeared to be a dark irregular shape in the cliff. Perhaps it was just a shadow. But as he watched the wavering light, the dark spot did not change. He was sure it was more than a shadow; it had to be a cave. Standing back up Bryan noticed faint lights in the darker reaches of Walker Valley below, reminding him that he had to descend for supplies and make an important phone call. Mentally stepping through the discoveries he had made, he definitely concluded it was time to bring in the troops.

Wasting no time, Bryan descended the rocky winding road into East Walker River Canyon. Once on the narrow paved highway he buzzed by the reservoir into the lonely town of Bridgeport. It was totally dark as he stopped for gas and food. Loading up on quarters, the store clerk wondered if he was headed for Reno.

Finding a nearby phone booth, Bryan mentally rehearsed what he was going to say. It would have to be short, less than thirty seconds so his call could not be traced. After dialing the appropriate string of numbers and plunking in the required sum of coins, the phone began ringing. Rachel answered.

"Is Tammy there?"

"No-o. Is this the master horseman?" she cryptically asked.

"I have to make this short," declared Bryan without answering. "Tell her to meet me at the 'Elbow.' They'll know where that's at."

"Is that it?"

"Yes, thanks Rachael. I have to go."

"I need to talk to you about Tammy; she's worse off than I thought—"

Bryan regretted having to hang up on her, but he had to. But what did Rachael mean by that statement? Was Tammy seriously ill or something? A pang of worry perplexed him. Apparently he had deeper feelings for her than he wanted to fess up to.

Driving back through the engulfing darkness to Masonic Road, Bryan made a simple camp for the night at the base of the mountain.

Next morning he woke to blue skies and frost. Without eating he decided to make an inventory of his climbing equipment and reorganize the back of his pickup. Timing his departure, Bryan drove further north on the highway to the turnoff at Walker River and proceeded on the well-graded dirt road to the site of the old stagecoach stop. Parking in a secluded spot above the bend in the river called the 'Elbow,' Bryan waited. It was possible that Josh and Tammy would be followed. He had to make sure. Bryan looked at his bearded face in the mirror. He didn't even recognize himself.

Nearly two hours passed, when finally a familiar vehicle appeared on the horizon. He immediately recognized Josh and Tammy as the vehicle came to a stop below him. They stayed in the Jeep for a minute and waited. Bryan noted they were heavily dressed. Having to make them wait wasn't pleasant for him. After ten minutes, he decided the coast was clear and drove on down to meet them.

Tammy was all smiles, decked out in a gray outfit with a matching cap.

"It's about time," roared Josh. "Is that you behind that beard?"

"Are you okay?" she asked.

"More or less. And you?"

"I'm fine," Tammy replied.

"Are you sure?" Bryan again asked.

"Why, yes!"

So, what's the skinny?" asked Josh.

"I've found Whispering Valley. I'm ninety-nine and forty-four one-hundredths sure."

"And the diary?" he further asked.

"I may have found its hiding place. But I need your help to get to it. I think it's in a cave two hundred feet down the side of a cliff."

"Amazing," remarked Josh. Tammy frowned and shook her head.

"We can't stay here," informed Bryan. "We better disappear back up into the hills. Follow me up, it's not too far."

"Josh, I'll ride with Bryan," she announced.

"Excuse my mess, I've been living in here for a few days," apologized Bryan clearing off the passenger seat.

On the road, Tammy informed him that it appeared to her that the FBI had a sudden change of interest in him. They hadn't even bothered to question her or Josh. It seemed they had suddenly been pulled off the case. Bryan was perplexed.

"Tammy, may I ask you a personal question?"

"You can ask—"

"Rachel said last night something about how you were worse off than she thought. What is she talking about? Are you sick?"

Tammy's face turned all different colors. She thought to herself: yeah, maybe love sick. "I'm not sick, nor do I have any kind of terminal disease. I'm fine."

"You look healthy enough," agreed Bryan, eyeing her. He noted a pink flush in her cheek.

"Bryan! I'm surprised at you," she replied folding her jacket across her chest. "I think you've been out in the wild much too long."

"Sorry, I was just worried that's all."

"No need." Folding her arms, she clammed up and refused to say a word till they arrived at the top of the mountain.

"What's wrong with you?" demanded Josh as he came around his vehicle and noticed Tammy.

"Your bearded friend here is acting strangely amorous."

"Well my land, Tammy, it's about time, don't you think?"

"What!"

"Out on Paoha, didn't he make some comment about your pretty legs? Did you complain then?"

"No, I guess not. But it's that look he gave me. Like a caveman, looking for a mate to drag into his cave."

"Ha, ha, that's funny," laughed Josh.

"The cave is this way," called out Bryan from further up on the hill. Josh and Tammy both broke out in laughter. "What's so funny?" he asked.

"Nothing," replied Josh, "we were just exchanging cave jokes."

"I'm sorry Bryan, I think I over reacted," apologized Tammy as she climbed the slope.

"I certainly don't want you angry at me, especially when I'm down the side of the cliff. One slice of the knife, and I'm a goner."

"You trust me don't you?" she asked mimicking Bryan's commonly used expression.

"Yes, I do. My life has been in the palm of your hand once or twice already."

Walking with them up to the edge of the cliff, Bryan showed them the sun layout and the Obelisk-like pattern that disappeared over the precipice. He next led them over to where they could get a glimpse of the cave from the far side.

"You'll have to repel down there," realized Josh.

"Well, Peter Pan, looks like you've finally found a practical use for your skills," commented Tammy.

"Yes, Tinker Bell. Truly spoken."

It wasn't long before they had the climbing gear all laid out. Josh helped Bryan by securing a set of 'friends' in the rocky outcropping to anchor the rope. Slipping on his climbing belt he clipped the carabiners into place. After adjusting the ropes he was ready.

"Tammy, I want you to guide the rope as I descend. And yes, you will have my life in the palm of your hands once again."

"Oh good, a chance to get even," she joked.

Bryan checked the sky, horizon to horizon. Tammy gazed down into the rugged valley several hundred feet below. He noted how she curled up the right side of her mouth.

"Promise me you'll be very careful," she asked.

"Don't worry, this should be a walk in the park." Backing his way over the edge, Bryan told her to smile. Finally she complied.

Pausing for a moment to make another adjustment, he noted that the weathered grooves of the sun symbol ended about three feet below the lip. Continuing down the fractured rock face, Bryan repelled, touching gently as he went. Half way down he stopped to inspect an odd looking vertical fissure in the rock lined with frosted black and white calcite crystals. The continued descent went smoothly.

He was rapidly nearing the end of the rope when he finally reached the opening of the cave. But something was amiss. The irregular shaped opening only penetrated into the cliff about five feet— there was nothing there. What next? Give up?

There was a bulge in the cliff to his left that he could not see beyond. Grabbing the climbing rope he pushed off and bounced his way across the face toward the protrusion.

Tammy noted that the rope seemed to be pulling to the right slightly. Suddenly, the main carabiner behind her broke with such force that it ricocheted off the rocks like a bullet. The back anchor held for a brief moment, but it too prematurely exploded. Tammy screamed as she grabbed the rope and it pulled her toward the edge of the cliff. Josh, who was down at the Jeep, heard the scream and came running. Sliding on her side, she was able to brace her feet against a short protrusion of rock. Three feet of rope slipped through her hands, burning them severely. Despite the pain, Tammy realized that Bryan was at the other end of that rope and his life depended on her. Bearing down, her hands went numb, but she was finally able to stop his decent. Tammy sensed she couldn't hold that position much longer. They were both doomed.

"No we're not!" she snarled. "Josh! Where are you?"

"I'm here!" Grabbing the rope, he ordered her to go get more anchors out of the pouch and set them. She could hardly open her hands. Tears streamed down her face from the pain. "Hurry!" Josh called again.

Stumbling, she dropped the bag and scattered its contents everywhere. Tammy hysterically tried to pick them up.

"The rope has gone limp!" yelled Josh.

"What? No—wait! He must be okay then," she realized.

Josh crawled out to the edge and peered down, but he couldn't see anything. Tammy hurried back over. Kneeling, she too peeked over the edge.

"You're one gutsy girl, you know that?"

"I wasn't till I started hanging around with you guys. Besides that's not the word we should be using here—it's the word, insane."

"Bryan must have gotten a hold somewhere down there," thought Josh.

They both called down to him. Finally a faint call drifted up to them saying he was fine.

"What's he up to?" she wondered.

"I don't know, but we better get the rope anchored again. The clip and the anchor should not have failed," replied Josh standing up. "Tammy, your hands! That's a bad rope burn."

"I know, it's all I can do to keep from passing out."

"I'll get the first aid kit. Hey, look at this! That's why they failed. They've been cut on the inside by a very fine blade, like a hacksaw or something."

"Sabotage?" Tammy gasped. "This is no movie, this is for real."

After securing the rope they waited. It had been ten minutes without a sound, except for an intermittent breeze.

Returning to the same instant when the carabiner broke, Bryan was in the process of swinging himself over the protrusion in the cliff wall, when suddenly the rope began to drop, taking him down with it. Before he could react his head slammed into the wall. Despite the piercing pain, Bryan managed to grab a wedge off his belt, and tried to jam it into a crevice, but instead another cave opening revealed itself. About three feet below the cave and off to one side, Bryan finally got a secure hold, and held on with only two fingers through the clip.

Painfully he held on. Tying himself off, he felt something that sent a twinge through his body. There was a discernible flaw on the inside of the clip, like a cut. Quickly, Bryan drove in a piton and transferred his weight to it. Wasting no time he worked his way up to the cave, and crawled inside. He heard calls from above, and yelled back that he was fine. What could have gone wrong up there? Blood was dripping off his face, but it appeared to be just a superficial wound.

Wrestling off his climbing gear, Bryan found his flashlight. The cave was in the shape of a distorted oval. It turned and followed the softer strata as it went in. He could hear his breathing echoing back at him. One hundred feet in, the tunnel enlarged into a room-sized chamber. Sweeping his light around, he noted how a portion of the cave tried to continue, but ended abruptly in a zone of fractured rock. To the right was a small clear pool of water about eight feet in width. Ominously waiting in the background was the back wall.

Bryan anticipated there would be something there. Flashbacks brought to mind the 'sun' symbol in the mine at Metallic City and on the canyon wall above the pool in the 'Oro de Cañon.' At first glance, nothing distinguished itself in the pitted and uneven wall. But drawing closer he made out the outline of both halves of the sun symbol. "Yes!" he exclaimed. But where would Captain Camino have hid the diary?

There was nothing visible in the room or its extremities. Past experience drew him back to the symbol wall. Holes were scattered throughout the back wall. Most were about four or five inches in diameter, running back in. "Of course," observed Bryan. Between the separated symbol halves and in the common position of the Obelisk was a fair sized hole. Going down on his knees he shined the light back in. It appeared that a stone was lodged about two feet in. What could be behind it?

Reaching in he tried to grip it, but its tapered shape made it difficult. Rotating his arm ninety degrees, it worked. The rock finally wiggled out. There was still something there, but how could he reach it? Bryan could touch it, but that was all.

Searching through his stuff, there wasn't much to work with, clips, pitons, and Band-Aids. No tools. Frustrated he had to think of something. Then it struck him, that by taking two pitons he could use them as pinchers, but it would be tricky. Getting into position, Bryan gripped the spikes with a finger between. What was the proper way to hold chopsticks? Shoving his right arm back in he could only feel the object. Several attempts to grip it failed. Going to his left arm felt awkward, but the grip angle was better. Successive tries allowed him to finally inch it forward. Reversing arms again, Bryan succeeded in pulling it all the way out.

It was a dried leather parcel, about four inches wide and six inches long. By the nature of the leather it must have been deerskin. Dried by the desert air it was very brittle. Bryan decided to pack it out as it was.

Getting his gear back on, he rambled back out to the cave entrance. Bryan made a mental note that the view from inside the tunnel was coincidentally lined up with a deep canyon across the way. Pausing at the entrance, he gave thought to the fact that Captain Camino himself must have stood in this very same place over two hundred years before, gazing out at the same panorama.

Yanking on the rope he yelled upward. Bryan was unable to see them, but he could faintly hear them saying the rope was secure. Connecting back up he was ready to ascend. Bryan could feel the side of his face still stinging as he self-assessed his physical condition. Moving the ascenders progressively upwards he soon climbed above the protruding curtain in the cliff wall. Bryan could see Josh now, waving. Waving back he signaled that everything was fine. It took another ten minutes for him to finally reach the top.

On all fours, Bryan crawled away from the edge of the precipice exhausted. Josh helped him free himself from the climbing gear as Tammy rushed over.

"Are you okay?" Tammy frantically asked, seeing the blood on the side of his face.

"Don't worry about me. Look at your legs all tore up. And your hands, they're all rope burned." observed Bryan. "What happened?" He could see the pain in her eyes and the dried tears that had streamed down her face.

She gently touched his face.

"She was a real trooper. She held on to that rope and refused to let go," informed Josh.

Bryan scooted up next to her and took her in his arms. He cuddled her to try to soothe the pain.

"You don't know how badly you scared me," shared Tammy.

"Oh, by the way, Bryan, look at this," informed Josh. "See how someone sabotaged your equipment, that's why the clip and the anchor failed."

"My climbing equipment was locked up in the cab of my pickup which was parked at your place, the whole time that I was back East," recollected Bryan.

"Tammy, you certainly took to heart what I said about putting my life in the palm of your hands," commented Bryan. "I owe you once again. How can I ever hope to repay you?"

"What I may ask of you, you may not be willing to give. Therefore I shall not ask."

"What?"

16

INDIAN SKY

"Musical notes? You're pulling my leg," replied Josh.

"No, I'm not. It's entitled '*Indian Sky*,'" informed Tammy.

"But what about the diary? What does it say?"

"There is a lot of hit and miss in his diary accounts. Sometimes he skipped months at a time. But basically it dealt with his interaction with the local Paiutes, and his feelings of depression being stuck there."

"Tammy! Cut to the chase. Was there anything in that parcel that guides us back to the 'Canyon of Gold'?"

"Yes, this!" she pointed.

"A sheet of musical notes?"

"The diary explains that the directions for the 'back door' route to the 'Oro de Cañon' are fully contained in this song."

"But there are no words!"

"Think about it. The Kuzedika Paiute didn't have a written language."

"Then how are we to know what the song says?" questioned Josh.

"Frankly, I'm at a loss," Tammy confessed. "I wish Bryan was here. I don't know if it's because he carries the Captain's genes or he just has some supreme capacity for logic. But he always seems to be able to figure these things out," she answered.

"Aha! What is this I'm hearing? You are surrendering in this war of the sexes?"

"I guess my heart is betraying me," she smiled. "Don't you dare say anything to him."

"When do we rendezvous with him again?" asked Josh.

"Tomorrow."

"It's getting colder, day by day. This can't go on much longer."

Tammy leaned against the doorway and watched her cousin leave as she thought about the special relationship they had formed with one another. A troubled feeling pervaded her as her thoughts shifted to Bryan's exiled situation in the Mono Basin. How much like Captain Camino, who likened his stay there to "a low sink of depression."

Josh and Tammy left early the next day to travel over to the isolated community of Lee Vining, where Bryan was staying in a small cabin on the outskirts of town.

Again Tammy thought about the parallelism of Captain Camino and Bryan. Both exiled in the same place, one sought power, the other truth. Perhaps it wasn't gold that was so valuable anymore, but right and wrong.

The town looked drab and cold under an overcast sky the following day as they drove into Lee Vining. An old deteriorated paved driveway led down to the cabin.

"We're going to have to stop meeting like this," declared Bryan who was standing in the doorway.

"You're telling me. If only they knew," teased Tammy, happy to see him.

"How are you?" asked Josh.

"Okay, I guess. Come on in."

Tammy glanced around the dimly lit room as she entered.

"Have you been followed or anything?" asked Bryan.

"No, which does seem odd. It's like someone blew a whistle and everyone backed off," answered Josh.

"Strange, I wonder what they could be up to?" questioned Bryan.

"Well, are you ready to hear about the diary?" asked Tammy.

"Yes, tell me!" he answered. "Here, sit down if you like."

"No, I need to stand for a bit, it has been a long ride."

It was good to see her again. Her presence and Josh's too was comforting to him. Setting her things on an old warped table, she turned to look out of a small window with a view to the southern mountains. She began by relating an overall view of Camino's colorful history that covered about two years. But there was nothing about the resurrection of his empire and its downfall, nor the intrigue that surrounded the Alamo. All those events must have occurred after the diary was placed in the cave. She finally handed him a copy of the Indian song.

"The directions to the 'back trail' are embodied in this song, apparently," informed Josh.

"No words?"

"No."

She refrained from saying anything to see how he would approach the problem.

"Musical notes have been kind of a universal language of sorts for centuries," Bryan thought out loud. "Four stanzas, each appears to be different, telling me they are probably distinct clues and in sequence."

Tammy shook her head in agreement and peered out of the window again.

"Is there something different about you today?" he asked putting down the paper.

"No-o," she answered smiling with her eyes and lips.

Bryan settled back into thought as he studied the song.

"Well, the Kuzedika had no written language so everything had to have been orally handed down from generation to— generation," he stated, pausing on the last word.

Suddenly he stood up. Josh and Tammy looked at each other quizzically.

"I hope we're not too late!" declared Bryan.

"Too late for what?" asked Josh.

"I think the point of all this is that we have to go to the source, the Kuzedika themselves. Once the musical notes are played, hopefully someone would be able to recall the song and relate its words to us."

Tammy began slowly clapping. "How is it that someone who only uses the left side of his brain is able to figure these things out?"

"Don't praise me. I'm going down in flames."

"Nonsense," objected Josh.

"Look, Bryan, we'll do whatever it takes to keep you safe, till all of this can get sorted out," encouraged Tammy. "And that time is coming soon."

"Loyalty to the bitter end, just like White Feather and Carlos, right?" he sarcastically replied.

"Something like that."

"I'm sorry," he apologized. "I seem to be wallowing in a sea of self-pity. You two have done so much for me. It's wrong of me to trip out and give up."

Bryan turned away for a moment and asked Tammy for her hand.

"Why? Are you going to propose to me?"

He smiled, "No-o, I just wanted to see how your hand was after that bad rope burn. Besides, I'm a fugitive on the run, and it wouldn't be right."

"You are not a fugitive," she replied extending her hand. "It's still a little red and sore, but the worst is over."

"You have such soft delicate hands."

"Okay, you two cut the mush," cried out Josh. "There are other things that we should be doing right now, such as finding out if there are any of the remaining members of the Paiute Tribe left that can tell us anything."

"Tammy, you said one time you played the clarinet, right?" asked Bryan.

"Yes, but its been—three years. Why?"

"If we do find someone to listen to us, someone has to play the tune."

"How many notes will it take for them to name that tune?" joked Josh.

"The actual instrument according to the diary was a flute, but I should be able to adapt," she thought looking at the sheet.

"Let's drive over to the Mono Basin Visitor Center and find out who we can contact," suggested Bryan grabbing his jacket. "I'll lay low in the backseat, while you two go in."

The Visitor Center was located just a short distance away, north of town, overlooking the placid blue lake with a view to the dark ranges beyond. The large brown building was of modern design, topped with a glass dome. It could not have been more than five or six years old. Only a hand full of cars was present in the parking lot. Bryan hid out of sight as the others went in. It must have been a good twenty minutes before they reappeared.

"We have two possibilities," announced Josh getting in.

"The only surviving descendants of the Kuzedika Tribe are a man and a woman," informed Tammy. "And look here, a plastic flute. A souvenir for kids, but it might work just fine for our purposes."

"That's good. We're in the ninth inning with two out, but we still have hope," replied Bryan.

Tammy volunteered to make the phone calls.

They only had to wait an hour for the first one, which took them to the south side of town, up on the hill. An elderly Indian woman met them at the door. The inside of her house was decorated with all kinds of basketry and brightly colored Indian memorabilia. Tammy became instantly excited, inquiring how the baskets were made. During a brief explanation she also learned that the availability of straight willow branches to make such baskets were now hard to come by, probably due to the increased salinity of the lake.

Steering the conversation around, Bryan questioned her about Indian songs. She personally could not remember them, but thought that Longtree possibly could. That is if they could get him to talk. He was much older than she was, but apparently had a keen memory. Living with his granddaughter's family, he did little but sit in silence and brood over the calamity that had befallen his people over the years.

Getting directions, they drove south out of town and followed the highway up Lee Vining Creek toward Yosemite. After two miles they turned off onto a dirt road that brought them down to a ramshackle of a house near the creek. It was evident the house had been added onto a number of times. The last addition remained unfinished; strips of curled tarpaper covered the exterior walls. Tammy glanced up canyon toward Yosemite's eastern wall as the wind stirred the colorful aspens along the creek.

A middle-aged woman met them at the door. Though of fair skin, her hair and certain features clearly showed her to be of Indian descent. With great curiosity she wondered why they had come. Bryan explained in a very direct way that they had the musical notes to an old Indian song and sought someone who could possibly translate it into words.

"My father's health is not good," she replied.

"It's important we try," implored Bryan.

"I'm sorry; it's out of the question."

As the woman turned away Tammy jumped in. "You can't turn your back on the great-great-grandson of White Feather can you?" she exclaimed.

"White Feather?"

The woman looked at Bryan closely, contemplating his features.

"You have to consider that there have been a number of generations since then. She was from the Pohono Tribe," informed Bryan.

Not totally convinced she asked them to wait. Returning after nearly a minute, she escorted them through the dark corridors of the house to a back room. Sitting in the corner was an old man staring obliquely toward the center of the room.

"Father, they are here now," she informed. "He's blind," she whispered as she left the room.

An awkward silence ensued. Breaking the silence, Bryan first introduced himself and then the others. Then he explained that they had the music to an old Kuzedika song, and would like to learn its words.

"It's entitled, 'Indian Sky,' " informed Tammy.

" 'Indian Sky?' " questioned the elderly man. After a long pause he continued. "It seems so strange you ask about Indian songs. No one has spoken of them in many years. So one of you claims to have Indian blood?"

"Yes, my great-great-grandmother was White Feather of the Pohono Tribe. She came here with Captain Camino a long time ago," answered Bryan.

"You must realize Indian songs were not just songs or stories. They were believed to be alive and to be shown respect. The songs were to be told in a certain way, the ancient way. How is it that you intend to play this Indian song?" he asked.

"Tammy will play for us," informed Bryan. "By flute."

"Play the song, so that I may remember."

Bryan smiled at Tammy, and she smiled back with her eyes.

"Josh, hold the music for me by the window, over here," she requested. "This is probably going to be a butcher job. She blew a few practice notes. "Okay, here goes."

Her first run through was slow and rough.

"Let me try that again."

In the meantime, Longtree's granddaughter returned and stood in the doorway, listening.

As Tammy played the succession of high and low notes, the flute seemed to speak. Stopping, she lowered the flute.

"How beautiful and sad," she commented.

Longtree's face was at first expressionless. Hearing it a second time seemed to finally awaken him.

"I have heard this song, but it was so long ago. I do not remember as I used to. Many of these old songs were stories that spoke of the Indian way of life—oneness with the earth. They were stories that taught a moral. In the Indian world all things were alive, everything from the utensils used to prepare food to the stars in the night sky."

Longtree paused as memories that were more than half a century old began to be stirred.

"None of the words were ever written down. Whoever recorded the voice of the flute likewise respected this."

"Can you give us at least a basic idea of what was spoken of in this particular song?" respectfully asked Bryan.

Suddenly, Longtree's right arm began to tremble. It seemed that he was agitated about something. His granddaughter rushed over.

"Grandfather, are you all right? Shall I ask them to leave?"

"No! Leave me alone!" he exclaimed pushing her away. "I had forgotten. Long ago, it was told that someone would come with the song of the Kuzedika and to that one was to be granted power and authority."

"Now we're getting somewhere," excitedly replied Josh.

"Why have you waited so long?" demanded the old man. "It was thought that whoever it was would come a lifetime or more ago. That one was to unite the Kuzedika with his Paiute brothers across the Great Basin. But it is too late—the Indian way of life is gone. He paused to reflect on that thought before going on.

"The melody of the flute was like the winds that blew free through the mountain passes; back when there was laughter in the voice of the many streams. I still remember the cedar bark huts, the sound of rain upon the roof, and the smell of pine on the morning breeze. Gone is that oneness with the Earth and those simple joys."

Longtree lowered his head and wept. Tammy wiped the tears from her eyes.

"I do realize now what song it is that you have played. It is the song of the beginning time. What was the name you called this?"

" 'Indian Sky,' " reiterated Josh.

"Yes, that sounds right. Indian Sky was also a term that denoted a time of peace, no enemies, no worries, no storms, when the skies were brilliantly blue, and the evenings fiery pink. When the future was bright, and man was at peace with the Earth."

"Not like the polluted war-torn world that we now find ourselves in," commented Tammy.

"I do not see how this old song will help you now," questioned Longtree.

Bryan explained that according to what they had come to understand was that certain information contained in the song would lead them to Captain Camino's lost hiding place. Bryan was careful not to disclose too much.

"Perhaps it's best you let the past sleep," he replied.

"The truth must be known," stated Bryan.

"This great-great-grandfather of yours may have been the one they called the Great Chief," speculated Longtree.

Bryan pondered the similarity of that thought with El Capitan in Yosemite, named after the 'chief'—the Captain.

"Yes, I believe so," agreed Bryan.

Longtree's thoughts returned to the Indian song. "Animals were respected same as people, and in Indian song and story they took on human traits and personalities. So it was long ago in the beginning time, there was Coyote, the Trickster. He was always getting himself into trouble. And usually there was a lesson in it for the listener. Coyote was a showoff and it was on one occasion when he was juggling his eyes to impress his lady friends that he threw them higher and higher until one of them stuck in the canopy of the night sky."

Tammy laughed.

"The Song is about how the Indian night sky came to be. So sad was Coyote's eye that tears fell to Earth. It so happened that the tears fell into the den of the snake—driving him out. He boasted, 'I will ascend to the tallest mountain and snatch Coyote's eye from the sky, so that all things can return to the way they were.' A bird of the canyon agreed that something had to be done. There would be no peace until Coyote's sadness was gone. So he said he would fly ahead and mark the trail by dropping seeds of a certain dwarf tree, and would wait at the top of the mountain for those who would come. But after a long time, no one appeared. Bird thought, 'What shall I do?' He could see the Great Bear being pursued by three Indian braves down in a canyon. There was little chance he would be of any help. But looking over to Coyote's eye he discovered that it did not move around the sky, but remained stationary. The only thing that Bird could think to do was to give Coyote's eye some company so that he would not be so lonely. So Bird flew up above the highest peak and began pecking holes in the night sky in the shape of animals. He did this gradually as the sky circled overhead."

The elderly storyteller paused.

"To this day Coyote's yellow eye can be seen in the north. Nearby is the Great Bear, along with the Serpent, and the Bird. They are all there. The moral of the story in this song was: no matter how hard one tries, some things can not be undone."

"Interesting," commented Josh.

"Thank you for that; your memory is phenomenal," praised Bryan. "Is there anything else you remember about the Song or the Great Chief?"

"No, not really. But I do believe this Great Chief spent time with Chief Tenaya, of the Yosemites, but it did not last."

After thanking Longtree and his granddaughter they left contemplating what they had heard. Longtree remained there in his room saddened, but thoughtful as the images and memories of long ago danced in his mind.

Returning to the cabin, Bryan built a fire in the small stove to break the chill. A south wind rattled the windows.

"This song is certainly a different wrinkle that the Captain is using this time, commented Josh. "But it seems that this song— 'Indian Sky,' directs us to the stars and constellations that resemble animals."

"It's another set of clues that involves animals," realized Tammy. "But you know, the song also seemed to highlight the circumpolar motion of the constellations around the North Star."

"Longtree mentioned that power and authority would be granted to the bearer of the song," reflected Bryan. "The Captain's use of the Indian Song may have been meant to serve two purposes: First, to lead someone back to the gold—the power. Secondly, to use that power in such a way to fight corruption and greed. Think about it—great change was sweeping the earth. Greedy empires were rising and falling, ever more rapidly. The riches and beauty of the West was not going to be ignored for long. A way of life was in danger. He didn't like what he saw coming. Apparently his attempt to create an empire that would protect their destiny, failed."

"According to what Longtree said there was supposed to have been someone who would come afterwards and accomplish what the Captain could not," recalled Josh. "But apparently no one came. Bryan, you may have been born one hundred and fifty years too late."

"If that was true we would've never met. And who knows where your lives would have taken you. But maybe it would have been best if you had never met me," reflected Bryan.

"No-o! The reality is that you are here, I'm here, and Josh is here, and what we have is something unique and special," argued Tammy. "The moral of the Indian Song was that 'some things can not be undone,' what is done is done and what is— is."

"But, is it really too late to turn some things back?" questioned Bryan. "It can't be done in a day that's for sure, but I would like to make that first step and try."

"You know, it's uncanny how many of the things you said were like bits and pieces out of the Captain's diary," commented Tammy.

"Oh, by the way, Tammy, you played the flute nicely," praised Bryan. "I found it somehow idyllic, along with what Longtree said about how the sound of the flute inspires hope like the winds that blow free through the mountain passes. I believe that hope has not been lost."

All fell silent for a moment, deep in thought.

"We first heard about 'Coyote's eye' up there at Tuolumne Meadows, remember?" reminded Josh.

"That's right, and the Great Bear," recalled Tammy. "Remember those two shooting stars that appeared to shoot right through the Big Dipper?"

"How could I forget? That's when you whacked me across the chest," replied Bryan.

"The Indian Song is not a riddle, but a story on how the stars came to be," stated Josh.

"Stars have been used for centuries for navigation," commented Tammy.

"Speaking of navigation, we better navigate over the hill before it gets much later," realized Josh looking at his watch.

Before leaving, Tammy paused at the door. "You know, even though this may be a shack, you've made it seem so cozy."

"I guess I've found my niche as a career bachelor."

"Oh? Is that so?"

17

URSA MAJOR

I t was morning, two days later. Clouds were dissipating from an overnight shower. Bryan watched as a coppery sheen spread across the lake. A certain calmness settled in as the sun slowly rose from the dark ranges of the Nevada desert.

He thought of his great-great-grandfather, who was held up here in this low desolate sink. How similar he felt, feeling trapped and depressed.

What secrets did the 'Indian Song' hold? Somehow the directions they looked for were embodied cryptically therein, among the stars and the constellations.

Restlessness was getting to him. He had to do something to solve this. It could be days before Josh and Tammy would get back to him after doing their research. How could he get his hands on a star map? The Visitor Center of course, he remembered. I can sneak over there just as it opens, he planned.

Bryan checked his wallet. The money inside was Tammy's. The reality was she was supporting him out of her savings. Had he thanked her enough? Probably not. It seemed that as things worked out, she was a better person than he was. Whatever rivalry they had, he felt the need to relinquish the entire honor to her.

Inconspicuously as possible, Bryan walked the half-mile through the scattered sagebrush over to the Visitor Center. Wearing a green jacket and a baseball cap he tried to make himself as unrecognizable as possible. Only two other persons were in the building as far as he could tell. Quickly finding what he needed and paying for his purchase he was out the door in a flash. The young woman behind the counter stared at him curiously and watched him go. He felt paranoid as it was, but no one followed.

Back at the cabin, he stoked up the fire and anxiously sat down to study the star guide. Looking at the northern circumpolar constellations, the *Big Dipper* was by far the most recognizable. At the tail end of the *Little Dipper* was Polaris, the *North Star*. Between the two Dippers was another constellation called *Draco*. It wound its way west in the shape of a backwards S. Beyond was *Hercules* and *Lyra*, and to the east was *Lynx, Camelopardalis, Perseus, and Cassiopeia*.

The 'Indian Song' made reference to the Great Bear, 'Coyote's eye,' the 'snake' and a 'bird.' 'Coyote's eye' was clearly explained to be the North Star. The Great Bear, as they had learned in Yosemite was the Big Dipper, *Ursa Major*. There were two obvious relationships. Two stars in the Big Dipper were directional to the North Star; and for an observer, the North Star was always north.

One of the other constellations had to be the 'snake,' and another the 'bird.' Both Draco and Lynx could be construed as a snake. As for the 'bird,' Cassiopeia was the strong candidate with its flattened M shape.

After staring at the charts for nearly an hour his eyes began to go out of focus. All the stars seemed to coalesce into one great mass. It was like picking out patterns in acoustical ceiling tile. Shapes appeared and disappeared in the grid. The stars formed such an irregular grid—open to the ancient and the modern observer to interpret any way they wanted. However, there was no mistaking Ursa Major, which included the Big Dipper. It was singular and distinct.

But what was the relationship of these constellations once he had them all identified? Nothing made sense, so far. Bryan wondered if Tammy and Josh were having any better success in figuring this out.

The rest of the day he just moped around, occasionally glancing at the star maps, and staring out the window at the distant sky and mountains. The sky would be clear that night he realized. Perhaps a better perspective could be gained if he viewed the stars and the mountains in their natural layout.

So it was, Bryan packed up his stuff, and at dusk drove north over Conway Summit into Bridgeport Valley, which he believed to be the suspect area to match earth and sky—the 'Indian Sky.' Stopping along the edge of Twin Lakes Road, away from the lights of town, he stepped out of the vehicle and was nearly run down by a speeding car. Where did he come from? Bryan wondered. He didn't notice anyone following him. The air temperature had dramatically dropped off after sunset. He could hear the roar of traffic headed north on State Route 395.

As the night canopy darkened, the stars began to dazzle ever brighter. He thought of Tammy, and longed for her tenderness and companionship. Why had he been so evasive? She was just waiting for him to say the right words, right?

Another car approached and whizzed by. Turning he let his eyes adjust to the darkness once again. In the northeast was the Big Dipper. From there his eye trailed on up to Coyote's yellow eye, the North Star. Following along the Little Dipper, Bryan became lost in the myriad of stars along the western horizon. To the east over town was Cassiopeia, just visible above the horizon. Viewing them in respect to the mountains didn't seem to help as he had hoped.

Driving up the road another three miles, he came to *Twin Lakes*. A black glassy sheen gave the lakes a mysterious aspect. Parking near the junction of the two lakes, he walked out on the isthmus that partially separated them. Bryan noticed the lights of Mono Village shimmering in the water as he continued further out.

"So quiet up here," he told himself as he stopped and turned.

Looking off into the northeast, the stars danced on the silent distant ranges. Stooping down close to the water, he could make out the faint reflection of the brightest stars. The surface of the lake steadied. Bryan recognized an upside down Big Dipper. The thought came to him that the Big Dipper was in a sense synonymous with the Lake. Both were basins, one real and the other imaginary. One held water, the other space.

Another thought occurred to him. "What if—"

Looking up he located 'Coyote's eye' and remembered how in the Song a tear fell from it—to the earth. If it did where would it have fallen? Somewhere beyond the high ridge that formed the north wall of the canyon, he reasoned.

But walking back to the pickup he discounted the whole idea. There were other lakes that would produce all different perspectives. Looking at a map under the dim dome light, he noted *Buckeye Creek* and *Buckeye Hot Springs*.

"Hot springs?" he spoke out loud.

Bryan recalled a passage out of the Captain's original diary that talked about "hot springs in the area."

Back on the road again he headed back toward town. In the headlights a sign caught his attention. It read: Buckeye Campground, with an arrow pointing left up some obscure dirt road. Driving on, it wasn't long before he was back in Lee Vining.

Before going indoors, Bryan turned to view the constellations of the north and the northwest. A small meteor sped across the blackened canopy.

Turning in for the night, he found it hard to fall asleep. Every time he closed his eyes, all he could see was the Big Dipper shimmering in the still waters of the Lake.

Bolting upright, Bryan jumped out of bed and searched frantically through his stuff looking for a map, knocking things everywhere. Finally finding one, he unfolded it and laid it out on the table. Grabbing a blunt pencil, Bryan focused on the map.

But he now realized he had forgotten whatever it was that had struck him. What was it?

"What a stupid bonehead," he told himself.

Then it came back to him. Locating Twin Lakes, he drew the shape of the Big Dipper so that the lakes fit inside the Dipper. Finding his star book, Bryan opened it up to the page that showed the Great Bear Constellation. He proceeded to draw in the tail as it was shown. It seemed to fit the curvature of the canyon. Then he realized that the two creeks that fed into the south end of the lakes fit closely the pattern of the Great Bear's legs. And leaving the canyon, along the main road was its head.

"Well, whata you know about that?" Bryan realized. "It fits, it's a superimposition of the Great Bear—Ursa Major!" he exclaimed out loud.

Laughing he thought about their experience with their own great bear up in the headwaters of that same canyon—how ironic. But wait, what was it that Longtree mentioned in the song about the Great Bear? Wasn't it something about three Indian braves chasing him in a canyon? Yes, it fits—"down in the canyon"—at Twin Lakes.

What was next? The 'Coyote's Eye'—due north. Drawing a line north, Bryan's pencil passed over Buckeye Hot Springs and beyond.

"Of course it all makes sense. Coyote's tears fell to the Earth." Tears can be warm and seemingly hot at times, he reasoned. Bryan recalled the next passage that told how the 'snake' was forced out and it eventually headed upstream. The star chart showed Draco in this position, making its characteristic backwards S to the north and west. Mimicking its shape, Bryan traced a bold line up the canyon curving north and crossing a pass into the Walker River Canyon and Paiute Meadows. The course curved westward toward Sonora Pass and back south along Leavitt Creek to Leavitt Lake and beyond. The serpent's head appeared to fit into the shape of *Emigrant Meadow*. Its head was made up of a triangular cluster of stars pointed west, northwest, pointing through Brown Bear Pass toward the *Relief Range*.

The guidebook showed how Draco was pointed in the direction of Lyra. Thumbing through the pages Bryan came to where it described the origin of its name. Skipping down through the paragraphs, he found that to the Greeks it was a lyre or harp, and in Asia it was viewed as an eagle or vulture.

"So it could be construed as a bird. Wow," realized Bryan. "It works."

He was stunned and thrilled by the depth of the intricacy. The Captain must have discovered how the constellations formed a celestial map of sorts. And when he heard this Indian Song, it was a natural—a marriage made in heaven so to speak.

Stumbling, Bryan slipped his pants back on, and rushed outside into the still dark night to view once again the heavenly masterpiece. The grouping of constellations had now moved into the far north and northeast. With new eyes it was now easy to trace the trail of stars to arrive at the top of the mountains, at Lyra.

Bryan knew what he had to do. It would be turning light in four or five hours. He had to pack a few things to last him through the next day and travel up into Buckeye Canyon before first light. Too excited to sleep he began making preparations immediately. Later he did doze off for a couple of hours before leaving the cabin about 4 a.m.

It took a good hour to travel over the hump, up the Twin Lakes Road, and north along the primitive dirt road that led to Buckeye Creek. The rough corrugated road contoured along the western foothills gradually gaining elevation. Glancing down, it seemed that the lights of town and those scattered throughout the broad valley blinked at him.

A small sign directed him to the right. According to the map it was another half mile. Climbing a short hill, the bumpy dirt road curved off to the left. After going about half a mile, Bryan turned around and stopped at the top of the small knoll. Turning off his headlights and ignition, he decided to wait for the light of dawn.

Back down on the dirt road a couple of miles south he noticed a pair of headlights. Suddenly the headlights went out. Bryan was instantly suspicious.

The air grew colder as gray dawn came on. Soon the first golden rays of sun broke forth out of the east, from the direction of Aurora. How appropriate it seemed—a golden dawn.

"How strange," spoke Bryan. There were colors being reflected in midair straight out from the hill to his left. Hopping out of the truck he tried to get a better look. Apparently there was mist rising from below. "It has to be," he told himself.

Scampering down the steep bank he could hear the roar of rushing water. And sure enough there it was just below him flowing out of a rock stratum and descending into a pool at the base of the steep hill. The water was moderately hot to the touch. Water vapor ascended and was caught by the early morning breeze.

"Coyote's tears," recalled Bryan, "and the snake den." Looking around the rocky landscape he could see how this could have been true.

Climbing back up to the road, he viewed the Canyon and its adjoining peaks. Bryan was sure this had to be the correct route; the Captain's return trail to the 'Oro de Cañon'—was via *Buckeye Canyon.*

Driving up into the brushy canyon past the campground, the road ended at a trailhead nestled in a small grove of leafless aspens. The campground was closed for the season; no one was around.

The plan was to march up canyon till he found confirmation or was forced to return. Throwing on his pack he was off. The air was crisp, and the sky was ever so blue. Thickets of brush protruded into the narrow rocky trail. This truly is snake country in this forsaken canyon, he thought to himself.

After a slight bend to the south the terrain began a definite curve to the north as patterned in the shape of Draco. The microclimates changed quickly as he progressed upwards through groves of Mountain Hemlock and Jeffery Pine. Soon Bryan was in shadow, finding frost along the trail.

As the terrain became more confining, he watched more carefully for the Captain's markings.

After two hours, he estimated he had gained over one thousand feet in elevation. The air had a definite bite to it. The trail grew steeper as it hugged the eastern wall. Sunlight intermittently appeared along the winding course.

Rounding a shelf of rock, frozen snow about a foot deep covered the trail, causing him to pause. From this point on, Bryan reckoned this was the way it was going to be all the way up to the pass. It wasn't going to be easy, but there was no way he was going to give up. The eroded trail disappeared under a sloped snow bank. Stepping up onto its granular surface he found it crunchy and hard, proving to be awkward and greatly slowing his progress.

Resting more often now afforded him a greater opportunity to study the rock faces that presented themselves. A recollection of Coleman's photographs recalled to mind that there were shadows on the left side of at least two of the shots. Because the sun could only shine along this slope during midday or after, it made sense to him that the theoretical rock face should face south, or southwest. The shadow also may indicate that the face could be recessed to some degree.

The snowdrifts grew deeper as he plodded ahead. His legs felt like lead weights. Resting again he pondered the thought that many of Coleman's pictures seemed to have been taken at an oblique angle, perhaps from below. Bryan remembered the '*Door of the Sun*' symbol in the 'Oro de Cañon,' and how high it was. The shadows that lingered along the fractured faces made it difficult to pick anything out.

Warmth from the sun caused the ice and snow to begin melting. Drips began to rain down along the slope. Large icicles hung in secluded pockets.

After another half hour of arduous climbing, Bryan decided he couldn't go any further. Crampons would be necessary to scale the formidable slope ahead. Failure was not in his vocabulary, but what could he do if the symbol was buried under tons of snow beneath him?

Reversing course, he found the downhill trek much easier through the softening snow. Bryan remained watchful. If Coleman had taken pictures in this canyon, it must have been in the summer when there was no snow on the trail. Standing on the trail he would've been looking eight or ten feet above, up to about his present eye level. So maybe, what he was looking for was right in front of him so to speak. Bryan turned around and re-examined the slopes behind. There was too much talus along that stretch.

Continuing on down there was more likable granite protrusions presenting themselves, but there was nothing there. Passing the pockets of large icicles, Bryan stopped and turned around. One of the pockets had a southwest-facing surface. The four-foot icicles were now beginning to drip from exposure to the sun.

"Could it be?" he asked himself.

Stepping up to the ice formations, he gave the closest one a swift kick but it was too strong. Finding a twenty-pound rock that had rolled down from above, Bryan hurled it and smashed the beautiful formation. Kneeling down, he could see a pattern in the rock surface, which was recessed about two feet back. He recognized a straight line and a descending curved line. To see more Bryan dug down through a top layer of frozen snow and another eighteen inches into softer snow. He ignored the cold water dripping on his back in the excitement of the moment. The curved line proved to be attached to a series of radial straight lines. Bryan was now convinced he had found an inverted 'sun' symbol.

"E-ha!" he yelled out in victory. The echo boomed down through the canyon.

Getting up off his wet knees, he stepped back to assess how it was located. Sure enough as predicted, the rock face angled and ran north into shadow.

"Thanks Ben, wherever you are, thanks for your help."

Bryan had forgotten about how tired and chilled he was. Sighting on three reference points, he made a sketch of this location before getting on his way.

In the glare of the winter sun, Bryan descended the slopes to soon drop below the snow line.

It all made sense now. The Hot Springs near the mouth of the canyon and 'Whispering Valley'—were both on a straight line across the north end of Bridgeport Valley. This was it! He had found the Captain's 'back door' route—the eastern access to and from the 'Oro de Cañon.' " Bryan tried to hurry despite his fatigue. He knew things were about to jump to light speed once again.

18

TRAIL OF THE ANCIENT DWARFS

"Where have you been?" Tammy demanded. "We've been waiting for you since about noon!"

"Well, I'm glad to see you too. I was out checking on a hunch," he explained.

"You're wanting to get yourself caught aren't you? Anyway, we've come up with some answers. Sit down and listen," she ordered still a little perturbed.

Bryan smiled and said nothing. Josh unfolded a map of the constellations and laid it out on the table.

"What have you been doing in here?" questioned Josh "There's stuff all over the floor."

"I'll explain in a minute," laughed Bryan.

"These are the significant constellations in the Indian Song: Ursa Major, Draco, and Lyra, all grouped together and forming what we think to be a schematic of the route we're looking for," Tammy pointed out.

"You're right, I agree," Bryan replied.

"What do you mean we're right? How do you know?"

"I'll tell you in minute, but first go on. What else did you come up with?"

Josh spoke up and continued, "In the 'Indian Song' there was reference made to the bird dropping seeds that would mark the route to the top of the mountain, right? Well, according to our research on birds of the eastern slope, there is one match to this scenario. It's the *Nutcracker*. It roosts in the Whitebark Pine and eats the seeds from its cones."

"Interestingly, the seeds are wingless and don't propagate themselves very well. The Nutcracker helps out, by dropping the seeds that pass through its digestive system, wherever they fly. And when this happens some will germinate and grow into mature trees," explained Tammy.

"These trees are at home in high elevation on the east slope, scattered up in the canyons, added Josh.

"There is one more thing. There are two varieties of this tree, one is a dwarf," informed Tammy.

"Dwarf?"

"Yes," she replied. "They are even rarer."

"Wow, I'm impressed," replied Bryan. "*Trail of the Ancient Dwarfs*," he pondered.

"Now top that," she challenged.

"Young lady, you dare challenge me? O-kay, I too have resolved the constellations, but I went a step further and matched it to an actual route in the mountains. Look at my map, it's already marked up."

Bryan walked them through the route as depicted by the constellations. He showed them how the head of the serpent, Draco matched the shape of Emigrant Meadow and pointed toward Lyra in the Relief Range."

Tammy sighed, "How do you do it? I give up."

"Out of pure boredom, I guess. But there's more."

"More?" questioned Josh.

"I went up into Buckeye Canyon early this morning to try to find a 'sun' symbol, as was shown in Coleman's photographs to verify that my hunch was true. And guess what?"

"You must have found one. That grin on your face is no mere accident," answered Josh.

"Well, isn't it good?" asked Bryan.

"Of course, we're all on the same team, right?" smiled Josh, winking at Tammy.

She frowned at the edges of her mouth and said nothing.

"This helps us to cut to the chase, we can go directly to Emigrant Meadow and go from there," realized Josh. "And I believe we can drive to within several miles of the site."

"That's true; there is a Jeep road up to Leavitt Lake and perhaps a ways beyond. And—I still have my Forest Service keys," Bryan recalled.

Now wait one idiotic minute here, let's go through a reality check! The first winter snows have already come. It's absolutely too dangerous!" exclaimed Tammy.

"We've hit a dry spell, no rain, no snow—nothing," replied Bryan. "It's an Indian Summer!"

"Oh no, you are not going to do it, and that's final!" she declared.

"Tammy, I appreciate your concern, but it's not final until I say it's final. What do you think, Josh, is it doable?" asked Bryan.

"Well, it didn't look bad when we came across the Pass this morning, there was even some bare spots," recalled Josh.

"Josh, whose side are you on anyway?" she fired back.

"Tammy, there is always a degree of risk, even in everyday life, but the way it looks now—it's not all that bad," answered Bryan.

Tammy looked at him and pleaded with her eyes. "Please don't do this," she begged.

"I can't wait! I can't wait till next summer. They're liable to track me down and throw me in the slammer any day. It has to be dealt with now, while the window of opportunity is still open."

"I understand its importance to you, but it's still not worth risking your life over," she argued.

"Tammy, I've been sitting here in a pool of depression, I have to make this attempt to keep my spirits alive. Don't you understand? I have to try."

Tammy knew she had to wager everything in one last-ditch effort. "Please don't. I'm begging you. Look, I'm lowering myself before you," she said taking off her shoes. "I humble myself at your feet—you win. I'm at your beckoning. But please don't do this."

Bryan reached down and gently brushed the hair on the side of her head back. "Tammy, I have to try. Please understand."

"Very well, if that's the way it's going to be!" she lashed out. "I'm not going to talk to you anymore. I was hoping though that our relationship was improving. But I guess it was never meant to be." Gathering her things she stalked out.

"You're going through with this aren't you?" asked Josh. Bryan did not reply. "I can't let you go by yourself."

"Let Tammy know I'm sorry. If I could arrange this any other way I would."

"I'm sorry too. I was hoping it would all work out between you two. Well anyway, if we're going to do this, we better do this fast."

"I agree."

"I'll be back tomorrow evening. Oh, by the way, thanks, it's going to be a wonderful trip home tonight," stated Josh as he headed out the door.

As Bryan watched their tail lights disappear up near the highway, he felt a rift in his heart become ever more painful. What power drove him to this madness?

As promised, Josh arrived after dark the following day a little perturbed about the whole thing.

"Josh, if you feel uncomfortable about this—"

"Yes and no—let's just finish this," answered Josh.

"How's Tammy?"

"She's pissed. She seriously considered turning you in to keep you from killing yourself."

"She wouldn't dare!"

"Think again."

"You're right, we need to wrap this up quick. We better leave tonight," replied Bryan.

"Tonight?"

"I think somebody is watching me, apparently day and night if my suspicions have any substance."

"Well, we need to figure a way so we can just disappear," thought Josh.

"If somebody is watching, they will probably expect us to light out before dawn, just as we always do. So tonight at 10:30, we'll turn off the lights just like we're going to bed, except we'll load up in the dark and leave with no headlights on."

"Like old times, eeh?"

"I wish we could go back to those times, when things were simpler," lamented Bryan.

Time dragged as they prepared for their nocturnal excursion, stacking their gear near the door. Both said little as they watched the clock.

"Anytime now, it's 10:15," stated Josh checking his watch.

After one final check, they killed the lights. It took a moment for their eyes to adjust to the darkness. Except for one minor tripping incident, they quickly had their gear stowed aboard the Jeep.

Hearing a truck approaching on the highway, Josh waited till the noise level was sufficient enough to cover the starting of the engine. Working their way out to the road, they headed north in the darkness. A weak glow on the eastern horizon indicated that the moon was soon to rise. The lights of Lee Vining soon disappeared behind them. About three miles out, Josh finally turned the lights on as a vehicle approached from the opposite direction. Climbing the steep grade up to Conway Summit, they soon passed a freight truck. Bryan looked back down into the black void checking for headlights, but none were visible. He wondered if someone could even be watching them from above, at the overlook. Interestingly, there was one darkened car parked there as they went by.

Nearing the top of the pass, the constellations loomed overhead. They had new meaning—almost coming to life as it were.

With little conversation between them it wasn't long before they had crossed the sleeping Bridgeport Valley to wind their way into the Sweetwater Mountains beyond. Rounding a curve they neared the site of the old burned-out cafe.

"It seems we've just about come full circle on this," commented Bryan as they passed by.

The road soon entered a valley guarded by tall dark stone sentinels, which the locals called Devil's Gate. From there, Camino's Sierra Highway descended to meet Highway 108, onto which they turned. Only a few lights marked the location of the Pickel Meadow Marine Base. Signs along the road indicated that Sonora Pass was open. Leavitt Meadow looked dark and lifeless as they ascended the switchback. The chilling air temperature began to affect their hands and face as they climbed. The faint roar of Leavitt Falls marked their location on the winding ribbon of asphalt.

"Keep an eye out," warned Josh, "it's going to be hard to spot our turnoff."

The Jeep roared in low gear up a steep straightaway, then turned left, followed by a corresponding sharp right.

"This is it!" yelled Bryan.

Josh turned sharp left, braking hard, and banging over a drainage berm that nearly threw them out of the vehicle.

"Whoa horse," called out Josh.

"I'm awake," laughed Bryan.

"There's the road," pointed Josh.

"Drive up to the gate, and I'll dig out the key," directed Bryan.

Once past the gate, Josh locked the hubs into four-wheel drive. The road was very difficult to follow in the darkness. Some sections were steep with loose rock, and as they gained elevation snow appeared out of the shadows to eventually cover the primitive roadway. One hill was particularly difficult due to a mixture of rock and snow. Sliding sideways, they slid into the trees along the right-hand side. Bryan was forced to push branches out of his face as they struggled upward.

Soon they had gained the plateau upon which Leavitt Lake sat. A partial moon rose from the east, highlighting the scattered snowdrifts upon the rocky landscape. The primitive road worked its way to the edge of the lake, which in the rarified moonlight appeared dull, covered by some kind of thin film.

The trail took them through a small drainage and climbed continually above the lake. The Jeep banged and rattled as they crept up to another locked gate.

"This road was built fifty years ago to mine tungsten," informed Bryan as he slipped out to unlock the gate. Bryan had more difficulty with this lock. "This hasn't been unlocked in a coon's age," he told Josh. After forcing it, it finally snapped open. He decided to leave this one unlocked for their return trip, if there was to be such a thing. "This road was built all the way to Snow Lake near Emigrant Meadow," continued Bryan as he jumped back into the vehicle, "but I understand it's impassable not far beyond Leavitt Pass."

Slowly, Josh eased the Jeep up the rock-strewn road, bucking and jumping. The grade was constant and fairly steep. He noticed how the cold was now creeping into his toes.

"I think you'll have to buy me a new set of tires after this," commented Josh.

"Oh, heck, I'll buy you a whole new Jeep, if we—"

"If we what? Make it back alive?"

"Josh, think about it. Have I ever steered you wrong?"

"You can't control the weather or hold the sun in the palm of your hand can you?"

Bryan watched the lake disappear behind him and said nothing in return. The incline moderated as they entered a treeless basin. Stars danced above an invisible horizon. Coming around a switchback, the steepening road appeared to ascend into the stars. A captivating view opened to them as they crawled up into Leavitt Lake Pass. To the south a vast arena of sleeping giants poised silently in the lunar alpine-glow, and looking back in the direction of the lake, volcanic silhouettes loomed in the darkness.

"Erie, it's almost like another world up here," commented Josh.

"A vast empire of rock and ice," replied Bryan.

Beyond the pass, the road narrowed to a mere ten feet wide, contouring around the mountain that loomed high above them. The left side of the trail dropped off into the infinite darkness below, perhaps hundreds or thousands of feet.

"This is as far as we go," observed Josh as he brought the Jeep to a halt in front of a significant rockslide, which blocked most of the narrow road. The headlights shined out into the black unknown void.

"Should be another nine miles to Emigrant Meadow," Bryan estimated.

"I hope the weather holds. The forecasts were a little iffy. Usually you would expect to find five feet of snow up here, and the winds howling over these passes driving the chill factor down to twenty degrees below zero," reminded Josh, still a little concerned.

"Except for the first couple of weeks, this has been more like fall weather," agreed Bryan jumping out of the vehicle.

"How much climbing gear are you taking?"

"A few basics," Bryan replied, slinging a coil of climbing rope over his shoulder.

After hoisting on their packs, they secured the vehicle as much as possible, and were off into the gloom along the mythical route of Draco. The trail wound its way down into a saddle that soon ascended onto a knife-edged ridgeline that appeared to be the main crest of the Sierra Nevada.

Their moonlit nocturnal sojourn under the stars seemed unique and adventurous. The sky dome descended to their feet displaying dazzling constellations, many submerged into the terra firma. It was as if they were walking on the stars themselves. Bryan looked up and thought about the 'Indian Sky' that revolved above them.

"Do you hear anything?" asked Josh.

"No, just your flat feet," Bryan replied. After two minutes, he also heard a strange sound. "You're right, I hear something too—kind of a roar."

The roar grew louder as they approached a low point in the ridgeline. It did not seem to be a sound that was produced by natural means. Rounding a large rock outcropping, they spotted something down canyon, hovering. A powerful spotlight was directed onto wreckage of some kind.

"It's a helicopter," realized Josh. "What do you make of that?"

"Don't know."

As the turbine powered chopper swung around, shots rang out striking something below them.

"What in the world?" wondered Josh.

"I wonder if this has some connection with all the recent helicopter incidents that we've observed?" questioned Bryan.

"Their shooting at something near that wreckage," realized Josh.

Another volley of shots was fired off, striking rocks and metal. Turning, the chopper and the spotlight moved away from them along the canyon wall.

"Come on, let's check this out," beckoned Bryan.

"Are you crazy?"

"Josh, their gone. We'll be okay."

"I'm not so sure."

Coming off the saddle they worked their way down through the rocks along the south side of the canyon. The roar of the helicopter continued to move away and finally ceased. After twenty minutes they found the mangled wreckage of a four-wheel drive vehicle vertically wedged in a wide crevice. Turning on their flashlights, the nocturnal explorers scoured the wreck for clues.

"It's been here for a winter or two already," observed Bryan.

"Whatever they were shooting at they must have hit. There are fresh blood spots under here leading out, and I assume they lead down canyon," Josh replied back.

"Josh!"

"What?"

"Don't you realize? This fits the description of Ben Coleman's rig, remember?"

"Yeah, you're right, but way up here?"

"Well, he apparently had found enough of the 'sun' symbols to get him this far," thought Bryan.

"You don't think he could still be alive?" wondered Josh.

"I don't know, but let's get back up on the ridge, and get on with this," prompted Bryan.

A slight breeze whispered through the saddle. The moon rose high in the star-studded expanse casting shadows that accented the strange formations that they now passed in the dark. Groups of Whitebark Pine appeared and disappeared in the gloom. It was nearing dawn as the two slowly worked their way along a rough zigzag course to the top of the next mountain. The cold seemed to be settling into their joints and bones. The coming sun would be welcome.

Once on top, the terrain grew gravelly as they approached a small placid lake. Its mirrored surface reflected the moon and the brighter stars, beckoning them to pause and rest.

"How many times has the sun, moon, and stars—the universe passed over this stationary plane?" wondered Bryan.

"Interesting thought, but I doubt it is far from being a stationary plane," commented Josh.

"Think about the ages of time in the past in which these same unchanging stars have glittered on these waters, while here on earth empires have risen and fallen."

"Are you going to take up philosophy now?' asked Josh.

"No, but it's interesting to contemplate."

With eager anticipation they waited for the first rays of sun to break over the horizon. As if from the Creator's own hand, color was restored to the earth. Everything about them began to glow gold and red. The crystalline sky above gradually softened from the star-studded blackness of space to that of the darkest of blues.

Turning their attention to the south, Emigrant Meadow came out of the shadows below them. It was a large sweep of land with a moderate sized lake on its east side.

"Draco's head," pointed Bryan. "It's next in the chain of stellar events. The head points toward those volcanic-like mountains on the right."

"From there I guess we're back to searching for more of the Captain's classic clues again," thought Josh.

"We'll definitely have to keep our eyes open for the 'sun' symbol, but this thing about the ancient dwarfs could be very difficult to figure out."

After an hour of recuperation it was an easy hike down into the treeless flat basin. A gentle cold breeze urged them to hustle on across the brown alpine grassland to its far west side.

Approaching a ridge of rocks, they heard noises beyond. Without discussion they crept up to a point between two rocks to take a look. Digging out a pair of field glasses, Josh focused them in the direction of the sound. A short distance away was a team of men dressed in silver-white protective suits loading bright yellow canisters onto a helicopter which was camouflaged by black netting.

"That crazy guy we met at Deadman Creek wasn't so crazy after all," realized Josh.

"Plutonium?" Bryan half-remembered.

"They're certainly not lemon sours."

"Let me see. There's a sunset symbol painted on the side of that helicopter—just like you seen before, remember?" discovered Bryan.

"Really? Let me see. Yeah, that's it! Interesting, they are hauling those canisters out from between two rock columns from a cave or something."

Bryan again took a turn with the field glasses. "Oh, wow!" he exclaimed.

"What?"

"Look along the cliff wall to the right, near that gully, about twenty feet up," directed Bryan handing him back the binoculars.

"The inverted 'sun' symbol!" he realized.

Bryan looked again at the symbol painted on the helicopter and the one carved in the rock. "How ironic," commented Bryan.

Suddenly a second helicopter appeared out of nowhere directly behind them. Ducking was to no avail, they were openly visible from that side. Scrambling along the rocky ridge they neared the side of the mountain that towered over the basin. Men with weapons quickly poured through openings between the rocks looking for them.

"Looks like we're cornered," observed Josh.

Suddenly there was another surprise—from above. A rockslide cascaded down the face of the cliff scattering those that had advanced toward them.

"This way!" yelled Bryan, pointing toward the small gully that they had spotted earlier.

"Yes, yes—go, go!" agreed Josh pushing him.

The boulder-filled draw twisted and turned giving them constant cover. It must have been a whole minute later when they heard gunfire striking rock some distance away.

"They must be firing at someone else," spoke up Josh, breathing heavy.

"Could it be our buddy from Deadman Creek?"

"Whoever it is, I'll be his friend."

Soon the roar of a helicopter could be heard again.

"They must be going airborne again," thought Bryan.

"Let's hide back up in here," pointed Josh.

Scrambling up into the secluded spot they waited. After a moment the helicopter made a pass to the south and then came over their general direction. Soon the drone of the aircraft was lost in the distance.

"I think they're gone," breathed Josh.

"It's unthinkable that anybody would even be up here," mussed Bryan. "For some unknown reason our paths keep crossing."

"There may be a parallelism here. It's like a change in the hierarchy of minerals."

"You mean from gold to plutonium."

"Yeah, both have to do with power. It's a curious thing though how they may be connected."

"Interesting thought, Josh," reflected Bryan getting up.

Continuing up into the rugged draw they finally reached the crest of the mountain range after a good hour of difficult climbing. In the early morning sun they looked out over Emigrant Meadow and the Lake. To the south loomed the sentinels of Yosemite—in the rarified haze. Over the crest, the head of Kennedy River Canyon could be seen below in partial shadow.

To Bryan it seemed so long ago that he had ridden those trails and looked up at the azure blue skies above East Flange Rock. He hoped all this would soon come to an end. As he thought of Tammy his heart felt a pang of regret.

A natural trail contoured along the cold north side of the mountain. A momentary breeze caught their attention. Ice and snow blocked their path in places. To the west, cirrus clouds were spread out above the horizon as musical notes upon a sheet of music. A recess in the mountainside revealed a variety of routes that ascended the near vertical terrain. There was no sign of any carved symbols along the way they had come so far.

"In the 'Indian Song,' the variety of trees mentioned were dwarf, weren't they?" asked Bryan checking his memory.

"That's right."

"It all makes sense then. Most everything on this north slope would be dwarf—due to the lack of sun."

"Snow does lay along these slopes into late summer," agreed Josh.

"What did Tammy call those trees we're looking for?"

"Whitebark Pine, I believe."

"Yes, that's what it was. So we'll need to watch for a dwarf tree with a typical pine needle cluster," stated Bryan.

"So far there have been very few trees of any kind," observed Josh.

Approaching a small stream they decided to split up. Josh volunteered to follow the stream, while Bryan went on ahead.

Josh stepped cautiously up into the rocky drainage. For the most part it proved to be very unimpressive. No trees, no significant rock faces, or any kind of plausible trail was noticeable.

In the meantime Bryan had followed the natural bench around a spiny protrusion in the mountainside to discover another niche in the cliff wall. A winding corridor led him back into an impressive staircase-like valley that progressively climbed out of sight. The heavily eroded terraces appeared to be notched into the ascending canyon wall. A puff of wind scurried by him buffeting the sparse vegetation that landscaped the narrow valley.

He hiked along the sunnier side to examine scattered trees that were about twenty feet in height. The needles were dark green and were clustered like a pine. But these trees were obviously not dwarf. Glancing across the way into the shadows, the trees appeared to be shorter up against the mountain. Working his way across a gully, Bryan realized that these were of the same variety, but much smaller—dwarf! Though scattered, they hugged the shadowy slopes that ascended out of sight. This could be it he thought.

Rushing back to find Josh, he soon led him up into the narrow valley to get his opinion. Josh examined a pine branch, and then gazed along the upward meandering course of the dwarf trees.

"It has to be!" thought Josh. It fits. This must be the 'trail of the ancient dwarfs!' "

"The weather is changing, we better hurry along," Bryan urged. "The 'back door' can't be too much further."

Driven by the excitement of their seeming discovery they quickly ascended the various levels of the natural staircase. Upon reaching a certain elevation the geology of the mountain suddenly turned volcanic. Below them the canyons deepened and ran off into Relief Basin. Momentary glimpses of the Obelisk now and then presented themselves in the far west, several miles distant. Gathering dark clouds around the Obelisk gave it an angry appearance. Though sparse, the trail of the dwarf pines continued, and after almost two hours they had reached the top of a bare volcanic ridge with breathtaking views, both north and south.

Before them arose a black giant, an ancient crater draped in white ash and black basaltic debris. The steep walls of this great fortress were solid, rising nearly vertical in places to eight hundred feet above them.

Bryan turned around and looked at Josh in realization of something.

"What?"

"On Paoha—remember—the *caldera*!

19

BEYOND THE CALDERA

"I have a feeling that we're finally here—at the Captain's 'back door,' " excitedly declared Josh. "I apologize for all my negativity."

"No need to apologize, the reality is you're right, we are in harm's way," replied Bryan as they mounted a succession of stair-step slabs of volcanic rock, which took on the appearance of overlapping layers of armor.

"This is like one of those movies where the dark castle sets high up on the crag. All we need now is a little thunder and lightning to fill in the scene," commented Josh.

"Your depiction may soon come true," pointed Bryan toward the gathering clouds in the west.

Now hugging the southerly wall of the caldera the course climbed steeply. Crossing a minor seepage that issued out of a crevice in the wall, their climb soon ended at a sheer precipice. About five hundred feet below was a small green lake situated in an irregular shaped crater.

"What did we miss?" asked Josh.

"Nothing that I could see," sighed Bryan looking back along the slope of the caldera that towered over them. "Let's try following this higher ledge on the way back."

A biting wind picked up as the cloud cover moved in. The temperature began to drop. Hurrying, they scampered along the narrow ledge that Bryan had pointed out.

"Another seepage," noticed Josh looking up.

Bryan glanced up the near vertical slope squinting his eyes. "It would almost appear that there's an opening up there."

"How big?"

"I don't know," answered Bryan.

"Are you prepared to go rock climbing?"

"Yes indeed."

Pulling off his pack, Bryan clipped a set of carabiners to his belt, tucked in a couple of pitons in his pocket, and shouldered the coil of climbing rope.

"This should only take a couple of minutes. I'll send the rope down if there is anything up there," informed Bryan.

Finding a vertical crevice, Bryan quickly ascended the weathered wall. Josh watched him approach to about where the hole was located, and then he suddenly disappeared. After a moment his head reappeared.

"I'm sending the rope down."

"Really?"

"Yeah, I think this could be it."

Josh tied Bryan's pack to the end of the rope, and pulled himself up the steep wall. As he neared the opening it continued to enlarge. Josh figured he must have climbed nearly eighty feet as he reached the irregular shaped portal that was approximately six feet high and four feet wide.

A scarcely noticeable outline in the rock adjacent to the right-hand side of the cave opening caught his attention. The figure was almost completely sand blasted away, but it was enough for Josh to confirm they were on the right track.

"This is it!" Josh exclaimed as crawled inside. The seepage soaked through the knees of his pants. The pain from the cold was severe.

"What?" came Bryan's questioning voice from somewhere further down in the cave.

"This is it," he repeated. "This is the 'back door!' "

Bryan came quickly toward him out of the darkness. "How do you know?"

"Outside on the outer wall, a faint symbol—didn't you see it?"

"No, I didn't."

"Most of it is gone, but it has to be!"

Bryan shook his head in agreement. In a moment of silence they could hear the rise and fall of the moaning wind outside.

"Find anything down in the cave?" asked Josh.

"Nothing yet. There's an ice floor a ways down. Let's take a look."

Josh found his flashlight and began the treacherous descent, which began about seventy-five feet in. Soon they entered a small to moderate sized cavern, whose ice floor glistened like polished glass. Josh searched the ceiling and walls with his light. Walking carefully on the ice they slowly examined the perimeter of the room.

"Josh, turn your light off for a second."

After he turned his light out, their eyes began to adjust to the darkness. Then it became apparent that there was a dull, bluish-green light coming up through the ice.

"How can that be?" wondered Josh, whose voice echoed.

"I'm not for sure, but it has to be light coming in from the outside, I would think."

"Look here, the light is strongest on this far side," discovered Josh.

"Solid ice, I'm stumped on this one," confessed Bryan.

Suddenly a muffled, oscillating sound came to them from the direction of the cave entrance. Hurrying back up to the cave opening, the sound increased. It wasn't the wind. About a quarter mile straight out was one of the enemy helicopters hovering.

"There's no way they could know we're in here," thought Josh.

"The rope, my pack—we left them hanging outside!" realized Bryan.

Grabbing the rope they began hoisting it up. Suddenly and most unexpectedly a fiery explosion impacted on the side of the caldera.

"They're shooting at us!" announced Josh.

"And not just with small arms either," was the reply.

After a moment, there was another hit scattering rocks everywhere. They could hear the position of the chopper moving to the east. Another explosion could be heard coming from around the opposite side of the mountain, followed by a closer one in the direction of the helicopter itself. Cautiously peering out of the opening, Josh and Bryan could see the aircraft in flames, spinning out of control toward the southeast side of the crater. There was silence followed by a violent impact and explosion. Metallic debris flew everywhere. Billowing black smoke from the wreck blew easterly away from the caldera.

"Wow, I wonder what happened?" spoke up Bryan.

Josh stuck his head out as far as he could and took a long look around.

"What a mess down there. The impact must have broken something loose," commented Josh.

"What do you mean?"

"It's hard to tell, but I see water gushing out from down near where we crossed that seepage."

Again, a menacing sound approached. The whine of another turbine-powered craft could be heard increasing out of the northeast. Hiding back inside the cave with their backs against the wall, they waited in suspense. Not only was there one, but now there was two. Both moved slowly around the caldera and finally disappeared.

"A person can't even come up here in the dead of winter and get away from it all," mused Bryan. Deep down he realized that Big Brother could also be right on their heels.

"Let's just keep moving," recommended Josh.

261

"Can we?" wondered Bryan. "How do we get through the ice?"

Back down into the ice room, the investigation continued. After several minutes a crackling noise soon became apparent.

"Josh, are you doing that?"

"No-o, that's not you either?"

"Not me. It's coming from everywhere now."

The crackling intensified, especially along the edges of the ice—turning to more of a groan. Microscopic cracks were gathering along its perimeter.

"I don't like this!" called out Josh. "We better back out of here!"

But it was too late. The ice floor exploded with large cracks instantly appearing everywhere. Josh being on the opposite side from Bryan quickly made his way back up into the cave. Within seconds the main floor began collapsing from the center outward. Bryan found a narrow rock ledge as a temporary haven as the ice floor caved away. Loud echoes resounded as large blocks of ice fell twenty feet or more into a pool of water below. Geysers of water splashed upward drenching almost everything in the cavern. As the turbulence subsided and the mist cleared, dim daylight was plainly visible below. Josh yelled for Bryan and received back an immediate reply that he was okay. It seemed that the pool elevation was slowly lowering.

"I'm going to tie off and lower myself down and take a look," announced Bryan.

"All right, but be careful. I can't come running to help you, you know."

Bryan thought about the fact that their separation may soon present a definite problem. Driving in a piton he was able to anchor himself. "I'm going down—next stop basement level."

As Bryan descended, Josh walked back to the 'back door' and peered out at the intensifying storm. The gusting wind had driven the chill factor at least down to zero. The possibility of getting trapped by the storm crossed his mind.

Meanwhile, Bryan had descended some twenty feet to the edge of the pit. Icy water lapped another four feet below. Turning around he could see gray light shining in through an irregular shaped opening in the wall. Landing among a group of large rocks, he loosely tied off his rope.

Stepping over the boulders, and up an incline he reached the opening. Venturing on out he found himself in the interior of the caldera. Dark clouds blew across the top of the bleak volcanic crest, some six hundred feet above. It looked to be like the proverbial lost world. Bryan envisioned prehistoric monsters inhabiting this austere landscape.

The floor of the crater dropped into a large sink that ran a quarter of a mile to the far wall. The floor of the sink was relatively flat, sloping gently to the northwest.

Traversing this prehistoric-looking crater he found himself following an eroded fissure that led him into a depressed area adjacent to the west wall. Looking up Bryan could see gusts of wind blowing snow and dust off the rim.

Caves began to appear in the basaltic walls. The first one was irregular and distorted. A cool breeze issued out of the second cave. Passing by, Bryan went on to discover one more separate lava tube. Since there were no exterior clues he decided to search at least the first fifty feet of each tunnel.

Retrieving his flashlight from his coat pocket he entered the last cave searching the floor and walls for clues. But after fifty feet of finding only bare rock and rubble, he went on to the next.

Bryan had only ventured in about ten feet when he spotted two makeshift torches leaning up against the left wall. Just above it was an unimpressive sun symbol, marking the way.

Thinking of Josh he hurried back. But after climbing back out into the open he realized things had turned for the worse—it was snowing. The wind gusted and the snow intensified. Stumbling back across the crater into the entry cave, he noticed that something was amiss. There was a large pile of rock near the edge of the pool, where there was none before. But more devastating than that was the fact that his rope was gone.

Glancing back up into the cavern he noted that the ledge of rock that he had descended from was no longer there, but was now under his feet.

"Josh! Josh!" Bryan called out. He could hear an echoing clamor coming from above.

"You're back," Josh happily acknowledged.

"Well, I've got good news and bad news," reported Bryan in an anxious voice.

"Good news first."

"I found a marked cave on the far side of the caldera. There are three caves, but it's in the center one that I found the sun symbol and a couple of torches. The bad news is that my rope is now buried under these rocks that I can't begin to budge. I'm stuck down here!"

"It's snowing heavy outside," added Josh. "What can we do?"

"Tell you what—since I'm stuck here, I'm going for broke. You'll have to go back and get help. A copter should be able to land in the bottom of the crater. Give me two days and I'll meet you or whoever out in the caldera."

"That is if the storm does clear in two days," replied Josh.

"It should. But anyway, I see no other viable course."

Josh sighed. "I guess, but what if I don't make it?"

"If that's the case we're both goners."

"Here, you better have this," responded Josh throwing him a bag of additional food.

"Thanks," replied Bryan taking a deep breath. "You better go. The trails will soon be impassable. Oh, one more thing—tell Tammy that I—"

"Go on say it!"

"That I'm sorry, and I love her."

"There, was that so hard?"

"Thanks Josh, you've always been the best friend a person could have."

"Bryan, snap out of it. Now buck up, I'll see you in two days."

Pausing in a silent stare, Josh finally turned and marched toward the cave opening. He felt his heart beating hard. Taking a deep breath Josh looked outside. The snow fell steadily, but was only now beginning to stick.

Another problem now presented itself. There was no more rope to safely lower himself to the bottom. However, to the left of the opening was a six-inch wide ledge that ran downward at about a thirty degree angle. He perceived that the trick would be to maintain his footing while leaning into the rock wall. The wind was also a factor—pushing him down the slope. But there was no other way. Blowing snow prevented him from seeing very far below. Just as well he thought.

With one long step he was out on the ledge. It seemed okay. Josh moved along the ledge with growing confidence until accumulating snow melt made his walkway increasingly more slippery. Suddenly the ledge ended, and he felt his chest heave. How far was the bottom? Could he slide the rest of the way? There was no other choice. The important thing was to keep his feet below him; otherwise if he went headfirst chances are his head would be cracked like an egg.

Slowly pushing off, Josh slid a few feet and stopped. Pushing off again, Josh slid further and faster, five, ten, fifteen feet. Then boom, he hit bottom. His legs crumpled up in front of him as he impacted. The rebound launched him forward to land face down on the wet weathered basalt.

Recovering from the painful impact, Josh looked at the punctures on his bleeding hands. Still a little dazed he stood up holding his right hand. Looking back up through the swirling snow, the dark caldera looked mysterious and menacing.

Following the wall, Josh descended, soon passing pieces of smoking wreckage. Could there be survivors he wondered? Meandering through the debris field of wreckage he heard no sounds, nor found any bodies. A flowing stream of water where there had not been one next caught his attention. Then he remembered that this must be where they had crossed the seepage earlier. Was there a connection between all these events? Could this be what triggered the collapse of the ice floor? If this is true there should be a marking at the outlet he told himself. Up close he scanned the surface surrounding the crevice. On the upper right-hand side Josh spotted it, a severely weathered miniature sun. So it was true, the shots and impact of the aircraft into the side of the caldera had loosened a dirt and stone plug that held back the pond of water which supported the ice floor. This was apparently the Captain's key to unlocking the 'back door.' It was a matter of hydraulics. Wonders never ceased.

Hurrying on, Josh discovered a respite from the blowing snow as he descended the terraces. Once he was back on the trail that skirted the north side of the mountain, the brooding storm again engulfed him. It seemed like an eternity before he reached Emigrant Meadow. The snow had accumulated to six inches in depth on the ground, which had been bare earlier in the day. His cheeks burned from the wind.

Crossing the Sierra crest, Josh stayed on the old mine road. The wind blew him sideways, then forward in alternating bursts. Cold penetrated his legs and joints, but he knew he had to keep going. Stopping would be curtains. Night was coming on, making it increasingly difficult to see.

The thought of reaching his Jeep was his focal point as he worked his way around the folds of the mountain range. Accumulations of snow had reached ten to twelve inches as he rounded the bluff expecting to see his Jeep, but it wasn't there. Josh reassured himself that it was still ahead, around the next bend. But continuing through a couple more turns, Josh believed he had already reached Leavitt Pass just above the lake. On the down slope he realized it was true. Someone had taken his vehicle. Or perhaps it was now two thousand feet over the cliff.

A twinge shot through him as he wrestled with this new reality, the reality that he may not make it. His energy was going quick; and darkness closed in about him. Snow blew sideways at him from the west. Josh wanted to lie down and sleep, but he had to continue on. He thought of Bryan, still inside the mountain, and Tammy. Both depended on him. The road descended. Though nearly dark he could see snow-bearing clouds above the lake being driven through the passes that separated the volcanic peaks.

Suddenly Josh froze in his tracks. Was he seeing things?

20

EMPIRE OF THE SUN

The snowstorm intensified. Bryan could barely discern his earlier footprints in the powdery snow as he trudged back across the caldera. It would be much warmer inside the cave he told himself.

Tammy was right. How foolish this turned out to be. Bryan looked up into the swirling snow far above him. Here he was two miles above the sea in the highest peaks of the Sierra Nevada with the onslaught of winter bearing down on him. The near vertical walls presented no plausible way to climb out, especially now that his equipment was lacking.

Ducking into the lava tube, Bryan shook off the snow. Pulling off his pack, he dug around for his flashlight. It was worth its weight in gold at this point in time. Retrieving one of the old torches leaning against the wall, Bryan examined it closely in the light. Though gray and deeply furrowed, the wood appeared to be from a tree that grew on the Pacific-slope. This was a good sign. Finding a match he tried lighting it up, but it took several attempts before it ignited and crackled to life.

After slipping his pack back on, he glanced out one last time out into the snowstorm, as if connecting one last time with the outside world. Stepping forward he was ready to begin the search. Bryan paused at the 'sun' symbol and reflected on its significance. Shadows danced as he waved the torch in front of him. A cool breeze issued out of the depths. His footsteps echoed as he descended the oval-shaped tunnel, which in certain sections was quite steep. Bryan scanned the walls for any additional markings, but found none.

It was close to a half mile in when Bryan discovered a left branch to the lava tube. It was also descending, but with one distinctive difference—there was no breeze, therefore he reasoned it was most likely a dead-end.

Continuing on down he entered a large room whose ceiling had partially fallen onto the floor. Water dripped from fissures in the remaining ceiling.

After another half mile, more connecting tunnels appeared, but they too as the first, had no air movement. Accumulated seepage formed a small stream that now flowed with him down into the depths. Somewhere far above, it was probably still snowing. He wondered if Josh had made it back safely.

At about two miles in, Bryan stepped out into a very large cylindrical tunnel that ran at an acute angle, downhill to the left, and uphill to the right. It was at least twenty feet in diameter with a small stream of water about four inches in depth flowing out of the great unknown. The cool breeze that he had been using as a guide now issued out of the upper reaches of this new tunnel.

Hopping to the opposite side of the stream, Bryan paused as he thought of the howling winds that descended into the cave system near the Obelisk and wondered if these in any way could be interconnected? Only one way to find out he told himself as he trudged forward into the gloom.

Bryan climbed and climbed, one mile, two miles and more. Large rooms opened up, separated by curtains of gray-black stalactite-like formations. In one such room, the roar of water led him to discover an underground waterfall with an extensive fore bay.

From there a set of terraces led him up into the largest room yet. There was something different about this high vaulted cavern. It was grand, like a palace. Archways lined both sides. Then the first hard clue appeared out of the darkness—a torch mounted in the left wall. Others soon revealed themselves as well.

Bryan stopped in front of a large flat wall. A vertical line appeared at about eye level. Raising the torch higher, he was bowled over by the sight of a very large full-circled sun symbol nearly eight feet in diameter with sunrays running radially in all directions. "Empire of the Sun!" Bryan exclaimed in excitement stepping back. There was no seam running through the equator of the circle, distinguishing between the symbol of the west— the sun rising—the 'Door of the Sun,' and the inverted 'sun' symbol that corresponded to the east—the 'back door,' but it was singular and whole. This was the same as it was on the Captain's medallion. A flood of memories returned and saddened him.

"So! Great-great-grandfather is this where you are?" he called out, his voice echoing through the caverns. The echo diminished and there was only silence. How ironic, the 'Empire of the Sun' in this dark cavern, he thought. But it really wasn't. This was but—the dark end to the fallen empire. This was where east met west, but it was too late—it did not endure. But the truth concerning Captain Camino and what he stood for, and the ugly secrets that history hid—had to be revealed.

To his left, Bryan discovered the remnants of habitation— old deteriorated kegs and chests. Much of the debris was unrecognizable. The camp covered an area about eight hundred feet square.

A sunrise symbol above an opening at the far end of the cavern beckoned him forward, but exhaustion was catching up to him. After igniting two more torches, Bryan turned his attention to appeasing the pain in his stomach and taking a nap.

He woke cold and stiff. How long had it been? It seemed hours. There was no way to know. There was no sunrise or sunset in this land of eternal blackness.

What next? The logical thing to do was push on to the Obelisk—the inner sanctum. Perhaps there was to be more discoveries on the way. Leaving two torches burning, Bryan ventured on into the designated tunnel. Water stains on the floor gave evidence that a much larger stream had at one time flowed through there. The echo of his footsteps clamored into the black void. The lava conduit became unusually steep, changing shape to that which seemed familiar—shelves along both sides.

Coming to the top of a rise, a small side cave opened to the left. Lava stalactites blocked the right-hand side, but on the left they had been broken off. Then it hit him—he had been here before—this must be the way up into the Obelisk. His heart raced. Taking a deep breath he crawled up into a vaguely familiar chamber. If this was true there would be a pile of rubble at the head of the slope, he reminded himself. And so it was, the pile of rock soon appeared in front of him as well as the cave entrance that led to the great cavern in the heart of the Obelisk. Sticking his torch through the opening he immediately realized something was different—there was no wind, no howling wind. Proceeding into the bottomless labyrinth that had at one time struck terror in their hearts, the silence seemed eerie. On the far side his torch fluttered, indicating that there was a breeze blowing out of the main cavern toward him. A low hum grew more audible as he drew closer.

Stepping into the high vaulted cavern a dull light emanated from the ceiling telling him it was still daylight. Bryan could now clearly see the volcanic orifices that at one time had howled and whaled. Now only a low moan issued from them. The snow appeared to have stopped, but the cloudiness persisted.

Everything looked the same as far as he could tell. Remembering the solar clock, Bryan walked to its location on the open floor. There were memories here. Moving to one side of the etching, he remembered how Tammy looked up into his eyes while he stood in this spot.

Turning, he made a beeline for the hidden room. Stepping over the fitted stones, Bryan again stood in front of the four-foot wide filament of solid gold and the engraved sunrise symbol across its face.

Josh rubbed his eyes—was he seeing things? There were lights below on what he believed to be the north end of the lake. The lights had a blue cast to them and they periodically blinked through the blowing snow. But could he make it? His forward step was more like a stagger. His numb feet felt like wooden clubs, kicking up the snow in front of him. Maybe by closing his eyes it would all go away, but it didn't. He had to keep on. Josh began counting his steps—trying to focus. As the minutes ticked off he felt more and more dizzy, and finally collapsed. Josh tried yelling, but nothing seemed to come out. His efforts to pick himself up failed. Was this a dream? Or was this really the end?

A resounding knock startled Tammy. Who could it be this time of the day she wondered? Opening the door part way she observed two men dressed in dark suits. Both looked to be in their early forties with signs of graying hair.

"Yes, may I help you?" she asked demurely.

"I'm Agent Woods, this is Agent Kelley," spoke up the man closest to the door. "We're with the FBI. Miss Holden—I presume?"

"FBI?"

"Yes," he replied flipping open his badge.

Tammy paused momentarily before identifying herself. "Yes, I'm Tammy Holden." Suddenly her cheeks flushed red. "Does this have anything to do with Bryan Anderson?"

"Yes, it does."

Her face clouded. She imagined that she was about to become the recipient of bad news like women during the war who received an unexpected knock at the door.

"Is he o-kay?"

The two men exchanged glances. "We really don't know," spoke up the second Agent. "But you need to come with us."

"Okay," she replied opening the door all the way. Her head was swimming. Grabbing a notepad she didn't know what to write. "Where are we going?" Tammy asked.

"To the airport—bring a warm coat," replied Agent Woods.

Getting on the way, Tammy rode in the back seat of their full-sized black sedan. She stared out rain-streaked windows, afraid to let her mind wander on the possible realities. She wanted to cry, but couldn't.

At Columbia Airport a small two-engine jet was waiting for them. Within minutes the white sleek craft roared off the runway rocketing over the green, wet foothills to finally ascend through the clouds into the bright sunshine and the blue skies above. They were the only passengers. It seemed like only minutes before she noticed that the jet had changed to a descending slope. She overheard someone mention Reno. And so it was they soon landed at the Reno Cannon International Airport.

Light snow fell as she was escorted over to another aircraft—a dark green marine helicopter.

"Bundle up miss, it's mighty cold where we're going," informed one of the airman as he helped her to get buckled in.

"Thanks," she replied.

Tammy noticed that the two FBI Agents did not board with her. Their job was apparently done.

After a few minutes the tower cleared them to leave. The whine of the turbine engine soon turned to a deafening roar. Leaving the ground, the craft circled and headed south passing over numerous ranches below.

How was Bryan? She had a sick feeling about this whole thing. Was she a widow without even first getting married?

A cold draft made her shiver. They soon passed over a range of low snow covered hills into Carson Valley. The helicopter shook from a strong gust of wind. The pilot and the co-pilot conversed, and then they looked back at her.

Where were they taking her she wondered? Something must have happened, but what? This was no celebrity excursion. What about Josh? He was with Bryan as far as she knew. A pang of fright ran through her. Bryan always told her to trust him. She was still mad at him for going against her wishes, but she had to have faith that they were both okay.

The chopper flew low paralleling the Sierran east slope.

"Brace yourself," called out the co-pilot, "it's going to get mighty bumpy through the Walker Gorge."

She braced herself as they entered the turbulent gorge. Erratic winds pushed them sideways causing them to fishtail in one direction and then in the other giving them unwanted close up views of the eroded sedimentary bluffs that lined both sides of the gravelly river canyon.

After five minutes of literally getting beat against the internal framework they cleared the gorge to enter a basin-like valley. At this time the pilot began calling to someone on the radio. But there was no reply at first. He kept asking if they should abort. The snow was falling much heavier now. They circled while waiting for a message. Tammy could see a narrow highway below covered in snow with no tracks. It led up into the mountains where the snow clouds were massing. Finally the radio crackled to life, and they were given the word to proceed.

Directly into the gale force snowstorm they plunged. Were they crazy? Their progress was slow, and visibility was near zero.

The co-pilot suddenly became frantic, stating he had lost GPS and was going to laser navigation. "Give me the beam," he kept calling for on the radio. Apparently they soon received the navigation beam that would bring them in. The storm was now a true whiteout. How could anyone fly in this?

After a good mile, Tammy could see a set of extremely bright lights ahead—streaming vertically far up into the cloud mass. As they closed in, Tammy could see the vague outline of buildings, tent-like structures, and military trucks. What was this place? A heliport target appeared within the tower of light. It continued snowing incredibly heavy as they landed.

"O-o-o-h! What a ride," exclaimed the pilot over the whine of the engine as it wound down.

The side door was soon opened and she was escorted to a low flat building in the back of the complex. Soldiers dressed in parkas and fur lined hats guarded the entryway. Within, military personnel busily rushed back and forth. Tammy was told to wait outside a conference room. Sitting, she waited nervously.

A door opened down the hall to her left. Two men appeared—one seemed familiar. It was the ranger from Yosemite she finally realized. He appeared to be under arrest, being quickly whisked away into another room.

After fifteen minutes people began leaving the room. Apparently a meeting had just broken up. Strangely, most of those coming out were not dressed in military uniforms but neckties and parkas. A tall thin man approached. He towered over her.

"Miss Holden, we're sorry for having to drag you up here in this storm, but circumstances have taken a turn. Follow me."

Tammy noted he did not introduce himself. Obediently she followed him down a hallway. Opening a door on the right he motioned her inside. It appeared to be an infirmary—beds were lined up in a neat row. A man sat on the edge of a bed facing away. She was guided to one bed in particular. The cover was pulled back to reveal a face that she had seen many times.

"Josh! My goodness is he okay?"

"He should be fine. We found him half frozen up by Leavitt Lake."

"Have you called his mother?"

"This has been a difficult operation—trying to keep the number of people involved in this to a minimum, but yes, we have."

"What about Bryan?" she demanded.

"That's why we've brought you here, to help us find him."

Tammy plunked down on the edge of a cot. "Why are you asking me? You're probably the ones who've been following him all along."

"True, but an unrelated incident ran interference, and we lost track of him."

"How am I supposed to know?"

"Well, for starters your cousin was muttering something about 'inside the caldera—two days.' "

"Caldera? Caldera. Hmm. Why is it you're so interested in this whole thing anyway? What are you after? And first of all, who are you?"

"We can't specifically identify ourselves, but we're with the Federal Government. And everything regarding this is classified at the executive level. Aren't you a bit interested in saving your boyfriend's life?"

"Of course! It's just that I'm tired of this whole thing. I begged Bryan not to go." Tammy paused as her emotions settled down. "The clues as we understood them directed us to Emigrant Meadow and to the mountains to the west of that location, possibly to the highest peak. That's basically all there is, except for a possible trail marked by dwarf Whitebark Pine."

"Good, let's look at some maps," he responded getting up. "Oh, by the way, my name is Joe.

Tammy smiled. "Is that really your name?"

"Yes," he smiled back putting his finger up to his lips, as if swearing her to secrecy.

In the conference room a middle-aged man with black curly hair and dark framed glasses peered at a computer monitor.

"Norm, I think Tammy has given us what we need," spoke up Joe as they came in.

Norm spun around in his chair. "Hello Tammy. Glad to meet you. Say, I've read reports on your adventures, and I must say I'm intrigued."

"Spying on me are you?"

"If only you knew," he smiled.

Tammy's face turned red.

Joe shuffled a few maps on the conference room table. "Here's Emigrant Meadow," he pointed.

Tammy moved her finger westward toward *Relief Peak*. "Right here somewhere."

"Contours show a partial crater on the west side and a probable one right on the very top. Norm, bring up the SAT on that quadrant," ordered Joe.

A strong wind caused the building to shake. The storm's intensity continued at gale force white out conditions. The lights flickered.

"Dang!" complained Norm looking up.

After a momentary delay an aerial photo showing a section of the mountain range in their area appeared on the screen. As Joe barked out a set of GPS coordinates, Norm typed them in on the keyboard. Soon another picture appeared showing Emigrant Meadow and Leavitt Lake.

"Zoom in right there," pointed Joe. "And again."

"Can I do that?" asked Tammy.

Norm paused and smiled. "Sure." Getting up he let her sit in his chair and explained the keyboard strokes necessary to complete the task. "You're quick," he commented.

"Look, this must be the crater, the caldera," pointed Tammy.

All three stared at the screen in silence.

"What did Josh say?" she asked.

" 'In the caldera—two days,' " answered Joe.

"In the caldera," repeated Tammy.

"It does appear that a landing in the crater is possible," thought Norm.

Norm had Tammy click the cursor on opposite sides of the crater and type in a set of instructions. The screen turned black with a set of coordinates and the distance across the caldera.

"One kilometer," Joe noted. "I would say that's probably what Josh was trying to convey."

"Weather could be the controlling factor," commented Norm.

"Two days would be tomorrow then, right?" questioned Tammy.

Again they stared out into the raging storm.

Bryan took a deep breath as he stood before the golden sunrise. So far there were no answers to his great-great-grandfather's last days. Turning he stepped into the room where the gold had been stored. Everything looked the same—the stack of gold bars—the gold dust that had spilled out onto the floor. Bryan walked around the table-like rock, topped with gold bars where he had found the original diary.

In a symbolic way he had again touched bases with the *Legend*—and its reality. Was there something here he had missed the first time through? After a while he realized the truth he sought must be elsewhere.

Before returning to base camp, Bryan followed the main lava tube up into the internal pool through which they had originally entered from the 'Oro de Cañon.' Only a trickle now flowed out of the regulated outlet. The opening to the outside was plugged solid. There was nothing left to do, but head back.

Returning to the base camp, he decided to search the lower reaches of the cavern. Bryan was awe struck by the beautiful rooms decorated by stalactite-like curtains. Clear pools of water dotted these lower rooms. But alas—as beautiful as they were, they were still empty.

Bryan consigned himself to the fact that there were no answers here for him, and he had to prepare for departure. It was all in the timing. Since it was daytime, he had to gauge himself—sleep sparingly—leave early, and travel the miles back to the caldera. And so it was, he rested, he slept, he walked around, and finally he decided to leave and wait for daylight at the caldera.

It took a good four to five hours to reach the cave opening. Night still prevailed. Just a sprinkling of snow fell. Bryan made himself comfortable as possible just inside the cave, and welcomed the arrival of day.

But when it did arrive he was not awake. At some point the winds began to pick up, whistling around the rocks. It was enough to awaken him. Stumbling outside, the weather was turning ugly again. Dark clouds were massing above. Bryan turned round and round studying the sky. Angrily he turned back to the cave realizing that there may be no rescue.

He would wait, and wait he did—all day. As the day wore on the storm grew worse. Bryan ate the last of his food; and then slept off and on through the following night. The next day offered no better hope as the snow continued to accumulate passing the three-foot mark.

Bryan could tell his strength was waning, but what else could he do but go back down to where it was warmer, and where water was plentiful. This was his darkest hour—what could he do to escape this dilemma? Was there another way to survive?

Bryan was fatigued when he reached the base camp and very thirsty. Stumbling his way down into one of the lower rooms he stooped down to get a drink.

"Eck!" he exclaimed. The warm water tasted like heavy metal. Must be some kind of geothermal activity still underfoot he thought to himself. Raising the torch he could see this was but one in a series of pools. But water was water, it was a necessity.

Suddenly there was a noise. Bryan froze. He listened intently for the longest time, but the noise did not repeat itself. Could have been a falling rock or something he told himself.

Still feeling drained, Bryan found a comfortable spot to lie down and rest. It seemed a bit warmer in these lower rooms. Using his pack as a pillow he soon fell asleep.

Sometime later, Bryan awoke. The noise had returned. Was he going nuts? The echo in these large rooms made it difficult to distinguish direction, but it seemed that it was coming from higher up in the cave system. Bryan struggled to his feet. He felt rested, but his overall strength had not improved. It was questionable if he had enough energy to make it back to the caldera.

Returning to the base camp he listened again. Had someone from a rescue crew found their way in? The sound that now resembled footfalls came again. Bryan walked in the direction he perceived it was coming from—the upper back part of the main cavern, a place where he had earlier found nothing. Perhaps it was just bouncing off the back walls. The sound drew him into a dark corner where he now noticed something that he hadn't seen before—a small crude hole in the wall about 2 inches in diameter. It wasn't natural the way it slanted into the wall to a depth of four or five inches. Moving to the left, Bryan found another one. Then it all made sense—these were used to hold torches. These obviously led to something at one time, but what?

Continuing along the wall, Bryan came to a low cavity. Stooping down to use his flashlight, cold air struck him in the face, and from somewhere beyond he again heard the sound that had been beckoning him. Bryan now believed he might have found another way out. With renewed energy he crawled through the hole to find a tunnel beyond. Water stains were oddly in evidence along the passageway. Bryan suddenly stopped at the edge of a sheet of ice. Looking beyond, large white gleaming icicles descended from the ceiling to penetrate into the ice floor. How odd it looked. A way through offered itself, and Bryan wasted no time in scooting across the icy floor to pass through.

"Oh my!" he exclaimed.

A grand staircase of encased ice ascended before him. Along its sides were magnificent icicles, some over one hundred feet in length. The castle-like decor beckoned him to ascend, but the icy steps proved to be slippery and treacherous. Pausing to rest he gazed upward at the height of the vertical dome that rose above him, being similar to the chamber within the Obelisk.

Hope kept him going—the hope that he would see Tammy again, to hold her and to tell her that he loved her. And hope— that Josh had made it down the mountain safely.

Continued climbing proved to be increasingly painful. His chest felt like it was going to explode. Whatever happened to that young man who thought he could run with boundless energy amongst the highest peaks? Steadying himself on one arm, he found that he had reached the top of the ice bound staircase. It was apparent that the water flowing out and down the rock staircase had been going through a freeze thaw cycle for some time.

Standing erect, Bryan surveyed the scene. An ice floor extended back in under the dome disappearing into the darkness. Walking out onto the floor, he found himself in a large circle of ice within the confines of the cavern. No escape routes appeared—the walls were solid. Holding the torch high, something reflective above caught his eye. Bryan wrestled the flashlight out of his coat pocket and clicked it on.

"Wow!" Bryan exclaimed as he ran the beam of light down the side of the dome. Seams or veins of gold radiated from the high point of the dome down the walls disappearing into the ice. He could follow one vein for a ways under the ice until its increasing depth put it beyond sight. This reminded him of the internal layout of the helmet they had found on Lembert Dome. Probing further out into the ice, two or three dark objects appeared below him. Interestingly the ice itself sparkled in the light.

"O-oh no!" he exclaimed.

Standing up he felt shocked. Could it be? He needed more light to verify, but from where? Looking around the room Bryan spotted torches spaced about twenty-five feet apart along the walls. Each was interestingly situated in one of the gold veins that radiated down from the ceiling. They lit stubbornly, but once they did the whole cavern came alive. The gold—the ice—it was like a palace.

Bryan walked around in a circle studying the objects. Two appeared to be long and narrow. And the third in the middle was small and square-shaped. Coming around he noticed his own scuffmarks on the surface of the ice. The surface must be frosted he realized. Taking his pack, Bryan wiped off an area above the objects. Getting down on his knees he could see more clearly. Clicking on the flashlight he peered into the icy depths.

A sickening feeling came over him as he realized he was looking at the body of a man. Bryan halted and collapsed sitting on the icy floor stunned. Was this what he had journeyed to see? Apparently it was. It must be the Captain—there was no doubt in his mind. The nagging question that had troubled him for so long was now answered. The empire and all that his great-great-grandfather envisioned had ended here in this golden cryogenic chamber.

Who was with him? Again he directed the beam of light downward to see a woman. It had to be White Feather—much older than her image that had been caught on canvas. Nevertheless her features were still striking.

What was the smaller object? Probing again, he discerned it to be a small chest that sat higher up in the ice very near the surface. The significance of it being set at a higher level lent itself to the fact that the box could be easily removed without disturbing the bodies. Again golden flecks glittered in the ice attracting his attention.

"Gold dust," realized Bryan.

Someone had sprinkled gold dust upon the different layers of ice as they formed. In some places it was heavily layered. It was even possible there had been an attempt to form a pattern.

Looking once again at the ceiling, Bryan now understood the full significance of this cavern. The veins of gold in the ceiling and walls were like rays ascending out of the sun, and the sun itself was the circular pool of ice that glittered gold. How closely it matched the design that they had found within the Spanish helmet.

Sounds clamored out of the ceiling, almost straight out from him. His light revealed two irregular shaped volcanic vents each about two feet in diameter. Bryan recalled similar orifices in the main cavern within the Obelisk—which the more he thought about, was probably close by. If this was true, the sounds that he was now hearing could mean that someone else was in the Obelisk at this very moment.

Without hesitation he hurried as fast as he could down the icy staircase and up through the passageway to the side tunnel. As he approached the great cavern within the Obelisk, fatigue again slowed him to a crawl. Lightheaded and dizzy, Bryan leaned up against a wall gasping for breath. He could see into the cavern, but nothing was visible.

Getting his wind back he yelled, "Hello, anyone here!"

His voice echoed and diminished. There was no return, only silence. Was he going nuts?

Stumbling forward, Bryan found his way back into the hidden room. Waving his torch to and fro he found nothing that seemed out of place. Retracing his steps he stopped in front of the golden 'Door of the Sun,' and lost himself in thought, mesmerized by the flickering light across the face of the symbol. But there was something there he hadn't seen before. The sheen on the surface inside the 'sun' looked tarnished—dull. Holding the torch up close, Bryan jumped back in shock. There was a dirty handprint glaring back at him. That wasn't there earlier was it? No, he told himself. Someone else was undoubtedly in here with him, but who? A creepy feeling came over him. Could his weakened condition be bringing on hallucinations?

Turning the corner, he watched snow gently filtering down through the volcanic vents in the ceiling. The storms continued. He realized there might be no escape. Bryan was unsure what to do—remain here in the past or return to the present?

He thought of the warmth in the lower rooms and decided to return there. Taking his sweet time it took him a good half hour to return to Camino's base camp and stand in front of the large full-circled sun symbol.

But all he could think of was rest, and the warm water that could break the chill in his bones. However, he realized something was amiss as he stepped down into the adjacent room. This was not the same chamber he had been in before. There was pools and running water, but different. Bryan could hear gurgling and splashing nearby. Following the sound he was led to an amazing fountain of water that gurgled out of a crater-like depression, leaping upward about two and a half feet. The water glittered in the light. Stooping down beside the pool he scooped up a handful of gold flakes out of the warm water.

"A fountain of gold!" laughed Bryan.

Moreover, the warm water was more appreciated than the gold. Dipping his arms and legs into the pool felt so good. Soon he had the idea to immerse his whole body in the shallow pool. Removing his clothing he did so. Lying back and relaxing, Bryan enjoyed the therapeutic waters.

How many days had it been since he had eaten? The ache in his gut was painful. His overall weakness had dropped to a very serious state. Holding up his arms he could tell there was a definite lack of coordination and strength in his muscles. But he resolved whatever strength he had left he was going to make an all-out attempt to get back to the caldera. Bryan relaxed and dozed off, dreaming of better times.

Suddenly a noise jolted him awake. Rising up he listened. Distinctive footfalls drew closer and stopped.

"Who's there?" called out Bryan.

There was no answer. The echoing footsteps again commenced, heading more directly toward him.

"Captain! What is it that you would tell me?" he again called out—frightened to no end.

Finally, he could see a light slowly approaching. Bryan stooped down low at the edge of the basin, cognizant of the fact that he was still buck-naked. A fearsome face appeared in the wavering torchlight. It was a bearded man—from whose eyes the flames danced. He didn't see Bryan yet, just his torch burning off to one side.

"Where are you?" the man asked in a gravelly voice.

Bryan now recognized him. He was the crazed man they had met at Deadman Creek. What was his next move?

Suddenly, Bryan leapt up out of the water, his arms above his head yelling: "I'm the guardian of Camino's cavern, beware!"

The man screamed and fled seeing the nude body of a man coming up out of the water coated in glittering gold. Bryan could hear him running and yelling for quite some distance, then silence. He wanted to laugh, but couldn't—his heart pounded.

Bryan realized he might have made a mistake by scaring him off. This crazed man may be his only hope.

Drying off as best he could, he got redressed and took out after him. Following in the same general direction it wasn't long before he had found him lying unconscious on the floor of the cavern. Apparently, he had tripped in his hasty retreat and hit his head. Bryan shook him and after a minute he came around.

"Ha!" he yelled again.

"Stop! My name is Bryan Anderson, I'm not going to hurt you," replied Bryan trying to calm him.

"You? I remember you—that night near Kennedy Meadows. There were two of you."

"That was Josh, he's gone for help. I'm stuck here."

"Are you crazy? You scared the living daylights out of me, coming up out of nowhere like you did—naked as a jay bird, all coated in something weird."

"Me crazy? I don't go around howling like a wild animal."

"I was on the edge of insanity for a while, I must admit."

"Answer me this: who are you and why are you here?"

"My name is Ben Coleman."

"You're Ben Coleman?"

"Yes, what of it."

"We were trying to find you. You had those pictures at the cafe, and then we found out you had disappeared."

"Yes, there were pictures," he recalled. "But what is your interest in this?"

"Captain Camino is my great-great-grandfather, and I've spent considerable time in tracking him down, trying to figure out why history has mysteriously chosen to forget him."

"Then we must we be related. You see, I am also a descendant of the Captain, and have been searching for a while. It was just a few days ago that I found a recently collapsed lava tunnel that brought me here. But after finding this hideaway and searching these caverns, it seems that I have failed in finding the Captain and any truth about his past."

"No, you haven't failed. Captain Camino is still here. But you must promise me one thing."

"What?"

"If I reveal this to you, you must help me back up to the crater so I can be rescued—unless you know a better way."

"I'll be glad to—if you likewise promise to tell me all you know about Captain Camino," Ben replied.

"Sounds like a fair trade. But what proof do you have that you are related to the Captain?" asked Bryan.

"Now wait a minute, what proof do you have?" fired back Ben.

Bryan slowly reached for the medallion that hung around his neck and pulled it out from under his shirt.

Ben's eyes lit up with recognition. "The Empire of the Sun!" he exclaimed. After a few moments Ben released the medallion and straightened up. Without saying a word he reached under his jacket and pulled out a key attached to a key chain.

Focusing on the key, Bryan could see that it was a skeleton key made of hammered gold. Then he recognized the pattern of the sun in its design. "Amazing," replied Bryan.

"I have no idea what this goes to," confessed Ben, "but I understand by the use of this key there are documents or something that have been preserved that have the power to restore the Empire."

"Absolutely incredible, another piece of the puzzle," realized Bryan. "But like I said, if you promise to get me out of here alive, I'll show you where these things are."

"My word stands," Ben reaffirmed.

"We need to keep all of this between us," added Bryan. "Now help me up. There isn't much time."

After standing up and steadying himself, Bryan had a sudden recollection. "Say, were you the one who ran interference for us when those nuclear freaks just about bagged us?"

"Yeah, that was me," he kind of laughed. "I had to do sometime because they were preparing to take the whole shipment out of the country—so it appeared."

"How is it that you got so involved with that?"

"It's a long story, but it goes back to when I was a 'nuclear freak' as you so aptly put it, working for the Government at Yucca Flats—the Nevada Nuclear Test Range. To make a long story short, I discovered a discrepancy in the plutonium inventories, and reported it to my supervisor." Ben grunted as he lifted Bryan up to the next floor level. "It was two weeks later when my supervisor had a fatal accident, and the next day his superior disappeared and was never heard of again."

"Wow, that's crazy. Just like one of those movies," commented Bryan.

"Crazy is not the word for it. Apparently whoever was behind the murders was not aware of my involvement. I kept to myself. In the meantime I had been going up into the Sierra looking for clues concerning Captain Camino, and it was on one of my weekend jaunts that I ran across another part of their operation. Apparently it was one of their hiding places for the stolen plutonium. Somehow they figured out that it was me who had been up there. Suddenly my job ended, and they began following me. I spent more and more time hiding out and looking for the Captain and his hideaway. But on one occasion they ambushed me and I barely got away. From that point on, I was definitely on the run."

"Okay, stop here," commanded Bryan. "The Captain and White Feather are through a tunnel—there," he pointed.

"White Feather?" he asked.

"His wife, don't you know?"

"I didn't know her name."

"Follow the ice laden staircase up to a pool of ice, and there you will find them—under the ice. Take my flashlight. And you'll see a wooden chest just under the surface. Your golden key may be just what is needed to unlock its secrets."

Ten minutes elapsed as Bryan sat there in silence. Suddenly, he heard pounding. It lasted for a couple of minutes and stopped.

Bryan recalled his trip to Bishop, and their examination of Ben's personal things. It substantiated the many things he was now being told. Bryan decided in his own mind not to discuss these matters with him at this time, even though the photograph hidden in the dresser continued to intrigue him.

Upon Ben's return, Bryan could tell he was visibly shaken. He held something under his left arm. It was a small wooden ornately carved box. He must have taken upon himself to extricate it.

"You dug out the chest," stated Bryan, who was somewhat surprised. Without answering him Ben handed him the box. Opening it up he found numerous documents and a few unusually large gemstones inside. "Wow, these documents may be what we need to set matters straight and establish our hereditary link," Bryan commented.

After a few minutes Ben again became more himself. He helped Bryan up and they began a slow trek down the lava tunnel. On the way Ben disclosed information about his family, and how his discovery of an old letter in his grandmother's trunk set him off on this crusade.

It seemed like an eternity that they had trudged through the dark tunnels. Stopping to rest, Bryan couldn't be sure if they were at the first or second junction from the caldera. His stomach cramped. He rolled over on his side from the pain. While this was going on, Bryan did not notice that something had startled Ben, and panicking he had run off. Finding that he had been abandoned, Bryan resolved himself to failure and imminent doom.

For two days Tammy had been watching the storm rage on without any let up. That same day, Josh had recovered enough to tell his story, confirming the location of the caldera.

The next day dawned clear and very cold. Tammy wasted no time in getting over to the main building to see what was up. Coming down the hallway she passed the open door to the Base Commander's office and overheard a few words on a possible rescue flight. Pausing by the door she next heard a rendition of potential risks and concerns.

"I'll fly that machine myself if none of you are man enough," challenged Tammy stepping into the office.

"Ha ha," they laughed. She recognized Joe and Norm in the group.

"Okay," agreed the Commander, "let's give it a try, if conditions remain stable."

"I'm going," announced Tammy. "You can't leave me behind."

"You're a civilian, the risk is too great," she was told.

"Look, my life is up on that mountain. I'll gladly risk everything!" she responded emotionally.

The men involved in the discussion turned away from her and argued among themselves in low tones. Finally they came to an agreement.

"You can go, but you must do exactly as you are told, okay?" announced the Commander.

"That statement is ironically familiar to me. I'll do everything as I'm told," agreed Tammy recalling memories that involved Bryan.

The flight was scheduled to lift off in one hour, and preparations had to be made. She was outfitted in cold weather gear and was given some general instructions in how it had to be worn. It wasn't long before the sound of an aircraft engine coming to life could be heard. Within ten minutes she had been buckled in, and the rescue mission was off.

The flight was extremely rough, and the engine seemed to have a hard time in developing any kind of horsepower. Frigid air poured through the cracks, cutting like a knife. Tammy could barely make out what she thought was Leavitt Lake below, covered by ice and snow. The overall view was beyond description—a vast field of sentinels piercing through a great mantle of white, turning gold in the early morning sun.

Their course now turned easterly. Tammy could now see the crater ahead, black, primeval, and edged in snow along significant joints. Invisible air currents pushed them around. Coming up over the crest of the caldera, the helicopter chattered as they battled winds blowing over the top. Descending, the pilot guided the airship into the crater, landing on a relatively flat snowfield.

Snowshoes were brought forward as equipment was being assembled by the side door. Snowshoeing was new to her. How hard could it be? It was only a short distance. Once outside she could see the special landing pads the helicopter was outfitted with.

Besides Tammy, there were four men who made up the rescue squad. Snowshoeing across to the westerly side of the crater they quickly located what they thought to be the right cave according to the information provided by Josh. The top of which was visible just above the snow. They could feel air issuing out of the opening. By enlarging the entrance they were soon able to slide down onto the cave floor. Turning on their lights, their beams crisscrossed examining the structure of the cave. Tammy knew what she had to look for, and sure enough there was on the left wall—the 'sun' symbol, confirming they were in the right place. They called out at the top of their lungs and then listened. No sound returned to them, except that of dripping water.

The decision was to press on into the unknown depths of the tunnel. After ten minutes they came to a junction in the cave system. Yelling again there was no response. Splitting up, one crewman went left and two went right, while the team leader and Tammy waited at the junction.

Nearly a half hour had expired when they heard footsteps approaching from the left side. When the crewman, finally reached their position he seemed pale and out of breath.

"What is it Morgan?"

"I found human remains at the end of the tunnel," he stammered.

A jolt went through Tammy.

"They appear to be extremely old," added the crewman.

Tammy could breathe again. Soon the others also returned—with no results. The cave appeared to continue on forever.

The Captain looked at his watch and then at Tammy. "Our two hour window is just about up. I don't know what else we can do. I'm afraid it's time to head back."

"No-o! He's still down here somewhere," she protested.

"Keep calling as we go back. That's all that I can think of," he replied.

Gathering up their gear, they slowly headed back. Tammy, following in the rear called out Bryan's name as loud as she could. Soon they were back at the cave entrance. She stopped and gazed into the black void unable to move.

"I'm sorry miss, we have to go," insisted the Captain.

"Don't you know I love him?" she broke out crying. "Bryan!"

Bryan stirred—was he having a dream? Was Tammy calling him? He heard it again. It was not a dream. He tried to call but his voice was weak. Bryan tried again, "Tammy, help." Crawling a few feet to one side, he picked up a ten-pound rock and smacked it against the floor, creating a loud resounding echo. Waiting five seconds, Bryan called out with all he had.

Crawling up out of the cave, Tammy broke down and cried again. Suddenly a sharp sound resounded out of the depths.

"Did you hear that?"

"Tamm-y, please—" coaxed the leader.

"I'm serious, listen!"

A faint "Tammy" could be heard.

"You're right," he realized. "Dan, John, all you guys, come on back, we may have something after all."

"Wait here," she was told.

Stepping forward a couple steps she peered after them as they rumbled down the tunnel calling out. Tammy prayed. Gradually the clamor of their feet faded away as they descended into the depths. The minutes ticked by, but it seemed like an eternity. She pressed her hands against her head as if it was going to explode.

Then she heard talking, a funny shuffling noise, and more talking. Their voices were getting louder—they were now returning. She couldn't stand the suspense any longer, and dropped to her knees.

"Hey sweetheart, we found your lover boy," came a call out of the darkness.

"Really?"

Coming into the light they were carrying someone between them. Tammy could see that it was Bryan—his face was strange, pale, and cold—his eyes closed.

"Bryan! Are you okay?" she asked. Tammy could see he was too weak to respond. "Don't talk, you're safe now." She was so excited and grateful she could hardly contain herself.

Quickly they hustled him up out of the cave and across the snow to the helicopter. Soon as the side door was slammed shut, the engine was fired up.

"Get under the blanket with him. Your body heat is just what he needs," she was told.

Tammy smiled, "I'll remove my jacket so I can warm him."

Snuggling up to Bryan, she found him to be like an iceberg and still unconscious. Tammy could feel a large lump under his coat. What was it? A box? What was he doing with that? Setting that aside she was able to snuggle up to him once again. She tenderly touched him on the cheek.

"My goodness, Bryan, what is this on your skin and in your hair—gold dust? 'Gold dust in your hair,' " she repeated recalling the words to the song. Tammy slipped her arm around his waist and drew him close. "You're safe now," she whispered. Tammy realized she had never been so close to him. Did she dare? Why not? Tenderly she kissed him. "Bryan, I love you, please never do this again." Tammy wiped the tears from her eyes and held him tight as she felt them lift off.

"There's someone else down there," spotted one of the pilots as they circled south of the caldera.

"Whoever it is they're sure on the move," commented his partner.

In the ensuing twenty minutes, Tammy confessed to him numerous things, thinking he was unconscious to what she was saying. Including how on that very first day they had met, she had fallen for him.

A crowd had gathered near the heliport waiting for them to land. Bryan was awakened by the commotion when they placed him on a stretcher and carried him out. Tammy put her jacket back on and then remembered Bryan's box. Following the procession out she caught up with Bryan as they stopped to let the crowd part.

"Hi there," she smiled. "You're going to be fine, just relax. Bryan, was there someone else up there with you? The pilots said they spotted someone else up there near Relief Peak."

"That was Ben Coleman. I have to go to Hell's Mountain and find him. He is family, the long lost part.

Reaching inside his jacket, he realized that the box was missing.

"Looking for this?" asked Tammy.

"Yes, hang on to it, because it has documents that may prove our rightful inheritance."

"Did you say, 'our'?"

"Yes, I did," he replied.

"Okay," replied Tammy who seemed to be a little misty-eyed. "What is important now is you. You need food and rest. Forget all this other stuff."

"Josh—did Josh make it?"

"Yes, he's okay. Josh is already up and around."

"Good," replied Bryan, laying his head back down.

Tammy noticed her mother and Bryan's parents standing in the crowd. She stopped to hug her mother, and to tell her that everything was fine.

After the hug, her mother held her at arm's length. "Tammy Holden! What is that on your lips? Looks like gold glitter."

Suddenly Tammy's cheeks flushed red as she cupped a hand over her mouth. "It's gold dust."

"Ha ha, really? Tamm-y, don't be so embarrassed. My goodness. You can kiss him all you want. And you two can get married and have all the babies you want. It's just I'm relieved that both of you are okay, or at least will be," her mother replied glancing over toward Bryan.

Tammy followed her mother's glance to see Bryan's mother and father talking with him.

"Oh, by the way, I keep meaning to give this back, here's Bryan's ten dollars. You'll need it."

"Mom? You actually kept it?"

Out of the crowd appeared a face familiar to Bryan. It was Mr. Gorbly! In a flash of realization it came to him that this man was not the person he thought he was. Expressionless, he approached without saying a word. The short older gentleman stopped next to him, peering down through his gold-rimmed glasses at him. He wiped his finger across Bryan's forehead and examined it.

"We need to talk," he finally stated, flipping open his ID—identifying him as a Federal Agent.

"I agree," replied Bryan. "Wait till the record gets set straight regarding the Alamo and my great-great-grandfather. I believe we have found the documents necessary to establish some new historical truths and my family's rightful inheritance. The phrase, 'Remember the Alamo,' will have new meaning."

"Are you saying what I think you're saying—you can't! There would be no end to the fallout from that," he replied in a frantic, but hushed tone.

"Like I said, we need to talk."

As the stretcher moved on, Mr. Gorbly, or whatever his true name was, stood there stunned.

Despite the medic's insistence on getting him in, Bryan asked for Tammy. Quickly complying, she gazed quizzically into his face.

"Tammy, I want you to know that I love you too."

"You heard that?"

"Yes, and all the other things too."

"Well, Bryan, it's all true.

"Tammy, I think it's time we go build our own empire. The past is gone—the future is ours. I have a feeling there is—'*Indian Sky*' ahead for us."

"Blue skies and glorious sunsets," she muttered. It was hopeless for her to choke back the tears. "Bryan! Look at what you have done to me—I'm such a sight."

"Tammy, you're the most beautiful sight that I could possibly cast my eyes on."

Wiping the tears away she bent down to embrace him, but stopped short noticing everyone staring at them.

"I don't care—let them stare. I love you—so very much. You just don't know." As their lips met the applause faded away.